Praise for Jayne Rylon's *Razor's Edge*

"Everything about this book was perfect, there was enough sexual tension throughout this story that when the characters finally gave in, whew! The sparks were hot and bright. I can't say enough about this story, it's a winner, you just won't find many written as well."

~ *Just Erotic Romance Reviews*

"Razor's Edge balances humor and eroticism perfectly... You won't want to miss the next installment of this guilty pleasure series!"

~ *RT Booklovers Magazine*

"Jayne Rylon has written a fantastic follow up story to the first Men in Blue book. This book is a lot of fun and has plenty of unexpected twists that lead up to a great ending. Though they can be read individually, after meeting the characters readers will want to read all of the books."

~ *The Romance Studio*

"Razor's Edge is an intense spicy thrill-ride. From the opening page you are on the edge of your seat. Jayne Rylon definitely knows how to write gorgeous cops guaranteed to make you drool. Razor's Edge is a pulse pounding adventure in and out of the bedroom."

~ *Joyfully Reviewed*

"There were so many shocking twisters, spine-tingling suspense and devilish sexual play. I just had to keep reading until the conclusion emerged."

~ *Romance Junkies*

Look for these titles by
Jayne Rylon

Now Available:

Nice and Naughty
Dream Machine

Men In Blue
Night is Darkest
Razor's Edge
Mistress's Master

Powertools
Kate's Crew
Morgan's Surprise
Kayla's Gifts

Compass Brothers
(Writing with Mari Carr)
Northern Exposure
Southern Comfort
Eastern Ambitions

Print Anthology
Three's Company

Razor's Edge

Jayne Rylon

Samhain Publishing, Ltd.
11821 Mason Montgomery Road, 4B
Cincinnati, OH 45249
www.samhainpublishing.com

Razor's Edge

Print ISBN: 978-1-60928-296-7
Digital ISBN: 978-1-60928-252-3

Editing by Bethany Morgan
Cover by Mandy M. Roth

First Samhain Publishing, Ltd. electronic publication: November 2010
First Samhain Publishing, Ltd. print publication: October 2011

Dedication

For my beta readers. None of my books would be possible without you. I can't express my appreciation for all the work you do to make my stories shine. I value your insights and your ultra-quick turnaround times (yes, Kelly Ludwig, I'm talking to you!). Patience has never been one of *my* virtues.

Special thanks to:

The real life Roeser for lending my character your name. If I set the bar too high, blame Antonio.

Michelle Boone for inspiring Ty's club moves. Can't wait until next time we roll the dice or start the chainsaw. Then we'll add spinning the pizza too.

Chapter One

Isabella swept bare necessities off the Qing dresser into her open toiletry bag. Her hand shook as it hovered over the cut crystal bottle containing perfume her father had given her on her wedding day. The memory of his secret smile and the shine of tears in his eyes as he prepared to deliver her to her waiting fiancé rubbed her face in the destruction of all the bright hopes she'd harbored that day.

Though it had only been two years, it felt like three decades ago.

Breaking her promise to take nothing of this life with her, she tucked the relic safely beside the single change of clothes she'd jammed into her oversized Gucci purse. Light winked off the polished surface in the ornate mirror, which towered over the furniture in the mammoth room. It drew her attention to her reflection—disheveled, black smudges staining the skin beneath her eyes, a maroon slash of blood drying on her split lip.

The clock on the wall behind her heralded the five o'clock hour. She nearly jumped out of her skin. She had to hurry. Malcolm could come crashing into their bedroom at any instant. When he realized she wasn't prepared to service his friend, he'd vent his fury.

As of last night, the straggling vestiges of the aristocratic veneer she'd fallen for had vanished. She regretted not being able to jam his balls into his throat, but the way he'd pinned her—with just one arm while she kicked and thrashed—had proven she stood no chance of overturning him in a physical matchup. She refused to allow anyone to manhandle her again.

After fleeing the jail that should have been her sanctuary,

she made one last stop. She flung open the teak door to her husband's study, striding to the Renoir concealing his personal safe. She keyed in the code he had never realized she knew then overlaid her meager belongings with the pile of cash he kept on hand for emergencies. This counted as one for sure.

Isabella limped through the hall as fast as the fire searing her ankle would allow, cursing the sprawling mansion that had never become the home of her dreams. Nothing so cold impressed her, no matter how many millions it cost. A cry tore from her throat when she stumbled over the marble stairs remaining between her and freedom. Pain spurred her to move faster while she had the chance. The tap of her heels echoed across the expansive entryway. She couldn't remember the house being empty before. Not even the butler lingered.

She had no idea where to go. Without her husband, she had nothing. Was nothing. Or so he had told her often, during the past several months of their degrading relationship. Hiding would be futile. With unlimited resources, Malcolm could hunt her no matter where she ran. No, she had to make sure he couldn't touch her. The pictures she'd taken would be a start. Alone they wouldn't stop him from seeking retribution.

She climbed into the silver Mercedes she usually rode in. An assortment of knobs baffled her. She tried each one, accidentally rolling down the window before adjusting the seat so she could reach the gas and see above the dash. Why the hell hadn't she insisted on driving herself anywhere in the past two years? Pre-Malcolm, the act had been a secret thrill since her father had attempted to shelter her from any possible harm.

Overprotective following her mother's accident, he'd coddled her. She hadn't had the heart to rebuke his attentions, sensitive to the debilitating fear of loss he'd often revealed when she became too adventurous. He'd meant well, but she'd married young, determined to stretch her wings. Too bad she'd jumped from the frying pan into the fire. Malcolm put her father to shame in the controlling department, and he hadn't cared for her at all despite his loving act upfront. In the end, she'd hurt the one man who mattered.

Her father.

Isabella's forehead thunked against the steering wheel before she turned the key in the ignition. She unclenched her jaw, wincing at the ache left behind when her teeth separated. If there was any other way… But, really, who else could protect her from the psycho her husband had morphed into? Swallowing her pride, she did the one thing she had sworn she'd never do.

Her phone weighed a ton in her shaking grasp. A cramp in her neck stopped her from looking over her shoulder again. Instead, she put the car in gear, took a shuddering breath and navigated the long, winding drive. Rapid thumps of her heartbeat echoed in between interminable rings. Damn it! He had to answer his personal line.

"Isabella, I'm in the middle of a meeting."

"Daddy…" She choked on a sob. Her only parent didn't seem to notice.

"I'll have to call you back in a few hours."

"No! Wait! I'm coming home…" But it was too late, the phone had already gone dead.

Tears she'd sworn she wouldn't shed obscured her vision as she flew along the wooded road. Every time a black vehicle rounded a bend in the oncoming lane she flinched, swerving toward the shoulder, terrified it would be Malcolm's Audi R8. An hour later, she had reached the freeway with no sign of her soon-to-be-ex husband. No cars, no calls, nothing.

A sigh big enough to flutter her bangs escaped her chest when she turned onto the cobblestone road to her father's estate and triggered the automatic gate opener. The leather steering wheel creaked as she flexed her fingers, noticing the tingles pervading them. How long had it been since they'd gone numb? She abandoned her car on the far side of the fountain, which acted as a centerpiece in the turnaround in front of the manor, then tore up the stairs to her childhood home.

Gerard opened the door before she reached it. He held out his arms. "Miss Bella. Are you all right?"

She clutched the older man, loosening her grip when the ridges of his bones—more prominent than she remembered—sent pins and needles through her recovering hands.

Safe. She was safe here.

"Isabella?" Her father's inquiry boomed from his study down the hall.

"Go ahead, child. Don't keep him waiting." Gerard patted her shoulders. A nudge in the right direction followed.

And suddenly she wished she had a slo-mo button for

reality to figure out what to say. How much should she tell her father of what she'd seen, of what had happened? The thought of divulging all the torrid facts had heat racing up her chest to her cheeks.

Her gaze traced the zigzagging lines of the parquet floor to the tips of her father's Berluti loafers. Wisps of her platinum-blond hair curtained her face, hiding the superficial damage there from his inspection. Anger heated her cheeks for the shame she knew she shouldn't feel, but she hadn't forced herself to raise her stare by the time he spoke.

"What's this about?" His stern tone created no wiggle room.

"I'm leaving Malcolm." She hardly recognized the scratchy wheeze as her own.

"I had hoped he was mistaken."

Her head snapped up, taking in the whole room. The bastard she'd married stood at the polished bar on the far side of the mancave, sipping two fingers of the Macallan aged whiskey he loved. More than he loved her. Hell, he'd never truly loved her at all. How could she have been gullible enough to believe he had?

Isabella backpedaled, horrified when the man who'd tried to auction her off—though he had more money than some small countries—winked at her from behind her father's back. Fury seethed beneath the surface of his calm façade.

A flash of recollection hit her hard.

Malcolm's face had contorted when she objected to his proposition.

"It's one time, baby. Even for your sweet pussy, five mil is generous. Especially since you just have to lay there and take it. It's about time you start earning your keep around here."

She blinked, unable to process his intent, but instinctive denial rushed out. "No! I'm not some toy to be rented to your friends. I won't do it."

His knuckles split her lip when he struck as quick as a snake, backhanding her. No one had ever dared to hit her before. The tang of blood burst over her tongue, leaving her reeling long enough for him to ensnare her wrist. Spittle dotted her face when he tugged her close.

"If you think this is bad, you can't imagine what he'll do to you—to us—if you don't please him, bitch."

Her jaw dropped open as she sputtered, "Daddy!"

"Enough, Isabella. Grow up. You're no rebellious, spoiled girl anymore." Her father heaved a sigh, steepled his fingers across his plump waist and decreed, "You can't come running to my home because you've had a spat with your husband. I'm disappointed, darling. You have to learn to work through your issues, not avoid them. Marriage is a sacred vow. If your mother were here, it would break her heart to see you give up so easily."

Easily! What did he know of the hell she'd suffered?

When Malcolm laid his hand on her father's shoulder, she flinched. That conniving monster had already stolen her salvation.

She ran in an undignified cross between a hobble and a lurch, ignoring the electric shocks shimmering up her leg. Nothing could hurt as bad as being returned to that madman. The sedate snap of footsteps behind her broadcast Malcolm's arrogance. But, really, there was no way out. She was trapped.

Isabella flew around the corner, heading for the gardens. Someone's hand covered her mouth at the same time his other arm wrapped around her waist. Her captor smuggled her into an alcove. "Hush."

Gerard.

"Down here, to the cellar. Head to the corner where you used to hide. The supply loading chute behind the storeroom shelves... I've left it open for you. Go. Now. I'll distract them." He whispered the frantic directions in her ear.

"What about you? What if they find out?" She yanked his wrist, trying to pull him with her. "You don't know what he's capable of."

"I'll be fine, little bell. Quickly." The time for debate had passed. The ominous snap of Malcolm's steady approach echoed closer in the marble hall.

"Th-thank you." She bussed his cheek before slipping onto the steep servant's staircase. She cursed the clatter she made when her ankle gave out. Thank God the rickety railing held.

Masculine voices cascaded through the darkness. She froze, holding her breath to avoid making a sound.

"Yes, sir. In the garden, Mr. Carrington."

The evil cackle she'd never forget from the night before followed Gerard's misdirection. "Good man. I'll have her under control in no time. Don't you worry. She won't be pulling this shit again."

When she heard the leaded-glass door to the yard fall into place behind her husband, Isabella hopped across the dusty floor on her good leg. She scrambled over the stacks of supplies to the nook where she'd often stolen away to read the exciting romances someone—she supposed it had been Gerard all along—had stacked for her behind the tins of caviar. Who'd have guessed, despite those steamy afternoon fantasies, that her prince would turn out to be such a toad?

She climbed the shelves, stifling a squeak when one of the bolts broke loose, nearly pitching her to the concrete floor below. Her fingernails ripped on the steel, destroying her French manicure, as she clung to the side in her best superhero imitation. Boosting herself into the bottom of the chute, she ignored the spider webs tickling her arms as she clawed up the slick incline toward the sliver of light rimming the opening about ten feet ahead.

For once, Isabella was grateful for her ultra-petite stature. No long-legged beauty would fit in the rat hole she crawled through. Her fingertips brushed the hatch, poised to shove it wide, when her purse—flung over her shoulder—caught on a rivet. She jerked to a stop. As she struggled to free the fabric, she heard someone bitching outside.

"How the hell do we get stuck with these jobs? We're supposed to be guarding the boss, not playing hide and seek with his fucking daughter."

A crude grunt came from a few feet to the left of the slatted opening. If she remembered correctly, bushes concealed the panel on the north side of the service road, parallel to the estate's driveway.

"I'd hide something in her if it wouldn't mean my dick hacked off with a rusty knife."

"It could be open season after this. I heard Malcolm is tired of her... ...renting her out... ...part of the ring..." His voice trailed off. Rustling brush obscured the rest of his explaination. But his meaning came clear soon enough. "...signed up a list of customers a mile long who want a taste. As if that'll keep his head off the chopping block with the big guy. If we find her, I bet he'll let us take a reward. Teach the princess a lesson."

Isabella prayed they wouldn't hear her gag, though the metal shaft surrounding her amplified every scuffle. The violent heaving of her torso ripped her purse loose. She knocked into the grate covering the chute with an elbow, cracking it further open. When her eyes adjusted, she caught a glimpse of one of the assholes outside rearranging his package before joining the other hired muscle around the corner.

About twenty feet away, across the gravel delivery zone, the backdoor to her father's ten-car garage sat open. Isabella took a deep breath. She counted down in her head, psyching herself up for the dash across the open grass.

Three... Two... One.

She burst from the duct, tucking into a ball as she landed in the mulch a couple feet below. A sprint for the garage exposed her, but no one seemed to notice. She grabbed a random set of keys hanging on the pegboard mounted to the wall. When she hit the unlock button on the dongle, the lights on a candy-apple red sports car flashed in response. Worked for her.

In the illumination from the car's lights, she popped open the door and slid inside. The supple leather interior cradled her abused body. She fit the key in the ignition. A mechanical grinding shattered the surreal silence of the unoccupied space. She blinked in the harsh light that streamed through the widening gaps where the garage doors receded.

Her fingers twitched as her foot inched toward the gas, but she reined in the panic making her teeth chatter before she could crash out of the breach. The noise of the V12 would alert the goons chasing her to her presence. Instead, she ducked below the custom dash and waited for the grinding of the openers to stop. As soon as it did, she hit the starter, slammed the car into first gear then peeled out of the bay.

Two burly men—she couldn't tell if they were the same ones she'd overheard—sprang to either side of the driveway. The breeze of her passing gusseted them as she nearly mowed them over. The roar of the powerful car announced her location to anyone within half a mile.

Isabella couldn't afford to hesitate long enough to bring the vehicle under complete control. Instead she shifted hastily, grinding the gears while trying to straighten out her trajectory. It wasn't easy. The machine had enough torque for a fleet of sedans.

She clipped the corner of the fence that penned in her

father's thoroughbreds before zipping along the driveway toward the main entrance. As she barreled past the front of the house, she spotted her father waving his arms. His mouth gaped in his flushed face as he roared at her to stop. She accelerated instead. Up ahead, the gate shuddered, beginning to close.

Isabella wrestled the shifter into third. The speedometer climbed as she raced toward the narrowing exit. There was no way she'd make it in time. She half-expected to smash into the wrought iron as she threaded the needle between the moving panels. It was a struggle not to scrunch her eyes and brace for impact.

None came.

She cleared the gate with inches to spare. A pursuer she hadn't noticed couldn't brake in time. He slammed into the deceptively strong tangle of metal with a terrible combination of a screech, a bang and the shattering of glass. Behind the steam rising from the destruction, some combination of her father's and husband's minions scrambled to clear the blockage. The walled perimeter effectively held them in.

They shrank in her rearview mirror.

The blockage wouldn't detain them for long, but she only needed a head start. She considered driving straight to the police. However, both her father and husband made sizable contributions to the force. After what she'd witnessed the other night, she guaranteed they had at least a few cops in their pocket too. She couldn't risk trusting the wrong person.

They'd left her one option, and she'd take it. No matter the cost to her father's businesses. She'd ruled out public humiliation earlier for his sake. His convenience no longer ranked on her list of priorities when the devil had his ear. She would never return to that man—either of them. If only her mother were alive...

Isabella punched the glowing phone icon on the steering wheel, uncaring if her father somehow listened in on the conversation. He couldn't stop her now.

"Call."

"Please say the name of the person you'd like to reach." The car's onboard computer prompted her to use the voice-activated controls in a tone entirely too pleasant for her current state of mind.

"Channel 9 News, bitch."

"Nametag not found. Please try again."

"Channel 9 News. Please."

She prayed this car had an equivalent, or better, system than her own. When ringing filled the cabin, she grinned.

"Newsroom."

"This is Isabella Buchanan Carrington. I'm on my way to your studio to announce my separation from Malcolm Carrington. Please have your anchor reporter on site. If you hurry, we can make an exclusive on the eight o'clock news."

She figured the clerk had never received a tip like hers before when the commotion of the newsroom droned on in the background for a solid ten seconds.

"Hello?"

"Is this a prank?"

"No. Now pay attention or I'm calling Channel 6. I don't have time to waste. Would you care to explain that to your boss?"

"Jake!" The panicked man bellowed in her ear, but she didn't care. "Get Steven on the phone, I need him in here now for breaking news."

"I'll be there in—" she revised her estimate as she jammed the pedal to the floor, "—twenty minutes. It'd be best if you kept this to yourself until then."

"We're sure as shit not going to leak it and end up scooped."

"Thank you."

"No lady, thank *you*."

Chapter Two

Isabella thumbed past the now-famous snapshot of her interview on the front page as she skimmed to the help wanted section of the Sunday paper. She'd hunkered down in this weekly hotel for three days, expecting someone to come for her at any moment. Every clanking pipe, honking horn or scratching rodent in the wall made her jump a mile high. So far, they'd left her in peace.

Her adamant statement complete with bloody lip, torn clothes and an iron resolve she hadn't known herself capable of had convinced enough people of her sincerity that Malcolm hadn't been able to make his move. Yet.

With her husband and father temporarily off her case, she needed to figure out a plan. Fast. The stash of money she'd pilfered wouldn't get her very far despite the shoestring budget she'd drafted up. She scrubbed her palms over her face. How could she have stayed oblivious to the enormous cost of survival relative to average wages, even in their mid-Western city, until yesterday?

How did most families make ends meet?

Isabella tapped her pen against the extremely short list of her marketable skills.

Charity event planning.

Personal shopping.

Modeling.

She figured she was royally screwed but browsed through the job ads regardless. She'd clean toilets if she had to. Any honest living beat crawling home to Malcolm and his deceitful, humiliating, perverted ways. Not to mention the other women who needed her help.

She shuddered.

Painter, secretary, landscaper, clerk...she could learn these trades, if someone would give her half a chance. So far, every establishment she'd contacted had disregarded her interest. One woman had outright cackled, assuming the call was a joke. "Yeah right, like that bitch would ever slum it enough to dirty her hands. She might break a perfect nail."

Tears had filled her eyes. Mostly because the woman wouldn't have been so far off from the truth less than a year ago. Others had rejected her because they didn't want their business turned into a circus with her as the starring freak.

She understood their concerns, but the neat stacks of hundreds she'd stuffed under her mattress—ignoring the gummy stains there—wouldn't last her more than half a year, even at her new standard of living. Plus, it would take far more than surviving to break free from her husband and fix the evil things he'd done.

Though she'd checked her accounts, she hadn't been one bit surprised to find each of them frozen. There had to be something she could handle. Determined, she turned the page.

The moment her eyes landed on the double-sized ad, she knew she'd found the perfect solution. This she could do. Here her personal drama would work in their favor.

Isabella grinned wide enough to crack her lip open a little. She didn't pay any attention to the iron tang. Already she formulated a plan. She'd need the right outfit, makeup, shoes... these things she knew about.

And Channel 9 owed her big time.

Isabella appraised her reflection in the mirrored doors of the station's elevator. The woman she spied was a far cry from the terrified girl who'd ridden up to the newsroom with her back to the corner mere days ago.

A slinky red dress with matching fire-engine lipstick, five-inch heels, brilliant blue eyes enhanced by drastic cosmetics, hair curled and piled sky high to make her appear taller—she meant business. The bell dinged, signaling her arrival. She forced her fingers to uncurl. She embraced the persona of the dignified lady her father had bred her to be.

The strut she had perfected by the time she had turned thirteen came in handy as she traversed the hallway as though it were a *haute couture* runway.

Chin up. She didn't deign to acknowledge the heads that turned from all directions as she passed by. Whispers accompanied her progress like the brush of silk skirts on one of the ridiculous ball gowns her father and husband had insisted on often for public appearances. She followed the sexy beat of Latin music to an open studio for her grand entrance. Hand on hip, she tossed her mane over her shoulder. She stood, waiting for the producers to notice her.

It didn't take more than half a second.

Activity in the room froze as people turned to gape. All conversation hushed. When she could be heard without raising her voice, she said, "I'll be auditioning for the instructor slot on the Pro-Am dance show. Latin round first?"

Two women to her right shot her death-ray glares then packed in their legwarmers. She ignored the vicious curses they slung at her when they deserted the studio. In their place, she'd be pissed too.

"Baby." A short, middle-aged man sporting enough gel for someone with five times his thinning hair grinned. She shied away from his outstretched arms and the double kiss he tried to plant on her cheeks. "You're a dazzling local celebrity embroiled in a scandalous divorce. No audition's necessary. Our ratings just shot through the roof."

Isabella concentrated on keeping her stiletto glued to the floor instead of kneeing the pompous asshole in the balls for his glee over her heartache.

"I will not accept this position without a proper audition." He had no clue if she could dance, never mind instruct someone else.

After the loss of her mother, who'd died when Isabella was eleven, her father had been determined to raise her as a proper lady. Part of her training in all things sophisticated had included ballroom dancing. The lessons her father had required were the single thing she'd enjoyed about the endless schooling in etiquette that had accompanied her traditional education.

She'd dedicated years to pleasing her father, making him proud. But it seemed ten times as important to ensure she deserved this opportunity. Especially because she hadn't danced since her wedding day. Malcolm had forbidden her from partnering with any other man, and he had a sense of rhythm on par with a drunken goat.

What if she'd forgotten everything?

She might try and fail, but things that were given could easily be taken away. Of that, she was certain. And she was damn tired of being beholden to people.

"I'll go last."

The producer shrugged. He reclaimed his folding chair at the single table in the room, facing the stage. Most of the other women trickled out. A smattering stayed to fight, unwilling to quit or hoping to see her choke. She could respect their determination.

The music resumed, and a candidate started her choreographed routine. Isabella appreciated the technique and lines of the obviously seasoned dancer, but she thought the movement lacked some fluidity and connection to emotion. As the dancers performed, her confidence increased. She could do this.

"Isabella Buchanan Carrington." The stagehand read her name off the list.

Showtime.

Isabella stood with her back to the room. She closed her eyes, shook out her muscles and rotated her stiff ankle as she waited for the music to begin. Thank God for ibuprofen. The introductory strains filled the space yet she didn't move, allowing the melody to imprint on her. Smooth and sensual, the Spanish rumba flowed through her. She synchronized her breathing to the phrases then leaned into the beat.

Her hips swayed to the sultry guitars before her arms joined in. Her abdomen rolled, accenting the percussion of the drums. The song called to her, sad and sweet at the same time. She opened her heart and allowed all her longing to pour out in her movement.

What would it be like to have a lover as achingly passionate as the music implied? Someone who lifted her up instead of tearing her down. Someone she could whisper her fantasies to at night without fear of recrimination or humiliation. Someone she could commit herself to heart and soul.

Isabella imagined such a man and how she could partner with him. Moving in unison or rocking in delicious counterpoint, together they'd set the night on fire. She leapt into the air, transitioned into a *fouette* then ground her pelvis in an instinctive lure for her imaginary lover.

As the music quieted, so too did her movements. She smiled to herself as she swayed, wishing she knew the satisfaction of sharing pillow talk and quiet moments filled only with physical exhaustion and absolute contentment. All things she considered a delicious fairytale.

But that didn't keep her from dreaming.

She sighed, releasing the last of her labored breaths into the quiet room. Terrified to open her eyes, she wondered at the lack of commotion that had followed the other auditions.

At the first resounding clap, her lids flew open. Suddenly everyone joined in, applauding her impromptu performance. Her knees went weak, dropping her to the stage as the crowd in attendance—as well as several people in the hall who'd gathered around to watch—rewarded her honest expression. Their approval meant more to her than she could have imagined.

The woman she'd observed earlier jumped onto the stage and approached with her hand outstretched. She helped Isabella to her feet and whispered, "You deserve this. I'll be watching the show and cheering for you."

"Thank you." She squeezed the woman in a brief hug as they headed toward the producer's table.

"Welcome to *Dance With Me.* You'll be paired with your celebrity amateur for your first rehearsal Monday morning. The winning instructor will receive a two-year lease on a building downtown to open their own studio. Good luck." The producer shook her hand with a wink. "I think you'll do just fine."

"I quit!"

Chief Leigh chuckled.

"For Christ's sake! I'm a cop, not some twinkle-toed ballroom dancer." Razor gawked in horror when his superior officers didn't flinch. They were dead serious.

"Listen, kid. You don't have a lot of options these days. Your cover is blown. We can't use your baby face to bust drug rings in the schools anymore. Not since you've been plastered all over the news this last year."

No one mentioned the reason why. They pitied him too much to talk about how fucking stupid he'd been—how he'd let his dick lead the way straight to hell.

After five months in rehab, thanks to the two bullets he'd caught with his chest and the one that had skimmed his thigh, James "Razor" Reoser had reported back to duty only to find the department planned to farm him out on some feel-good publicity stunt as a hometown hero. Some damned hero. Maybe they didn't trust him with real police work anymore.

He wouldn't blame them.

But why were Mason Clark and Tyler Lambert in on this meeting? They'd been at the core of the fiasco that had landed his ass in the hospital for months. Thank God his fuck-ups hadn't cost them, or their woman, their lives in the end. He never could have survived that.

"They're screwing with you, Razor." Ty broke the tension, letting him off the hook. "There's more here than some bullshit assignment."

The chief nodded. "If you think you're up to it..."

"I am." Razor didn't need the man to finish.

"I have one last undercover op for you." His boss retrieved a manila folder from his desk and handed it over. "You've heard about Mrs. Isabella Buchanan Carrington leaving her husband?"

"Uh...yeah." Razor scrubbed his hand through his hair as he tried to recall the society news. Not exactly his usual cuppa. In fact, he fast-forwarded through those stories to reach the local sports scores on his DVR most nights. But the second the captivating woman's picture had flashed on his screen a few days ago, her interview had fascinated him. Or at least he'd studied her luscious mouth as she recounted her sob story.

Disgust had rolled through his gut when his cock stiffened for the first time AG—after Gina. All for a damsel in distress who'd probably staged the whole drama to leech cash out of the sucker she'd married while she schemed to run away to Mexico with the pool boy.

"She'll be your partner on the show."

His stomach cramped.

"Is this some kind of sick test? To see if I can keep my hands to myself?" Razor hated that they might think him incapable of remaining impartial. More, he feared they were right.

"Not exactly."

"That's not very reassuring," he grumbled.

"Let's say there are advocates in the administration for your early retirement."

"Fuck! I'm twenty-four, sir. I'll be the only retired rookie in history." Just when he thought his destiny couldn't decay beyond miserable. Now he'd have unemployed to add to crippled and gullible.

"It's not going to come to that. You need to regain your edge, that's all." Mason clapped his giant hand onto Razor's slighter shoulder. He always felt like a freaking hobbit compared to the hulking man. "You've got this. Ty and I will have your back."

"Tyler, brief him." The chief monitored the city playing out on the other side of his seventh story window.

"Isabella Buchanan Carrington. Age—twenty-two. Height—five-foot-two. Blond, amazing sky blue eyes, I'm guessing 32C..."

"Ty!" Mason wasn't in the mood to fuck around.

Razor appreciated his focus. Regaling the movie-star looks of his new mark couldn't possibly help.

"Yeah, yeah. She comes from money. Lots of money. Married more money. We've been after Malcolm Carrington for years, but had no luck proving he's supplementing his inheritance with dirty deeds. Yet, his tastes run to more expensive shit than he should be able to afford. And, believe me, that's saying something. He's been involved in Buchanan business for years. The night Isabella turned eighteen Carrington was spotted wining and dining her at The Summit. Gossip columns billed them the perfect couple despite the fact he's nearly fifteen years older than her."

Razor couldn't imagine that kind of lifestyle. Hell, he'd have to save for the next five years to have an appetizer at the swank restaurant. He supposed extravagance helped when attempting to snag the hottest, richest lady in the state. Hell, maybe the country.

"When she turned nineteen, Carrington proposed in front of a quaint gathering of five hundred guests at Rolling Greens, the country club both he and pops belong to. The platinum couple was engaged for a year and married the day before her twentieth birthday."

"This guy was on a schedule, huh?" Razor blew out a sigh.

"Seems like it. Didn't hurt that she was set to inherit some of her mother's cash either, I bet." Mason's disgust for Carrington rang through the room.

"Set to?"

"Seems when her mother died in an accident at their mansion, a clause in her will left her share of the wealth to the daughter. Unless Isabella were to marry into a family better off than hers—hard to conceive of—in which case old man Buchanan could keep the dough to support himself in retirement. Like the bastard needs it."

"Lambert, that's enough." The chief beat them at politics every time. One reason he'd made the grade and they never would—never wanted to.

"What kind of douche takes from his own kid, even if he's allowed?"

"Move on."

"So the babe gave it all up for her husband. Who, by the way, was spotted by one of our watchers with another woman in the garden at his own fucking multi-million dollar reception. Paid for courtesy of daddy's new stash, I'm sure."

"And she fell for all this bullshit?" Razor could have kicked his own ass when the three other men in the room stared at him without uttering a single word.

When he thought the supercharged atmosphere might spontaneously combust, the chief said, quietly, "Malcolm could be an expert con man. What chance would a sheltered girl have against a shark like him?"

"It looks like she might be wising up now." Mason added.

"Or she was in on it from the beginning." Razor scrubbed a hand through his hair and tried to ignore the subtext. "So why do we care? Yeah, maybe they shat on her one time too many and she decided she wants out, maybe demanded her nest egg, but there's nothing criminal here. Just greed. All of their greed."

"On the surface, you're right." Tyler snatched the briefing. "But lately we've been picking up some chatter. The joint Carrington-Buchanan holdings are vast. They're into lots of legitimate businesses and a few that skirt the line. This time they may have gone too far. Ever hear of Black Lily?"

Razor paused. Should he admit that? In front of his boss and his superior officers? Who already had reason to doubt his judgment when it came to sex? Fuck it. No sense in lying now. "Uh...yeah. I know what it is."

"Ever been there?" Mason arched an eyebrow.

"Maybe once or twice."

"Malcolm Carrington is the proud owner of the establishment. On paper. Lots of people say Buchanan has controlling interest but doesn't want the trail leading in his direction." Tyler winked at him. "Again, nothing illegal about people enjoying consensual BDSM scenes in a private club. However, we've heard rumors of something...darker going on in the reserved rooms."

"What do you mean? Prostitution?" Razor had heard whispers the last time he'd visited—forbidden offers—but it'd been a while.

"Worse." Mason spoke through clenched teeth. "They're allegedly trading sex slaves in the dungeons. Offering test drives, rent-to-own deals and other arrangements I can't comprehend. One of our moles reported seeing someone resembling Mrs. Carrington on site."

Razor cursed under his breath. One psychotic woman who thrived on power games was enough for any man's lifetime. He'd barely survived Gina. They wouldn't sic another on him, would they?

"We need to know if she's involved or if she can slip us information. With trouble in paradise, she could help us crack the case, bring Malcolm down."

"And you think *I'm* going to be able to figure out the truth? You think I can fucking tell if she's lying—if she's up to her perfect tits in trouble or masterminding the plan? We all know I can't tell jack shit when it comes to the femme fatales of the world." He hated the panic squeezing his vocal chords until his pitch rose.

"I believe you can." Tyler looked straight into his eyes as he offered the reassurance Razor never could have asked for but desperately needed. "You won't get fooled again. We'll be at every show, watching, helping."

"You're on the case. You better get your act together." The chief didn't stray from his place at the window. "I won't be able to overrule the administration again."

"It's all about your edge. You have to hone your instincts. Jump back on the horse." Mason nodded in Razor's direction. Not a single trace of doubt tinged the more experienced cop's expression.

Razor didn't have a choice. He was being pitched into the lion's den. Again. "There's just one thing..."

"Yes?" The chief hesitated a moment before answering.

"I don't do sequins."

Mason and Tyler's laughter boomed through the office. The chief pivoted, flashing a hint of a smile. Ten tons lifted from Razor's shoulders. If he could pull this off maybe things could return to normal.

Chapter Three

Razor spent the next two days preparing for his initial meeting with his new teacher. He read the department's files on all the players at least a dozen times, did some extra research into the Black Lily online and jacked off as much as humanly possible to ensure he could keep his libido under control.

Though he hadn't had much of a sexual appetite while recovering in the hospital—followed by a lack of time for indulging as he spent most of his waking hours rehabbing in the gym, returning home dog tired—he didn't seem to have any trouble now. Every time he saw Isabella Buchanan Carrington's flawless face he sported a hard-on so rigid he impressed himself. The file of photos he'd amassed in his dossier showed her off in sparkling evening gowns, her brilliant smile flashing as she laughed on the arm of her über-rich, asshole husband.

He'd made up for months of abstinence in one short weekend the likes of which he hadn't experienced since he'd activated his broadband connection his freshman year in college. In fact, he might be developing some chafeage. Despite the epic release he'd granted himself, he feared he'd fall into his old ways as soon as he met the tiny blond bombshell in person. Why did she have to be the most beautiful woman he'd ever seen? Something about the gleam in her eyes sucked him in as surely as her doll-like features or that downright sinful mouth.

At five-eight, he wouldn't win any height competitions. He'd always aimed for lean and agile over big and bulky, but this waif would make anyone feel like the Jolly Green Giant. Delicate and petite, she'd fit perfectly in his arms...

Shit.

He didn't have time to take care of his raging arousal again before he left for their pre-arranged meeting place in one of the unused TV studios downtown. Unable to stand pacing the confined area of his apartment one second longer, he grabbed his leather jacket to ward off the early spring chill before taking the stairs from his third-story landing two at a time.

Razor straddled the neon yellow and black Suzuki GSX-R750 he'd bought himself instead of a car. When he'd worked undercover, it'd enhanced his badass image. These days, he reveled in the freedom he found flying along country roads on the maneuverable bike.

As he navigated the rush hour traffic heading into the city, he let his mind wander. A mistake when he realized how many parallels he'd drawn between Gina and Isabella.

Gorgeous. Check.

Keeping secrets. Check

Used to having men wrapped around their little fingers. Definitely check.

Somewhere in the past forty-eight hours, he'd made up his mind. Princess had to be in the know. Maybe she had pushed her luck, insisting on a larger share of the take, until dad and hubby kicked her to the curb. He'd dug up the press conference on his DVR, glad he never deleted things until he was about to run out of space. The crocodile tears she'd manufactured hadn't moved him.

All right, so what if that was a big fat lie? He'd watched the damn segment no less than fifty times, trying to build resistance. He attempted to embrace the numb void he'd experienced between drug-induced periods of sleep in the hospital. But no matter how many times he'd rewound the program, he flinched each time that single tear trickled down her battered cheek. So he'd thrown the remote across the room. It had cracked the drywall and left his tuner stuck on the home shopping network. *Damn it.*

If she had nothing to hide, why wouldn't she answer the reporter's questions about the injuries evident on her face and hands, or the reason behind her sudden separation?

The legal mumbo-jumbo she'd spouted about the media affecting the outcome of her divorce proceedings reeked of bullshit. After all, she'd been the one to call the press conference. No, something didn't add up here. That conclusion finally tamed his arousal, leaving him frigid as a glacier.

Razor parked out front of a non-descript building next to a gleaming, red Enzo Ferrari. He winced when he noticed the white scuff on the front quarter panel. After drooling over the machine behind the cover of his tinted visor, he tugged his helmet off and glared at the wall of windows facing him. Somewhere up there she waited. And he was ready to face the music.

Isabella studied the man on the motorcycle, thirty feet below her. Even from here, she could detect the unyielding set of his compact shoulders. When he shook out his wild hair from under the helmet, her breath caught in her lungs. Until he glowered up at her with unmitigated fury. She staggered several steps from the window.

She'd seen that potent concoction of anger and bitterness on another masculine face, not long ago. And she never wanted to witness it up close and personal again.

Focus.

Now was not the time to permit her doubts to bubble to the surface. Especially not because of a random stranger. She swore she'd make the most of this opportunity, prove to the world—or at least herself—she could survive on her own. She didn't need the riches of others to thrive. Not when she had the spirit of a fighter and a stubborn streak a mile wide. And especially not when the life of luxury she'd known came with such a high price tag.

Dear God, she had to do something. Had to find some way to stop them...

Her frantic thoughts made it impossible to think clearly.

Take it one step at a time. Do well today and think of the rest later.

To calm herself, she selected a mellow piece of music then began to stretch, warming up. Her partner should arrive within the hour. She reviewed the beginner choreography she'd assembled over the weekend so they could sprint right out of the gate. It'd been a long time since she anticipated something as much as she did this morning.

The barre on the mirrored wall seemed high to her, but she could reach it while balancing on the tiptoes of her uninjured foot. She'd taken so many things for granted. Outside of the custom-made studio her father had ordered for her in one of the outbuildings on their estate, everything seemed a little odd. She adjusted as best she could. The stretches were more difficult in this position. It would tone her core strength faster.

Isabella bent at the waist, reaching for the ankle on the barre as the light strumming of harps helped her get her zen on. With her eyes closed, she didn't see the man approach, but she heard his careful footfalls come to an abrupt stop when he turned the corner.

Two and two collided.

She jerked upright so fast she lost her balance, crashing to the floor flat on the ass he'd had a perfect opportunity to ogle.

A gentleman would have offered his hand, drawn her to her feet and made sure she hadn't hurt herself. This man did none of those things. Instead, he scrutinized her with such contempt, she felt like a bug about to be squashed.

Didn't it figure? The motorcycle man. Her partner. One and the same.

Had the studio intentionally given her the competitor least likely to be trained? Did she make a better story as a failure?

Refusing to believe something so despicable to be true, Isabella hauled herself from the dusty hardwood before brushing off her black leggings. She stepped forward, extending her hand. If nothing else, she knew a hell of a lot about manners. When he refused to shake in introduction, she let her wrist fall to her side with a shrug.

"I'm Isabella Buchanan." She had decided to drop the Carrington. Nothing about the name inspired her to claim it any longer. Though he continued to stare at her with bitter loathing tainting his milk-chocolate eyes, she refused to be cowed. "And you are..."

"Razor."

Terrific. A monosyllabic, motorcycle-riding, dance-hating Neanderthal named after a cutting implement. Piece of cake.

"Nice to meet you, Razor. The producers left instructions for us, but I thought I'd wait for you to arrive so we could go over them together. I admit, I've never actually seen *Dance With Me* before. I'm curious to discover what we've gotten ourselves into." She chided herself for the nervous titter that escaped before she could subdue it. "Are you ready to begin?"

"Why not?"

"Great." She ignored his sarcasm and his stinking attitude.

"Please change into your rehearsal clothes so we can make the most of our time. We have the space for five hours today before the next couple arrives. Since you're early, we can fit in almost six if we settle in quickly."

He looked at her as though she had nine heads. "Unless you want me naked, this is all I've got."

Isabella decided not to acknowledge his crude remark when he looked chagrined enough for them both. She scanned her partner from head to toe. Every part of him—from his stiff leather jacket to his snug jeans to his motorcycle boots—more inappropriate than the next for their purpose. But damn if the bad boy ensemble didn't outline one of the finest bodies she'd ever spied. He was so different than any other man she'd met in her prior life; she found herself oddly and immediately intrigued.

Just what she needed.

"You'll have to do this in your socks for today. Tomorrow, we'll find you proper shoes." She tried not to think about how many groceries she could have bought with that money. Her contract stipulated she'd only be paid for the number of episodes they appeared in. As the worst couple was eliminated each week, she needed them to stay in the running as long as possible if they couldn't win outright. A little investment up front would pay off in the end. She had to believe that.

Dead silence surrounded the rasp of her unwilling partner untying the laces of his boots with yanks hard enough she swore the little plastic caps on the ends popped off. He kicked the heavy footwear into the corner, rattling the mirror on the wall.

Oooo-kay.

"Can we cut the petulant-child crap here, Razor? You're pissed. I understand I'm probably not the person you were hoping to see today. If you want to call the station, it's not too late to have them hook you up with someone less...controversial."

Though she'd started her rant with a decent amount of steam, it had bled off by the end of her magnanimous offer. If he took her up on it, she'd be right back in the pile of shit she'd started out in days ago. Plus, she really hadn't had time to worry about public opinion until the disgust in his almond eyes telegraphed exactly what he thought of rich daddy's girls who'd fallen from grace. He wouldn't be the only man who held her in such low regard.

She'd been lucky to find this job, never mind another. But she couldn't waste time. Not when innocents counted on her success.

She turned, prepared to gather her belongings. He reached for her. His broad hand had nearly grazed her arm when he stopped short. He retracted his shaking fingers.

"Damn it, I'm sorry. I didn't mean to come off all caveman."

Isabella almost crashed to the floor again when his impish smile brightened his whole face and turned her knees to jelly. The light expression took years off his militant face. She realized he couldn't be much older than she was.

"Talk about a bad first impression. Can we start over?"

Afraid to speak, she nodded instead.

"Here's the thing. I'm doing this on orders." He ruffled the dark brown spikes of helmet hair persisting at the base of his skull. "I...uh... Well, shit. I'm not unfamiliar with drama, and I hate being shoved into the limelight when people were beginning to forget about my fu...um, screw-up."

She studied the strong lock of his jaw and his classic Roman nose as something tickled her memory. The way his palm massaged his chest, in an awkward gesture she'd swear he didn't realize he indulged, tipped her off.

"You're the police officer..."

"Ding ding ding. We have a winner." The loathing flowing from him resonated with her. She took a step in his direction, but he retreated at an equal pace. "I'm the dumbass the smoking hot psycho-killer duped. You know, the bitch who shot me with my own gun when my pants were around my ankles then attempted to murder two of my squadmates and the love of their lives. They won't let me resume active duty until I take one for the force, make amends by leaving a good impression on the public through this joke of a show."

"I'm sorry," she whispered. She shivered as she remembered the macabre interest Malcolm had taken in the story. The garish pictures on the news had sickened her. Blood spattered in every direction. This man's blood. No one could understand better how the betrayal of someone you thought you cared for blistered your heart. The way it slashed your soul. But her pity didn't interest him, and he didn't offer her any in return. Not that she would have appreciated it if he had.

Isabella gave him a minute to pull his act together. She glided to the corner of the room, sitting cross-legged near the stack made by her bag, the CD with the music selection they'd been assigned to use and a packet of instructions. After several long, tense moments, he followed, dropping to his haunches beside her spot on the floor—careful to keep their knees from touching.

Maybe her bullshit meter had been permanently fried, but he seemed genuine when he met her questioning gaze and murmured, "Thanks."

She smiled, deflecting the intensity he leveled at her with a joke. Though, she wasn't entirely kidding. "You might want to hold off with your gratitude. I have every intention of winning this title, and I'll do whatever it takes to whip you into shape."

"Why is some cheesy competition so important to you?"

She nearly forgot to answer him as she inhaled the succulent combination of leather and soap wafting from his skin. How could it be possible to be this attracted to a man after knowing him less than five minutes, of which he'd spent a solid fifty percent pissing her off?

"I guess I want to prove I'm more than a beautiful but useless trophy." She certainly wasn't about to cry to him over her money issues or clue him in to her worst nightmare—that her father would allow Malcolm to reclaim her before she could rescue those poor women.

This time he'd make her pay. Double for the humiliation she'd showered on him by going public. If he found out she'd discovered his sordid business, or how much it upset her, he'd start making others suffer for her transgressions too.

"Is that why you left your husband?"

Isabella refused to confide in her partner, no matter how gently he asked. No matter how she wished she could trust someone—anyone—because when it came down to it, he was still a cop. And, holy God, what if her father or husband had sent him? What if they'd been biding their time to put her off guard? What if it had nearly worked?

Razor's abrupt change of heart had her instincts prickling. Well, two could play at this game. She would spoon-feed him what she wanted him to see, to know. Nothing more and nothing less.

"We should get to work. The camera crew is coming around the hand-off time to film snippets of us practicing and record a couple candid quotes to use in commercials for the new season. I want to run through our entire routine today. We have until Wednesday to prepare. That's not a lot of time." She tore open the envelope then tipped it upside-down. A note card fluttered to the ground where it landed face up.

Isabella Buchanan and James Reoser: The Waltz.

"Well *James,* it looks like we'll have to pretend to be dignified. What do you know about the waltz?"

"First, only my mom calls me that. Second, are you serious? The waltz? About as much as I know about designer purses, *Izzy.*"

She couldn't help but grin. Her lack of interest in fashion had been one of the many disappointments she'd delivered to her father and husband. "Well, I'd have a hard time telling a Louis Vuitton from a Coach handbag if they didn't stamp those handy letters on them. But, lucky for you, I do know how to dance the shit out of a waltz."

A heartfelt laugh escaped Razor's trim yet solidly-put-together chest. "I love it when a good girl talks nasty."

"I wasn't allowed to curse at home."

"Most kids aren't."

Isabella zipped her not-so-angelic lips before she revealed too much. God, he made it easy to run her mouth. At least he hadn't caught that she meant either her father's or her husband's household. Thank God. She'd have to watch herself around Razor. He put her at ease too quickly—too completely—for her own good.

"I want to see you move."

"What?" James cocked his head, trying to keep up with her change of topics.

"So, you don't know the waltz. I can teach you steps no problem. I have to see you dance. To anything. Show me what you've got."

"Oh, hell no. I don't think so."

"If you can't shake it for me, how will you perform in front of a studio audience and all the live viewers at home on Wednesday night?"

"Son of a bitch." His face drained of color as though he

seriously hadn't considered that aspect of their task.

She reached out to take his hand, but he snatched it away so fast she thought he might punch himself in the face with his fist.

"Hey, never mind for now. I didn't mean to freak you out. I just need an idea of how much work we have to do and where we should start." Isabella flipped on the radio next to her. La Roux's "Bulletproof" poured out of the crappy speakers. "Do you ever dance at parties? Or maybe hit the clubs?"

The idea of a carefree night on the town seemed unbelievably alluring to her. If she'd had the opportunity she would have gone out every weekend. How could she be twenty-two and already have so damn many regrets?

"Uh, yeah. That's hardly the same thing. I mean, there's a lot of alcohol involved before I venture on the floor and..." He glanced toward his toes as he left the thought hanging.

"You're usually chasing a woman so you have added incentive, right?"

Could her hardass partner actually be blushing? She couldn't resist teasing him.

"If it helps, I could wear a really short skirt and wiggle around in front of you."

"No! Shit, don't do that." If she hadn't spotted the bulge in his pants—for which he made no apologies—his insistent denial might have ground her ego into dust. All her life she'd been complimented on her beauty. Sometimes it had intimidated men or women who couldn't see past her genetic good fortune. Never before had it seemed to anger someone outright.

Razor shot to his feet, turning his back to her. She smiled as it reminded her of her audition for the show. Whether he acknowledged it or not, she had an awful lot in common with this damaged man.

"This is stupid." He bitched as he peeled off his armored motorcycle jacket with deliberate efficiency, but he didn't stop. Isabella thanked her lucky stars he couldn't see her eyes bug out when she caught sight of his faded T-shirt clinging to the defined muscles of his shoulders and trim waist. A gasp nearly choked her when her stare traced the contours of his biceps to his hands, which tugged the cotton into place over the exposed swatch of his bronzed lower back. "Don't suppose you ever saw *Napoleon Dynamite*, huh?"

She had to gulp to prevent the whimper threatening to escape her tight throat. "Nope."

"Welcome to D-Qwon's dance grooves..."

Isabella had no idea what he kept muttering about. She didn't have any spare brain cells to decipher his rambling. She'd only ever seen one man naked until last week. Hazy images assaulted her, but she buried them. Malcolm kept himself in shape. Tall and broad, he had never seemed half as powerful as the man an arm's reach from her now. She wondered what Razor's caramel skin would taste like if she licked it.

She shook her head violently to erase the obscene images from her mind. Maybe her husband had been right to keep her distant from other men. He'd always claimed Isabella would be out of control, too sensual for her own good. She'd learned to suppress her desires when she noticed they turned Malcolm off faster than a kick to the crotch. She never would have poured salt on the wound made by his shortcomings.

When faced with something as tempting as the man before her, she had to draw on the reserve she'd worked hard to cultivate. For all she knew, he had a girlfriend. He'd avoided so much as shaking her hand. Plus, hello, she was married until her lawyer came through with no-fault papers and she convinced Malcolm to sign them by whatever means necessary.

So why the hell couldn't she stop imagining this man caressing her?

Here and now, the only thing that mattered was surviving this week of competition. Isabella allowed some of her fear from *that* night to seep into her awareness. Trusting the wrong person could prove fatal and yet she daydreamed about a near stranger.

Her recklessness chilled her as though ice water ran in her veins. And not a moment too soon.

Razor's fists unclenched, his shoulders dropped and his tight ass began to sway at eye level as he—hallelujah—kept time with the music. His thighs bunched and released beneath the fabric of his jeans. He didn't try any fancy moves. He didn't have to. The simple play of his coordinated swaying spoke volumes.

This she could work with. As long as she began their session instead of drooling over his eleven-on-a-scale-of-one-to-ten buns. Before she could consider her actions, she slapped his firm rear. “Nice job, teammate. Now we need to find out what you’re like in hold.”

Chapter Four

Razor's heart fell to the soles of his filthy socks when the little princess curtseyed then extended her arms to him. He'd never ached to accept an invitation so badly in his life. Not the one offered by her posture. The one burning in those azure eyes.

No doubt about it, he was screwed.

If his attraction had been basic, all about her looks, he could have written it off. The instant chemistry between them, though, made it a million times harder to dismiss. Ms. Isabella Buchanan got him right off the bat—his moods, his bad jokes and his need for space to avoid poisoning his surroundings with the self-loathing rotting his gut after the long winter months.

How the hell could he battle their instant connection?

Now she stood, waiting. Waiting for him to take her into his arms with hope shining from the depths of her soul that he understood even a sliver of her in return. Damn it, he did. Or at least, he thought he did. Unless it was all an act—a con intended to disarm him.

Fuck. He hungered to touch her—skin on skin—so bad there might as well have been a giant magnet in each of his hands, drawing him toward their counterparts in hers. He stepped closer, near enough his breath fanned tendrils of her hair.

The light strands did a piss-poor job of concealing the fading bruise on her cheek. He smothered primal instincts, which shouted for him to claim her and force the barbarian who'd infused doubt into something so magnificent to count the cost.

After all, his intelligence outweighed preprogrammed

reactions. Had to, if he were to survive.

Crazy women had no boundaries. Isabella's sketchy side of the story might not exist in the same universe as the truth, though the fact Malcolm Carrington had declined to comment on her departure had the public scratching their heads.

Razor had come prepared to hate her. Or—better yet—to feel nothing at all. What coursed through him now was definitely not nothing. It was something.

Something monumental.

His palm hovered a millimeter from hers for an eternity. Their ragged but synchronized breathing filled the time until he surrendered, allowing forces of nature to bring them together. Isabella's fingers folded over the top of his then squeezed. Her other hand rested on his shoulder blade, searing a hole in his shirt. Before he lost all control and slammed them together from collarbones to shins, she broke eye contact and cleared her throat.

The pulse pounding in her wrist caught his attention as they both concentrated on acting impartial for a solid fifteen seconds. When he thought he might have to excuse himself or risk embarrassment the likes of which he hadn't known since middle school, she jerked his hand. His elbow stuck out to the side at an awkward and uncomfortable angle.

Razor saw her mouth moving. He had no idea what instructions spilled from those glossy pink lips as he mentally recited his new mantra: This could all be for show. She could be sumptuous but deadly. Don't trust her. Ignore your dick. Ignore your dick. Ignore your—

"James! Are you listening to me?" She wrenched away a moment after repulsion clouded the summer sky of her eyes. "I can't teach you anything if you don't open your ears and quit looking at me as if you'd like to spit in my face."

Her prim and proper schoolmarm scolding made him harder. How the hell fucked up was that?

He hated the wobble in her voice as she finished her verbal smackdown. Regardless of her guilt or innocence, he hadn't been raised to hurt a woman. "I'm sorry, Izzy."

"You realize we've known each other less than an hour and already you've apologized twice? We don't have time for this nonsense." He suspected she spun around to hide her reaction. If so, she covered it well. She popped the CD into the cheap stereo. After setting the track to loop, she snagged a broom from the corner with the rest of the supplies. For one surreal second, he thought she intended to take a swing at his head with it.

Instead, she sauntered over in time to the sweeping orchestral introduction that could have come from an old black and white movie or a classy commercial for something he could never hope to afford. He liked it instantly.

"What is this?"

"'At Last' by Etta James."

"Nice." His grin cut short when she hoisted his arms into that torturous shape then jammed the broomstick into the vee of his elbows, behind his shoulders, until he stayed pinned where she'd put him. "What the hell?"

"Perfect." She grinned up at him. The dazzling display stole his breath, allowing her to continue steamrolling him. "Now...shut up and dance."

Razor sputtered when her hands landed on his hips and molded him into position. She might as well have shoved the broomstick up his ass. He'd never stood so straight in all his life.

"Now, place your right palm on the center of my back, between my shoulders." When he didn't move, she glared at him. "What? Do I smell or something?"

He couldn't help but crack up when she did a quick pit check. Princess was busting with surprises.

"Touch me. Now, Razor."

Fuck if that didn't bring to mind all sorts of forbidden temptations.

She squirmed beneath his bicep where it dangled off the torture device behind his spine. His hand reached out without the conscious green light from his brain. It spanned most of her shoulders.

"That's...fine." She swallowed hard as she stiffened her frame, mirroring his pose by resting her tiny fingers on his shoulder. Her other hand clasped his, folding over the ridge made by his index finger. He marveled at the difference in their sizes. A baby bird couldn't have seemed more delicate in his grasp.

Razor peered at Isabella's face, close enough now he could kiss her with no effort at all. In the hushed atmosphere, she whispered, "Feel the beat of the music. *One* two three, *one* two three, *one* two three."

The romantic melody could have been the soundtrack for a child's fairytale. The steady thump resonating through him originated from the pounding of his heart...or his cock. At least that's what he thought until her counting blended with the soft lullaby and Razor found he could definitely hear what she meant.

"Oh, yeah." He tapped on the base of her neck with the pad of his middle finger. "It doesn't seem like such a slow song should go that fast."

"Yes, yes. It does." She beamed. "You have it. Now imagine walking forward, three steps at a time. Starting with your left foot. Left, right, left, pause. Right, left, right, pause."

He'd no sooner thought about it than his body began to move as though he'd done it a million times before. The instant he stepped forward, she stepped back. They moved as one. Their graceful promenade bore no resemblance to bopping from side to side with the bass in a club. Hell, the times he'd really gone for the bump and grind had nothing on the intimacy of dancing like this. When he reached the far wall of the studio, he turned, unwilling to let Isabella go. She flowed with him like water over a rock in a stream.

"Very good." She beamed up at him when she squeezed his fingers. "Keep your arms locked, maintain the basic step and I'll follow wherever you lead."

Goddamn, did she know what she did to him? How such a sweet promise nearly made him drunk with longing? Razor closed his eyes, feeling instead of thinking for the first time in months. A rough breath bellowed his chest, pressing it against the dual mounds of lush but perky breasts. When had he cradled her so close?

The pebbled tips of her nipples branded his ribs, obliterating his concentration. He tripped. To avoid smashing her, he stutter-stepped and ended up tangling their legs beyond saving. They were going down.

Razor shrugged the broom off. He smothered her in a bear hug. He rotated so his side absorbed the brunt of the impact. The air whooshed from her with a pronounced, "Oomph."

"Shit! Izzy! You okay?" When her shoulders shook beneath his palms, he wondered if he hadn't somehow hurt her.

But when she lifted her head, there was no mistaking the

childish exhilaration flushing her checks and brightening her eyes for anything harmful. She draped over him, propped on spread hands that kneaded his chest.

"I'm better than okay, James. You did great. We're going to kick some serious ass Wednesday night."

Before he could react, she lunged over him, bussed his cheek—stroking every inch of his body with hers—then sprang to her feet. He shook his head when she offered him a hand up, as though he wouldn't drag her to the floor again if he accepted. Not that parts of him objected to having her close, maybe beneath him next time.

Damn it. When she gazed at him with those wide, innocent eyes, he couldn't believe her capable of involvement in something as base and disgusting as a sex slavery ring. Could this sprite sell out other women to those who would inflict horrors guaranteed to mar their souls forever?

It seemed utterly impossible. And that's when he knew he'd already lost all objectivity. In less than one hour, she'd planted the seeds of major doubt in his ironclad conviction of her guilt and treachery.

"I need air." He tried to ignore the shock he caught in her expression before spinning away.

"What did I do, James?"

The flare of regret at her dismayed whisper didn't assuage his guilt. Instead, it fanned the embers of his annoyance, transforming his lack of caution into a raging bonfire of self-recrimination. Especially when he had to stop himself from returning to her and begging her to forgive his temper.

"I told you. Don't call me that," he snapped as he stomped from the room. "Give me five."

"Be ready to learn choreography, you jerk." Her undignified shout rang along the hallway as he slipped into the stairwell.

He respected the strength it took for her to focus on the task at hand when he'd obviously hurt her. Or at least surprised her. If only he could do the same—block out the desire clamoring for his attention to the detriment of his common sense—they'd be set. He needed a little time to clear the scent of her strawberry shampoo, the sound of her lyrical laughter and the feel of her lithe, young form locked in his arms from his system.

Then maybe he could think straight.

Isabella splashed icy water from the bathroom sink onto her cheeks and the nape of her neck. She fanned herself with a wad of coarse paper towels. When that didn't help, she cranked open the grimy window, blasting her damp skin with brisk spring air. Nothing worked. She gawked at her rosy cheeks in the cracked mirror. Could she be having hot flashes thirty years too early?

Damn it. No.

Could she rationalize the heat burning her up as if she had a triple digit fever?

Damn it. No.

There was only one valid explanation. The reason had stormed from the closest thing she'd had to fun in years for God knew what reason. Fickle men. She'd never figure them out. Had she become so pathetic and starved for attention that anytime someone glanced at her with a tiny bit of interest, or a truckload of hunger, she caved?

Okay, so Razor looked like an avenging angel and carried some serious scars. She still shouldn't allow him to affect her. Isabella couldn't afford to depend on him, to have his opinion matter so much. Not so soon after she'd finally torn herself from Malcolm's influence. She wouldn't make the same mistake again, trusting another person for far too long when her instincts screamed at her to run. No, she had ruined her life with blind faith once. She wouldn't do that again.

If Razor screwed up, she'd call him on it. If he earned her respect, she'd give it. But never again would she surrender her soul to someone who didn't deserve it. Who wouldn't care for it.

Isabella laughed at herself as she returned to the practice room, ready for round two. What the hell was she doing, thinking of souls and forever? All she had to do was dance with this surly man for a few weeks. After that, she'd never see him again.

Before she could chastise herself for the sinking in her stomach at the thought, her cell phone rattled from the depths of her bag. She rifled through the contents—ace bandage wrapper, tracksuit, car keys—as the insistent buzzing drove her nuts. Why was it that whatever she needed most was the last thing she could set her hands on in this damn duffle?

"Got you." Her grin morphed into a frown when she

unlocked the screen of her Droid and read the message waiting there from Nobody.

Don't get too cozy with the cop. I'm watching.

Another buzz.

Nice ass, btw. I'll keep texting if you'll keep bending over like that.

She whipped around, her frantic gaze flying from window to window. It was no use, their training space faced no less than four high-rises huddled around a central courtyard. Each towered above their spot on the third floor. There had to be dozens of vantage points in the neighboring properties.

The creeps tingled along her spine as her breath sawed out in unregulated gasps.

When a tap rocked her shoulder, Isabella yelped. She almost jumped out of her skin.

"Ohmygod!" She stumbled from Razor, who cocked his head, a mix of amusement and concern in his gaze.

"Sorry." He scrubbed his knuckles over his creased brow. "Shit, I wish I didn't have to keep saying that."

Her heart slammed in her chest, preventing her from responding.

"Look, I didn't mean to get so riled up before. Hell, I went outside in that nasty alley without putting my boots on. I wasn't trying to sneak up on you." He reached out to her when she stood there, shaking. "Sit down before you fall, Izzy."

She slapped his helping hand then crashed to the floor, her legs curling beneath her.

"You have a right to be annoyed. I acted like an ass."

Tears stung her eyes so she closed them, afraid to let him see—afraid she'd permit him to gather her close and soothe her where her secret observer could note every detail. No matter what happened between them, Isabella swore she wouldn't tangle this man in more trouble than he'd already had.

"Son of a bitch, your face is beyond pale. I never knew what *ashy* meant before. Breathe, Isabella."

Razor's tender caring only made things worse. She bit her

lip hard, a technique she'd perfected to distract herself with the small pain when she couldn't afford to show her emotions in public. Malcolm had taken sick pleasure in insulting her where she couldn't hide during their relationship.

In the beginning, she hadn't understood why he goaded her, almost as though hoping she'd swipe at him. It took a while but she'd figured out it happened at events her father also attended. The power must have gone to his head each time she heeled.

Why had she stayed so long? What if he never granted her freedom? Was she putting Razor at risk? If he suspected what she'd seen...

"Maybe we should call it a day. If we lose this week, you'll be home free." She cursed the tremor undermining her authority.

"Maybe we shouldn't."

Great. *Now* he tapped into the stubborn determination she'd sensed in him from the moment they'd met.

"This is important to you. It is to me too. I need to show the community they can rely on me. I'm going to continue to serve them—to make our city safer. It's all I've ever wanted, and I'm willing to earn their trust. Your trust."

If her thoughts weren't racing a million miles an hour, trying to maneuver them both to the safety he claimed to uphold, she might have delved deeper into his compulsion to reassure her of his commitment. Why did he look at her so intently?

Did he suspect all she hid from him?

Suddenly, she could no longer stand to peer into his warm eyes. She broke their too-intense connection as she struggled to her feet. When his hand landed on her arm, she shook it off.

Isabella caught a glint of a reflection across the way. At least she thought she had, in either the eighth or ninth floor of the black-glass building. But when she peered at the spot, nothing shone in the sunlight. Wishful thinking and the shimmer of tears had manufactured the flash.

She heaved a sigh.

"That's it, Izzy. Take another deep breath. Calm down, okay? I'm not angry with you. I'm not going to hurt you. Shit, you must think I'm a total asshole to flinch like that." The soothing timbre of his speech did help some.

Her brain kicked in again as adrenaline receded. The message had warned her off getting too cozy. It hadn't instructed her to drop out of the competition. If she did, whoever Malcolm had sent to pester her might become equally angry. God only knew what they wanted from her. Better to play it safe. Keep on as she had been while ensuring Razor kept his distance.

That she could do. Malcolm hadn't attempted to touch her in months.

"Fine. Let's continue where we left off. We have a lot of work to do if you're going to be presentable by the day after tomorrow. Where's the broom?"

"Izzy..."

Isabella stomped out the fuzzy glow his nickname lit in her belly. She cut him off with her best imitation of her etiquette coach, who'd had the most annoying method of lecturing out of all her snobbish teachers. "Next, we'll focus on rise and fall as you memorize the opening sequence."

She ignored the irritation etched into the grim set of his jaw and his grumpy mutter, which she would bet he hadn't intended for her to overhear.

"Fine. If that's how you plan to be. Probably for the best..."

Four hours later, Razor ached in places he'd never imagined could be sore. Of course, that was in addition to his not-quite-healed injuries, which throbbed like a son of a bitch. Physical therapy couldn't compare to ballroom dancing. Hell, half the stuff Izzy had him attempting seemed more in the realm of contortionism than nobility, which—she'd informed him in what he was coming to think of as her hoity-toity voice—was what the freaking waltz had been designed to showcase.

She had morphed into a serious hardass since his outburst. He supposed he deserved it. Plus, it made resisting her easier. She felt like a board in his arms instead of the supple young woman he'd danced those initial steps with. Some unwise yearning urged him to recover a bit of their earlier closeness. Eight weeks of this could freeze his balls off.

If she were trying to sucker him, would she take this approach? It sure as hell didn't sound smart, but what the fuck did he know of women, demented or not? He couldn't figure out a damn thing. He'd toed the line too. Hell, he'd practically pushed her away when he needed to learn more for the investigation.

"Once more, from the top."

"You said that five times ago." Razor battled fatigue, but he worried more about the strain weighing on Isabella. Her shoulders slumped between run-throughs. Last time around she'd stumbled, crashing into his chest before snapping back as though burned. Lunchtime had come and gone. She hadn't accepted any of the peanut M&M's he'd scored from the vending machine in the lobby and their bottled water had run out over an hour ago.

"Do it right and we'll call it quits for today." She rotated her ankle while they waited for the music to begin again.

A handful of inches from her sweaty yet adorable face, he detected a chink in her stony façade. The vulnerability she finally relaxed enough to let him see had him spilling his guts in a flash. "I'm really glad you're my partner."

"Because you wanted more gossip associated with your name?" She sniffed, shaking her head. The reaction had him tucking her closer, no matter how bad he stunk.

"No, because I enjoyed spending time with you today."

She grimaced as she massaged the base of her spine. The motion thrust her breasts at him. After hours of dancing, plastered together, he thought he'd be immune, but the mouthwatering sight derailed his train of thought.

"You relish being bitched at for hours when you've done a great job?"

He had to think twice about what she'd said.

"You think I did great?" Razor overcame the resistance in her hold with minimal effort. He reached around her dainty waist to rub out her cramp.

Both of them ignored the music they knew by heart now anyway when it droned out the waltz once more. He anchored her to his side until she practically rode his thigh. At least she'd gotten used to his hard-on bumping into her, because he had no chance of hiding it.

"Yeah," she sighed. "You're amazing."

The primal side of him cheered when she went lax in his hold. For the first time since morning, she rested against him. Pliant, warm, tired and sexy as hell, she conformed to each plane and ridge of his body. Just like he'd known she would.

"You're not doing too bad yourself, teach." Before he could consider the consequences, Razor's palm cupped her jaw, tipping her face up to his as his other hand continued the slow circuit over her spine.

The dazed look in Isabella's striking eyes beckoned him. He leaned closer as his thumb traced her high cheekbone.

"Mmm," she sighed. "You smell like chocolate."

"Probably taste like it too," he whispered a hairsbreadth from her lips.

The racket caused by something smashing on the floor had them jumping apart like startled jackrabbits. Razor shoved Izzy behind him with one arm while he reached for the gun he wasn't wearing with the other. *Fuck.*

He'd gotten so caught up in the moment he hadn't heard anyone approach. Two shadows flickered in the hallway as he prepared to defend Izzy from the intruders. He crouched, calculating the best line of attack, when a freckle-faced kid stumbled into the room.

"Damn it, Freddie!" A rotund dude in a garish Hawaiian shirt and cargo shorts, despite temps in the low fifties, followed two steps behind. "How many times have I fucking told you? Take the lens shade off *before* we get inside. You don't need that shit in here and now we missed the shot. In this market I can hire a new intern anytime I damn well please. Make yourself useful for once. Buy me some donuts while I tape the commercial clips. That shit's all you're good for."

Razor wanted to pound the dickhead twice. Once for his treatment of Freddie and again, harder, for the leer he flung in Izzy's direction.

"Man, you're my hero. Half a day in and you're scoring some of that fancy pussy."

Razor snarled as he prepared to set the man straight.

"No, James." The combination of Isabella's gentle plea and her arm wrapped around his waist stopped him dead in his tracks. She cuddled up to him. His blood boiled when she murmured into the nape of his neck, out of sight, "The camera's recording."

"Jealous? It's not like you'd know anything about that, shithead." Okay, mouthing off was immature. But the slam made Razor feel a little better when the weasel squinted in an overweight version of his Aunt Maria's evil eye. "You could only dream of a woman like her."

"Come on." Isabella lurched from behind him to fling her belongings into her giant purse. "We're finished here."

"Uh, uh." The cameraman grunted. "We gotta can some shit to use for the show."

"How's this?" Razor flipped the man off. He knew better than to stoop to this level, but the grueling day of endless frustration—both in learning something so novel and being trapped in such close proximity to a woman he wanted desperately and could never have—ate at him, finally finding a place to vent.

The bastard laughed. His lurid attention migrated from Isabella's sweet ass to scope out her headlights beneath the damp white T-shirt she wore. That's when Razor's fingers curled into a fist. He believed in the law, in doing things the right way, but sometimes a good fight solved problems with less paperwork.

"I'm leaving. If the producers need a sound byte, they know my number." Isabella brushed past his posturing and strode from the room, forcing him to choose between rearranging the dirtbag's greasy nose and making sure she was okay.

"Fuck with her again and I'll have you downtown for harassment before you can blink. She's not a toy, made to amuse any man eager for a cheap thrill."

"What else do you think a broad like that sees in some work-a-day cop? You're more pathetic than me if you think she's looking for anything other than a rebound fuck. You're in the right place at the right time, bro. Live it up."

Afraid there could be some truth to the man's venom, Razor stormed from the studio, racing to catch Izzy. Damn, the girl could move quick when someone fired her up.

He burst into the lot as she collapsed into her Ferrari. He cringed when he imagined their current sweaty state meeting the supple Italian leather. She hadn't had a chance to put on the spare clothes she'd brought.

She slammed the door, making him wince again, as he neared. He scowled when the snick of the locks engaging reverberated through the deserted lot. Was she afraid of him?

He crossed the last couple yards at a more sedate jog to tap on her window. When she refused to turn her head, her blatant dismissal couldn't have been more obvious. The tinted windows made it hard to tell for sure, but he thought she might be crying. The possibility drove him nuts.

He refused to budge when she revved the engine. Finally, she cracked the window then begged, "Please. James, let me go. I'm fine, okay."

"No, it's not fucking okay. You shouldn't have to put up with shit like that." He didn't mention their almost kiss. If it had a tenth of the effect on her that it'd had on him, her insides probably felt like they traveled in a dinghy over rough seas.

"I'm used to it. It happens all the time. I ignore it. Please, back off. People will see us talking."

His head snapped back as though she'd roundhoused him. "Oh. Yeah. Right."

"I didn't mean that like it sounded. I..." But she didn't continue. Really, what else was there to say?

When he spun toward his bike, itching for the open road, she raised her voice so it would carry. He didn't turn around, but he slowed.

"Practice isn't scheduled until the afternoon tomorrow. I'd like to spend the morning buying you the proper attire. Meet me at the Pyramid Mall, outside Wrightman's, at eleven?"

Two minutes ago, he'd have granted her whatever she asked for. Now... why should he? Oh, right, it was his job. "Not afraid someone will spot us together there?"

"It's not what you think. I have to go. Now. Please, be there."

He tried not to glance over as she peeled out, but he couldn't fucking help himself. The misery in her expression made it impossible to deny what he'd already known. He'd show up at the damn mall, or anywhere else the princess requested his presence. Because he had to figure out if Ms. Isabella Buchanan was the devil in disguise or the woman of his dreams.

The cool metal of the gun settled into his grip like an old friend as he trained the crosshairs on his target. He'd been instructed to frighten. Wound but not kill. How many times had he been given that exact order when someone lacked the balls to ask for what they really desired? Stealing the life of something so beautiful seemed almost a shame. The prospect made him feel like a great safari hunter taking down a cheetah.

Isabella Buchanan would be a prize kill.

His prey stepped into his line of sight. The man's finger curled, tensing on the trigger as he drew a steady breath. In the fraction of a second he needed to eliminate her, a crash sounded from below, breaking his concentration.

The fucking cop. The do-gooder raced from the building, heading for the target. When the sniper looked back, she'd already hidden behind the cover of her car. Even if he could be sure the bullet would stay true through the sheet metal, or that he'd hit her behind the tinted glass, destroying the vehicle seemed crude. They'd only made four hundred of them and half of those had probably been crashed by now. Maybe, after she had been terminated, he'd buy the car and keep it as a momento.

Being wasteful wasn't his style. There'd be plenty of other chances to complete his assignment. He'd promised his employer he'd finish the job by the end of the week. Time enough to make it perfect for them both.

Chapter Five

Razor rode until his arms and legs went numb enough he worried he might crash his motorcycle. When the freezing evening air finally registered, he headed for home. Day one of his new life had been a hell of a reintroduction to undercover work.

At the apartment, he parked then hopped off his bike. At least he tried to. His thigh had stiffened beyond belief. It took some working over the scarred area, plus two more attempts, to clear the seat. Once he had, he found himself gazing at the twilight sky, smiling as he recalled the highlights of the afternoon.

Terrorists could rip his fingernails off one by one before he'd admit it to the guys at the station, but he'd enjoyed the hell out of dancing with Izzy. Even when she'd tried to shut him out, electricity had sizzled under the surface, ready to arc between them when she let her guard drop.

Every time he'd mastered a difficult step she rewarded him with those delicious dimples and serious approval. By the mid-point of their session, she'd upgraded the choreography to incorporate more advanced tricks.

Razor danced up his sidewalk, practicing her precious rise and fall with the heel-toe action inciting his muscles to cry uncle. It'd been a while since he believed he could succeed at something. So what if it was a stupid contest—one he wasn't a true competitor in?

He had no idea why it mattered, but he needed to give his partner a chance at her dream. It must be the way she looked at him, as though she noticed the wounds no one else could see. The ones on his soul.

She empathized because she had scars too.

He'd swear on it.

What he couldn't decide was how they'd shaped her. Or him for that matter. What did either of them have to offer the world after sustaining irreparable damage? How would they act now that their ideals had shattered and reformed?

Razor swung wide as he practiced the dip Izzy had taught him. Without her weight to counterbalance him, he staggered a little.

"It could use some polish, kid."

He fumbled when he caught sight of the familiar man loitering on his steps. Jeremy Radisson sat on the landing with his legs stretched out over the stairs. From the glint in his friend's eyes, Razor knew he'd been busted big time.

"Shit. You're not going to keep this to yourself, are you JRad?"

"Oh, hell no." He grinned. "What fun would that be?"

Razor would have taken a whole load of crap instead of the glum resolve that coalesced on the computer whiz's face, dampening his teasing.

"Fuck me."

"No thanks. You're not my type. But, yeah, you're probably not gonna like this." JRad climbed to his feet and made things worse. "Why don't we head inside?"

"That bad?"

"I respect you. I think of you as my little brother on the force. That's why you should hear the truth from me before you face it in front of the chief and the other guys. I can wait until the briefing tomorrow morning, but then I have to share what I found."

Acid clawed at his stomach as he fished in his pocket for his keys. He opened the door, waiting for JRad to pass. The older cop went straight to the fridge and removed four beers as though he lived in the apartment. He joined Razor in the connected living room where he'd plopped onto the hand-me-down couch he'd inherited from Mason and Tyler when they moved in with Lacey.

"You planning to start on that?" Jeremy nodded to the bottle Razor had nearly broken in his grip. "Or you want the news fast?"

"Both." He used the edge of his coffee table to pop the top off his beer before downing half the contents in one long swig. "Go."

"I...uh...hacked into her phone today."

"Before you had the carrier's permission?" Razor rubbed the knot of tension in his neck.

"We have a warrant, but...yeah."

"JRad, that kind of shit is going to land you in trouble one day." They'd had this conversation before. Right now, he didn't care. He needed facts. Enough of all this emotional guesswork.

"I know." JRad looked chagrined. Still, the rules never stopped the nerd. He loved a challenge when it came to breaking and entering on virtual premises. "Anyway, I hate to tell you, but I think she might be dirty."

The serious concern on his friend's face deflated Razor. He crashed into the cushions of the sofa, flinging a forearm over his eyes as though he could block out the world. As an afterthought, he snagged his beer. He drained it before exchanging it for the full bottle.

"Why?" The question sounded more like a croak to him. JRad understood.

"It sounds like she has a handler."

"Fuck!" The vehemence of his anger and disbelief combo-special surprised them both.

"Tell me you aren't invested after a single day."

When Razor didn't answer, JRad cursed. The hiss of Razor's second beer opening ricocheted through the room.

"Damn it, I should have come down there. I tried to call. Your cell went straight to voicemail. I should have stopped in as soon as I intercepted the text messages."

"When did they come in?" A sinking suspicion grew in his gut.

"Around eleven."

"Son of a bitch!" That had been right about the time of their meltdown, when he'd bolted from the room and left her reeling. "I should have realized something had changed. She acted funny when I came back in. Fuck, she seemed terrified. I thought I'd startled her...you know, that she's jumpy after whatever shoved her from the nest last week."

JRad permitted him to ramble without asking for

unnecessary details. "I could see her being frightened. The tone definitely threatened with a hefty dose of jealous asshole, 'Don't get too cozy with the cop. I'm watching.' The dude also talked some shit about scoping her ass. Felt like he knew her. Maybe not. Maybe it's a psych out. I wouldn't put a lot of money on it, though."

Razor thought of at least a dozen scenarios that could paint Isabella innocent, then shook his head. He refused to wear rose-colored glasses. "If she were clean, she would have showed me that shit, right? I'm a cop for God's sake. I could help her if she were in trouble. Right?"

He peeled his arm from his face to glance at JRad, willing his friend to provide the barest shred of hope. Both men had stood in their friends' house and bought a psychotic woman's story hook, line and sinker. Neither cared to make such a grievous mistake again. JRad had answered Lacey's frantic call that night while Razor had lain in a pool of his own congealing blood, terrified—not for himself, but for the brothers he had failed. And their woman.

Instead of false promises, JRad asked, "Want another beer?"

"Bring them all."

The slave trembled with anticipation as he knelt in artificial darkness behind the satin and fur of his blindfold. Gentle hands guided his shoulders to the raised section of the padded bench. Leather restraints bolted to the far reaches of the contraption encircled his wrists. His cock throbbed, releasing a stream of pre-come that trickled toward his thigh.

Familiar scents—leather, sweat and sex—perfumed the air. He dragged in a greedy lungful and held it. The assistant shoved his knees further apart as she positioned him in the ideal pose. She lodged a spreader bar between his legs to ensure he remained where she'd placed him. He arched his spine to present himself for her approval. She always cared for him when he behaved and doled out appropriate punishment when he deserved it. He understood he reflected on her—her training, her handiwork.

"Very nice, slave." She patted his ass, her hands trailing along his flank to cup his balls in her supple palm. Her dainty hand had no trouble gripping all of his junk at once.

He knew better than to move, though he yearned for nothing more than to thrust himself into her grasp. He must save his arousal for the Master. Perhaps if the Master was pleased, he would allow the woman to bring his slave satisfaction as he sometimes did. If not, the slave would be made to wait, to suffer unbearable lust that rose inside him like leavening bread until the next session when it would erupt in raw desperation.

God, how he loved those times. He would do anything—had done unspeakable things—to be escorted to a plane of existence where nothing mattered except submission, soaring on endorphins boosted by the manufactured ecstasy the Master doled out so sparingly.

He whimpered behind the ball gag stretching his jaw. Surely he had earned satisfaction.

"Quiet. You'll have something to cry over soon enough."

The slave stifled a moan when the blunt tip of a smooth device probed his asshole. He couldn't decide if it would be worse for her to shove it deep in one stroke or take it away. His muscles went slack as he relinquished his fate to her.

"Ah, yes. You *are* my favorite pet. So obedient."

Pleasure swamped his senses when she daubed lube against his tender hole in reward. Slick gel stole his breath with its coolness. The promise of heat to follow had his fingers clenching into fists where they lay, trapped.

He was not disappointed.

The pressure returned at his ass. He pushed out, welcoming the intrusion. It stretched him wider and wider as it sank to the base and yet he yearned for more.

"That's all there is for now." The woman crooned in his ear. "You know the Master likes to destroy some of your resistance himself."

And the slave loved it too. The bite of pain along with penetration made the act so much more intoxicating. He couldn't deny his implicit surrender then. Nothing made him hotter faster.

She checked the fit, her gloved finger teasing his anus around the imbedded object. When she was satisfied, he heard the familiar glide of nylon accompany her motions as she wove the attached straps through the loops on the modest cock ring strangling his straining erection, ensuring he could not eject the plug. His equipment paled in comparison to the Master's, but he hoped it at least plumped to its full capacity in a display of his rampant eagerness to please.

Although, the Master did delight in belittling him for his shortcomings.

The Dom would often fuck him harder after teasing him about his tiny prick or his inability to please his wife.

He had no chance to will the stubby flesh to subside when the rattle of chains rang through the quiet room. Knowing what would come next, he still cried out when the teeth of chilly metal clamps latched on to his sensitive nipples. If he squirmed, he could force the links connecting the pinchers to his cock ring to brush the nub of his dripping hard-on. The stimulation coupled with the pain generated by the motion would be enough to set him off.

But he didn't dare move.

His trainer verified the grip with one firm yank on his chains that set his cock swaying. When everything held, she whispered, "Prepare yourself. He's coming for you now."

The woman petted his hair until the initial shock of adrenaline subsided. He could hear the clink of metal, as he shivered, over the pounding of his heart.

"Please him so I may take care of you afterward. I would enjoy that very much today."

"Yes, ma'am." She would understand his garbled response through the gag. After all, she was an expert.

The moment the Master entered the room, the atmosphere changed. Though the slave couldn't see, the steady clomp of heavy boots approaching in a familiar gait told him all he needed to know. The man arched his back, flattened his shoulders and held the perfect posture as steps ringed him. The Master observed and critiqued his possession.

"Very nice job, Lily." The Master's tone resonated. Full of smoke, it reminded the slave of fine, aged whiskey.

"Thank you, Sir."

"You may observe from behind the mirror if you wish."

"I will, Sir. Enjoy."

"Don't I always, dear?" The Master chuckled, waiting for the woman to retreat to her observation post before proceeding.

The slave tensed when footsteps neared his head, grateful

for the straps anchoring the plug in his ass when he clenched on it. The Master unbuckled his gag, letting it fall to the floor. In the next instant his blindfold vanished, ripped away with one wrench.

The dim lighting of the dungeon seared his pupils for several moments. When his sight returned, the hard length of his Master's veiny cock—framed in crotchless leather chaps—filled his vision, front and center.

The man lunged forward as far as his restraints would allow to engulf the delicacy with his salivating mouth. He swallowed the shaft to the root, reveling in the growl his Master made.

"Ah, yes. That's better. You missed me?"

The slave swallowed around the plump head, inviting the Master into his throat.

"I couldn't come sooner. Your failure angered me. I would have broken you."

The slave froze, terrified the Master would leave him again.

"But everyone makes mistakes. You will atone for yours."

Harsh fingers gripped his hair, tugging painfully to hold him in place as the Master fucked his mouth. The rocking set his nipples and balls on fire as the rigging enhanced the vacillation. He could service the Master like this for days on end. When the Master's abdomen tightened before the slave's eyes, the Dom yanked his cock away, abandoning his slave's throat. Spittle from the slave's mouth stretched before breaking. The glistening strand draped onto the nest of graying pubic hair that ringed the Master's ultra-thick shaft.

"So, tell me. Have you done as you were instructed?"

"Yes, Sir." His raw whine had been caused half by the rough treatment of his throat and half by his terror of disappointing the Master. "I hired..."

"I do not wish to know the details. Plausible deniability." The Master paced toward his rear. The slave hung his head to watch between his legs as the Master took his place there. "Just tell me it's been done. No fuck ups this time."

The Master accompanied his stern command with a hard slap on the slave's ass. He writhed, nearly begging for more.

"No, Sir. No fuck ups. I've done as you asked."

No sooner had he spoken the words than the Master

released the straps and extracted the plug from his gaping ass. The Master plunged inside the partially opened orifice until he buried the enormous length of his cock in one long thrust. Sparks of pain and pleasure radiated from the slave's channel as he imagined himself impaled on the glorious erection.

"Then you may take me."

"Yes! Thank you, Sir." He wept as the Master began to fuck him with brutal strokes, exactly how he loved it. This is what he lived for. This is what he had bargained so much of his soul for. The dark craving he'd always possessed, this man had recognized and began fulfilling more than fifteen years ago.

As the Master exited his prime, things had gotten shady for a while, until they had funded development of the drug. The savior of all they both needed. Yes, it had made the Master edgier than ever, but the slave welcomed the return of their sessions. How could he live without this? He wished the untamed fucking could last forever.

All too soon, the Master's balls grew taut where they slapped the slave's tense sac. The Dom's fingers tightened on his slave's hips as he rode with wild abandon. Though forbidden to come without permission, the slave edged toward the point of no return. At the last possible moment, the Master turned rigid behind him, spewing his come into the depths of the slave's bowels, searing the slave's prostate with seed as he roared out in completion.

The slave panted, dying for the single touch—the single word—that could have him joining in the rapture, shooting his own meager load to the bench beneath him. He was not granted such a reprieve.

Instead the Master withdrew, wiping his cock on the slave's thigh. When he turned to leave, the slave could not stand to be silent no matter the punishment he might have to endure for speaking out of turn. "Please, may I come for you?"

The Master sneered in disgust. "Absolutely not. Until you return my daughter to your household, you deserve no reward. Have you forgotten the terms of our arrangement? You keep the bitch close, and I give you what you need. I've upheld my end for over a decade, fucking you, training you, making you the centerpiece of lavish orgies. You've had responsibility for her for four short years, and you've already lost control of one tiny girl. You say you've done as instructed. Soon she will be scared right back into your arms, if not your bed, but who can blame her there?"

The Master stared pointedly at his slave's crotch.

"She is mine. She is valuable. Take her back. Her and *everything* she left with. This time I'll make sure she earns her keep. We've already strengthened the formula of the drug and prepared a list of clients who are willing to pay top dollar for a turn with her. We'll secure a lifetime supply for ourselves. You cannot afford to disappoint me again, Malcolm."

Isabella figured the odds of Razor showing to be one out of ten at best after the way she'd bungled things. Still, she dressed and styled her hair with more care than she'd taken in weeks. She tried to convince herself she did it to prepare for the stop she had to make before going to the mall. That didn't explain why she chose the sweater closest to the color of her student's eyes from her sparse stack of clothes, folded atop the broken chair in the corner.

She sighed in regret when she opted for classy pumps instead of her highest heeled boots, which she hadn't been able to leave behind. The confidence boost would have come in handy, but she'd overdone things the day before and her ankle protested. Loudly. The ace bandage she'd supported it with at her practice with Razor didn't seem to help as much today. Maybe because the flesh around the joint had swelled to epic proportions before she could ice and re-wrap it.

It'll be better by this afternoon.

She hoped she wasn't lying to herself about that one.

For now, she shoved aside her lingering dread. If she could execute her plan for the morning, maybe her ability to dance wouldn't matter as much by lunchtime. At least, not as more than a matter of pride.

Isabella appraised her handiwork in the speckled mirror, making a mental note to pick up some cleaning supplies on her excursion. From what she could discern through the grime, she'd done a respectable job of painting on her high-class camouflage. She marched over to her unlevel coffee table then refolded the certificate there along the existing creases before slipping it into her purse next to the envelope containing her leverage. Her stomach churned when she touched the documents. Using them could mean the difference between long-term escape or surrender.

Isabella gulped to swallow the knot in her throat, which threatened to strangle her. She strode out the door, engaging the half-assed lock behind her. Her mind zipped between choreographing more difficult transitions in the waltz, her insane attraction to the hot-headed—and hot-bodied—cop and anything else that would keep her occupied so she didn't have to consider nightmares that paralyzed her with hurt, terror or disgust.

Distracted, she failed to notice the shady guy lurking behind the stump of a dead oak tree at the bottom of the half-rotten staircase, which led to the street where she'd parked her get-away car. He stepped directly into her path. An undignified squeak burst from her before she could catch it. The panic she attempted to repress must have shone through, regardless.

"Hey there, pretty lady. No need to freak." When he held out his hands—covered in fingerless gloves, which might get cleaner if he rolled them in the dirt—Isabella tried not to cringe at the odor that wafted her way. The man could have a story not so different from hers for all she knew.

"I'm sorry, sir. You surprised me, that's all." She attempted a smile. The expression morphed into a grimace when the gap between her lips allowed her to taste his rankness as well.

"Sir!" The man doubled over with a hoot. "Ain't nobody ever sir'd me before."

Isabella edged closer to her car, eager to jump into her errands. She had limited time since she intended to reach the Pyramid by eleven, even though she expected James to stand her up.

"I like you, pretty lady. Was gonna shake you down for some spare change. You know, piss on your mailbox when you blew me off. But you ain't nothing like the other rich-bitch types I seen downtown."

When she winced, he waved his hands, amplifying the toxic fumes surrounding them like a black cloud.

"What's your name?" She cut him off before he could apologize. Why should he when she'd seen her father or Malcolm trod past less fortunate people like they didn't exist. Hell, half the time, she hadn't been treated much better.

"People call me Stinky." He grimaced. "But my momma named me Leo."

"It's nice to meet you, Leo. I'm going to be late if I don't hurry. Are you planning on being around tonight?"

"Nowhere else to go."

"I'll bring dinner. What's your favorite?"

"I ain't had a juicy steak in years." His dull eyes sparkled for a moment before he grunted. "I'd be glad for anything I don't have to dig out of the dumpster. Something warm would be heaven."

"I'll see what I can do." Isabella gave him a wave as she beeped open the car. "I might be late, sorry."

"Something to look forward to. Almost as good as food." He peeled his holey knit cap from his matted hair then fashioned her an awkward bow. "Drive safe, pretty lady."

Isabella darted in and out of traffic, loving the growl of the engine. It turned the heads of men—young and old alike—as she passed by. She ignored the pointing or gawking when a couple recognized her behind the wheel.

One of her greatest worries had been that her partner would hound her, asking uncomfortable questions she wasn't prepared to answer about her personal life. Razor hadn't pressured her much, and she hadn't pestered him for the gruesome details of his fiasco. Maybe that had created the foundation for their instant bond.

She didn't think she'd ever be able to discuss what had happened with anyone. Except maybe her lawyer, if Malcolm didn't cave under the pressure of her bluff to splash his indiscretions from newsstands to billboards unless he did as she demanded.

Isabella thought of the grainy black and white pictures in her purse. Clear enough to damn but fuzzy enough to allow room for doubt. Her husband could afford a whole team of high-priced lawyers to refute her claim.

She'd be lucky to snag one. *If* her meeting went well this morning.

After double-checking the flashy titanium sign against the page she'd torn from the phone book, she unfolded herself from the low-slung beast of a car. How did any man—never mind a tall, heavy one like her father—fit in the contraption? Hell, he'd probably never touched the toy. He simply enjoyed owning what others could not.

The whir and zing of power tools screeched into silence as

she progressed to the building. Before she'd gotten halfway there, three men in suits had appeared out of nowhere to hold the door. From inside the garage, a smattering of mechanics practically drooled. She grinned when she realized they leered beyond her, to her ride. Perfect.

"Ms. Buchanan." A salesman greeted her by name. It behooved luxury businesses to familiarize themselves with the high rollers in their city. She thought he took it a little far when he bent to kiss the knuckles of the hand she extended in greeting. The middle-aged brownnoser attempted to steer her toward a plush office, but she didn't have time for the requisite coffee and chit chat before getting down to business.

"If you'll excuse me, I'm on a tight schedule." Besides, it'd be better if he knew she meant to play hardball. Just because she looked like a freaking powder puff didn't mean she had to act like one anymore.

"Of course. How may I help you today?"

"I'd like to sell my car. Quickly." Isabella thought she might have heard the cha-ching of an imaginary register as the man calculated his potential bonus. She gave him credit for managing to keep his shit-eating grin from showing. Mostly.

"That shouldn't be a problem, miss. If you'll leave it here for us to detail, I'm sure I can line up a buyer within days."

"I'd prefer you to solicit bids for a sale by the close of business today."

The salesman's faux smirk wilted a smidge. "Ma'am, rushing this kind of transaction is not in your best interest."

"Thank you, I realize it won't maximize either of our profits. However, I'm in a hurry. I'm willing to sacrifice a bit in order to tempt someone into buying something ridiculously overpriced, which they could never justify in a thousand days of deliberation."

When he continued to drone on about return on investment as though she hadn't expressed her opinion on the matter, she crossed her arms over her chest and tapped her toe on the marble tile.

"Can we cut the crap, Mr. Nathwell?" she read off the embossed business card he'd handed her. "I realize you'd like a big fat commission from this sale, but something is always better than nothing. And that's what you'll have if you can't execute my wishes in the sale of the vehicle by this afternoon."

The older man's jaw hung slack as he reevaluated her. After several long seconds, he granted her a terse nod. "I understand. Let me take down a number where you can be reached then I'll arrange for someone to drive you wherever you need to go while we show the Enzo."

After no more than five minutes, George—they were now on a first name basis—shook her hand with a firm grip as he looked her straight in the eye. "I appreciate your business, Ms. Buchanan. I hope you don't mind me saying this... You're really nothing like I assumed you'd be. You remind me of my own daughter."

The sincere smile he flashed transformed his somber features into a kindly visage more appropriate to her ideal of grandparents—she'd never known any of hers—than a high-end auto shark. Tears pricked her eyes in an instant of weakness when she could least afford it. Instead of pouncing on her, George patted her wrist. He murmured, "You're going to do fine on your own, dear."

"I'm trying my best."

Chapter Six

The pounding in Razor's brain punished him for his overindulgence. He should know better than to attempt to drown his bad judgment. It had never worked before. When he flipped up the visor on his helmet, sunshine stabbed the recesses of his skull like a red-hot poker. What the hell was he doing here when he should be crashed on the floor of his apartment like JRad?

Oh yeah, he was working. Stupid piece of shit.

If he could have kicked his own ass for forgetting that yesterday, he would have done it. Twice. He'd wasted the entire day flirting, dreaming and dancing with the enemy when he should have been gathering intelligence to lock the conniving bitch away for the rest of her long, lonely lifetime.

Speak of the devil. Some freaking rich dude in a Bentley pulled to the curb. He circled the understated sedan to assist the princess in alighting from her chariot. The tool laid a giant smacker on Ms. Buchanan's lily-white knuckles, eliciting a giggle that sank the chump further into her clutches.

She obviously had a thing for suckers old enough to be her daddy. Or maybe they just had to be rich enough to be her sugar daddy. Razor tried to ignore the spike of jealousy accompanying his disillusionment. He feared the sarcasm in his tone couldn't be fully attributed to loathing—or the grumpiness that went hand in hand with a killer hangover—when he shouted, "Don't wait up. I probably won't bring her home before you fall asleep watching Judge Judy."

The bastard ignored him, turning to Isabella instead. That smile she'd worn, the one so huge you'd think she'd received the best Christmas present of all time, had vanished. She nodded at whatever the guy said then grasped him in a reassuring, one-armed hug. Razor ground his molars as the car rolled away. The resulting pain didn't impair him enough to blind him to the threatening glare the driver leveled at him as he passed by.

He stood rooted to the sidewalk near his motorcycle, insisting Izzy come to him. The strategy didn't pay off when her slinky hips shifted from side to side, encased in well-worn jeans, and her luscious breasts swayed beneath a sweater that tempted his palms to discover whether it felt as soft as it looked.

A far cry from workout garb. Holy shit.

Razor spun from her when her platinum hair billowed around her in the gentle spring breeze, denting his iron resolve to ignore the simulated magic between them.

"Good morning to you too, James." She didn't wait for him, keeping her pace steady as she headed for the front entrance to the posh shopping arena. He'd never ventured inside the mall, which catered to premium boutiques and designer labels.

"Stop calling me that." He broke into a jog to erode the distance she'd put between them. Immediately, he regretted it when his stomach cramped.

"Stop acting like an overbearing jerk."

He flung out an arm to keep the heavy bronze door she dropped from crashing into his chest. The jarring impact sloshed the contents of his turbulent guts. At least the interior of the building seemed dim in comparison to the cheery fucking morning, granting him some reprieve from the marching band pounding a beat in his head.

"So I'm supposed to stay silent as I trail far enough behind Your Highness that no one realizes we're here together? If you want, I could flash my badge so I look like paid protection. Give you some excuse to be seen with..."

Isabella startled him when she stopped mid-stride. He nearly plowed into her, catching himself by placing a hand above her elbow on that fuzzy sweater. The damn thing did feel like touching a cloud, more downy than it looked. She must have interpreted the gesture as an invitation. Before he could initialize evasive maneuvers, she'd planted herself less than a half-inch from him and wrapped her fingers around the base of his neck.

He didn't resist when she tugged him lower to peer into her turquoise eyes.

"I'm sorry for how what I said yesterday must have sounded. I like you, Razor. Yesterday was the most fun I've had in years. Please, don't make my comment something it wasn't so you can use it as an excuse to shut me out."

How the hell could he argue with her frankness? If she lied, she deserved an Oscar for that performance. But if she meant it...

"Tell me what you did mean, Izzy. What's going on here?"

She nibbled the corner of her lip. Her laser stare faltered before she glanced into the distance. In case miracles could happen, he tried to stay open-minded, letting her witness his acceptance and how fucking badly he wanted to help her—needed this sweet yet fierce girl to be innocent.

The flex of her throat as she swallowed hard drew his attention to a hand-shaped mark. Halogen lighting in this facsimile of a tropical paradise revealed discoloration he hadn't noticed there yesterday.

"What the..." he said at the same time she whispered, "My husband..."

Before either of them could finish, a gaggle of over-processed glamour babes with more plastic parts than a case of Barbie dolls shrilled from behind them. Their miniature dog, which looked embarrassed to sport a diamond collar and a ridiculous bow in its fur, ran for its life. It attempted to hide between the tiny gap separating his and Izzy's legs.

She scooped the shaking animal into her arms and rocked it. He understood completely when it tried to nuzzle into the v-neck of that sinful sweater.

"Smart little guy," he mumbled as he patted the puppy on the head with one finger.

It wagged its frizzy tail then stood up to lick Razor's hand and Isabella's cheek, which had somehow migrated extremely close to one another. They both laughed at the sensation.

"Aren't you the cutest dog ever?" She coddled the lucky bastard while she lavished it with baby talk and rained kisses on its fur.

Bad enough when he'd envied gramps earlier, but now a dog too? Holy shit he'd sunk to new lows.

The pack of airheads tottered over on their absurd, spike

heels. Instead of the grateful thanks he expected, the ditz in the front started waving her arms and having a conniption in Izzy's general direction.

"Oh, gross! I just had him groomed. Now you've gone and messed up Gabbana's mousse."

Isabella's face fell. This time he had someone else to blame for making her unhappy.

"Listen, lady, maybe if you took more time to play with your dog rather than treating it like an inanimate object, it might not abandon you for someone with an iota of affection to spare."

"How dare you talk to me like that?" She looked down her fake nose at him, her voice rising an octave or three. "Do you know who I am?"

"I do, Rosalie." Isabella brushed past him to set the quiet animal into the woman's purse-slash-dog-carrier. "He didn't mean anything by it. Do me a favor, okay? When you're bored with the dog, make sure he ends up in a good home? If you can't find anyone, I'd be glad to take him."

"Can't afford your own Yorkie Poo now that your daddy sided with Malcolm?" Her passel of robo-bimbos generated the laugh track Rosalie expected. "I'd feel bad for you, since you're clearly batty. I mean, who forsakes the best catch around to slum it with losers like this? Then again, maybe I should thank you. In fact, I already planned to offer your poor husband my support through this trying time."

"Be careful," Izzy warned.

"Is that some kind of threat?"

"No."

"You can't have your cake and eat it too, cow."

Razor bristled at the way the socialite slammed Isabella. The warning touch on the small of his back distracted him before he could defend her. The bitch switched her attention to him with a sick smile that had his balls shriveling.

"We'll see what Mr. Carrington thinks of my 'capacity for affection'." She flashed her garish claws when she mimed air quotes.

"Great idea. Maybe he'll sign my divorce papers that much faster." Isabella gave the poor puppy one last little finger wave before spinning gracefully on her heel and strolling away as though she didn't have a care in the world.

Razor had to struggle to catch up with her after being caught flatfooted. By the time he reached her, she'd taken a place on the shiny escalator. He ignored her luscious ass, presented at eye level as he stood a few steps below her. "Shit, are you okay? Who was that witch?"

"I'm fine. She's no one important. One of my father's vice president's daughters. I've known her all my life since her dad tries to kiss my father's ass every second of the day. She's always hated me for it. It's the dog I feel bad for." She sighed as she turned around. "I wasn't allowed to have pets growing up. I mean, my father had the horses, but they hardly count. I remember one time I snuck a stallion some carrots. Apparently they're on strict diets to enhance their performance. The animal inhaled the whole bag. It got colic and almost died."

He put his hand on her shoulder in a panic when it looked like she might cry.

"I couldn't sit for a week after that. Only because my father lost the cup he'd been coveting. He didn't care about the animal. He'd sold it before he left the event grounds. That adorable dog is going to be the same. It's another *thing* to them. Nothing more."

"And what about you, Izzy? What were you?" Somehow he knew the answer.

She didn't deny it. Instead, she sniffed and shrugged.

Her resilience impressed him. She'd recovered by the time the mechanical staircase set them on the second floor of the ritzy mall. She turned away to swipe at her eyes, fixing the makeup threatening to streak across her pale cheeks with surreptitious flicks of her short, blunt nails. Razor pretended not to notice while he surveyed the area.

Lush palm trees grew from the ground floor to tower over the three-story atrium. Waterfalls, fountains and streams splashed along the indoor garden, drowning out the more pedestrian sounds of conversation with white noise.

On the second floor, a man in a black trench coat scoped out Izzy for a longer than Razor was comfortable with. When he took a giant stride forward to break the guy's line of sight, the other man shifted to preserve it. Another step, another shift.

"Which way are we going? Let's move." He hated to rush her, but the hairs on the back of his neck stood up. The mall had dropped lower, if possible, on his list of places he wanted to spend more time than necessary.

"Sorry, James." She reached out. He didn't object when she tucked her hand in the crook of his elbow. "The ballroom specialty store is around the corner. They're expecting us."

Razor hustled her in the direction she'd indicated, keeping one eye on the man. He lost the guy when they cut through a group of sophisticated women carrying more packages than Santa. Concerned, he pushed Isabella faster along the walkway. He regretted the rapid click of her heels, clocking what had to be an uncomfortable pace.

She never complained.

They didn't have much farther to go. He could see the window dressing of *Dance With Me's* largest sponsor within spitting distance.

"I didn't think you were this excited about new shoes and a costume," she muttered from a few inches to his right as he practically dragged her across the final stretch of marble.

"What costume?" He threw a questioning glance over his shoulder.

"Did you read the rest of the studio's information packet last night?" She arched a perfect brow in his direction, slightly out of breath from their sprint.

"Hell, no. I was so..." Shit, he'd almost confessed to tying one on. If he did, he'd have to lie about why, and he wasn't up to that challenge at the moment. How could everything seem so different when she was around? Polar opposite from last night's shit storm.

Razor shook his head, instantly regretting it when stars cluttered his vision. He faced forward—in time to see the man in the black trench coat emerge from the shadows cast by the pillar outside the storefront. On instinct, he tucked Izzy out of sight.

"James..."

"Shh. Trust me, please. Stay right here." He situated her behind another solid column before reaching into his Nirvana touring jacket for the concealed gun he carried. He prepared to address the suspect in his most authoritative cop voice. As the Sig was about to clear his zipper the guy turned, leveling something in his direction.

"Put it down," he shouted. Razor had no desire to be shot. Again. Even worse, what would this crackpot do to Isabella if he weren't here to stop it?

A flash of light nearly blinded him. Holy shit, had he been hit? He transported to the night months ago when it had taken his stunned mind several instants to realize the blood pouring over his hands was his own. That the fire searing him came from within.

This time, no pain followed. The only thing he noticed was Isabella's light touch on his hand. Damn it, he'd told her to stay put.

"Come on. He's taken his picture. This isn't worth our time. It's okay, James. It doesn't matter. We're okay."

Her gentle murmur eclipsed the pounding of his heart. "Picture?"

"Just some journalist from one of the gossip mags hoping to make a quick buck." She winked as she tugged him inside the shop. "He probably thinks you're my new boyfriend."

"Darling!" The shop manager rushed to her side, breaking her hold on Razor's clammy fingers before she could object. "We're so glad to have you. I'm Arthur, and this is Eileen."

No doubt he hoped she'd drop cash with every step she took. Unfortunately for him, she could only afford to splurge on a decent pair of dance shoes for Razor in addition to the studio's clothing allowance. Before she could set the shopkeeper straight, he skipped right to business. He handed her off to his assistant, who herded her into the dressing rooms on the other side of the modest dance floor occupying the center of the store.

He flipped the sign on the front door from open to closed. "You'll have our undivided attention. Nothing but the best for you, love."

Isabella winced. That sounded expensive.

The pair of merchants ushered her and Razor into a room with mirrors in every corner. They were led to separate stations filled with tape measures, pins and mannequins though no dividers partitioned the space. She flinched when the kind-faced woman nudged her waist.

"I'll need you to take off your sweater and jeans for the proper measurements."

Isabella balked. Out of the corner of her eye, she caught James stripping without a modicum of self-consciousness. She tried not to watch, but couldn't tear her gaze away from the hard muscles he revealed when he tugged his T-shirt over his head with one arm. His other hand dropped to the button of his faded jeans as he kicked off his sneakers and, in ten seconds flat, he stood impatient in a pair of grey boxer briefs that hugged him in all the right places.

Her appreciative gaze roamed across his tight ass and powerful thighs. She drooled over his reflection in the mirror. Isabella lingered at the bulge distorting the front of his underwear before devouring the contours of his six-pack. His lean muscles reminded her of a big cat—sleek and dangerous. The scars marring the flesh above his ribs and chest had her gasping.

How had he survived that kind of damage?

Beside her, the seamstress fanned herself with a book of fabric samples.

"Disgusted?" He probably hadn't intended to growl the question.

"Nope. I don't think that's the description I'd have chosen." Her cheeks flamed as she finally pried her stare away.

Arthur laughed, "Oh, honey, you can say that again."

Razor spun to face the obvious appreciation in the older man's eyes. Isabella tensed, wondering if he'd be offended. Instead, he barked out a laugh. "Thanks."

An evil smile tugged his mouth into the irresistible smirk of a naughty child."Your turn, Izzy."

When she hesitated, Eileen came to her rescue. "We can wait until they're finished if you'd prefer."

It seemed Razor had gained an ally with his frank acceptance. Arthur argued in his favor. "If you're going to be partners, you might as well learn to see and touch each other intimately. If you have boundaries between you, you can forget winning this competition. Dancing is about more than the steps. You need magnetism. Looks like you have it. Use it."

"Yeah. What he said." Razor waggled his eyebrows. The gesture should have made him look ridiculous—antagonizing her while in his underwear. Somehow, it didn't. She envied his confidence. "What are you willing to do to win, sweetheart? I double-dog-dare you."

Isabella sucked in a breath to steel her spine. Do it quick, like a Band-Aid.

She whipped her sweater over her head, heeled off her shoes then shimmied out of her jeans without unbuttoning them. Not a single sound fractured the silence in the room as she concentrated on the lush carpet she curled her toes in. She focused on keeping her hands lax at her sides while she waited for the onlookers to recoil.

"What the hell did he do to you?" She jumped when Razor spoke, ragged and harsh, near her ear before sinking to his knees at her feet. His broad hands cupped her hipbones, angling her until she faced him. The harsh light beside the tailor's mirrors exposed every tiny mark and flaw.

The two shopkeepers receded, leaving them to settle things in private.

"Disgusted?" She mimicked his earlier tone.

"More like furious. There's no way you could have done this to yourself." He traced the faded bruises and shallow cuts, which crisscrossed her abdomen and back, with tender strokes of his fingertips. She forgot to worry while she tried not to purr beneath his petting until his mumbling penetrated the glow she basked in.

"Why on earth would someone do this to themselves?" Her mouth hung open as she wondered what kind of drugs he smoked.

"I gave up trying to figure people out about the time I woke up in the hospital looking like Swiss cheese. The woman who shot me...she paid people to beat her so we'd believe her story."

Isabella covered her mouth with her palm as she imagined someone so deranged. No wonder Razor sabotaged their budding friendship anytime she drifted too close.

"Can we pretend you never saw this?" She waved a hand at her torso. "I'm not proud of marrying someone who permitted this to happen."

She trailed off as tears threatened for the second time in one day. So not her style.

"You're not responsible for someone else's actions. Mason, Tyler and Lacey have been telling me so for months. Seeing this, though..." He surprised her by laying a series of kisses over the worst of her injuries, right above the frilly pink lace of her panty line. She tangled her fingers in his shaggy hair when he licked a slice on her belly, her knees weakening in the wake of the silky heat. "God, you should have told me before. This had to hurt yesterday, with you sweating and me grabbing you...practically mauling you. For Christ's sake, I'm a cop. Whatever's going on here, let me help you. Trust me. Tell me."

He lifted his mouth from where it brushed her skin with every word to look into her eyes. Though he stopped short of saying please, everything about his bearing screamed of his desperation as loudly as if he'd begged.

"I *do* trust you, James." She could no longer imagine him taking bribes or condoning corruption. No way.

Some of the tension seeped from his shoulders.

"But I won't mix you up in another scandal. I respect you too much for that."

When he began to argue, she laid three fingers over his lips. They were moist from soothing her.

"It's done. I'm divorcing Malcolm. It's not worth worrying about." She half-expected God to smite her for the gargantuan lie. She would figure out how to help the others—a way that didn't risk such a good man. If she confessed, he'd go straight to his superiors. At least one of them had to be on the take. They'd hurt him because of her. "Please, let's finish what we came for so we can arrive at the studio on time for practice."

He squeezed his eyes closed, resting his forehead on her tummy for a solid thirty seconds while his thumbs rubbed delicious arcs over her sides. He lavished comfort, which she soaked up like a desert pelted by rain after decades of drought. Things she'd assumed long dead stretched and blossomed under his care. Content, she allowed the intimate moment linger far too long.

"Okay, Izzy. If you change your mind, you can tell me anything." His monotone response seized her throat. They both knew she didn't intend to take him up on the offer.

How could she when confiding in him would put him in danger? Malcolm's spy could be anywhere. Until she rid herself of her husband, she could never take a chance. Not with someone who mattered more to her with each passing breath. She'd rather weather Razor's disappointment a thousand times over, even though it made her feel like scum, than place him in the line of fire.

The store manager cleared his throat loudly before reentering the room. She giggled and Razor grinned when the man peeked around the corner as though they might be doing it in the middle of the dressing room. Now there was a thought to tuck away for later daydreams.

"Ready for measurements?"

Chapter Seven

Razor prowled the rows of displays while he waited for the designers to figure out a dress style to flatter Isabella—hell, even a burlap sack would look great on her rocking body—while concealing the evidence of the horror she'd endured at the hands of a man she should have been able to trust implicitly. He rubbed his temples to calm the raging ache there, but knew better than to blame the pain entirely on his hangover.

His blood pressure had shot through the roof imagining someone hurting that girl. In an instant, he'd forgotten everything he'd learned in the past year and surrendered to instinct. He'd barely stopped himself from offering her solace, searing away the world-weary dullness in her beautiful eyes and replacing it with something passionate, something white-hot.

"Why don't you have a seat? She could be a while longer." Arthur hovered nearby like a mother hen.

"I can't. It's hard enough to stay out here when I want..." He forced himself to leave the thought unfinished.

"Yeah, I can tell. Will you at least take some of this?" The man tossed him a container of ibuprofen from behind the counter.

"If you have some water around here I might even kiss you for this."

"Only in my dreams, I'm sure." Arthur smiled as he extracted a plastic bottle from the mini-fridge Razor hadn't noticed before.

He shook some pills into his palm then chugged them. Hopefully they'd kick in soon. When he held them out in return, the shopkeeper shook his head.

"You better hang on to those. She's going to need them for that ankle, especially if you two plan to work much more before show time tomorrow."

"What'd she do to her ankle?" Razor imagined her slipping off one of the hemming blocks in the fitting room.

"I assumed she'd sprained it during your practice session yesterday. It's wrapped up tight, but she's favoring it."

"It was like that when we came in?" How the fuck had he missed her injury?

"Yep. Don't worry. I imagine it's hard to concentrate on details around her. Hell, even I can see she's stunning."

Isabella's emergence from the dressing room spared Razor from answering. A huge grin lit her face. "Your team works miracles, you know? If the computer mock-up is anything like the real deal, I can't wait to wear their creation."

The wattage of her full smile blasted them both, leaving them putty in her elegant hands.

"Did you try on the shoes, James?"

She'd delegated the task to Arthur, who'd enjoyed Razor's outraged reaction when he realized the torture devices had heels. As if he was a woman.

"Think of it like this. When she puts on four or five inch stilettos, she'll be too close to your height for the proper posture. With these, you'll maintain the optimal differential. You two really are perfect together."

He'd ignored the mumbo jumbo he didn't understand in favor of imagining Izzy's sexy legs in killer spikes and how they'd fit together if they were doing a little horizontal tangoing. It would be an ideal matchup.

"Yes, he fit best in the black pair you suggested. Nice eye, Ms. Buchanan."

"You've been such a tremendous help, Arthur. I can never thank you enough." She strode right over to the man, wrapping him in a hug. This time Razor detected the slight hitch in her movement. Son of a bitch, he should have picked it up sooner even though she covered it well.

The merchant smiled at her as he returned the embrace with an awkward pat on her back. Good thing for Arthur it seemed entirely platonic.

"No thanks necessary. Could I ask one thing...?"

"Of course," she separated to smile up at Arthur.

"Can I see you dance?"

"What? Right now? Right here?" Razor panicked at the thought of performing for someone.

"You *are* going to have to do this in front of an audience tomorrow night. Plus, we can see how the shoes fit without risking another trip to the mall. We don't have time to waste."

Damn her sound logic.

"We also don't have our music."

Arthur overruled Razor's last-ditch objection with a wink. "Who do you think provided all the selections?"

He gestured to a CD rack with built-in headphones in the far corner of the floor then pressed a button on the store's overhead system behind the counter. "Here it comes."

Isabella waited for Razor in the middle of the dance floor, an adorable smirk highlighting her plump lips. "I *triple*-dog-dare you."

"Well, shit. I can't keep my man card if I pass up a triple-dog-dare." He laughed as he crossed toward her. Funny, the ridiculous shoes actually gripped decent on the polished hardwood. For the hell of it, he stopped short, executing his best imitation of a bow from some old black and white movie he'd watched when he had trouble sleeping several weeks ago. He hadn't expected to enjoy the sappy flick as much as he had.

Hell if she didn't curtsey in return as though she'd done it a million times before. Probably had. He shook his head as he held out his arms. Isabella came to him, fitting gracefully into the frame he made for her. With Arthur looking on, Razor felt honor-bound to perform well. Izzy didn't need a bad rap as an instructor.

Neither one of them could afford more trash-talk at this point.

The opening strains of music surrounded them. They moved together. After no more than five seconds, he'd forgotten all about technique, their miniature audience and the fact that he probably looked like a poser. He gazed into Isabella's eyes, relishing the way her slender body moved against him.

Razor imagined what it would have been like to have lived in simpler times. What if he had been born privileged and could claim any woman he wanted? This woman. He danced to impress her, to steal a forbidden touch here or a handful of curves there.

When they reached the end of the choreography, he dipped her—as they'd practiced—into a drastic bend, which highlighted her flexibility over his tensed bicep. Only this time, he didn't stop there.

Razor planted his hand on her shoulder while the other lifted to support her head. He ran his palm from the crown of her head backward, gathering the silky fall of her platinum hair. The soft waves teased the sensitive skin between his fingers as he descended while pulling her tighter to his chest.

Though it took an instant, time seemed to slow to a crawl. She watched him come nearer with a dazed smile on her beautiful face. Before he knew what he intended, he tasted the strawberry gloss on her full, slightly spread lips.

One sample could never suffice. He squeezed her close, hardly registering her fingers clenching on his back and around his neck. Instead, he focused on her sweet hesitation, as though unsure of how to kiss him in return. Had her husband never indulged in this fine confection?

He nuzzled her mouth with his, coaxing her into responding as he wished.

When Izzy caught on, she turned voracious. She nipped his bottom lip then sucked to soothe the miniscule hurt. He chuckled into their kiss, letting his tongue dance with hers.

"Ahem."

The not-so-subtle faked throat clearing startled Razor enough that he nearly dropped Isabella on her perfect ass. Snapped back to reality, he yanked her upright. He lunged away so quick, he tripped in the heeled shoes.

"So sorry, Ms. Buchanan." Arthur's cheeks had turned maroon. "I didn't think you'd appreciate broadcasting your private exchange on the news."

He gestured over his shoulder to the film crew peering in the shop window.

"They just arrived. They're doing a behind-the-scenes piece on *Dance With Me*," he finished with a shrug.

"Th-thank you, Arthur." Isabella's voice shook.

"Why don't the two of you use the service door?" Eileen waited near the dressing room to show them out. "No need to waste any more of your rehearsal time. Though, really, I don't think you need it. You're fabulous together."

"Perfect," Arthur agreed. "We'll do the rest. Your dress and tux will be waiting at the studio tomorrow evening. Good luck."

"The shoes..." Isabella objected, but she sounded like he felt—disoriented, breathless and gooey inside.

"Take them. You two are going to do more for this store than any ad we've purchased."

Isabella's infectious laughter had him mirroring her grin as they scrambled down the metal fire escape hand in hand. "Never snuck out of the house as a teenager?"

"Kind of hard when your father has cameras everywhere and an entire security force patrolling the grounds. When certain guards were on duty, I'd slip into the garden for unauthorized walks at night. That was as far as I could go. There are a lot of things I've never done."

He hated it when her dimples disappeared. Why had he mentioned her past? Hell, half the time he forgot who she was and where she'd come from. She seemed completely unpretentious and grounded. How could that be possible?

"How about riding a motorcycle? Ever done that?" Ah, the adventurous spark returned a secret glint to her eyes. Sexy as hell.

"Nope."

"Want to try it?"

She bit her lip then nodded as they reached the edge of the parking lot.

"Come on." Razor threw one leg over his motorcycle. He patted the seat behind him. The bike barely dipped as she climbed aboard, leaving as big a chasm as possible between them. "That's not going to work, Izzy. Let's try to keep you from bouncing off, okay?"

He groaned when she scooted close, her thighs bracketing his as she plastered along every inch of his ass and back.

"Better?"

He had to try twice before he wheezed, "Yeah."

With what he hoped was a stealthy shift, he adjusted the length of his hard-on where it jabbed the folds of his too-tight jeans. Razor kick-started the motorcycle. He raised his voice to carry over the engine, which roared to life beneath them. "Hang on, princess."

Izzy banded her arms around his abdomen. She delighted him by laying her cheek on the fabric of his touring jacket between his shoulders. Most inexperienced riders couldn't pry their terrified gaze from the road, spooking at every tiny bump or turn. Isabella stayed calm and relaxed as he pushed off to navigate the somewhat heavy afternoon traffic. She counterbalanced the lean of the bike, following his lead with the same effortless grace as she did in the waltz.

Even when he reached the highway and opened up the throttle, she molded to him without tensing or clutching his chest in a death grip the way some women had when he'd caved to their relentless harping for a ride. In fact, he'd never found it very enjoyable to tote someone along on his excursions. He savored his independence. Somehow, having Izzy with him didn't seem like an imposition.

The heat of her core radiated into him despite the brisk spring air. They leaned forward, into the speed, together. If riding alone hadn't always guaranteed his hard-on, the weight of her supple breasts on his back and the tendrils of her lustrous mane fluttering in front of his visor would have had his cock filling in a rush.

Razor glided into the ample gap left by a truck exiting the road. In the bug-eye lens of his side-view mirror, he caught a glimpse of a non-descript Ford. Familiar to him, since the force used similar cars for their undercover work, he'd noticed this one behind them near the mall. He found it a little odd to see the vehicle tailing them regardless of the lane changes he'd made on the more maneuverable motorcycle.

Had the chief sent someone to babysit him?

The idea rankled enough to stir his impulsiveness. No matter how foolish it made him, he indulged the whim, bucking his recent attempt at maturity.

He removed one hand from the grip to squeeze Izzy's fingers. She nodded against his shoulder then clung a little tighter. Now he had to follow through. Acceleration would be a better outlet for his testosterone than the alternative. After the sizzling kiss they'd shared in Arthur's store, Razor swore setting the sheets on fire with Ms. Buchanan would do the trick, but the ramifications would be unacceptable.

At the next safe opportunity, he revved the engine, gunning it past the tractor-trailer, which hogged the left lane, up the slight incline in the road. An RV behind them formed a rolling roadblock.

Fuck off. He aimed mental daggers at the poor schmuck obeying orders as the dude swung over the rumble strip for one last look at their retreating backs. He hoped it wasn't JRad, Matt or one of the other guys from his division. He didn't mean to cause them heartburn with the boss, but it sucked donkey dick. They didn't trust him enough to see to his charge on his own.

Then again, if it hadn't been for Arthur's intervention, who knows where that kiss would have led him. Probably straight to hell. At least he'd have had fun burning there with Izzy. Until he surfaced to the shame of falling for another woman with a shady past.

Why couldn't she come clean to him? She'd wavered in his hands earlier when he'd examined the marks blanketing her otherwise flawless body. They looked new, but mostly healed. Superficial. Whoever had marked her had intended to frighten and cause pain. Not to scar her. By the fear he'd glimpsed in her eyes, they'd done one hell of a job.

Either her innocence had been validated or she'd gotten involved in something bigger and badder than she could handle. Christ knew it wouldn't take much. No matter what she'd become tangled in, Izzy didn't possess the guile that had made Gina's stories so believable. She couldn't lie worth shit. When uncomfortable, she stalled, clamming up instead of crafting some ingenious tale. Her bluffs might as well have been fashioned out of glowing neon.

So maybe she had no part in her husband's affairs. Or maybe she simply sucked at the game.

He blew past the exit leading to the studio as frustration made his head so hot he thought steam might fog his helmet. The lure of the open road had him winding along his favorite combination of curves, hills, dips and bridges in the state park outside the city limits.

Pine and the fresh scent of last night's rain replaced exhaust fumes and the bitter aftertaste of regret before long. They could spare twenty minutes for him to clear the interference in his mind. Otherwise, he'd be no good to either of them. If nothing else, the last half-year had taught him how to win control.

Razor looped around the circuit, taking turns at the top-end of wise, always riding the fringe of excess. Didn't it figure? He wasn't exactly known for his tact like Tyler or his calm reasoning like JRad—impulse was his trademark.

Why should driving be any different?

By the time they'd circled around to the front gate again, he aimed them onto the highway for the return journey. Five more minutes and they'd be face to face, chest to chest and toe to toe. Now, he'd be able to lock away the lust that had gripped him earlier to ensure things stayed all about the case at hand.

At least that's what he thought before he rolled into the dilapidated lot behind the studio. That goddamn sedan perched, pretty as you please, in the corner. As if he wouldn't spot it behind the brush. Now his fellow officers thought him unobservant in addition to young and reckless. He'd give them two of the three. The last one he'd fight for.

He considered himself a damn good cop in the making. Sure, he could use some more experience, but why else would they have granted him this second chance despite some doubters who expected him to blow it? Someone saw potential in him.

Razor planted one booted foot on the pavement with enough force to send tremors zinging through his damaged thigh. He left his helmet in place while Izzy peeled her lithe frame from his, leaving him cold and exposed. No chance he'd let those assholes spot the hunger she sparked in his gut.

When he finally allowed himself to glance at her windblown face, he thanked the powers that be for having the presence of mind to wait. Her rosy cheeks and glittering eyes tempted him to run off on an escapade he knew she'd welcome as much as he would.

Had she smothered that part of her nature in her socialite world?

Razor forced his fingers to uncurl. He tried to act nonchalant as he stripped off his gear.

"That was amazing! How did you learn to ride? Do you think I could...?"

"Don't mention it." His gruff response seemed overly harsh, but he couldn't stand to listen to her laud him when he'd had ulterior motives. Besides, he had to take care of this shit before it bubbled out of hand and he didn't need her around to witness him get dressed down.

"Why don't you head in? Warm up. I have to make a call..." He trailed off, unwilling to take the lie further. He hadn't mastered the art anyway, if her dissipating smile gave any indication. The pair of them could benefit from a set of decent poker faces. Neither one seemed capable of real deceit. Though he'd worked undercover for nearly two years, something in him had changed when those bullets pierced his flesh.

To her credit, she didn't call him on it. He wanted to chuck his helmet when her spine straightened, replacing her loose-limbed openness with stiff formality.

She surprised him when she shook off some of the reaction with a sigh. "Is everything okay?"

As okay as coming home to a steaming pile of dog shit in your favorite chair. And that's how he felt, as though he'd crapped on the cease-fire they'd forged together. Especially since he couldn't level with her now.

"Fine. I just need a minute. Please."

Isabella nodded. She had his chest cramping all over again when she trailed her fingers over his cheek before walking away.

He rolled his head on his neck, wincing at the pop and crackle of several vertebrae, to drain the lingering effects of her touch. He stormed toward the copmobile, ready to vent his frustration on someone who knew how to fight back. Hopefully, it'd be Matt. He moonlighted as a bouncer, though he rarely had to do more than fling that I-can-kick-your-ass-with-one-hand-tied-behind-my-back glare in some little punk's direction before they found somewhere else to cause trouble. Or maybe Clint, Razor's usual sparring partner at the gym.

The guys had taken it easy on him since he'd reappeared at their fitness sessions. No more. They'd gone too far this time. He didn't appreciate someone holding his hand or shadowing his every move. He wouldn't stand for being babied. He didn't need training wheels on this first assignment since his grand fuck-up.

Ready to make himself clear, he drew up short when he realized the car had been abandoned. No one, familiar or otherwise, sat in the driver's seat. He hauled his phone from the inside pocket of his jacket to speed dial JRad.

"Who is it?" He didn't bother with a greeting when the other man picked up.

"Who is what?"

It hurt that his friend played dumb instead of cutting the crap.

"The man who drew the short straw and has to keep an eye on me." He scrubbed a hand through his hair then gave up. Nothing could truly tame the mess his helmet had made. "Is it Matt? Clint? Who?"

"Slow down there, Razor." The sound of typing in the background supplemented JRad's placating tone. "I'm pulling up the schedule. As far as I know, you're flying solo. The chief didn't assign anyone to you in our briefing this morning. Kid, there's no one here."

"Someone tailed us. Now this piece of shit is sitting right here in my face. Someone's watching, officially or not."

"What piece of shit? Give me something to go on." JRad donned his computer whiz hat, always eager to search for the answer.

"Black. Taurus. Late nineties. Plate number 87HN21."

More clattering keys. "It's not ours."

"What the fuck do you mean it's not ours?" Razor swiveled around, searching for tracks or some sign of the driver who'd done a lame job of camouflaging his ride. He laid his palm on the hood. Still warm. "It's the same one I saw earlier. I'm sure of it. Left headlight's misaligned and the motor's been off less than twenty minutes, I'd say."

"Registered to some dude who died two weeks ago. Supposed to be taken in for overdue taxes. Hasn't been picked up yet. It's not us. Take cover, Razor. Where's Isabella?"

"Son of a bitch! I sent her inside by herself. Dispatch Mason, Tyler, Matt... Christ, anybody."

"Wait for backup before entering." JRad's warning huffed out as though he sprinted along the hall to the detectives' unit.

"You know I can't. Just send someone. Quick."

Chapter Eight

Jeremy's shouted curses trailed from Razor's phone as he disconnected, already tearing up the stairs to the third story. At the landing, he forced himself to slow. He strained his ears for any indication of something out of place, but his heart hammered too loud for him to be sure of the all clear.

Nightmare visions of his bloody handprints crawling across the safe house carpet threatened his composure. The memory of agony staved off only by the hope of alerting his partners of the danger he'd placed them in fragmented his focus. The terror chilling him now mingled with the trauma of that night until he staggered under the combined weight of dread laced with pain. He didn't have time to clear the cobwebs of doubt and fear ensnaring him. Izzy needed him. Now.

Keep your shit together.

In a crouch, he fisted his pistol in a two-handed grip, inching toward the studio at the end of the hall.

Stairwell, clear.

Bathroom, clear.

Hallway, clear.

Clear but with no sign of Isabella either. He snuffed the panic threatening to shatter his concentration, rounding the corner braced for the worst. He peered into the shadowy corners of their rehersal space with frantic sweeps of his trained gaze.

What he faced almost surpassed his macabre imaginings.

Isabella rounded on him. The soft smile tugging the corners of her pert lips vanished when her mouth gaped open. Horror transformed her blue eyes into glaciers. Before he could yank the sight of his gun—which followed his laser focus—from between the icy pools, she stumbled backward.

She went down. The *whap* of her skull hitting the barre on the mirrored wall cracked through the open space. She scrambled from him in a grotesque crabwalk. Her instant reaction would have sent his heart plummeting through the floor if it hadn't already been relegated there by his own disastrous blend of past and present.

"Izzy! Shit. Don't freak." Razor flipped on the safety. He rammed the muzzle of his gun into his waistband as he rushed to her side.

She didn't hear his pleading. Instead, she shot him a look so full of disillusion and panic, he thought he'd wither on the spot. How could she think for one instant he'd harm her?

"It's okay." He held his hands, palms out, toward her as he slowed his charge to a timid creep. "You're safe, sweetheart. I'm an idiot. I didn't mean to scare you. Shit, Izzy. I'm a douche. I'm sorry."

His soothing nonsense must have worked because she collapsed into a tiny heap and clutched her chest.

In the next instant, he skidded to his knees beside her before scooping her into his arms. He squeezed her until she squeaked then forced himself to let up a tad.

"Wh-what..." she couldn't finish the question. Her teeth chattered too violently.

If he hadn't believed himself two seconds from a heart attack, he might have provided a calm and rational explanation. In this condition, he had no hope of affecting cool and collected, so he skipped ahead to the most important point.

"Christ, Izzy. I would *never* hurt you." He framed her face with his shaking hands, stroking her cheekbones with numb fingers. "Never. Do you understand me?"

She hesitated before surrendering a timid nod. Her gorgeous eyes filled with tears. When droplets seeped from the corners, over his knuckles, Razor's heart broke. He knew exactly how she felt. In the moment when her gaze had locked with his in that doorway, all his doubt had been blown away.

This woman knew the soul-deep stab of betrayal. Just as he did.

And he'd made her think she was about to live through it all over again.

Fuck.

Nothing short of an act of God could have intervened to

prevent him from comforting her. Without hesitation, his mouth descended, intending to absorb all her aching misery and the lingering anxiety he'd inadvertently caused.

Izzy gifted him with another new experience when a kiss became all about giving rather than taking. For years, he'd partied hard with women who threw themselves at him for a chance at a night of no-strings sex. He'd earned his reputation as a fun-loving man who respected his partners and always left them satisfied.

Razor wouldn't have understood if someone had told him it could be like this. Actually, he'd damn near busted a blood vessel ripping mercilessly on Tyler when his friend had argued the existence of a bond this pure. Irresistible. As soon as his lips met Izzy's, Razor paused, waiting for her to claim what she needed.

Adrenaline swooshed through his system, borne on frantic pumps of his blood. He held stock still until she showed him what she desired. Where their earlier kiss had been gentle, exploratory, this encounter had more in common with an explosion. One part each—despair, longing, relief, lust—and a double helping of the camaraderie he would never have expected to find in this siren, mixed into the perfect chemical reaction.

Izzy crawled onto his lap for better access. She plundered his offering like a pirate unleashed on a huge stash of loot up for grabs. Her tongue raided his mouth, stealing tastes of his teeth and the roof of his mouth with bold swipes that caused his cock to throb. When he attempted to return the favor, she stopped him cold by sucking on his tongue, rasping her teeth along the sensitive muscle.

Razor guided her knees to either side of his hips. He palmed her ass while she ground against his hard-on. He would have loved to tease her perky breasts while she poured herself into their full-contact kiss if slipping a hand, or a sheet of paper, between them proved possible.

Desperation tinged her initial veracity. It melted into something sweeter the longer she rode him. Writhing in his arms, she unleashed the sensual storm that had been brewing between them since the moment he'd crossed the threshold into this room yesterday. Hell, ever since he'd caught the snippet of her interview on his TV.

And with Izzy, when it rained…it poured.

She moaned, a feral sound, as she buried her hands in his hair then rocked against his chest. Her hips glided in a seductive figure eight. The motion had him ready to beg for mercy.

Until he heard a faint rustle from the other side of the room.

In a flash, he'd shifted her slight weight to the crook of his left elbow while he snatched the gun from his waistband. He aimed in the direction of the scuffle.

"Whoa." Matt skidded to a stop so fast Clint almost barreled over him. "It's us, bro."

Razor relaxed, avoiding the concerned gazes of his cohorts. Partners on the force and buddies who enjoyed nights out on the town—though he hadn't tagged along since the incident—the men seemed more like brothers than co-workers. They knew him well. Any attempt to conceal his lip lock with Isabella would be futile, even discounting the attention to detail every good cop possessed.

The picture he and Izzy made in the mirrored wall—clothes rumpled, hair standing on end, lips swollen and red—screamed of imminent, hardcore sex. Not to mention how he clutched her in the shelter of his torso while sporting an erection it would be impossible to miss from across the room.

If they hadn't come to his rescue, no one could say what might have happened.

The two men took turns cursing under their breath, shifting from foot to foot, inspecting the water-damaged ceiling tiles and otherwise offering all parties involved a chance to recover. Isabella nudged his biceps. She climbed to her feet to stand on her own. He followed her lead, though his legs wobbled a bit.

"Would anyone care to fill me in?" Isabella whispered. Her voice didn't crack.

Razor held out his hand, glad when she accepted it, entwining their fingers. He rubbed his face with his other. "Izzy, this is Clint. That giant bastard next to him is Matt. They're officers, like me."

"Nice to meet you both." He would have laughed at her relentless manners if she hadn't followed up the prim and proper routine with, "Now somebody better tell me why James felt it necessary to scare the shit out of me and cover his ass like this."

"James?" Matt barked out a bass laugh.

"Is that your real name?" Clint acted shocked.

Razor nodded at their handoff. They weren't sure what story to give. So he did the dirty work while sticking as close to the truth as possible. "All this is my fault. I must be a little jumpy. I thought we might have been followed here, and I overreacted."

His resignation was genuine. Rusty instincts had nearly caused him to blow his cover. Despite them, his belief in Isabella's innocence persisted. No one could fake the raw, honest emotion he'd detected in her split second of pure reaction. Only, now, he didn't repay her in kind. Sickness tarnished the gleam she had inspired.

"Followed?" Color drained from her cheeks in a rush.

"There was a suspicious-looking vehicle outside, ma'am. Razor played it safe, that's all. Nothing wrong with being cautious." Clint let him off the hook a bit. "He called for assistance, and we were closest. Our beat's less than a mile east of here. So we came to check it out. Nothing to worry about. The car's gone. The building's secure."

Razor sighed. The rest of the team probably combed the outlying property as they spoke. They'd have covered most of the area before sending Matt and Clint into a dangerous situation.

"Maybe we'd better call it a day."

"There's no need to do that, Ms. Buchanan." Matt crossed his tree-trunk arms over his chest. "If it'd put your mind at ease, we could have a patrol car swing by now and again to keep an eye out."

Razor read between the lines. Someone had been stationed outside to watch his back. Though he'd been fired up when he thought they sent a watcher on the sly, relief eroded the dregs of his lingering unease. He could trust the men in blue with his safety. And Izzy's.

"Unless you're tired of me stepping on your feet, I say we keep working." He smiled at Isabella before turning serious once more. "I didn't mean to frighten you."

She shushed him with a hug that stunned him silent. Was *she* comforting *him*? Could she sense the ghosts haunting him?

Acid churned in his stomach.

"Whatever you say next, don't apologize. I understand what it's like to check over your shoulder all the time."

The other guys retreated, giving him space to accept her gesture and whisper a response. After all, she seemed close to divulging pertinent information. The officers knew better than to jeopardize his assignment.

Son of a bitch. He had to make the most of the opportunity. God help him, he craved untangling her secrets more for himself than in support of the investigation. "Why, Izzy? What are you running from?"

Isabella blew out a sigh. She opened her mouth. Then she closed it again. She peeked over his shoulder in Matt and Clint's direction before shaking her head. "Nothing."

Close but no cigar. She wouldn't tell him. Not now, not like this.

"Are you up to practicing some more? I'm afraid of disappointing you, Izzy." Truer words had never been spoken. If this ridiculous contest allowed him one avenue to live up to her expectations, he planned to knock the waltz out of the park. Maybe someday, when the shit hit the fan, she would realize he wished he could do more than something so insignificant.

Besides, if they danced, he could touch her while pretending he sacrificed for the sake of the job. Now that someone from the force kept an eye on them, he'd have to revert to his best behavior. Their surveillance would relegate him to the straight and narrow. No way would he put his career at risk. Again.

"Sure, we can put in more time on the double reverse spin."

Did he detect a hint of disappointment in her response? What else did she have in mind? An afternoon of sweaty sex instead? After their smoking kiss, who could blame her?

"It was very nice to meet you, Ms. Buchanan." Clint waved from the doorway. "Sorry to barge in."

"Call me Isabella. Please. And thank you for making sure we're okay. It's nice to find out there are real good guys in the world."

Razor couldn't blame the partners for their googly eyes when she flashed them a hint of her spectacular smile, which illuminated her extraordinary features. Any man would be dazzled by her beauty, especially when combined with her grace and easygoing personality.

A trifecta of perfection, really.

"If you insist, *Isabella.*" Matt winked. "See you next time we pass by. In about an hour or so. Good luck whipping this guy into shape."

"If he gives you any trouble, you let us know." Clint's teasing jab hung in the air between them as the cops vanished.

Razor stayed frozen in place until the fireproof stairwell door slammed behind his friends. "Izzy..."

"You don't have to explain." She embraced him from behind, reminding him of her absolute trust on their wild ride earlier. Faith he didn't deserve.

When he didn't respond, she deserted him, leaving cool air in her wake. He struggled to draw deep breaths while she fiddled with the stereo until the opening strains of their song floated throughout the room, breaking the silence.

He held out his arms, and she came into them.

They communicated on a level more expressive than language, every synchronized step and turn reaffirming their bond—the affinity he would obliterate with his pretense. He hadn't dreaded a loss so much since the ride to the hospital when the EMT had informed him his chances were slim to none. He hadn't had the spirit to mutter an apology for the guy to carry to his friends, whom he'd failed.

There had to be a way to protect Izzy, to collect the information the department required and avoid hurting either of them. Hell if he could figure it out, though.

"Stop thinking so much. Go with your emotions."

Could she read his mind now, too? Doubtful. Or the spitfire would be kicking his ass instead of fixing his posture.

Isabella winced when she laid into the arabesque turn, pivoting on her bad ankle.

"That's it. We're finished. You've had enough." Razor possessed eagle eyes when it came to her reactions this afternoon. His scrutiny made her feel like a diamond under a jeweler's loupe, all flaws evident. Since their smoking kiss, he'd tuned into her thoughts as though he had a persistent connection straight into her brain.

"I'm okay. Don't use me as an excuse to quit. The show is

in less than twenty-four hours."

"We're ready. Besides, how well do you think we're going to do if your ankle is swollen to the size of a loaf of bread and you can hardly put any weight on it?" Razor snapped at her. She deserved it. He had a point.

"Fine. But we'll start early tomorrow." She hated her petty need to win something. It demanded he offer a compromise. She had to retain a modicum of control.

"Fine," he grumbled. Exhaustion hounded him as much as it did her. Neither possessed enough energy for a proper argument.

They gathered their jackets. When she headed for the stairs, a firm hand gripped her wrist.

"Take the elevator or I'll throw you over my shoulder."

She rolled her eyes, but changed direction.

"Let me lead. It's getting dark out. You wouldn't want to trip and hurt yourself again." Irritation colored his directive. She'd refused to explain how she'd sustained her injury no matter how many things he'd tried to suggest.

Isabella didn't have to be a rocket scientist to realize the earlier scare had him spooked. She didn't call him on it. No need to embarrass him despite the overbearing asshole he'd imitated. Guilt had eaten at her all afternoon for not coming clean about the threatening messages she'd received yesterday from someone who could very well be lurking nearby this instant.

No news was good news, right? She hadn't heard a peep since then. Still, the hairs on her nape insisted someone was watching. Biding their time. Razor's freak-out had been justified. She wished she could confess without putting him in greater danger than she already had.

Especially since holding out gambled more than the two of them.

Matt and Clint had stayed true to their word. They'd stopped in from time to time to check up on her and Razor. The duo had reveled in flinging shit and talking trash until she kicked them out for disrupting. Every time the cops appeared, her partner stiffened, fumbled a step he'd nailed repeatedly or forgot sections of their routine.

He didn't seem like the type to give a crap what others thought of him, so why the change?

In any case, the guys had treated her like she imagined they would a kid sister, doling out smiles and ribbing her and Razor mercilessly. She figured she'd sunk to the level of sewer sludge for jeopardizing them all.

The elevator slowed near the ground floor.

Razor tugged her out of alignment with the center seam of the doors. They opened to the empty lobby, which did seem a little creepier in the dusky light filtering through the dirty windows. She shivered.

Satisfied no Bogeymen lurked in the shadows, Razor ushered her from the building and headed for his motorcycle.

Isabella called, "Goodnight." She veered onto the cracked sidewalk leading toward the road, but she hadn't made it more than two steps before his hand landed on her wrist again.

"Where do you think you're going, princess?"

"Uh, wherever I choose." She studied the site where his touch scorched her skin through the leather of his riding gloves.

"By yourself? Where's your car?"

She'd hoped to wedge a little space between them before contacting the dealer. The lack of updates from George had her biting her nails. Something must not have gone as planned. She didn't fancy hashing things out with Razor so close. She'd only open the door to more questions she couldn't supply him the answers to.

"I took it to the shop this morning to have the scrape on the side panel repaired." George had promised the mechanics would address it before showing the car so it wasn't really a lie. Right?

"So you're traveling home by pumpkin?" He careened his neck in an obnoxious faux search. She had to bite her cheek to keep from laughing. No need to encourage the man.

"Is that what you call the bus?" She actually hadn't thought beyond touching base with George. Her mind spun so fast with worry, it didn't leave room for much else. If she couldn't produce a sizable wad of cash in hand, she'd have a hell of a time convincing a lawyer—at least one who had any chance of winning—to represent the case she hoped to build.

"The closest line is over on Henderson. You're not walking that distance through this neighborhood, in the dark, on a sprained ankle." He crossed his arms over his chest. "Get on the bike, Izzy."

"I can't. I'll hail a taxi." She scuffed the dirt with her good foot as she wondered how expensive a ride across town could be. "I have to run some errands."

"Patience is not one of my virtues, princess. Why don't we cut the bullshit? Tell me what you need to do. I'll drive you wherever you want. Or tell me straight up to fuck off. Tell me the heat we've been tiptoeing around all damn day doesn't mean jack to you and I'll disappear. Otherwise, let me in. Let. Me. Help."

When she didn't answer right away, he threw up his hands. The slump of his shoulders as he spun away had her stopping him despite her best intentions.

"Wait!" She whimpered when she lunged after him. Her ankle chose that instant to give out.

"Damn it." Razor hauled her into his arms as though she weighed nothing at all then carried her to his motorcycle. He seemed to understand her predicament when he settled in front of her. Without probing for more info, he asked, "Where to?"

Isabella dropped her forehead to his back, hugging him tighter than the ride required. His whole torso jerked in surprise when she murmured. "Carnot's, please."

"You have a *date*?"

She couldn't help but chuckle at his instant outrage. If he'd thought about it for two seconds he'd have realized she could never appear for a dinner liaison at the prime steakhouse dressed in faded jeans after hours of exertion. Unless he'd never been inside the swank eatery. This could be more fun than she'd thought.

"Hell no, but I'm hungry. Come on. It'll be my treat." Screw living in penury. She'd make do somewhere else. Scrimping would be worth it to return a fraction of his kindness.

When he started to object, she reminded him, "You said you'd take me wherever I chose."

He muttered something that sounded suspiciously close to, "Yes, Ms. Daisy," before peeling out.

"Why hasn't she contacted me? When are you going to make your move?" The whining of the weasel on the other end of the phone announced the expiration of the assassin's grace period.

"I had to ditch the plan this afternoon. They were on to me. I didn't figure you'd appreciate it if I were caught, *boss*." He snarled the last word though the fool probably wouldn't notice his disgust. The buffoon had no idea how these things worked. "I have something else lined up. Should kill two birds with one stone. I'll have the goods returned to you tonight. She should follow soon after."

The man disconnected before waiting for his employer's approval. Malcolm Carrington didn't deserve his respect. Everyone knew old man Buchanan pulled the strings there. Always had. Now *that* was a man he'd hate to cross.

He inspected his tools for tonight's run. A walk in the park. His apprentice had spotted his marks heading into Carnot's for a juicy steak dinner no more than thirty minutes ago. No one finished dining at the prime establishment in less than two hours. More if they went for the infamous triple layer chocolate cake.

Meanwhile, he'd be in and out in twenty minutes or less with the help he'd hired. Nothing like a little breaking and entering—with some destruction of private property thrown in for good measure—to spice up a Tuesday night.

The man grinned as he tugged on his ski mask and black nylon gloves.

Chapter Nine

Razor slowed as he approached the ornate portico covering the grand entrance to Carnot's, an ultra-exclusive restaurant he'd heard you needed to make reservations for months in advance.

Unless your name started with B and ended with uchanan apparently.

When the princess noticed where he headed, she tugged on his jacket. She shouted—loud enough for him to hear over the engine with his helmet on, "Go around to the kitchen entrance."

Figured she didn't care to be seen arriving with a blue-collar guy. Something in his chest crumbled every time he remembered his station around her. She made it too damn easy to believe they were equals and the connection arcing between them like a livewire jolted her, too. Hell, he'd swear it burned so bright you could spot it from space.

She sprang from the bike the moment it rolled to a stop, hobbling for a couple awkward steps on her stiff ankle before he could catch her. No way would he let her out of his sight, though. He propped the bike on its stand then ambled after her, allowing her to think she'd slipped away.

When he joined her in the whirlwind of activity overflowing the stainless steel and marble prep area, she had already found some dude in a chef's hat to hug. Damn if she wasn't free with those. The woman would snuggle up to anyone. She loved to touch and be touched. Worse, her genuine affection made suckers left and right melt into puddles of goo, willing to go to the ends of the Earth to make her happy.

Knowing it to be true, her open nature continued to work on him time after time. Damn if he wasn't the biggest sucker of them all.

"No problem, Ms. Buchanan. Three house specials to go. Coming right up."

Razor stalked closer, earning a scathing glare from the cook. "What are you doing in my kitchen?"

"Stefan, this is James Reoser. He's a police officer and my partner on *Dance With Me.* The new season starts tomorrow night."

The guy scanned him head to toe before nodding, though the tension in the air hadn't diminished much.

"Uh...need to...use the restroom." Isabella tossed the obvious fib over her shoulder as she scurried for the swinging door into the main area of the restaurant. Through the gap, Razor watched her hustle—eyes lowered, shoulders hunched—to the door marked Ladies.

She should have waited to fumble her phone from her purse until she had hidden behind the cover of the shiny brass door. Who the hell did she plan to call? Why didn't she want him listening in?

Before he could brainstorm possibilities, Stefan started in with the third degree.

"What are you doing with Bella? You may be a cop but you don't know what she's been through. Not really."

"And *you* do?" Razor's hackles rose at the thought. "Maybe you should fill me in, buddy."

The asshole had the decency to look chagrined.

"She's a regular. Over the years I've seen enough to determine the men in her life treat her like shit. They smothered her, never let her talk out of turn or indulged her flirtatious side. It's not her fault she's sheltered and doesn't see their true colors. Look, man, all types come in here. Her dad and that pussy husband of hers are two of the worst. They might've had her fooled for a while, but she's finally doing the right thing. Don't screw it up for her. Don't make it harder. She's a good girl. There's nothing for you to bother her over. I'd bet this whole shop she's not involved in whatever the hell you're digging around for."

In two seconds flat, this guy tallied the score. Razor had to collect Izzy and beat it the hell out of here before Stefan could tip her off. Otherwise, the case would be ruined and she'd never forgive him. Suddenly the latter seemed the worse of the two consequences.

"Could you answer a couple questions if I send someone over? Believe me, I'd like nothing more than to put those bastards away where they can never touch her again." The vehemence in his growl must have convinced the chef.

"Yeah, have your guy stop by after the dinner rush. Around eleven. I don't know how useful it'll be, but I'll share anything I've seen or heard if it will help her out."

"Thank you."

Stefan shook his proffered hand in a firm yet reasonable grip as Isabella returned through the swinging door. The pasty hue of her skin, devoid of the flush she'd worn in, had chills assaulting his spine. Razor wondered who she could have spoken to in those brief minutes to make such an impact.

He and Stefan exchanged a worried glance.

"Chris! You have that to-go order? Take the filets from table ten."

"Everything okay, Izzy?" Razor held out his hand to her. She latched on to it then sidled close enough to lay her head on his chest, wrapping her arms around his waist.

"Yeah, just tired." Even though he recognized her excuse as she studied the floor, the exhausted sigh she released when she rested against him had him counting the seconds until they could be on their way.

The easy familiarity she exuded around him made him wish they were heading to his apartment for dinner in bed instead.

He stroked her tangled hair while the assistant boxed their food. Something had shut her down. The urge to tuck her somewhere safe and force her to spill bubbled inside him. Some deformed part of his brain refused to insist she air her dirty laundry. He needed her to come clean on her own.

"I've got you, princess," he whispered into the hair at her temple.

He couldn't say how long they stood huddled in the corner, out of the bustle. It probably had been more than two minutes. Time flew by as he relished holding her.

She blinked at Stefan when he handed her a fancy maroon bag with gold-foil lettering.

"Enjoy, Bella. Rest up before your big day tomorrow. I'll be voting for you."

This time she didn't relinquish her hold on Razor to hug Stefan goodbye. Razor's chest puffed up when the other man raised a brow.

"Thank you, Stefan. Your support means a lot."

"Come back to the dining room soon. And bring your cop." He shrugged a shoulder in Razor's direction. "I think you were lucky to snag him as a partner. He'll treat you right."

Isabella chewed her luscious lower lip then surrendered a hesitant nod. She fished in her purse for her wallet. Razor grunted when Stefan waved her off. He supposed it was true what they said. The more money you had, the more stuff you scored for free.

"I appreciate it, Stefan. Let's go, Izzy."

He wrapped his arm around her shoulders to steer her to his bike. After stowing their dinner in the saddlebag, he cupped her chin in his hand. "I don't know what happened in there. Always remember I'm trained to protect...and serve."

She winced then turned her head to press a sweet kiss to his palm. "Will you please take me home? After dinner, I'd like to talk if you're still interested in listening."

If he could have blindfolded her for one minute, he would have performed a ridiculous dance of joy complete with fist pumping, hip thrusting and maybe even a little crotch grabbing thrown in for the hell of it.

Razor enfolded her in a bear hug with the potential to crush a weaker being. He peppered her checks, eyelids, nose and, finally, mouth with quick pecks. "Thank you. Thank you. Thank. You," he whispered between each resounding smack of his lips.

She giggled, but her gaze was dead serious when it met his. "No, James. Thank *you.*"

He climbed on before her, asking over his shoulder, "Where are you staying?"

"On Seventeenth Street."

Razor completed a mental review of the neighborhoods in that section of the city. He dismissed most outright. "On the north side of the outer belt?"

"Ah, no. Seventeenth and Lakeview."

"Holy shit, Izzy. Do you have any idea how many calls pour in from that district? And how many more incidents should be reported but aren't 'cause the residents think drive-bys, domestic violence and drug wars are acceptable parts of daily life? Do you have a death wish?"

"I've kept to myself and no one's bothered me. Besides, the room came with a pet rat."

"Jesus Christ. Did you sign a lease on this shithole?"

"A weekly agreement. I needed something fast and obscure where people don't ask a lot of questions. Unlike someone I know." He couldn't be sure in the glow from the streetlamp but he thought color stained her cheeks. No use fighting about it now. He'd go on TV naked before he let her stay another night in some fleabag, rent-a-room.

He'd move in with JRad for a while so she could squat at his place if push came to shove.

They'd take a ride, eat their steaks, hash things out, then gather her stuff and move her somewhere safe. The trip should have taken about ten minutes from the heart of downtown. They made it in half the time as they whisked through the city streets without loads of traffic to jam them up. Razor gritted his teeth and signaled. He turned onto her street. Boarded up windows, broken glass and graffiti became regular landmarks in the urban scenery.

As they approached, he prepared to ask for a more specific location. Then he spotted the gleaming, cherry-red Enzo sitting at the curb. Its fresh wax gleamed in the light from the full moon. How in the hell had it made it this long without ending up stolen or vandalized? The sports car cost more than an entire block of this neighborhood. The residents probably assumed it was a trap.

He cut the engine then jumped a solid three inches off the seat when a car in the driveway behind them backfired.

Isabella slid from the motorcycle. She headed into the shadows before he'd finished parking. She had a bad fucking habit of trotting off without waiting for him.

From the corner of his eye he caught a glimmer of motion heading in her direction.

"Izzy!" He called out as he sprinted the ten feet to her, knocking aside the man who'd charged. They crashed to the ground in a tangle of limbs. Razor grabbed the guy by the scruff of his neck and pinned the assailant's arms to his hips. A noxious stench, worse than the odor caused when Clint deposited a fish in his desk as a welcome-to-the-force prank, enveloped him.

Despite his gagging, he realized Isabella gaped at him as though he'd squashed a kitten. She motioned for him to desist.

"Leo! Are you okay?"

Who the fuck was Leo?

"I didn't do nothing. I swear!" The dude stayed on the ground after Razor crawled off the stinky jumble of ripped fabric wrapping the man's slender frame.

Razor cringed when Isabella crouched beside the man after shooting him a glare that screamed, "How could you?"

His pulse slowed to somewhere near normal. The rushing in his ears receded. That's when he realized the man staggering to his feet looked more likely to keel over from hunger than to mug someone. In fact, he swayed like a tree in a windstorm.

Razor brushed Izzy aside as she attempted to brace the man. Even his emaciated frame would be enough to knock her off balance on that ankle. The homeless man shied from his supporting grasp.

"Sorry about that. We've had a kind of crazy day. I thought you were—" Shit, he didn't quite know who they were on the lookout for. "—someone else."

He led the man to the curb then helped situate the bum on the cracked stairs leading to the street.

"Are you sure you're all right, Leo?" Isabella hovered nearby.

"Yeah, yeah, no problem. Nothing wrong with a man who takes care of his lady."

Neither one of them bothered to correct the man's faulty assumptions. Izzy edged toward his bike. Did it offend her to hear Leo talk about them like a couple?

"I think I have something to make it up to you." She returned with one of the Carnot's takeout boxes.

"Hot damn! I mean... Dang. I can smell some tasty dead cow from here."

Razor thought if Leo's smile spread any further he'd risk tearing his perma-frown.

The man did a respectable job of disguising his sniffle behind the sleeve of one of his assorted coats. "You remembered my steak?"

"Not just any steak, Leo. She brought you the best prime beef in the whole fucking city." He probably owed her an apology for the insulting thoughts he'd harbored while driving her over to the restaurant. Spoiled. Too good for a run through Mickey D's drive-through. When really she laid claim to one of the biggest, softest hearts of anyone he'd ever met.

Who would've guessed compassion could be such a turn-on?

"Watch your language, son. This here's a gen-u-ine lady."

Razor grinned at Leo's exaggerated pronunciation, but truer words had never been spoken.

"Do you need somewhere warm to enjoy your dinner?" Isabella went one step further, inviting Leo inside. "This place isn't much. Still, you're welcome to join us."

"I couldn't accept, Ms. Bella."

Razor would be lying if he didn't admit to some relief over that one. Leo seemed nice, and sane enough, but Razor wanted Izzy alone—protected and willing to talk.

"Why not?" Though small, she had a truckload of determination on her side.

"Don't like confined spaces much. Besides, you got company." Leo had already cracked open the clamshell housing his meal. Steam poured from the opening. The man stuck his nose into the plastic and inhaled so deep he had a miniature coughing fit.

Izzy went to retrieve the other two meals along with the plasticware Stefan had tossed on top. The instant she turned around, Leo picked up his steak with his grubby fingers and took a giant bite.

"Heaven on Earth!" He managed to choke out around the juicy meat. "I'm good right here. With the five of you in that flat, I'd never catch my breath."

Neither would we, Leo. Razor chastised himself for the nasty reaction. Thank God, for once, he hadn't spit out his thoughts before filtering them. The chief said he had verbal diarrhea sometimes. He didn't mean to offend yet he found himself perpetually walking around with his foot in his mouth.

"Hang on. Rewind." His mind stopped wandering long enough to process the rest of the man's statement. "Who are you talking about? There are only two of us. Not five."

Leo paused mid-bite. Mashed potatoes plopped into the

container from where he'd piled them on his next helping. "You're not expecting anyone, Ms. Bella?"

Razor's stare shot to her in time to catch her shake her head. Thank God again.

"Three men in black suits came 'round about the same time your car showed up. I saw 'em checking out the mailboxes. You know half at least don't have numbers no more. They said they'd give me five bucks if I pointed out your room. They were dressed real nice. Not like people who live here. I thought you'd already come home. That you'd slipped by me. On purpose."

He spoke faster and gestured with his steak until some of the potatoes spilled onto his gloves as he started to hyperventilate.

"It's okay, Leo. Maybe they're people I know." Isabella tried to calm the man.

Both he and Razor understood the visitors were no welcome party. He dug his phone from his pocket in a flash.

"This is James Reoser, badge 98237410, requesting backup at Seventeenth and Lakeview. Suspected breaking and entering."

"He's a cop?" Leo replaced the filet in its packaging as though it were a crystal vase. He clutched the container to his chest as he stumbled into the shadows.

"He's a friend. You have nothing to worry about. You haven't done anything wrong." Izzy's reassurance didn't have any effect. The man started to fade into the murky background.

"I'm sorry, Ms. Bella. Didn't mean no harm. I didn't know you weren't looking to be found. Thanks. For the steak. Thank you, nice lady. Gotta go now. Gotta go."

Razor set a personal record when he drew his sidearm for the third time in a single day on duty before snagging her upper arm to keep her close. "Don't argue. Safer if he leaves. Stay right behind me."

His hand coasted along her arm until their fingers met. Then he wrapped hers around the waistband of his jeans, inches above his ass. "Hold on and don't let go. I don't want to lose you in the dark. We have to move. We're out in the open, a blatant target for anyone coming along those stairs."

When she didn't respond, his nerves sizzled. "Say it, Izzy. You will *not* let go."

"I'm right behind you, James." Her promise wavered, but

held. They jogged toward the cover of the wooded yard. When they hunkered together beneath a giant oak tree, Razor peeked from behind it. Silver-blue rays of light crisscrossed a window on the second floor, about thirty feet from their hiding spot.

He jerked his head toward the building. "Your apartment?"

Isabella snuck a glance over his shoulder. "I'm not certain. If it's not mine, it's one right next door."

"Son of a bitch." He slammed his hand, the one without the gun, against the gnarled bark of the tree. "What do you have in there?"

"Nothing much. A couple changes of clothes, some makeup..."

"Cash?"

"Uh..."

"Now's not the time to lie, princess. You suck at it anyway."

"Jerk! Yeah, yeah, okay. What money I have is up there."

"How much?" Jesus, the minutes ticked by and the flashlight beams continued to bob through the open blinds. If she'd only stashed the basics, what the hell were they searching for? He ached to bust through the rickety door on her exterior landing and force them to spill. Leaving her alone simply wasn't an option.

Come on, guys. Hurry.

"Twenty-five thousand, give or take."

"Jesus." More money than he'd ever seen in one place, the sum was nowhere near enough to warrant an operation of this scale when a simple smash and grab would have sufficed.

"I know it's dumb to leave it lying around. I didn't have any..."

"No, Izzy. You don't understand. There's something else. Think!" His harsh whisper cut through the night.

She blinked at him, her blue eyes as wide as an owl's in the starlight. But she never had time to deliver her confession.

Chapter Ten

Razor couldn't say for sure which happened first, the flash or the bang. He would always remember the vibrations most. The entire earth shook as though it were the centerpiece of some colossal god's snow globe. Heat and blinding orange light flared into the inky sky, hot enough to singe his eyebrows. He had time to think, *This is going to hurt*, as he flew through the air. Then he crashed into the trunk of a tree some undetermined distance from where he'd started.

His arm whipped out, by some miracle finding Izzy still attached to him. She hadn't let go. In the same motion, he rolled, blanketing her with his body. His biceps pillowed her head as he wrapped around her, trying to block every exposed inch from the debris raining all over them.

Bits of stone, metal and flaming wood crashed into the dirt beside them. A groan escaped him when a chunk larger than the rest smashed into the armored section of his touring jacket, which protected his ribs. He couldn't hear the sound he knew he made.

The blast had deafened him.

So, when someone surprised him by grabbing his shoulder—yanking him to his feet—he popped up, swinging. No way in hell would he let them reach Isabella without a fight.

The familiar face about to become intimately acquainted with his fist had him pulling his punch at the last possible second. Instead of the right hook that would have guaranteed a broken nose, his knuckles glanced off Mason's cheekbone.

Strong arms hooked his elbows, dragging them toward the center of his spine. Tyler Lambert shouted in his ear. "Enough! It's us."

He sagged in the other man's firm grip. The world spun as though he'd split another case of beer with JRad. *Whoa.*

Razor calmed his respiration, inhaling a huge breath and holding it, while he watched Mason pluck Isabella from the minefield of smoldering shrapnel surrounding them. The ringing in his ears subsided enough to permit the wail of approaching sirens to slice through the din.

Cheap building materials, which had probably never met code, blazed, wafting up a cloud of foul, carcinogenic, midnight smoke visible against the blackness.

Tyler attempted to drag him toward the road. Nothing, not even the seasoned cop, could force him to abandon Izzy. "Mason has her. She's okay. You're okay. You're both okay."

The repetition began to sink in. His tunnel vision cleared, allowing him to catch the disbelieving glance Mason shot Tyler. The pair interfaced on a level beyond working together. Razor knew they were lovers along with the woman they shared. And, in moments like this, he'd always envied their bone-deep bond.

"What? What's wrong?" As soon as Ty turned him around, he realized what they were thinking. A three-foot section of aluminum siding had sliced straight through the thick trunk of the tree they'd hid behind. It had ricocheted off before burying itself at least three inches into the hard-packed dirt right about where his legs had landed.

He squinted at the sheet metal, noting the placement of his boot prints. One on either side of the projectile, about twenty or thirty inches behind the point of impact. A tiny fraction to the left, right or—God forbid—a couple inches higher and he'd have been singing soprano. If he hadn't bled out.

"Close one." All three men went white as a sheet while they considered a fate almost worse than death.

By the time they reached the curb, a host of support vehicles and staff crawled like ants across the scene. Two fire trucks and their respective crews battled the flames while an ambulance screeched to a stop not twenty feet from where they stood. Mason loped toward it, carrying Isabella. Why hadn't she squirmed from his hold by now? It wasn't like her to stay so motionless.

Razor clambered after them as fast as he could while battling the grey haze threatening to obscure his vision. It streaked with the blue and red strobes. A couple steps behind, he arrived in time to watch Mason set Izzy on the gurney he remembered all too well from his rush to the hospital last year.

The rag-doll flop of her limbs terrified him. Had she been hit after all?

"Sir. We need you to stay out here."

"Like hell." Razor stormed through the restraining arm the paramedic threw into his path. He half-knelt, half-collapsed by her head while the tech in the ambulance popped the cap on a vile. A potent whiff of the smelling salts brought him around pretty damn quick.

Thankfully, they did the same for Isabella. She groaned before bolting upright, searching the interior of the ambulance. "James!"

"Right here, sweetheart. I'm right here." He covered her fingers with his then rested his forehead against hers. His eyes closed as he offered up a prayer of thanks—something he hadn't done during the coldest winter of his life.

An hour later, Isabella nuzzled into the warmth of Razor's taut pecs from her perch on his lap. They huddled together, wrapped in the ugliest poop-brown blanket she'd ever seen. The coarse fabric had become her new favorite thing as it bound her to James, providing a convenient excuse to lounge in his arms while they watched her first home as an independent woman burn to the ground.

Smoke stung her eyes. More than irritation had her sniffling for the third or fourth time since they'd started the process of answering endless questions, signing papers and spacing out between requests. The hypnotic caress of Razor's fingers on her thigh couldn't alleviate her dismay.

"Shh." He rocked her and cradled her head on his shoulder. "We'll replace your stuff. Insurance might cover some of the cash."

"Don't have insurance." Her breathing hitched again. "Don't care about that..."

"You're not lightheaded or dizzy again are you?" His concern brought on several more sobs.

"No. Not me. J-Jerry."

Razor stiffened beneath her. "Who's Jerry? The fire chief said everyone made it out."

"My rat. He probably cooked, didn't he?"

His shoulders bounced beneath her clutching fingers.

"Are you *laughing*?"

"No. Definitely not." And by definitely not he meant hell yes.

"James!" Tears overflowed, tracking across her soot-streaked face. She no longer cared. Too tired to dash them, she let them pour. Stupid as it might sound, the varmint had been the closest thing to a friend she'd had since she left her father's house, and Gerard, behind.

"You're something else, you know that? Somebody tries to kill you and you're worried about a rat." He angled her face until she held his gaze. For all his teasing, the melted-chocolate of his eyes seemed solemn. "I've never met anyone like you, Izzy."

She tried to tug him closer. The cover wrapping them tight wouldn't permit her to lift her arms. It didn't matter, though. He leaned in, sipping from her lips in the seductive rhythm he'd taught her this morning.

Malcolm had never enjoyed making out. He'd peck her cheek in public when required. The handful of times she'd attempted to capture his mouth, he'd avoided her like the plague.

Razor didn't seem to have any of the same reservations. He savored her like fine wine before settling in for something more intense. This time the tears she shed were borne of joy. For years she'd feared she would never know this euphoric exchange during her lifetime. She'd doubted her ability to please a man. What if she was good to look at but not good to love or good to fuck?

Certainly her husband had lost interest in record time after their wedding.

Shoving the awful memories from her mind, she opened to Razor, facilitating his navigation of the swells of pleasure she floated on. When she licked a spot at the corner of his mouth, he showered her with moans of encouragement.

Beneath the concealment of their blanket, his hand skimmed from her hip, up her ribs, to cover her breast. The tip hardened at his exploratory touch, filling her chest with a sweet ache the likes of which she'd never experienced before. Every cell in her body came alive when infused with his energy.

The press of his obvious arousal at her hip had her

squirming in his hold, attempting to straddle him as she had in the studio. His cock had felt huge against her pussy, even through their jeans. Right now, she desired nothing more than to steal another hint of forbidden pleasure.

"I see you two are recovering." A smooth masculine jest broke her out of the moment.

Razor flinched, his arms steeling so quick the motion would have shoved her away had they not been tethered. Was he embarrassed to be seen with her?

Hell, she *was* a married woman. How would it make him look to be caught playing tonsil hockey with her? Again.

"JRad. Great timing." Despite his grumpy greeting, Razor didn't object when she peeled the cover from her shoulders and separated them. The cool night air did nothing to temper the boiling of her blood. "Isabella, this is Jeremy Radisson. He's one of the best e-nerds in the business. JRad, Isabella."

"Nice to meet you, ma'am." The cop's grey eyes turned sympathetic as his gaze crossed hers. No matter what he thought of Razor's lack of judgment, he didn't vent his disapproval at her, unlike the men most familiar to her. Both her father and her husband had legendary tempers. When they fell in a mood, anyone and everyone could be subjected to their wrath.

"A pleasure."

Both cops chuckled. She refused to act impolite no matter the circumstances of their introduction.

"I came to tell you, you're free to leave. The arson team is ramping up. There's nothing more you can do here. We'd prefer Isabella stay with someone who can guard her. The chief says you're to take her home with you. Matt and Clint will stake out. A team has run through your apartment already. You're clear."

Razor scrubbed his hands over his face. "You're cool with bunking at my place?"

"If you don't mind having me there." She took several awkward steps toward her car, which miraculously hadn't been damaged, before he responded.

"You're welcome anytime, Izzy. Anytime." A smile began to cross his lips when he continued, "A few things..."

"Conditions?"

"Yeah. Number one, we gotta salvage those steak dinners. Two, I only have one bed. Three, I really, *really* want to..."

She held her breath while he made her suffer. Would he ask for something she couldn't give?

"...drive your car."

JRad laughed, grasping his trim waist at the ridiculous request. "You're unbelievable, rookie."

"Hey, how many people do you know who can say they've driven an Enzo? She's gorgeous. Powerful and superior in every way."

When he described the Ferrari with such fire in his eyes, Isabella would have done anything to transform into that hunk of metal and glass. No one had ever desired her so badly. Or maybe Razor did?

She took a step in his direction, her fingers itching to explore, licking her lips at the idea of one more stolen kiss. He beamed at her, not running from the link pulsing between them. In fact, he'd started to drift in her direction.

"This is Peggy Springfield with breaking news. I'm on the scene of an apartment fire at Seventeenth and Lakeview."

Isabella watched Razor's eyes dilate until his pupils eclipsed his irises. The booming narration of the reporter, who'd managed to breach the police crime scene lines, grew louder by the second. Isabella froze, terrified to turn around and draw attention. Too late.

"Mrs. Carrington. Can you corroborate reports suggesting it was your apartment targeted in this arson attack?"

Before she could bark out, "No comment," Razor had tucked her against his side. He pivoted, sheltering her with the bulk of his body. From beneath his arm, she watched a wall of intimidating male flesh coalesce to provide instant sanctuary for them both.

Mason, Tyler, Matt, Clint, Jeremy and several firefighters assembled within moments to stand shoulder to shoulder, feet spread, arms crossed over ripped chests, blocking the woman's approach. Mason twisted, shouting, "Get her out of here."

Isabella crouched to snag the handle of their Carnot's bag, now somewhat crumpled. She succumbed to the pressure of Razor's hand on her spine. As they crossed to her car she caught Jeremy's mellow lecture providing a quasi-official statement. "Ms. Buchanan is not involved in the incident at this time. We have begun the early stages of investigation. The chief will issue a press release at such time as there are concrete findings to report."

The rest of his subtle smack down dissipated when Razor ushered her into the passenger seat of her father's car. She'd almost forgotten the terrible news she'd received in the elegant bathroom of Carnot's. George had informed her that although all the paperwork for the car had been in the glove compartment, he couldn't sell the thing unless her father signed the title over to her.

The genuine regret in his apology had meant the world to her as he'd explained the legal details of the transaction. Embarrassment had choked her. Oblivious to something so basic, she'd wasted the kind man's time, though he'd sworn it'd created no imposition.

Her options had narrowed considerably with the blow and ever further after she'd observed her pathetic start at a new life going up in smoke. Now it seemed she had to choose. Trust in the man fate had paired her with or surrender before anyone else paid the price. Remaining free, without making progress, would doom others to a life of terror she couldn't feign ignorance toward. Her conscious couldn't endure trading her happiness at the price of their misery.

One person could be behind tonight's attack. He'd meant to threaten her, to show her she hadn't won. He wanted her back and he'd go to any lengths to drive her home.

Too bad Malcolm cared only for the cash she could net him. In some twisted way, it would have seemed better if he'd stalked her because he cared. If he had a single shred of affection for her she'd return willingly, even knowing what he demanded.

She shuddered in the imported Italian leather seat.

Razor slid his hand from the gear shifter to her knee for a reassuring squeeze. His kindness sealed her fate. She couldn't, in good faith, subject this man to more danger than she'd already put him in. Her survival instinct refused to allow her to accept the life her husband mandated she lead. Hell, her own father had fallen to Malcolm's guile. No one could stop him.

Lights from oncoming traffic and the city around them dazzled Isabella's unfocused eyes. Her insides felt as heavy as if they were cast in lead. Her earlier folly smacked her in the face. Telling Razor the truth was selfish. Negligent. She'd have to continue to lie to protect her new friends and hope a solution presented itself. Their gracious acceptance and protection meant the world to her. No way would she risk bringing them harm.

She had no hope for herself. Once Malcolm realized she would never cave, he'd eliminate her to keep her quiet. He'd proven the extremes he'd employ this evening.

Her time was limited. She should make the most of it tonight. In the morning she'd have to slip away before anyone innocent became tangled in her mess.

Chapter Eleven

"Come on, Izzy. We're here." Razor bent to scoop her into his arms. She shook her head then climbed from the amazing car without accepting his helping hand. She'd been so quiet on the ride, he didn't understand what had changed. He had a hunch it couldn't be good.

"Let me walk."

"The medic said you should stay off your ankle. Plus, your shoes blew right off your feet." He clenched his jaw as he considered how close she'd come to disaster. Shit, if it hadn't been for her philanthropy in feeding Leo, they probably would have come upon the intruders before they'd finished.

That wouldn't have ended well.

She began to fabricate another lame excuse. Instead of bickering, he shoved their dinner into her arms with her purse, cradled her against his chest and headed for his apartment.

He nodded to Matt as they passed the man's post at the bottom of the stairs.

"Mason and Tyler had Lacey drop off a few essentials for Isabella. Try to manage a good night's sleep kids." The veteran couldn't claim immunity from the princess's charm either.

"Thank you for...everything." She peeked over Razor's shoulder with a weak smile of gratitude as he continued climbing the stairs. "Goodnight, Matt."

Razor kneed the door shut a little harder than necessary. He carried Isabella to the couch instead of depositing her inside the entryway. Not that the two strides made much of a difference to her. His grip refused to relax until he absolutely had to relinquish his hold.

He figured he owed Lacey big time when he noticed she'd

shoved his dirty laundry into one corner of the room, unpinned his Playboy calendar from the wall and cleared the scarred coffee table of the crushed cans that had littered it when he left this morning.

God, how could something so distant have been a mere twelve hours ago?

Isabella sighed when she rummaged through the floral canvas tote bag beside a note with her name on it. Shampoo, conditioner, lotion, pajamas and God knew what other feminine junk filled the sack. “Could I use your bathroom? I’d do anything for a shower right now.”

If she’d been any other woman he’d gone home with, Razor would have had a nasty suggestion or twenty starting with the two of them soaping each other’s backs. Maybe the fact that they were in his apartment, where he’d never brought a woman, had him checking his tongue.

Or, shit, maybe he was finally growing up. A little bit. That’s all, he promised himself.

Then again, maybe no woman before had mattered like Izzy did.

When he realized she sat there, gazing at him with questions in her beautiful eyes, he shook his head to clear the pesky thoughts.

“Yeah, of course. You don’t have to ask. My crappy one-bedroom apartment is your crappy one-bedroom apartment.” He spread his arms to gesture to his miserable excuse for a kingdom.

“Hey, it’s a giant improvement from Seventeenth Street.”

“That’s no joke.” He scrubbed his face to try and clear some of the visions flashing in his memory. The cracked sidewalk, Leo, boarded windows, flames shooting into the sky…

“Why? Why there? Why now?” He must be more tired than he realized if the questions slammed through his barriers. So much for the restraint he thought he’d cultivated.

Instead of granting him a smidgeon of insight, Izzy heaved a giant sigh. She slipped the handle of Lacey’s bag onto her grungy shoulder and turned toward his bedroom. All hope he’d harbored that she still intended to talk to him evaporated in an instant. “Is the bathroom this way?”

“First door on the left. There are extra towels under the sink.” Only door on the left, but whatever.

Razor crashed onto the couch with one arm behind his head, grimacing when the alluring scent of her wafted from the cushion. His cock inflated in a flash. He tried to ignore the aftereffects of adrenaline, but the patter of shower spray echoed through the thin walls, reminding him that her luscious body stood bare and dripping less than twenty feet away.

He visualized how her peaches and cream complexion would turn rosy under the warm water, steam curling around the curves of her dainty yet strong calves and thighs. The firm cheeks of her ass would tempt him to lay a teasing spank on them, jiggling the globes a little.

A groan escaped through his clenched jaw as he snuck his hand beneath the waistband of his too-tight jeans. He spread his legs, dangling one sneakered foot off the edge of the cushion to permit his engorged flesh some wiggle room. His fingers dipped into his boxer briefs to fondle his hard-on. They swiped the bead of moisture from the tip and painted it over the swollen head. His fingertips stroked his balls while his palm massaged his shaft, his breathing turning ragged.

What if they had showered together? Would Isabella notice his growing erection? Would she be generous and wild or shy and endearing this time around? It boggled his mind that she could bounce between the disparate sides of her personality. Almost as if she wanted to fly but didn't know how. Had her husband never indulged her innate sensuality?

If he were married to a woman like her, he'd never stop her from doing as she pleased with him. He could picture her naughty smirk as she prepared to obliterate his restraint. She would lick droplets off his pecs, raking her sharp little teeth over his pebbled nipples while her fingers walked along the taut surface of his clenched abdomen.

His cock flexed as though reaching out to meet her hand. She'd wrap it around him, her grip tight as she attempted to encircle him with the delicate fingers that had tormented him for two days. Every time he'd cupped them in the awkward ballroom hold or felt them stroking his shoulder through their turns, he had a desperate urge to experience the contact under his clothes.

Isabella's ultra-smooth skin had never known a day of work in her life. Pampered and perfect, it would caress his shaft. The sensation of her suds-filled hand stroking him would be almost as good as tunneling into her soaked pussy. Or between the unexpectedly voluminous breasts, which had overflowed his hands beneath the blanket at the crime scene earlier.

Maybe she would kneel before him, guiding his throbbing shaft to her cleavage. He'd glide between the slick mounds of her chest while she smiled up at him or bent her head to lick the salty fluid oozing from his tip. The heat of her pert mouth would tease him until he had to have more, take more.

Razor would grasp her upper arms, lifting her to her feet then higher, urging her to wrap her legs around his waist. He'd bury himself in her tight pussy with one long lunge that would leave her impaled on his cock. He'd ravage her lips—tasting the intoxicating sweetness he'd only begun to sample today—while he pumped into her heat.

Her ass would fit his hands as he raised and lowered her, grinding against her each time he penetrated to stroke her clit and drive her beyond her polite aloofness. When she cried out for mercy, scratching his shoulders with those manicured nails, he'd shift, pinning her to the molded plastic of his cheap shower stall.

After he had her where he wanted her he'd really begin to fuck.

"Izzy," he moaned.

"Yes?"

The soft reply from the other side of the room had him yanking his fingers from his pants fast enough to burn his knuckles on the denim. When had she finished her damn shower? Had she seen him jerking off to forbidden fantasies?

He didn't think so when she padded around the end of the couch to peer at him, head tilted to the side. The platinum strands of her damp hair hung nearly to the waist of her low-riding sweats. The cropped edge of the matching sassy top tempted him to reach out and circle her cute belly button with the tip of his index finger. Or, maybe, his tongue.

Shit! He slammed his eyes shut.

If he hadn't already hovered on the edge of exploding, that image would have propelled him there. Razor sprang to his feet, bent over due to the steel rod in his pants. He snagged his jacket off the arm of the couch where he'd laid it, clutching the nylon to his stomach, hoping she hadn't adjusted to the dim light of the living area after the stark white of his utilitarian bathroom.

He pinned his jeans to one hip as he limped toward the privacy of his bedroom. When the hell had he undone his fly?

"Are you okay, James?" She trailed after him, but he slammed the door in her face.

"Fine!" He hadn't meant to shout. Hopefully she'd assume he'd raised his voice to allow it to carry, though the cardboard-quality doors wouldn't require any extra decibels. "Be out in a few minutes."

Razor dropped his jacket. He shucked his jeans and briefs before he'd crossed the three steps to the bathroom. Hopping on one foot then the other, he peeled his socks off. He yanked his shirt over his head before reaching around the clear plastic curtain for the knobs with his other hand.

Within seconds, he stood beneath the steamy water, which beat into his hair. His head hung, his nostrils flaring as he inhaled the sweet scent of fruity shampoo. One hand throttled his throbbing shaft, angry red for having abandoned it so close to the mother of all orgasms. His other palm had barely cradled his drawn-up balls when he began to stroke his erection. He swore it had never been so hard or so plump.

He'd made less than five full circuits, his grip squeezing on the tip with each stroke, when he lifted his head and caught sight of a tiny handprint on the steamy surface of the shower wall. Exactly where Izzy would have to brace herself if he spun her graceful back to his chest and slid his cock home from behind.

The base of his hard-on tingled as he imagined laying open-mouthed kisses, licks and gentle bites along her neck. His hand would splay on her flat tummy, anchoring her in place to accept his intensifying thrusts. From there he could tease her swollen folds and engorged clit on either side of the shuttling mass of his cock until she shattered around him.

His head tilted back, exposing the ropey tendons of his neck as he imagined the spasms of her orgasm drawing him into the brightest pleasure he'd ever lived through. Come jetted from his cock, splattering on the wall, not too far from the evidence she'd left of her presence. The proximity had spurt after spurt of seed launching from his balls in a climax that wrung him dry.

Next thing he knew, Razor knelt in the shower, his ass

resting on his heels. He struggled to catch his breath. His hand naturally landed on top of Izzy's print, causing him to wonder if she might have done the same.

A light knock on the door startled him. "James? I thought I heard something. Are you sure you're all right?"

"Much better now," he called.

"Yeah. My...shower...helped, too. Hungry?"

"Starved."

"I'll start reheating dinner if that's okay."

"Sounds great. I'll be out in a few." He'd emerge as soon as he could stand again and had cleaned the mess he'd made, not to mention himself. First, he needed to catch his breath. Then he could manage those tasks. Jesus, no one had ever gotten to him like simply the thought of her had.

Now he had to play house with her too? He considered switching duties with Matt for a few hours. Every instinct rebelled. No matter what the right thing to do was, he couldn't force himself to retreat. The remnants of his orgasm swirled around his knees before circling the drain and disappearing.

He wished he could say the same for his arousal. The fire in his gut lingered, razing his objectivity. If only she would open up to him, maybe he could explore this attraction.

And maybe pigs could fly.

Isabella appraised her handiwork with a critical eye. It held up beneath the scrutiny considering she'd never cooked a meal in her life. Okay, so she'd simply reheated this one. You had to start somewhere. She'd done her best to sort out the jumble their meals had become in the fray, plating the steaks on an artistic bed of potatoes and beans topped with an arrangement of crisped onions.

She'd eaten enough fancy dinners in her life to know what worked and what didn't when it came to presentation. Stefan would approve, she was sure of it. While the entrees had warmed, she'd spent her time rummaging in Razor's cabinet. A dusty bottle of wine with a screw top and two mismatched candles had rewarded her search.

A neon green mountain bike and a set of free weights occupied the nook intended for a dining room table, so she used a hand towel to form a strip-runner down the center of the coffee table. Then she arranged two place settings on opposite sides of it and stole a couple of pillows from the couch for them to sit on while they ate.

She wandered to his iPod docking station and fiddled with the controls. The backlit screen proclaimed he'd set One Republic's "Secrets" on constant repeat. The soulful strings called to her, so she left the music on low.

Isabella dusted off the candles, placing them artfully on the table. She brought over the two glasses she'd discovered—one an old-fashioned coke glass and the other sporting a chip big enough she feared she might cut her lip while trying to drink. She'd barely finished folding a pair of paper towels into a decent imitation of the diamond silverware pouch Gerard preferred for napkins at grand events when Razor appeared from his bedroom.

Isabella had a moment to doubt herself as he surveyed her work—would he think it a pathetic attempt at seduction instead of a friendly gesture of gratitude—before his warm gaze landed on her.

"Damn, is this my apartment? Huh. Who knew it could look like this?" He tugged her into a brief, one-armed hug and dropped a quick kiss on her forehead before releasing her. The spicy mix of his soap and the man beneath had her salivating far more than the aroma of the steaks.

He frowned when he took in the motley assortment of silverware and the oddball glasses. "I should buy some decent stuff. Maybe you can help me pick out a couple things sometime."

"I like how it's real, used." She plucked a fork from her side of the table and examined the bent tines. "People have eaten with this. It's not for show. The experience, the history, means something. When everything is new and perfect there's no tradition, no culture, no..."

She broke off when she caught the curiosity and, worse, condolence in his warm eyes. "Sorry. I'm tired. Not really thinking. Let's eat before everything turns cold again."

They carried their plates to the impromptu settings before digging in. She carved a chunk of tenderloin, popping it into her mouth with a hum of appreciation.

"Holy shit." Razor's reverent groan set the butterflies in her stomach in motion again. "I always figured places like Carnot's to be overpriced bullshit. This is the best thing I've ever eaten."

A ridiculous thrill tingled along her spine. She had never been able to give her father or Malcolm something they couldn't acquire themselves. Making this man happy, over something as trivial as a meal, made her feel ten feet tall.

She devoured a quarter of her steak before surfacing for air again. Today had worked up a heck of an appetite in her. When she reached for her glass, she found it remained empty. Years of stringent rebukes stayed her hand. If she had broken protocol and poured her own drink, Malcolm would have been mortified. As she deliberated what to do, James raised his head from his mostly cleared plate.

How had he eaten so fast? She imagined him choking on an unchewed piece of steak while she attempted to perform the Heimlich maneuver and died of dehydration while in the process. Her imagination had landed her in trouble often.

"What are you thinking?"

"Hmm?" She stalled. "Nothing."

"When are you going to start leveling with me?" Tension crept into the temporary peace of their meal. His LieDAR functioned flawlessly around her, busting her every single time she tried to evade him. Even about something silly.

She couldn't stand to ruin the easy companionship they'd shared by divulging her unflattering daydream so she blurted the lesser of the two evils. "I wondered if you intended to open the wine."

"Oh, damn. Were you waiting for me?" He wiped his broad fingers on his paper towel before reaching for the bottle. "Christ, Izzy. You have to help me out here. What do I know about manners? If I fuck up, tell me."

"I wasn't worried about maintaining decorum." Good thing since dropping the granddaddy of all curses at the dinner table had to rank high in the top ten list of no-nos. "I...uh...didn't want to offend you."

She cast her glance to the floor, afraid to confirm she'd acted too forward.

"Princess, you could fart in the middle of dinner, and I would only laugh. I have about as much class as a ten year old. Though, I gotta be honest, you make me wish I had so much more."

Her jaw dropped open as her gaze flicked to his. He was serious. She tipped over, curling on her side on his industrial-grade carpet. She'd never laughed so hard in all her life. The residual stress she'd bottled seeped from her one giggle at a time until she lay boneless on his floor, tears streaking her cheeks.

One of his sexy bare feet nudged her knee.

"Glad you enjoyed that." He extended a hand to help her sit up as he grinned across the table at her. "My friends tell me I don't know when to shut up. They're right. I know they are. But I can't help myself sometimes."

"It must be liberating to be able to do whatever you want, say whatever you want." He had become her hero. Razor had everything she'd ever longed for—friendships earned, not bought, and the freedom to do with them what he would.

He shrugged. "I find myself in trouble a lot. I figure at least I'm not a phony."

Isabella's smile faded a little. She'd lived a lie for so long she didn't know what remained beneath the tangled fabrication of the perfect daughter or the perfect wife.

"Hey now, those dimples are cute, but I'm not a fan of your frown. How 'bout some wine?" Razor held the bottle toward her, jiggling it. "Let's go crazy, Izzy. Forget these shitty glasses. Open it yourself. Slug it straight from the bottle. I *quadruple*-dog-dare you."

How could she refuse? The metallic rip of the perforated top snapped through the air as it separated. She touched the green glass to her lips and chugged several gulps of cheap Merlot. The tannic concoction relied on too much sugar to disguise the inferior blend. Nothing had seemed so delicious to her before.

"Do I get some too?" He raised a brow as he studied her drinking.

When she tipped the bottle upright, a single drop trailed over her fingers. Razor clasped both her wrist and the bottle, one in each hand. He licked the burgundy stain from her knuckles, causing a riot of passion to warm her insides on top of the wine's effect.

He accepted the vessel, tilting it toward his mouth. His lush lips encircled the neck, inducing her jealousy. She noted the flex and play of his throat, wondering how he could make drinking sexy. The combination of his scruffy cheeks and his strong hand, which palmed the bottle, had her parched.

To distract herself, she cut her remaining steak in half,

transferring the thicker piece to his plate. She would never eat all that.

"If you expect me to politely object, you're in for a rude awakening." Razor swiped a rogue drop from the corner of his lips. He popped his thumb into his mouth to suck it clean. While she sat entranced, he started in on her addition. "And if you don't finish all yours by the time I'm through here, I'm likely to beg for more. Remember, no manners."

In the end, she had him polish off several more bites. Mostly so she could feast on the action of his throat as he savored each morsel. They passed the bottle back and forth between them as they joked about trivial things, enjoying each other's company. Any time a hint of unease snuck into her thoughts, Razor distracted her with some silly comment or another of his endless questions.

When she raised the bottle and nothing came out, she peered into the bone-dry depths.

"Uh oh."

"What's wrong, princess?"

"I think I broke another *fucking* rule." She laughed at her own joke, but not as hard as Razor did.

"Let me guess...women aren't supposed to get hammered?"

"More like, a true lady shall never become intoxicated in public. One glass of wine per event shall suffice." She stuck her nose in the air as she preached in her best imitation of her etiquette instructor while he deposited their dishes in the sink.

"Good thing we're somewhere private, huh?"

She blinked into the tawny eyes closing in on her when Razor returned, teasing her in his official cop voice.

"'Cause I think you're about three times over the snooty limit, ma'am."

She giggled at him, loose enough to dance on the table. A yawn surprised her, distorting her chuckle into an odd noise that inspired her to laugh harder.

"Time for bed, Izzy."

Chapter Twelve

Razor's pronouncement would have panicked her if she could have thought a little more clearly.

"Couch looks comfy," she mumbled.

"It is, but you won't be testing it out tonight. I'd like you with me. Close by."

His declaration guaranteed some fabulous dreams. "Okay."

"No, don't *okay* me. What do you want? You can tell me to go to hell. Matt's covering the front. Clint's at the rear. You'd be safe here."

She should have snatched the out and relegated their attraction to a place she could handle. But some of his impulsiveness had rubbed off. If tonight was her only chance, she had to grab it. "I *want* to sleep with you. I mean..."

"I know what you mean, princess." He lifted her from the rug. "It's what I had in mind too."

Isabella tucked her legs around his waist. She rested her head on his shoulder, trying to ignore the pulsing in her core where she rode him as he walked them into his bedroom. The limited space, decorated in various hues of blue and grey, seemed cozy and intimate.

Razor balanced her on one hip while he fluffed the covers. Then he tucked her beneath them. She burrowed into the worn cotton sheets and the imperfect pillows until they'd conformed to her shape. Everything smelled of him. Scrumptious. She glanced up with one eye to see him observing her from where he stood, on the opposite side of the bed.

"Change your mind? Should I go?" Isabella began to push up though her entire body protested abandoning the nest she'd made.

"No. No, you're good there." He sank onto the mattress—half the size of the monstrosity she'd shared with Malcolm, which had resulted in an acre of lonely distance between her and her soon-to-be-ex. The warp in this cozy pad shifted her toward Razor. "Sometimes it's hard to believe you're for real. That's all."

His hand cupped her shoulder, steadying her as he went horizontal.

"Sorry, this was my brother Andy's bed. Been handed down a bunch of other times I think. It likes to suck you into the center." He flashed a sheepish smile.

She didn't intend to complain.

"I always wondered what it'd be like to have a brother or sister." She imagined an older version of Razor and shivered. With a couple years to flesh out the remnants of his boyish charm, his dashing good looks would refine. He'd turn into more of a heartbreaker than he must already be.

"It's great and a pain in the ass all at the same time. I have three brothers, two sisters, a bunch of cousins and an assortment of nieces and nephews. I'm the youngest of my siblings. By the time I came around, I was pretty much left to do as I pleased." His devilish grin had her imagining him running amok and loving every second of it. He flopped over to stare at the ceiling. "I miss them like hell. This was the first year I couldn't make it home for Christmas. They thought about coming out here, but Mary had another baby two weeks before and my grandparents aren't up to the flight. I couldn't stand for them to split up because of my stupid mistakes."

Isabella could have blamed the sag for tugging her closer to his side. What sense was there in that? She nestled into the crook of his arm, laying her cheek on his chest. The steady beat of his heart echoed in the stillness of the night. Her fingers traced a soothing path along one of his scars through the thin material of his faded T-shirt.

"It's not your fault..."

"I'm *so* tired of hearing that shit, Izzy."

"Let me finish. I understand what it's like to be blindsided by someone you trust. No matter how much physical agony you've endured at their hands, it's the indignity that stings most. Despite what anyone says, you keep replaying things in your mind, wondering if you missed a clue. If you'd looked a bit harder maybe you would have seen it. How many other people knew what you were oblivious to all along? It's infuriating. And mortifying."

He shifted, rolling her to her back while he levered onto his elbow to peer into her eyes. "That's exactly it. How do you know? What did that fucker use you for?"

His fingers buried in her hair as he held on, bonded by their shared experience.

"Money, I think." She gulped. "I'm not a hundred percent sure. Greed's the only thing that makes sense. Talk about humiliating. It's not as if he's Leo, needing the cash to survive. Malcolm has piles and piles to swim in if the mood strikes."

Her gaze flicked over Razor's torso to avoid looking into his eyes. He lay so immobile she thought he might have stopped breathing. She should have shut her mouth and gone to bed, but for once, she didn't feel so damn alone. In the morning, she'd try to believe the alcohol had spoken for her. It'd be another lie. At this point, what was one more?

"See, growing up, Malcolm always hung around. He was my father's protégé in their business dealings. After my mother died, he acted like a friend to me. Nothing more. A lot of times I felt like Rapunzel locked in the tower. He broke the monotony, the isolation.

"No other kids stayed in the main house where I lived. I had no one to play with, no one really to talk to. Unless my father trotted me out for show like one of the thoroughbreds at a social event where I had to make him shine, no matter the cost." She closed her eyes when Razor skimmed his fingertips over her brows and cheeks.

"Malcolm never looked through me. Even when other associates buzzed around, he'd take time to say hello. Really talk. Or at least that's what I thought. Now I wonder if he ever cared or if he planned, all along, to own me someday. When I turned eighteen, someone might as well have flipped a switch. He asked me on a date the same evening. He'd never shown any interest, not a hint of anything more than companionship."

She drew in a shuddering breath filled with the clean scent of Razor. He hovered over her, petting her hair, kissing away the tears dampening her cheeks. "Self-control isn't his strong suit. I should have known."

"You were so young. Sheltered. Innocent."

"Don't bother making excuses, James. You know as well as I, they don't help."

"Son of a bitch. This is different..."

"It's not." She covered his lips with her fingers. Instead of arguing, he nibbled them, offering something better than rational debate: healing, soothing heat.

"I thought he'd waited until I had matured. He seemed proper, formal. Now I think he scrambled for any excuse to avoid touching me. I mean, I asked him to...experiment..." Isabella grimaced when she couldn't spit it out. Razor understood.

"I lost my virginity on my first date with Sue Ellen Diamblo in the backseat of my brother's Mustang when I was sixteen." He grinned. "You don't have to hedge with me, Izzy. I'll never judge."

"Malcolm turned me down flat. Said we should wait. That a lady never has sex before her wedding night."

She thought she heard a muttered, "Stupid bastard."

"He rushed, preparing for the big day as soon as manners would permit. I assumed he was as eager as me to start the new phase of our life. During the wedding planning, he said all the right things—how beautiful I looked, that he didn't deserve me. Did all the right things." When she tried to avert her face from Razor, he cupped her jaw in his hand, holding her in place.

"Your shame is wasted around me, princess." Gentle kisses stole her breath and her doubt, erasing her embarrassment. "Hell, I let some crazy bitch shoot me point blank after she'd admitted to attempting a hit on Lacey. Let's call it even, huh?"

He rubbed their noses together and would have sealed their lips, but she had to finish. Each word lightened the load about to crush her. "You don't understand. On our wedding night, I practically assaulted him. In the beginning, things seemed normal. He reacted...or tried. But when I laid, passive, on the enormous canopy bed in the presidential suite of our honeymoon hotel, waiting for him to take charge, he turned cold. I didn't know a lot. I tried..."

"To seduce him?"

She winced and nodded. "I stripped for him into the ivory lace lingerie I had special ordered from Paris. I'd heard several of the maids talking about how their boyfriends loved it when they put their...you know, in their mouths. I would have attempted it—"

Razor growled from beside her. She couldn't restrain the tide of confusion and raw emotion now that she'd started the telling.

"The moment I knelt at his feet, he freaked. He screamed at me to stand up, never to do it again. He threw the vase with my bouquet to the floor. I remember watching the red rose petals scatter, mixing with several droplets of blood, which oozed from a slice in his thigh. He'd cut himself on the shards. I felt so betrayed after dreaming about our wedding night for years. I'm not proud of this...I lost it. I slapped him. Hard. Quick as that, he came over to me. He ripped those panties I adored and his tux. I begged to see him, to take our time. He knocked my hands aside and mounted me instead."

"He hurt you." Razor's breath buffeted her cheek as he blew out huge bursts of air.

"No, he didn't. Not at all." She gazed deep into his eyes as she promised. That truth was the best she could offer. "I couldn't even tell if he was inside me."

"What do you mean?" He cocked his head.

"He rolled over, yanked me on top of him then ground himself against me. I grabbed his shoulders to keep from flying off. My nails gouged him. He shouted and moaned. In less than fifteen seconds the whole disaster was finished."

"Jesus Christ, Izzy."

"I don't think he had anything to do with it." She'd started trembling as she always did when she remembered the dead silence that had rung in her ears while she waited for Malcolm to fall asleep so she could escape.

Razor gathered her into his arms, rocking her against his chest.

"I froze, taking shallow breaths until I heard his snores. I thought about running. I think I was in shock. Plus, where would I go? I'd never been on my own before. I looked down and noticed his..."

"His cock."

"Yeah, except...he's tiny. Abnormal. It's not his fault. He was born that way. It obviously affects him deeply. He hadn't had the courage to tell me before I'd sworn my soul to him, 'til death do us part.

"How could I leave him to suffer alone? He'd been there for

me when I needed a friend. The only person who bothered to talk to me like a human being instead of an expensive decoration needed someone on his side. Together, we could work it out. At least that's what I chanted while I cried myself to sleep."

"Ah, shit." Razor's fingers tightened on her. "You're too damn sweet for your own good."

"The next morning he apologized. He told me he'd always had issues. I asked if there were other ways we could both reach satisfaction. He said it was impossible for me to please him. He'd understand if I took a lover as long as I was discreet. Malcolm wouldn't tolerate my affairs reflecting on him or my dad and their new joint ventures." She caught the sob before it escaped. "He swore he'd never touch me again. He hoped we could remain *civil*. I knew, right then and there, he'd never loved me at all. He'd negotiated a merger, nothing more."

"And despite it all, you stayed for two years. Because you care for him."

"I guess. I gave my word in front of all those people." She nodded. "There were times I'd think our friendship mended and grew. He seemed ready to open up. I'd start to hope. Then he'd turn cold, mean and reclusive. Sometimes he disappeared for days on end. I should have left him at the beginning. I guess I was scared. Unprepared. A little spoiled, too. The idea of roughing it frightened me."

"So why now, Izzy? What happened? Why did he hurt you?" The fingers of one of his strong hands clenched her hip where he'd glimpsed the marks on her earlier. "Why is he chasing you?"

His sincere questions shattered the illusion of boundaries in their midnight confessional. History had led them right around to the present. A present she couldn't divulge.

She shrugged.

He didn't push.

She'd fantasized about discovering one special man to share everything with. It could so easily be this man. But—no matter how much she'd spilled—if she went any further, she'd trade her unburdened soul for his safety.

Isabella couldn't transact such an unfair exchange.

In her marriage, she'd chosen to stick it out, hoping to heal the friend her husband had been before everything went to hell.

She'd never had a chance. *Her* mistake.

Like Razor, who'd eaten his hospital-issued Christmas Jell-O alone, she refused to impact the people who cared for her—the *person* who cared—simply because she'd been dumb enough to believe her friend had ever really existed.

So instead, she used Razor's sympathy and the genuine spark glowing between them to divert his curiosity toward assuaging some of her own.

Isabella cleared her throat, glad for the wine coursing through her veins. Now they'd discover whether he'd really meant it when he'd sworn she never had to be embarrassed around him or when he promised her lack of decorum wouldn't offend him. Because what she planned to request had to be at least a million times more uncouth than passing gas at the dinner table.

"Can I ask you a favor?" She whispered since they lay close enough for their lips to touch at her question.

"Anything."

"I've never been with anyone other than him. Just that single, disastrous encounter. I never took the lover he blessed. I knew I couldn't split my heart from my body and have any chance at reconciliation. Plus, I gave my word, and it didn't feel right. Even now. It doesn't. Not really."

She feared the desolation shredding her insides might pierce through her rambling. All hope she'd harbored for a peaceful resolution had dissolved earlier tonight. She had some grainy black and white photos, but no cash to leverage them against a powerful man with unlimited resources who refused to grant her freedom. The temporary shield she'd created out of a web of limelight and bad press during the past week wouldn't make him any more pleasant to deal with when he dragged her home either.

Thank God she had stopped relating her saga before revealing why her husband wanted to reclaim her when he had no intention of making her a true wife.

"I respect that." Razor put a little space between them, though the sparse distance didn't generate enough buffer to matter.

"I can feel...you." Heat raced up her chest and cheeks at the admission. She'd tried to ignore the thick length of him pressing into her thigh. No success there.

"Sorry, I'm not gonna lie. You're gorgeous, Isabella. After two days together, you get me. I'd swear you took some thoughts straight out of my mind. We work together like we've hung out for years. You're funny as shit, generous and adorable too. Underneath everything, I sense something wild in you. Something untamed I would give my left nut to see unleashed."

"James..."

"I've never wanted a woman as much as I want you right now. Together we could burn bright enough to chase away both our demons. So, yeah, I'm hard for you. Doesn't mean I have to do anything about it if you're not ready. Let me hold you."

She'd waited her whole life to hear someone say these things and mean them. Cruel fate destined, now that it'd happened, she couldn't throw caution to the wind and claim what she craved most. Her eyelids squeezed shut to stop the renewed flow of disappointed tears.

"Am I making you uncomfortable?" Razor shifted the lower half of his body, stealing the warmth beginning to thaw her frozen core.

"Yes. No." That's not what she'd call it. Her breasts hung full and heavy, her pulse grew erratic and her legs refused to stay still as she squeezed her thigh muscles in an attempt to quell the ache in her pussy. "That's not what I meant. I wondered..."

"Spit it out, Izzy."

"Can I see you?" She blurted the request before she could talk herself out of it.

In the dusk of his bedroom, Razor's feral grin turned her insides to molten lava. "Anything you want. Whatever you need and nothing more."

Her eyes dried out as she gaped, unblinking, while he kicked off the covers. He stripped his shirt and jogging pants from his compact but powerful frame without leaving the bed. Though he lay bare, completely exposed, she locked her gaze on his defined chest. In her peripheral vision, she saw his hands fist in the sheets at his sides.

"Touch me. Explore, Izzy. I won't move unless you tell me to."

How could she get that lucky? "I'm afraid I'll hurt you."

"You won't."

"Or leave you unsatisfied."

"I can take care of myself when you're through." His reassurance rasped as though he'd swallowed funny.

Isabella paused to consider her options. The side of the scale holding her guilt rapidly rose as the heavy weight of her genuine desire pulled her toward temptation.

You're married!

To someone who never intended to honor his vows.

"Go ahead, princess."

Just a little. A taste. She leaned in, closer, closer.

Isabella started at his lips, with the smallest of kisses she hoped conveyed a fraction of her appreciation. She trailed her fingers over the strong bend of his jaw, along the corded tendons of his powerful neck to the bold lines of his collarbones. When she laid her cool palms on his steamy pecs, he hissed.

She recoiled, crossing her arms. Her hands tucked between them and her breasts to keep from mauling him again. "Sorry."

He talked over her apology. "Shh. No harm. It felt great, that's all."

"You sure? Your nipples are hard." She blushed so furiously she probably looked like one of the fire trucks that had raced to their rescue at her apartment.

"I noticed. Why don't you see what they feel like?" His wistful sigh intrigued her.

"Do you like it when a woman plays with them?" Isabella sat on her haunches beside his hip, leaning forward once more. She drew a tentative circle around one with the tip of her finger.

"Hell, yeah. Though most don't."

"Why not?" The bristle of jealousy prickling her at the thought of his many previous lovers came as a surprise. She had no claim on this man.

"I guess they never took the time to learn a guy's body like you are, princess." He moaned when she stuck her finger in her mouth. She sucked on the tip to heat it, hoping to prevent shocking him again. "You have no idea how sexy you look right now. Strong, curious and open."

This time she paused at his scars. The skin hadn't fully healed yet, leaving them puffy and red. She placed more butterfly kisses along the ridge of his injuries, loving the warmth and taste of him.

"Don't." His harsh exhale had her peeking up. He'd slammed his lids closed. "They're nasty. Move on—"

"No, James, they're not. You're so resilient. To come back from this..." Isabella paused, stroking the unblemished flesh on either side of his wounds. She sighed, covering his left hand where it gripped the sheet. "It's amazing. Gives me hope."

"Dumb luck. Nothing to get excited about."

"Lucky for me. For your family. For everyone who loves you and everyone who will. Someday you'll realize these scars aren't a reminder of your mistake. They're a badge of courage." She dropped one last kiss on the worst of the marks before sliding lower.

How much more could she push the boundary without violating her values? Nothing about the sensual exchange felt wrong. She decided to roll with the pure attraction—the only honest thing she'd ever shared with a man. Something so glorious couldn't be depraved. Could it?

She teased his upper abs while she debated. His taut muscles mesmerized her. When she followed the ridge of one rib toward his abdomen, he jerked, laughing. "Tickles."

The musical quality of his amusement had her smiling in return. "I won't take advantage of you."

"I wish you would." His hips arched on the bed. She avoided peeking at her goal. "But I understand why you can't. I'm good. Keep going. If you want to."

As though I can stop now.

Her hands splayed over his belly, relishing the contraction of his lithe body. His chest rose and fell beneath the harsh breaths he took, every movement a dance of coordinated sinew that had moisture soaking her new cotton panties. The foreign sensation had her squirming, which spread her arousal.

She could kneel here and watch this magnificent man all day, though she must be tormenting him. Unwilling to rush through a once-in-a-lifetime opportunity, she closed her eyes then spun toward his feet.

"Holy shit." His muffled curse had her stiffening until he clarified. "Izzy, you have an amazing ass. I wish you didn't have those damn sweats on."

Could she give him what he hungered for? It seemed only fair.

With her shoulders braced on the squishy mattress, she

turned her head to the side and licked the protrusion of his anklebone. She studied the light brown fur sprinkled over his calves and knees—anything to distract herself from how vulnerable she'd be in a moment.

Isabella reached behind her, tucking her fingers beneath the waistband of her pants. She slid the fabric over her ass to her knees. The scrap of her pink bikinis wouldn't provide much coverage from his greedy stare. She wiggled out of the confining fabric. Razor's groan encouraged her to go for broke, shedding her snuggly shirt as well.

The chill night air swirled between her legs and over her breasts. Nothing could extinguish the flames raging there. He'd have a perfect view of her silhouette in the scattered yellow light of the streetlamp outside.

"Fuck, yes. More perfect than I imagined. Izzy. So beautiful." His reverent whispers dripped with desire she longed to satisfy. "I don't think I've ever been this hard. No more stalling, princess. Look at me. Take whatever you want."

She drew a shaking breath then pivoted, kneeling so their legs alternated, one of her knees on either side of his muscular thigh.

"Oh, my God. You're *huge*." Before she could stop herself, her fingertip ran the length of his thick shaft. The steely flesh covered in soft skin jumped beneath her light contact.

A strangled gurgle from Razor had her freezing in place. His fist knocked against the mattress as he battled for control. Finally, he answered. "Average."

"I don't think so." How could anything larger than two handfuls fit inside a woman? If he told the truth instead of being modest, things with Malcolm had been far worse than she'd realized. But she'd heard there were alternatives. "James? Even if Malcolm couldn't..."

"Penetrate?"

"Yeah. I could have pleased him other ways, right?" Despite Razor's patient understanding to this point, she feared he might laugh in her face. "And the same for me?"

"Hard, sweaty sex is great, Izzy. I won't try to kid you. If I couldn't get it up, or didn't have anything *to* get up, I don't know how that would screw with my mind. But for me, it's more about who I'm playing with than putting tab A in slot B. I don't have a favorite position, or orifice, like some guys. It's all about the moment. Believe me, there are a lot of possibilities when you're creative."

"So, I could make you have an orgasm with just my hand?"

She spoke theoretically, but he choked out, "Yes. Please."

Another step on the slippery slope. Still, how could she reject him? "Tell me what you like."

"Cup my balls in your palm. Gently." Razor watched her. He didn't beg or plead or try to grab her hands or move from where he'd fixed himself. The choice was hers.

The weight of his testicles settled into her grasp. She sighed when they shifted, drawing closer to his body.

"Roll them in your fingers a little." His hoarse suggestion had her pussy aching.

They played with fire, but she still drew her limits. The line in her moral sand clarified. She would not allow him to make love to her even if she skirted the fringes big time now. Denying the opportunity to experiment a little would have killed her.

"Yes. Just like that. Now curl your fingers around the base of my cock. Grip it tight."

When she did as he instructed, he bowed beneath her hands. His pelvis thrust, dislodging her momentarily. His legs bent, planting his feet on the bed. The motion wedged his thigh against her soaked underwear.

It was her turn to gasp. Fireworks burst inside her as sensations she'd never experienced overpowered rational thought. Razor's moan helped return her to reality though her insides had turned to jelly.

"You're soaked. Steaming. Ride my leg while you stroke me." Instinct kicked in, putting her body on autopilot while her brain floated in a sensual fog.

Isabella matched the movement of her hand to the rock of her hips, grinding herself on the bunched muscle of his thigh.

"That's it. Tilt forward if you can. It'll feel better if you rub your clit on me. Maximize our connection at the top of your pussy."

She lost track of what her fingers explored in the mindless pursuit of an elusive bolt of lightning, which traveled along her spine when she moved perfectly on him.

"There you go, Izzy. That's the way."

She picked up the pace as the pressure built within her.

"You're a natural. So sexy."

The sight of his cock tunneling through her fists ratcheted the need higher. When she made a particularly vigorous arc with her pelvis, her hands slipped over the blunt tip of his erection. Slippery cream coated her fingers, easing the glide of her hands.

"Ah! Shit." Razor's arms locked straight, his teeth clenched and his head rocked from side to side in the pillow. "Again. Do it again. Squeeze the head. When..."

He trailed off, unable to finish. She thought she grasped the concept. Another spurt of lubrication rewarded her escalating manipulation. Watching him dissolve under her care fed her own arousal until she thought she might die from bliss, if such a thing were possible. Her heart pounded, and so did the sensitive flesh between her legs.

Without shame, Isabella pressed the sweet spot against him. She timed the contraction and release of her fingers to elicit the greatest response from her test subject. His hungry gaze locked on hers when he growled, "Izzy. So close. Can't hang on. Stop now if you don't want..."

She wasn't about to stop for anything.

Instead, she redoubled the most seductive dance of her life. Grander than any symphony, the chorus of pants, moans and moist skin on moist skin created a soundtrack for her to keep time to.

She honed in on the perfect motion to maximize her pleasure. Razor's impressive cock expanded further, making it impossible for her fingers to meet around his girth. The veins gained definition a moment before he roared her name.

The sight of his surrender to ecstasy—seed erupting in milky strands to decorate his sweat-slicked muscles—forced her over the edge. She screamed when her whole body curled inward then exploded into a million rainbow colors more beautiful than she could have imagined.

Pleasure crested in wave after wave of euphoria until she found herself held tight in Razor's arms. She'd fallen from her perch, but he caught her. Kept her safe through the storm of passion they'd generated together.

Had it been real, or an amazing dream?

When Isabella regained some semblance of control, her breathing returning to normal, she swiped her finger through the evidence of his release. She brought it to her lips, devouring the salty sweet taste of his come and humming her approval.

"That's the hottest thing that's ever happened to me, Izzy." Razor squeezed her shoulders in a bear hug. "You're amazing."

She tried to answer. Twice. Exhaustion glued her mouth shut, preventing her from admitting how much their sharing had meant to her. How much he meant to her.

Even if she had to abandon him come morning.

Chapter Thirteen

Razor stretched to work out the stiffness cramping his muscles. Would there ever come a day he woke up pain-free? When his chest flexed, the unmistakable weight of a woman curled asleep there shifted too.

Izzy.

She'd damn near drained him with her innocent seduction and the uninhibited achievement of her own pleasure for what he would bet was the first time.

How could someone as alluring and sensual as her never have had an orgasm? It boggled his mind despite her midnight sharing, which had helped to unravel some of the mystery. Some. She hadn't divulged everything. He'd swear to it.

Guilt tainted the stunning memory of her education.

She'd had too much to drink. Hell, he'd purposely taken only tastes of the cheap wine. It didn't affect him as much. Used to drinking, he also weighed twice what the pixie did and he'd gorged on tons of steak. Shit, it had been delicious.

Encouraging her to spill her guts under the circumstances had been reprehensible enough. Allowing her to jerk him off after claiming to support her no-cheating edict had his dirtbag-o-meter pegged at an all-time high.

As punishment, he forced himself to sacrifice quality snuggle time. He bundled Isabella under his comforter, trying not to jostle her too much. Maybe his imagination and ego teamed up to play tricks on him, but she looked rested—healthier—this morning. She could use all the sleep she could bank.

Razor couldn't say how long he watched her curled in his bed despite his fairly urgent need to piss, made worse by the cool morning air seeping into his crummy apartment. A rustle from his living room caught his attention. On instinct, he crouched then grabbed his Louisville slugger from the closet before investigating.

What kind of idiot left his gun out of reach when trouble lurked nearby? Izzy had consumed his focus, no matter how he'd coached himself to remain aloof.

He choked up on the wooden handle before peeking into the living area. Someone had slung the contents of Izzy's purse across the coffee table where the two of them had shared their amazing meal. The intruder wouldn't barrel past him. No matter what they wanted from Izzy, they were about to have a hell of a fight on their hands. Failure was not an option where his girl's safety was concerned. He'd go down swinging if he had to.

Sometime during the night his instincts had roared to life. What had Mason called it? Claiming his edge? His confidence, which had disappeared for half a year, returned in a rush. Isabella's innocence could not be questioned. Not after what they'd shared. He'd move heaven and earth to eliminate any threats to the amazing woman he'd discovered.

The trespasser switched on the ugly fluorescent overhead in the kitchenette, blinding him for a second. He raised the bat, prepared to knock the bastard's head for a grand slam. Except he recognized the voice mumbling uncharacteristic curse after curse. The profanity shocked Razor more than the identity of the man who'd entered uninvited.

"JRad? What the fuck?" he whispered to avoid waking Izzy. The lack of volume didn't hinder his annoyance from flashing out loud and clear. Though Razor meant business, the absolute dread on the other man's face had nothing to do with the rookie's threatening stance or the near bludgeoning he'd almost bestowed on his mentor.

"Sorry, kid." JRad's head tipped back until it banged into the freezer hard enough to scoot the appliance a fraction of an inch closer to the wall. "I didn't want to find these."

"What are you talking about?" Unease slithered up Razor's spine.

"You two looked so good together yesterday, asleep this morning. You fit. Isabella seemed like such a sweet girl. And it was cool to see the old Razor put in an appearance. I don't blame you for falling for her after meeting her. I just thought I'd cover your ass. You know, be extra cautious after..."

"Snooping again?" The revulsion instigating his nausea had little to do with his friend's legendary penchant for gathering info through whatever means necessary. It stemmed from the certainty he would hate the fuck out of what he was about to hear.

"I didn't think I'd find anything. Not a scrap. I swear."

When JRad glanced away, Razor noticed the manila folder open on the counter. He snatched a glossy photograph from his friend, ignoring the slight crumple his fist made in the heavy paper.

"Is this..."

"I wasn't sure either. Had to flip on the light for a better look. Now I wish I hadn't." Jeremy scrubbed his knuckles over his scrunched lids.

A grainy, black and white version of Malcolm Carrington knelt, naked, at the feet of a petite woman. Latex boots with mile-high heels encased her shapely legs. Her pale, pale thighs glowed in drastic contrast at the top of the frame. The quality of the image made it difficult to say for sure but Razor thought the man might have been in the process of licking her soles. A studded collar encircled the guy's neck. Chain linked him to the leather loop encircling his Mistress's wrist.

"No!" Razor clutched the phantom pain zinging through the scars on his chest with one hand as he scanned the half-dozen damning images littering his countertop. In each, Isabella dominated her husband, humiliating him while doling out extreme punishment. Even worse, she got off on it. Big time.

How else could he explain the picture of her honey drenching the leather whip-handle embedded in her pussy while Carrington supported the other end with his teeth?

No rationalization he manufactured could will away the worst scene—her slave, face down, his back welted and oozing blood in several spots, while the knotted tips of her cat-o-nine dangled, ominous, between the man's legs. Nothing could horrify him more. Or so he thought until he uncovered the shot featuring Malcolm in a sling, his asshole stretched around the tiny wrist of the woman fisting him.

Holy fuck!

Well, at least she hadn't lied about one thing. The man's cock looked more like a giant clit than a penis. Razor gagged as he catalogued the hysterical rapture on Carrington's face. He forced himself to avoid studying the woman abusing Malcolm's trust, taking advantage of his condition.

His pride couldn't handle admitting his faulty judgment.

Razor had nothing against kink. Serious forays into the darker side of passion intrigued him. Yet, something about the man was off. Really off. Even in the pictures, Carrington's dementedness jumped out at him. Any Dom, or Domme, who capitalized on the situation couldn't hold his respect. And they sure as hell couldn't be the innocent the little witch had convinced him she was.

Isabella had been crafty, avoiding including any identifiable features in the photographs. It didn't matter. He recognized her build. The photographs seared his eyes. No wonder Carrington had resorted to such desperate measures to search his wife's—his Mistress's—shithole hideout and annihilate what remained when he hadn't found what he sought.

The pictures slipped from his fingers. He stood rooted to the floor, wondering at the rapid gasp of his hyperventilation.

"Razor..." JRad took one step toward him, kicking his limbs into motion.

"Need some air. Fuck. Should have searched her stuff. *Mistress* Isabella." He met the man's gaze long enough to reject the pity lurking there before groaning, "Thank you."

He limped from the apartment. Sparks shot through his thigh with every staggering lurch. Jeremy would keep her from leaving and he couldn't stand to occupy the same space as her for a single minute more. He burst out his door then crashed down the stairs.

Mason leaned, arms crossed over his chest, one hip against the retaining wall at the edge of the parking lot.

Shit! Avoiding the man would prove impossible.

"What's up, Razor?" His friend hailed him from across the vacant lot.

"I fucked up. Again." Despite the stiffness in his joints, he spun around. He punted Mrs. Crabczyk's obnoxious garden gnome a solid forty feet through the air. The damn thing bounced before landing right side up with a friendly wave that had him pulling his hair while trying to ignore the pounding in his toe.

"Jesus H. Christ! I can't do anything right. Fuck it, I quit.

For real this time." His throat tightened. He dropped to his ass on the brown grass, which hadn't begun sprouting quite yet, his fury morphing into something less manly.

Great, like I need something else to be ashamed of.

When the scuffed running shoes Mason preferred filled Razor's downcast vision he closed his eyes. He pressed his fingers over the bridge of his nose. A pounding headache coalesced behind his temples.

"I take it JRad found more than he hoped to on his little look see?"

"You have no idea."

"It caught you off guard?" Mason surprised him by plopping onto the dewy lawn beside his knee.

"Clark. Don't turn shrink on me. This is all your fucking fault." He sat on his hands to keep from waving them at his fellow officer like his grandmother in a fit.

"Huh? How do you figure?"

"Your bullshit about my edge. You got me pumped. Might as well have played 'Eye of the Tiger' before running me up the *Rocky* steps."

Mason barked out a laugh. "That movie rocks."

"Figures you'd think so." He scrubbed a hand through his bed-head hair.

"What's your problem, Razor?"

"In real life, Rocky would have had his ass kicked. And every time he staggered to his feet they'd have taken him to the mat again and again until he learned his fucking lesson. There's no coming back."

"So you're saying my pep talk worked? Sweet. Ty's been ragging on me to develop my interpersonal skills. Guess I showed him."

There was no help for it. Razor threw his arms over his head then crashed to his back, sprawled on the lawn. He prayed for a freak meteor strike to put him out of his misery.

"Look, Razor. Kidding aside, every guy on scene yesterday jumped to help your girl. It's in our nature or we wouldn't work these shit jobs. Yes, it makes us susceptible to being played, but I'm okay with my hero complex. We're extra cautious these days. Especially you, me, Ty and JRad. Despite that, she didn't trip any one of our feelers. And I don't believe for a second the heat shimmering between you was an act for this assignment. Maybe there's another explanation..."

"No way. I saw..."

He didn't have the chance to fill the other man in because Tyler shouted from around the corner. Mason scrambled to his feet, bolting toward his partner before Razor had moved a muscle. Sort of like his foolish ass had leapt to Izzy's defense less than an hour ago. Must be nice to love someone who deserved it.

He struggled to follow, dreading what they would find.

Isabella never slept past seven. So when she rolled over and squinted to protect her throbbing head from the rays streaming in the roadside window, she panicked. Until she recalled the night before and the man who'd made it the best of her life. Her distress morphed into dread. It had bile burning a path up her esophagus. Or maybe her upset stomach was a side effect of all the wine she'd imbibed.

Either way she might have already blown her chances for escape.

She nuzzled the indentation in the pillow next to hers, dropping a light kiss to the center of it before rolling to her feet. She tested her sprained ankle, much better today.

Checking around, she couldn't locate her clothes. Although they'd been ruined by the fire, she couldn't risk sneaking into the living room for Lacey's replacements. She'd have to wing it in her borrowed pajamas. She imagined Razor rounding up breakfast when she heard movement in the kitchen. Without much time to decide, she reviewed her options. She could stay. Every second she associated with James put him in more danger. She could run. Without the pictures in her purse, or her car keys, she'd be screwed.

Not that she wasn't already there.

No cash, no lawyer, no place to hide... The odds weren't in her favor.

Her lack of money rendered the photos useless. Plus, her car screamed for attention no matter where she went—not exactly conducive to living on the run.

Footsteps neared the bedroom.

Isabella braced herself, prepared for her opportunity to slip away.

The steady stride faded once more.

She had to act now. With less than she'd had the last time she'd fled her home, she scurried to the window, eased it open then popped the screen. When the light aluminum frame bounced onto the pavement twenty feet below, she winced.

Good thing she had practice climbing out. Unable to roam far, she'd entertained the need for a moonlit stroll in the gardens on the occasions she couldn't sleep. She craned her neck, grinning when she spotted a beefy oak tree about five feet away. If she could lean a little closer...

The downspout bolted to the siding less than two feet from Razor's window would make an ideal handhold and stepping stone. As long as her weight didn't rip it apart. Without much to lose, she evaluated the drop. Worst case, if she could slow herself at all on the pipe, she might have a slender hope of surviving in one piece.

Isabella stole one last glance at Razor's room over her shoulder, swearing she wouldn't cry until she had made it away. Until she'd removed him from danger. She tucked through the opening and balanced on the sill while grasping the outside of the casement with her fingertips.

The longer she hesitated the more likely she was to lose her balance and fall. So, without analyzing the situation too much, she hopped to her left and shoved off the pipe toward the oak tree. The branch caught her a little higher than she expected. She'd almost missed her mark. It slammed into her ribs, knocking the wind from her. She managed to cling, draped unceremoniously over the bark.

Air flooded into her chest with a painful wheeze, distracting her from the inferno in her fingertips, a product of clawing the limb for dear life like an unwise kitten out of its league.

She had to hurry.

Isabella scooted toward the trunk of the tree. She made quick work of stepping down the spiraling branches until she hung from the lowest one. She dropped the remaining four feet below her dangling heels, rolling into a somersault to avoid absorbing the full impact on her recovering ankle.

Tears streamed over her cheeks when she peeked at Razor's apartment. She'd never forget that man. Not a difficult feat since she didn't stand a chance of lasting through the week.

Maybe her father would listen to reason this time?

She jogged toward the road, hoping to spot a taxi to drive her to her father's estate. Otherwise, she'd head for the gas station she'd glimpsed yesterday to beg for a phone call.

Isabella hadn't crossed more than twenty paces when someone shouted her name.

How could she have forgotten Razor's friends? She hadn't detected them lurking in the yard, but they'd maintained their watch. Instead of slowing, she sprinted in the opposite direction from the noise. As she neared the front of the building, someone streaked around the corner, nearly bowling her over. She dodged the pursuer. When she twisted to check his proximity, she plowed straight into a sturdy male chest.

A chest she'd recognize anywhere. "No!"

"Oh yes, princess. It's too late to run. You're not going anywhere."

She lashed out, kicking at Razor's shins until he grew sick of her antics and tossed her over his shoulder. No matter how hard she squirmed, she couldn't break free of his relentless hold.

"Be still." The raw command shocked her more than the stinging swat of his palm on her ass.

She obeyed, slackening in his hold. Why fight anymore?

She'd lost on every count.

"What the hell is this about?" Razor shoved a photograph in her face.

There'd be no point in denying it now. "Blackmail."

The last trace of her selfless lover from the night before vanished behind a stony mask. "You admit it?"

Tears choked her, preventing her from responding.

"How fucking hard did you laugh behind your sugary mask last night? You manipulated me into lying there and behaving myself, didn't you? You loved towering over me, being on top while I fucking let you do whatever you damn well pleased."

The self-loathing twisting Razor's lush mouth into a vile sneer spurred her into action despite the raised eyebrows and bugged eyes of the other men in blue.

"Hold on. You have this wrong." She reached for him, but he evaded her like she had the plague. "Can we talk about it in private?"

Her cheeks flamed.

"You'd like that, wouldn't you? No one around to smack some sense into me. Alone, you could con the fucking loser who gets jerked around by his cock all the time?"

"Stop saying those things about yourself." Isabella's temper rose to the surface, escalating with his insults.

"Or what? You'll bring me to heel? Teach me a lesson or two? *Mistress*?"

Oh, crap!

"You think *I'm* the woman in those pictures?" She slapped her fingers over her gaping mouth. One of the other men, she thought it might be Mason, laid a restraining hand on Razor's shoulder.

"Is it you, Isabella?" This time JRad interceded.

"No! No, it's not me." She stared straight into Razor's gaze, shuttered behind lowered lids. The understanding he'd promised had vanished. "How could you think that?"

"What little there is visible of the Domme looks an awful lot like you." Jeremy continued to mediate, navigating them through the tricky situation. "If it's not, why didn't you show these to Razor? If your husband is cheating on you, mistreating you, the kid would help you. We all would. Tell us what's going on. Who did you plan to blackmail? Why?"

"I can't say." She dropped her face into her hands. It did look bad. Really bad. "It's my mess. I can't live with involving anyone else…hurting anyone."

"You don't think it's a little too late for that?" Everyone turned from her to Razor at JRad's question.

His chest heaved. Bunched muscles quivered beneath the steadying hands of two of his comrades. A pang squeezed her heart.

"Don't try to turn this shit around." Razor refused to believe her.

She didn't blame him. The thought of losing her only ally drove her to desperate measures.

"Okay, I admit it. When we met, I didn't confide in you because I didn't know who to trust. My husband and my father aren't opposed to greasing palms. How should I know which cops they've bought?" She winced when the guys grimaced.

Before they could object to the insulting implication, she hurried on. "And when I decided for sure none of you were on the take, I couldn't stand to repay your kindness by putting you at risk. Malcolm's watching me. He's waiting. Biding his time. He'll come for me. And he won't care about collateral damage. Damn it, you were there last night. You saw what he's capable of. He doesn't play fair. None of you will stand a chance."

JRad slouched onto the cushion next to her while Clint reached out to cup her knee.

"Don't fall for her bullshit." Razor's rejection stung more than she could have imagined.

"Kid. Enough." Mason cut him off before he could rant, but the grooves around his clamped mouth made her realize words alone could never persuade him. She'd fucked everything up.

Her lungs filled to bursting before she sighed.

"I can prove this isn't me." Isabella clenched one of the pictures—the one of the whip lodged between the Mistress's legs—in her shaking fingers.

Razor glared at her. No matter what she said, he wouldn't budge. Determination etched into the grim lines of his face. He seemed ten years older than he had the night before.

"How, Isabella?" Clint knelt in front of her to peer directly into her eyes. Mason tensed behind him. The spark of hope and trust she glimpsed in Clint's gaze bestowed the courage to do what she had to. Maybe then they'd understand.

"I'm a virgin," she whispered. The coppery tang of blood blossomed on her tongue. "James can examine me."

"Oh, no. Oh *hell* no." He recoiled, almost crushing Tyler in his haste to backpedal.

"You're serious?" Clint unclenched her fingers from the couch cushion, enfolding them in his solid grip. JRad claimed her other hand.

Despite their support, she found it impossible to glance away from the horror contorting Razor's face. "This is another trick. She knows I can't resist. I'm easy. I'll wedge my fingers in that tight pussy and forget about everything else. I'm not doing it."

"Razor!" Matt barked the ineffectual reprimand.

Isabella cursed the tears spilling over her cheeks. "I don't blame him. Just release me, please. Don't lock me up where Malcolm can attack me like a caged animal. Please. I trust you.

But not everyone on the force is as honorable as you guys. Don't send me where they can hurt me. You don't know what I had to do to escape last time. I'll never break free again."

A flicker of regret shifted across Razor's face. He shook his head as he turned his back on her degree by degree.

"I'm sorry, baby, we can't allow you to leave." JRad squeezed her numb fingers.

"Please, I'll tell you everything." She swallowed hard.

"Convenient." Razor's bitter sneer launched shivers along her spine. "Had enough time to construct an elaborate story, huh?"

She drew a shuddering breath then scanned over each cop in turn—Tyler, Mason, Clint, Matt, Jeremy. "He won't believe me until one of you checks. I understand why. I don't care about modesty or pride anymore. My word is all I have left. Someone do it."

Each man avoided her laser vision as she fixed it on them until Tyler broke the silence. "We need to know the truth."

Isabella sighed. "Thank you. Can we use the other room? Or do you all want to watch?"

"Whoa, I'm not volunteering." He fanned his hands in front of his chest. "Lacey would kill me. Mason's out too."

"If we do this, does it guarantee anything?" Clint rubbed his thumb over the back of her hand.

"I'm not really sure." Mason rubbed his chin. He turned to Tyler, asking, "You've taken a virgin before. Could you tell?"

"Definitely. I don't know if you always can though."

"Maybe we should phone-a-friend," Clint suggested.

JRad nodded as he faced her. "Lacey is a nurse. She would know."

Matt tossed the handset of Razor's cordless phone to Mason. Isabella clamped her eyes shut and tried to ignore his conversation.

"Hey doll, how's your day going?" Pause. "Yeah, everything's good here. I have a kind of weird question for you."

Isabella winced.

"Can you tell if a girl is a virgin by feeling her up? Yeah, that's what I meant...manual examination of her hymen." He chuckled, "I know, not what I thought I'd be doing today either. So, talk to me..."

After a series of ominous sounding affirmations, he ended the call with, "That's sort of what we thought. Thanks, doll. I love you. Yep, I'll tell him. Bye."

"What's the verdict?" Tyler wondered.

"She loves you too."

The two men stared at each other with stars in their eyes a moment before returning their attention to the room.

"Lacey says a manual exam is not definitive. Especially not when someone untrained tries without the proper tests. She also said, if the hymen is intact it's a pretty sure thing, though it's elastic. She warned we're more likely to obtain a false negative or some shit. Basically, there are things that could have caused it to rupture besides sex."

Isabella's face had heated enough to fry eggs by this point. She spoke up anyway. "I'm telling you I can meet the highest burden of proof. Will you at least agree to that?"

"Uh, yeah. That whip is shoved deep. No woman could take it and have a full hymen left." Mason cleared his throat when he caught her wince. "Sorry, Isabella."

"I-I've heard of...reconstruction." Everyone's head swiveled in JRad's direction. "What? I have the Internet. I read stuff. But, yeah, that seems drastic even here."

Tyler choked a little before adding, "We can have an official exam performed later. We need to know now if she's telling the truth before we follow any deeper into her explanations. We've been here before, guys. It's too easy to believe what you want to hear."

"You're fucking crazy. All of you." Razor slammed his fist into the wall. Still, he didn't call them off. "JRad, take her in my room."

She glanced at the computer specialist and nodded, trying to maintain a brave face when she wanted nothing more than to cower beneath the sofa or dash out the door. If she thought she had any chance of slipping past the squad of ultra-fit men in blue, she would have attempted it.

"For the record, I trust you right now." Jeremy brought her fingers to his lips and kissed her knuckles. "I'm so sorry for this."

They rose together, neither one rushing as they shuffled into the bedroom.

"Razor." Mason froze them all with his stern address. "Go

with them. If she's brave enough to do this, you should be too."

Isabella expected her partner to object. Instead he approched, his possessive snarl surprising the hell out of her. "If you insist. But when JRad is sporting a black eye *you* can explain it to the chief."

"Hey, don't deck the messenger." Jeremy tried to lighten the mood. He failed miserably.

"Keep it together." Tyler clapped Razor on the shoulder as he passed by. "Allowing your fear to blind you to the truth is as bad as believing a lie. Maybe worse."

"Let's finish this shit." James stalked past her without sparing a single glance in her direction.

Chapter Fourteen

Razor strode around his bed to stick his head out the open window. The fresh air couldn't clear his mind. Not when he studied the drop to the pavement below. His guts clenched at the hazard Isabella had endured to avoid dealing with him.

When JRad murmured reassurance to her in the background, Razor slammed the pane closed. Annoyance pummeled him. The racket caused her to jump several inches off the floor. A handful of damning photographs depicted her debauchery in black and white. How on earth could he feel guilty about the fake kicked-puppy thing she had going on?

Why did he ache to believe her act despite the evidence? Christ, how could she have played him so bad the night before? Maybe he'd drunk more than he thought?

JRad hesitated, giving Razor a what-the-hell-do-we-do-now glare over Isabella's head. Fuck if he knew. He absolutely refused to touch her. He shrugged.

"Quick is best. Like a Band-Aid, right?" Before either of the guys could approach the little con artist, she'd shucked her sexy pajamas, complete with torn knee and tree-bark stains.

Razor cursed himself for wincing at the matching scrapes on her knees, the rivulets of blood running down her shin and the bruise already forming along her ribs, below her breasts. None of those things had marred her perfect skin the night before.

"Jesus. Isabella, you're hurt." JRad's resistance didn't fare as well as Razor's. She had his fellow officer sucked into her deceptions already. Good thing he had come along, otherwise the witch would probably have talked JRad into confirming she had her cherry without so much as one poke.

"I'm fine." She held her chin up, her defiant scowl causing his moronic cock to stir.

"What happened here?" JRad brushed his fingertips over the faint scratches remaining on her taut abdomen.

"Can we talk about it after...? I'd rather not have to tell the story twice." A cross between a hiccup and a sob slipped past her guard. Or at least she made it seem as if it had.

"Of course, baby." JRad offered his hand to help her recline on Razor's bed.

The older cop propped her on the two puny pillows topping Razor's mattress then skimmed his hands along her sides, dragging her scrap of underwear with them in a practiced move. JRad didn't hesitate, and Isabella capitulated in the wake of his innate control without reservation. Observing the power exchange riled Razor beyond belief.

Watching JRad touch her—positioning her on the mattress so her heels reached close to each edge—had Razor's skin crawling with the urge to knock his friend away from the petite woman lounging there like something straight out of a wet dream. He concentrated on relaxing his fists at his sides when her pretty, pink pussy spread before them.

"You're unbelievably beautiful, Isabella." JRad spouted a string of infatuated nonsense similar to the crap Razor had ran on about last night. Right around the time she'd flashed her sweet ass at him.

Only, she didn't melt at the compliments as she had for him. She lay, stiff and unyielding. Her wide-eyed gaze locked on the stippled ceiling. Rapid, shallow breaths shattered the awkward silence. He growled when he realized he stared at her heaving chest.

"Razor, come over here. Hold her hand. Do something." JRad's demand almost sounded like a plea. "Stop thinking for two damn minutes and give in to what feels right."

"Because that's worked so fucking well for me," he grumbled as he took a step in their direction. Damn it if her discomfort didn't tug him closer, whether he chose to soothe her or not.

"It's not all about you, Razor." JRad's mild reproach stirred remorse and defiance.

"You're right. This is about the truth."

"She's scared." JRad trailed his palm over Isabella's toned

thigh, accustoming her to his touch. She didn't move a muscle or make a peep. Her jaw clenched tight. The white of her knuckles glowed in the dim light. "Distract her."

Razor groaned as he sank onto the bed beside Isabella. She finally shifted, her fingers seeking his. They grasped his hand in a death grip. Shit, they froze him solid. Before he could consider, he chaffed them. When the brisk motion didn't help, he brought them to his mouth. He blew warm air over the chilled digits.

She angled her head to offer him a weak facsimile of her brilliant smile. "Thank you."

He tried to ignore the shivers wracking her, chattering her blinding-white teeth. Impossible. Son of a bitch, he couldn't resist her even when his mind screamed red alert.

"Are you ready, baby?" JRad's fingers circled closer to her mons, inspiring a haze of jealousy to overlay Razor's vision. It condensed when the man crawled between her spread legs. Who knew JRad could be so dominant, so controlled?

"Y-yes." She had to try several times before the shaky assertion fell from her lips.

"I'll be gentle. I promise."

Razor had to clench his hand onto his thigh to keep from shoving JRad away when the tip of his friend's blunt finger traced the seam of Isabella's labia. What the hell was taking him so long anyway?

JRad lifted his head, meeting Razor's glare. "She's tense. Dry. I don't want to hurt her."

"Shit!" His head fell onto the bed. What had he done to deserve this kind of torture? She sure as hell hadn't had the same issue last night.

"Just do it." Tears streamed down Isabella's face. "Get it over with. Please. Hurry."

"No, Isabella." JRad kissed her flat belly. "That's not how you want this to happen. Trust me."

"Look at me." The directive burst from Razor's chest before he could change his mind. When her face tilted in his direction, he closed his eyes and imagined the delicious heat they'd shared the night before. He pretended it had been real then stole one last taste of her luscious lips. He should have known it felt too good to be true.

The moment their mouths fused, some of her apprehension

seeped from her delicate frame. She conformed to him, her arms winding around his neck. Her tongue darted out, laving a spot he hadn't realized he bit.

"I'm so sorry," she whispered between nibbles. "Should have told you everything. I should have asked you for help. I've never had someone I could count on before. Someone strong enough to stand up to Malcolm or my father."

He deepened the kiss to keep her from saying anymore. Her genuine-sounding confession had his instincts crying out for him to comfort her, to shelter her.

What would she do when JRad couldn't find her maidenhead? Claim it'd torn sometime in the past two days? Maybe when she'd done her Spiderman impression earlier? He took her without restraint as he recalled the drop he'd measured out his window.

At least she'd saved him from burning in hell. If she'd been innocent, it'd be damn hard to swallow his own deceptions. His job had mandated his lies. He'd done it for a higher purpose than cold, hard cash. Unlike his little blackmailer.

As if the reason mattered.

"That's better." JRad's reverent whisper cut through his whirling thoughts. "A little more, Razor. Turn her on."

The illusion could only survive a few minutes longer. He might as well take the opportunity to say goodbye to the girl he'd thought he had such amazing chemistry with.

His hand wandered along the elegant curves of her jaw and neck then lower to palm her pert breast. Her nipple strained against the lacy bra covering it, beading at his touch.

When she sighed, he eased his tongue into her mouth, memorizing her taste. Izzy responded, granting him free rein to do as he pleased. He paused as his chest tightened. She returned the seductive kiss, luring him to continue. Her hand buried in his hair, dragging him closer to her softness, her warmth.

Lost in rapture, the tap of JRad's elbow against his hip startled him. Both he and Izzy peeked through the chasm he'd put between them when he jerked. JRad stared with dilated pupils while he sucked on his index finger. At least Razor wasn't the only fool in the room.

"Ready?"

"Yes," she sighed beneath him, her hips arching toward

JRad.

"No," he groaned at the same time. He couldn't bear for the exchange to end so soon.

JRad quirked an eyebrow.

Razor ignored the man. He rose more fully over Izzy, devouring her lips. She tensed beneath him when Jeremy made his move. To counter, Razor stroked across the dip of her waist, aligning her with his torso.

"Jesus, she's so tight. Tiny." Sloppy sucking drew his attention to the juncture of her thighs. JRad had withdrawn the tip of his finger to moisten it further. "And tastes delicious."

"Are you okay?" He hated that he'd asked.

Izzy nodded but winced when JRad replaced the digit at her entrance.

"Lick her."

His friend hummed. He nuzzled her dewy flesh, giving her the chance to object before his lips parted. His tongue explored the apex of her slit, circling the hard bud of her clit.

Isabella's heels drummed on the mattress. Her hands tucked beneath Razor's T-shirt to rake his shoulders with her kittenish nails, urging him to reclaim her mouth.

Is this what sex was like for Mason and Tyler when they shared Lacey? He never would have guessed it could be such a turn on. But, when she shuddered in his arms at the barest contact of JRad's seeking hand, something inside him roared in satisfaction. Dictating her enhanced arousal went straight to his cock. It throbbed in his jeans, galvanizing his wish to bury himself in the slick satin his friend explored.

Izzy panted into their kiss. He pinched her nipple when she rubbed against him like a hungry cat. Her thigh shifted, making room for JRad to delve deeper while increasing the pressure on Razor's hard-on. He figured his friend must have made some progress when she cried out, trembling beneath him.

"Is everything okay in there?" Clint called from the living room. When no one could catch their breath to answer quick enough, the door crashed open.

"Holy shit, that's hot." Matt groaned.

Tyler jumped to the rescue, shutting the cheap hollow-core. The thin door didn't obscure Mason's bellow. "This is a fact-finding mission not a goddamn orgy. Do it."

"Ignore them," Razor growled into the curve of Isabella's neck. He licked a trail to the sensitive spot behind her ear. "JRad?"

Terrified the man had already tunneled far into her body with no obstruction, he held his breath while waiting for a response.

"Only in to the first knuckle." JRad rasped. The bed rocked in time to the other man grinding his hips into the mattress. Razor couldn't fault his appetite.

"More. Please, more." Izzy squirmed in his hold as though nothing had happened. The dazed quality of her beautiful blue eyes made him wonder if she'd noticed the rest of the men in blue.

"Give her more, JRad."

His friend nodded, dragging his lips over the glistening folds of Isabella's pussy. He pumped his hand between her legs. She gasped at the same time JRad yanked his gaze to Razor's.

"I can't. I'm in as far as I can go. She's telling the truth." His friend shuddered, his finger lodged in place as he trapped the flesh of Izzy's thigh lightly between his teeth.

Razor growled at the possessive display. "Enough."

"I've never taken a virgin." JRad tensed, his little head obviously having grappled control from the big one.

"And you're not about to today," Razor snarled. Relief mixed with an undeniable need to claim her. His heart pumped with victory he hadn't allowed himself to imagine possible. It hadn't been her in those pictures. She hadn't lied to him.

"Oh, God. Someone help me. Touch me," Isabella begged.

Shame overrode his lust and domineering instincts when he realized they'd abandoned this intoxiating girl on the brink of ecstasy. "Sorry, princess. Hang on. I'll take care of you. *We'll* take care of you."

JRad bent his head once more, sipping the juices dripping from her now. Isabella moaned, peering at Razor so he could witness her surrender. His friend must have done something naughty with his tongue because she squirmed beneath them before putting a restraining hand on Razor's chest.

"Wait. Not yet." She panted. "Feel for yourself, James. Believe me."

After the shitty way he'd treated her, her generosity awed

him.

"I do. I believe you. It's myself I can't trust." Razor framed her face in his palms. He pressed a kiss to her lips, aching because he couldn't be more gentle. "So sorry. Won't doubt you again."

She drew her knuckles over his cheek. "I understand. Didn't give you much choice."

"When I saw..." He cursed under his breath. "Lost it. Then you ran."

"Shouldn't have." She shook her head and promised between ragged pants. "Never again. Please. Touch me."

He licked the tear that beaded on her flushed cheek before worshipping every part of her on his path to her pussy. JRad shifted to one side though he refused to budge from his station between Izzy's legs. Razor didn't blame the officer who feasted on her sweetness like Leo had on his Carnot's steak.

Razor bumped into his friend, impressed by the vast difference between JRad's hard-muscled body and the soft resilience of Izzy's thigh, draped over his shoulder—although he'd never admit it. JRad's hips kept time with the slow advance and retreat of his index finger in Izzy's pussy.

Her legs flexed in rhythmic waves, which broadcasted the imminence of her orgasm. Razor couldn't wait for JRad to finish. The seductive scent of Isabella overwhelmed his inhibitions, reeling him in. Before he knew what he intended, his finger probed her entrance beside JRad's embedded digit.

JRad hadn't been kidding about how tight she was. Fuck, would Razor hurt her if he pressed beside his friend's hand? He hesitated until Izzy shifted, wedging the tip of his finger inside her.

"Yes!" She screamed loud enough for the neighbors four units over to hear, never mind the guys in the living room. "More!"

He tunneled a tad farther, noting the shallow depth of JRad's penetration. After swearing to himself he'd be the one to make love to her first, he acknowledged the act should be special, something more than the crude finger fucking they gave her now.

They'd grant her release, but leave her intact.

Razor gritted his teeth. He proceeded to ease into her channel while JRad stroked beside him. He worked her entrance bit by bit until he nudged her hymen. The elastic membrane flexed then held. Nothing could eclipse how erotic the proof of her innocence was to him.

"Let me taste her."

JRad lifted his mouth from her soaked flesh. She protested. Her head surged off the pillows as she searched for the reason the suction on her engorged clit had discontinued. When she spied them changing positions, she shuddered around him. The instant his tongue lapped at her, she tensed. She hung, strung so tight he feared she might snap—suspended on the edge for a couple of heartbeats—before the mouth of her pussy clamped around him and JRad in contractions strong enough to expel his friend's finger.

JRad didn't seem to mind. As he watched her convulse around Razor, he increased the arc of his hips on the bed. "So sexy. Shit, I'm going to—"

In the next second, his face contorted in a grimace while he grunted his release.

Razor gawked as his cock lurched. He tried desperately to pretend it didn't ramp him up to watch his conservative teammate blow his wad in his pants over the woman who'd captured Razor's interest. Yet, in the next second he found himself reaching to free his hard-on.

He pressed soft, open-mouthed kisses to Isabella's abdomen as he rose to straddle her limp form. When the heat of his groin pressed to her chest, she blinked up at him and smiled. She licked her lips then opened her mouth, inviting him into paradise.

His hand cupped her jaw, his thumb stroking the slick heat of her cheek. "You're sure, princess?"

She sucked his thumb, flicking her tongue over his knuckle. When he withdrew she whispered, "Teach me."

With a groan, he fed his cock to her inch by inch. She struggled to take too much on the initial pass and gagged. In a flash, JRad appeared by her side. Razor had forgotten the man existed.

JRad cradled her head, supporting her neck and adjusting the angle so Razor slid in easier. Already on edge, it wouldn't take much to set him off. Izzy knocked him away from the brink when her teeth scraped him a bit as he retreated.

"Careful, baby." JRad coached her. She reached out and

squeezed his friend's supportive hand although her gaze never left Razor's. "Wrap your lips over your teeth."

Razor could never have provided the coherent assistance his friend did. He'd owe the man a year's supply of his favorite microbrew for escorting Izzy through this.

"Good, very good." JRad stroked her hair, calming her until her throat relaxed and Razor's cock plunged to the limits of her mouth. "There. Now, if you can, try to lick the underside of his shaft as he moves."

Fuck! It made him ten times hotter to be the subject of JRad's manipulation. When his friend nodded at him, Razor pumped his hips a bit, letting Izzy slurp on him like her favorite treat. His balls tapped her chin, sending a riot of sparks up his spine.

"Ah, you've almost got him now." The corner of JRad's mouth turned up in a wicked grin. "Here's a hint. The spot just beneath the ridge on the head is the most sensitive. Suck the tip of his cock when he's at the top of a stroke. Make him work to bury inside you."

"Son of a bitch!" Razor growled at the intensity of his pleasure when Izzy did as instructed. A spurt of precome escaped his clenched muscles. His princess hummed around him in appreciation of his flavor.

"Do you want him to come in your mouth?" JRad watched out for her. "If not, you'd better stop now. He's close. Look at the cords in his throat and the way his hands are clamped on his thighs."

Instead of pushing him away, Isabella shook off JRad's hand. She clenched Razor's ass in her dainty yet firm grip. She devoured him, tightening the ring of her lips to strangle the head of his cock before swirling her tongue along the underside of his shaft. When he bumped the rear wall of her throat, her lips settled around the base of his straining erection. His sac gathered close to his body, preparing to erupt.

"Swallow him, baby." JRad drove the final nail in his coffin. "Now."

Izzy followed orders, dragging Razor into orgasm. He tried to pull out, to be tender, but she refused to permit him to retreat. He came so hard he thought his head might explode as he poured his semen down her throat. She swallowed, ingesting every last drop of his desire.

Even when he finally came to his senses, she continued to lave his softening flesh, cleaning him as she brought him to Earth gradually.

"You're a natural. This guy is one lucky bastard." JRad dropped a kiss to Izzy's forehead, in greater proximity to Razor's cock than any man had been before. Neither of them seemed weirded out, though. When JRad slid from the bed, he grimaced at the wet stain on the front of his jeans. "Damn it. Too bad you're so fucking short, kid. I'm stealing a pair of cargos. I'll clean up then hold off the squad until you're ready to rejoin us."

They exchanged a long look. Something momentous passed between them. Razor knew a bond had formed that could never be broken. He wanted to thank his friend. Unnecessary words would only cheapen the situation. JRad nodded, turning to rummage through Razor's dresser for a minute before slipping into the bathroom.

Razor tucked his cock into his jeans. He covered Izzy with the comforter when she began to shiver. He snagged a three-quarter sleeved baseball shirt from the top of the rusted radiator. On her it'd be better than a nightgown.

When he reached the side of the bed, he sat, unable to face her. He dropped his head into his hands, his elbows braced on his knees.

"Please don't beat yourself up over this." She kneeled behind him, laying her cheek on his shoulder. "I threw you for a loop. I couldn't stand to endanger you. Or your friends. Still can't. It's not exactly a great way to repay the only man who's ever cared about me."

"But you promise to tell us everything, right?" Stress eroded some of the relief from his orgasm. "Let us decide how to handle this. It's our job, you know. Despite what you might have heard on the news, some of us are pretty good at it."

"I trust you." She wrapped her arms around his chest. "I swear I'll explain it all. What I know anyway. The truth is..."

He shifted in her arms, turning to face her. "What, sweetheart?"

"I'm so tired. I couldn't keep this up for long on my own."

"Come here, Izzy." He dragged her into his lap, nuzzling the cloud of her hair. "You don't have to stand alone. We're here to help."

"I'm ready to talk." Her sigh dusted his neck. "Can we head

into the other room now?"

"I thought you'd never ask." Razor cupped her cheek in his palm. He kissed her with all the affection he could muster. It wasn't half of what he'd like to give. "Arms up."

He slipped the shirt over her head. A ridiculous thrill filled him when she swam in his clothes. Then he gathered her into his arms.

"If it starts to be too much, say the word. I'll make them stop."

"I'll be okay." She patted his chest before snuggling closer. "As long as you're with me."

"No worries there, Izzy. I'm not leaving your side for anything."

"Thank you, James."

"Anytime."

Chapter Fifteen

Razor carried Isabella to the sofa. He sat, angling her close to his pounding heart. She caressed the scars beneath his shirt, regretting the strain she continued to burden him with.

After a couple of cleared throats and a host of shuffling feet, Mason forged through the awkward silence. "Isabella, if you never..."

He glanced at his partner for assistance.

"Consummated your marriage." Tyler supplied a polite alternative.

"Yeah, if you never did that, you can file for an annulment. We googled it to be sure. I don't think you need these pictures to break things off with Malcolm, honey. Maybe you'd better tell us how you came by them. And why—"

"You don't understand." She cut him off before he could speculate further. "He'll fight me leaving."

Razor gripped her tighter to his chest when she shuddered.

"He still loves you?" Clint's innocent question broke her heart.

"He never loved me."

"Ah, sweetheart, things might be in the crapper now but I'm sure that's not true. What did he do, cheat on you?" Matt patted her knee.

She scanned the faces ringing her, surrounding her with their strength. Jeremy sat by Razor's side, rubbing her feet from his spot in the middle of the couch. Clint took up the far end. Mason and Tyler perched on the scarred coffee table facing them, while Matt kneeled on the carpet beside the couch.

It was now or never.

"He's accepting bids on my virginity. He hopes to sell me to one of his sleazeball friends."

She whimpered when Razor's fingers gouged her bruised rib and her scraped knee.

Amid the curses and sick expressions, Jeremy remained the voice of reason. "Start from the beginning, baby."

"I already told James about my marriage. You saw the pictures. Malcolm isn't emotionally or physically capable of a traditional relationship." She took pride in her calm explanation. "The two-second version is that I'm unbelievably gullible. I thought he wanted me, instead of a permanent partnership with my father. His shortcomings wouldn't have mattered if he loved me. We could have figured things out. I tried to stick around, to help him..."

She gulped past the knot in her throat. How could she have been so stupid?

"The fucking asshole doesn't deserve you." James squeezed her as though he'd never abandon her. "Explain what you said before. What makes you think he'd do...that?"

The raw fury in his quiet question frightened her. She glanced around at the other men in blue for help. All of them together could restrain Razor if needed, right?

Mason crossed his tree-trunk arms over his mammoth chest, nodding in her direction.

"Malcolm's been in a great mood lately. Almost like old times. We were growing closer, I thought we might start overcoming some of our issues. One night, he asked if I would go out. I thought he planned an early anniversary celebration. He suggested I wear a little black dress, a pair of Jimmy Choo's, my grandmother's pearl necklace, the garters and silk stockings I'd ordered hoping..."

She cleared her throat when Razor growled.

"He even encouraged me to use the perfume my father gave me as a wedding gift. It's one of a kind, made special for me. Supposed to last a lifetime. I can't begin to guess how expensive it had to have been. Only for special occasions. I was nervous. I hadn't eaten lunch. Something about the fragrance set me...off balance."

Isabella caught the squints and frowns the guys shared. She couldn't stop to consider why or she'd never have the nerve to finish.

"Leaving the house is foggy. He blindfolded me. A surprise, he said. I do remember climbing into Malcolm's Bentley as he held my hand, but nothing after that. Until I woke in a dark room. I couldn't move..."

Panic seized her throat. Shivers ran down her spine as though the cold metal still shackled her wrists and ankles to the inclined slab. She'd struggled to free herself until blood trickled over her toes.

"Izzy." Razor returned her to the present with a shake.

Isabella hated the sobs choking her and the pity radiating from the men surrounding her. She buried her face against Razor's warm chest.

"You're safe here. He won't touch you again. I swear it."

She focused on breathing steady and slow while someone, probably Jeremy, massaged her shoulders and Razor stroked her hair. When spots stopped dancing behind her lids, she sat up straighter and tried again.

"I was bound. To some kind of platform with manacles. I tried to escape. Nothing budged. I only managed to wrench my ankle and shred the skin beneath the restraints."

Razor cursed. Jeremy touched the ace bandage on her leg.

"Before I could really freak, someone emerged from the shadows. A woman. *That* woman." She gestured with her chin to the photo crumpled on the coffee table. "She introduced herself as Lily. I think she shook my hand as though nothing odd had happened. I suppose I could have imagined it between the fuzz in my brain and my fear."

"That's fucked up." Clint grimaced.

"No kidding. Even more odd, the lights were off when she snuck in. I begged her to release me. She refused. The sadistic bitch stuffed my underwear in my mouth to make me shut up and lectured me to listen to her. I couldn't understand everything she said. She talked so fast. So quiet. The room kept spinning."

Isabella reached out to grip Razor's hand before she came to the worst part. He laced their fingers, rubbing his thumb over her wrist.

"I remember her saying more than once, 'It's only a showing'. As if I'd know what the hell that is. Well, I didn't anyway."

"Son of a bitch." Mason barked. Tyler refused to meet her

gaze.

"Am I the only moron who doesn't know either?" Razor's gaze flicked between each of his teammates. No one answered him.

"Voices approached, echoing from a hallway or something. Lily jammed an envelope under me. I couldn't really focus—didn't know what she'd done. She pinched my nipple—hard—until I couldn't ignore her, then told me not to move. Not to allow them see what she'd given me."

Isabella couldn't prevent her blush, ridiculous or not.

"Lily kissed me. Smack on the lips. She encouraged me to stay strong."

Someone to her left wheezed, but she couldn't stop now.

"Malcolm entered the room. He joked around, laughing with the fake chuckle he trots out around his clients. A second later, light blinded me. By the time I'd adjusted, eight—or maybe nine—men huddled around me." She didn't realize she'd clamped onto Razor's hand until it jerked. His fingers sported crescent indentations from her nails.

Funny, the men hovering near now didn't spook her one bit.

"Do you remember anything else? Can you tell us? Details, Izzy. Anything to help us pin down a location or the scum involved."

How could she have gotten lucky enough to stumble into Razor and the other men in blue right when she needed them most? Could there be a God after all? Isabella had harbored some serious doubts lately.

"Malcolm announced he'd been saving me. Like a fine wine. They chuckled, as if they attended a cocktail party in our mansion instead of a *showing* in the dungeon. Almost made me puke. My torso heaved. The edge of Lily's envelope pricked my back, and I remembered her instructions. Don't move. I chose a spot on the black, painted ceiling and decided not to tear my gaze from it no matter what. So I didn't see a ton. Stupid."

"You did what was necessary to survive." Mason nodded at her. "Smart, not dumb."

"It became almost impossible, though." She rushed on. "He had someone with him, an expert. They examined me. The modified speculum felt like they'd extracted it straight from the freezer."

Crap! She must be losing it if she'd said that aloud. The cops' horrified regard stole some of her disassociation. She ignored them, choosing instead to stare at the juncture of her and Razor's hands.

"When they had certified my innocence, they raised a toast to the best man winning. One of them spoke up. A big guy. He sounded somewhat familiar. I tried so hard not to listen to them—to stay strong like Lily had ordered. He requested another test. Of my pain threshold."

"We have to bust these sick fuckers."

She dismissed Razor's interruption. If she stopped now she'd never regain her composure to tell them the rest.

"Every one of them laughed when he said virgins who spread for rich men were a dime a dozen. They wanted someone who would put up a fight. Give good sport. That's when they started taking turns slapping me, pinching me and yanking my hair. The only thing keeping me from losing it was Lily's urging in my mind. Stay strong. Don't move..."

"Jesus Christ."

"It pissed them off that I didn't react despite their escalation. When they didn't break my resolve, one of them drew out his pocket knife. They cut me. And poured whiskey on the wounds." She paused to sniffle before snot ran down her face, adding to her humiliation. Someone handed her a tissue.

"I saw the marks." JRad added while she blew her nose. "They're everywhere on her abdomen. Dozens of shallow slices. Meant to sting like hell but not scar. How the fuck could anyone do that?"

"You don't have to say anything else, Izzy." James shifted as though to remove her from the crowd. "Enough."

"It's okay," she whispered. "There's not a lot left."

"You're sure?"

"Yeah. I can handle it, James."

"I'm not sure I can." The sheen of tears in his eyes surprised her.

She pressed a delicate kiss to his clamped lips. After hugging him tight, she rested on his shoulder. "I thought I had reached my limit. I opened my mouth to scream, to cry, to beg them to stop. I almost moved, to hell with whatever that crazy lady had told me. But she showed up again. She shouted over their catcalls and the grunts of some of the men who had started touching themselves."

"Shit!" Matt stalked from their group into the kitchen.

"Lily called them off. She warned them they were too close to ruining someone's merchandise without having paid for it. They gave her some lip about riling them up until she offered them free service upstairs, whatever the hell that means." Isabella sighed. "In any case, it was effective. She proclaimed the bidding open for twenty-four hours then ushered them from the room."

Relief had nearly knocked her unconscious.

"I heard her talking to Malcolm. Like a child. Similar to how she'd talked to me. She told him to run along and play since he'd pleased the Master for once. He seemed hesitant. She shooed him off, after promising him she'd look after me. Of course, he didn't hang around."

"I'll kill that bastard." James vibrated with anger beneath her.

"I would gladly settle for breaking free of him." A tear splashed onto their joined hands. She couldn't say who it belonged to.

"Lily untied me. She apologized. Swore she'd had no idea they intended to hurt me. She didn't have time to stay or she'd risk raising suspicions. Still, she hurried to clean the blood off me, bandage the area and wrap the envelope between the layers of gauze. While she worked, she told me I had a thirty-minute window. The next day...last Tuesday...at four thirty."

"The day of your press conference."

She nodded at Tyler.

"Malcolm thought she would bring the buyer then. She planned to delay him until five, the best she could do without raising suspicions. They'd cleared the house to protect the bastard's identity. She told me why Malcolm wouldn't be home along with some other stuff. I can't remember. All the details sank into the haze in my mind when she led me to a room. It held dozens of beds. Women were chained there. Not moving much or fighting. They looked at me like I looked at them—listless, dazed and defeated. I *had* to help them. That's all I could think about. I think I tried to set them free. Someone slapped me. Lily? I don't know. I couldn't focus. I think I passed out, or zoned. When I came to, I had my dress on. Malcolm had dumped me on top of our bed in his mansion and disappeared.

My bad ankle had been lashed to the bedpost."

Jeremy traced the edges of the support there with the tip of his finger.

"I would have thought it all some crazy dream if not for the bandages, the envelope and my throbbing ankle. No way would I take some psycho bitch's word for it and wait for the next day. I tried to break away. It was no use. When a couple hours had passed with no change, my panic started to evaporate. I could think a little clearer. I ripped the envelope out of the bandages and stuffed it between the mattresses. Thank God because not ten minutes later, Malcolm stumbled into the room with a huge grin on his face."

She shuddered. "He seemed drunk...or...something. I couldn't help it. I freaked. I screamed at him, tried to kick him. He pinned me to the bed, snarling in my face. He told me it was about time I started earning my keep. He refused to let me ruin his plans. When I argued, he backhanded me. That's how I ended up with the black eye the reporters loved so much.

"Not exactly husband of the year material." Isabella couldn't help the sarcasm pervading her speech. "But, hey, the craziest bastard of all has to be the one who planned to pay upwards of five million for the right to rape a virgin. At least I wasn't dumb enough to marry *him*."

"Izzy—" Razor's tortured groan couldn't stop her.

"It's not about me, James. Please, now you know. You guys have to help me. You have to help *them*. No one else will." She sighed. Relief wilted the determination she'd powered herself with these past few days. "Those women need us."

Razor rested his palm on the cool door when he called softly, "You okay in there, Izzy?"

A sniffle migrated through the thin barrier separating them. He ached to hold her, to comfort her. She shouldn't have to suffer alone anymore. Never again, if he had anything to say about it.

"Can I come in, princess?"

The lock *snicked* a moment before the knob rotated. He squeezed through the crack she'd created to admit him. Izzy sat cross-legged on the floor, her knee blocking the door from swinging all the way open in the confined space.

Once inside, he relocked it before joining her on the braided rug Lacey had bought to dress up his sink. Their shoulders rested on the cabinet beneath the basin. For the space of several breaths he didn't speak, opting to sit in silence while she tore off another strip of toilet paper to blow her cute nose.

When she finished, he set his left palm face up on his knee. She entwined their fingers, squeezing his hand and hanging on. Thank God.

Razor hated to make things worse for her. He had one more shred of bad news to share before he could help her recover from the chaos of the morning. At least now she'd be better protected. The guys could work in the open around her. Of course, she didn't realize he'd been on the case all along. Guilt burned his conscience. No matter how he'd framed it, the chief had refused to grant his request to brief Izzy on all the facts. He'd been ordered to maintain his cover.

For the first time ever, he hated his job.

"Go ahead, James."

His head swiveled until her watery gaze met his. "With what?"

"Whatever it is that has you rubbing your scars. I can take it."

His right hand froze in its circuit across his chest.

"We sent Clint undercover as an agent from the studio to pick up Gerard from your father's estate. He told your father you'd asked for the butler to come to the taping. We planned to ask him questions en route." Izzy had identified the man as a witness who could corroborate most of her story. She'd told them of how the butler had assisted her when she'd fled. How her father had not. "I'm sorry, Izzy. He's gone. He quit."

"What? That can't be right." She frowned as she angled toward him. "He has nowhere else to go. I asked him to come with me when I moved in with Malcolm. He declined. He's lived at the estate almost all his life. His wife headed the cleaning staff while he managed the outdoor crews years ago. When she died of breast cancer, I think he... Well, he told me once, leaving would be like saying goodbye to her memories. He said he could never do that."

Razor cursed under his breath.

"You have to believe me. He's in trouble. I know it." Izzy sprang to her feet in the tiny enclosure, pacing to the tub and back. "They were soulmates. They stared at each other across the room when they thought no one watched. Touched each other every chance they could—a caress while transfering a basket of laundry, a peck on the cheek while passing by or strolling arm in arm while they walked in the garden at night. If it weren't for them, I wouldn't have known what real love looked like. That it existed at all. They—"

"Shh." He grabbed her around the waist, tugging her close. "I understand."

"You do?" She peeked from beneath those thick lashes at him.

"Yeah." He nuzzled the corner of her lips. "I'll never go to sleep in my bed without remembering last night. How hot you were. How sensual. How sweet."

Izzy blushed. She wrapped her arms around his neck, dragging him closer for a kiss that speared straight toward his heart. He wished he could show her what it could be like between them. He'd sacrifice another Christmas with his family, maybe five or ten, to make love to her. To take away a fraction of her pain.

He wouldn't make a move though. He wouldn't beg her to reconsider.

Razor would rather die than pressure her to abandon her values despite the fact her bastard husband didn't deserve her consideration. In his mind, the fuckwad hadn't truly married her. He'd conned a young, unsuspecting virgin into signing away her life along with her wealth. Simply to own her. A priceless trophy he didn't really want.

Izzy separated their lips long enough to whisper, "Am I doing something wrong?"

"No, princess." His hand flexed over the firm swell of her ass. When had it wandered there? "You're perfect. Being around you drives me crazy. I want to make you burn. It would be so easy for us both. You've locked all your passion inside. I don't know how you did. It's hard for me to follow your lead."

A fresh tear squeezed from her puffy eyes. "Can I tell you something else?"

His heart skipped a beat at the dread creasing her pale brow. "Anything."

"I ran in here because I was scared you'd see. They'd see."

"See what, Izzy?" Razor smoothed her hair off her checks, tucking it behind her ears.

"Even though I felt sick when they touched me... Even though I've never been so scared in my life..." Her graceful throat flexed. No sound came out.

"You were aroused?" His arms banded around her, absorbing the shivers wracking her body.

She nodded against his chest. "How fucked up am I? From the moment I put on the outfit Malcolm had picked out to the time I woke up in my bed, something pulsed through me. Beneath the fear, confusion and pain, it lingered the entire time. Desire. Hot and dark. Forbidden."

"You're twenty-two years old. You'd never had an orgasm." He had to pause to catch his breath when he remembered her first. "Adrenaline can do extreme things. I think it's natural for your body to react—"

"It didn't feel natural. I couldn't resist it." She shook her head. "Plus..."

"What, Izzy?" He tipped her face up so she could see his acceptance. Nothing she admitted would change his opinion of her bravery, her generosity or her compassion. Those things mattered to him, not some crazy physical reaction she'd had while under extreme duress.

"When I came to in the dungeon, I thought Malcolm had tied me." A deep flush crept up her neck to her cheeks. "I thought if that's what it takes... I kind of liked it."

"Lots of people enjoy being restrained by a trustworthy partner." He groaned. "It's called bondage."

"Have you tried it?" Her genuine curiosity made him hard as steel.

"Yeah." He decided to give her as much of the truth as he could. "I enjoy strapping a woman to her bed. I've gone to clubs a couple times before. Maybe even the legitimate side of the one you were at."

The thought had his pulse slowing a tad. Had women suffered in the basement while he played with a willing partner above them? What kind of cop did it make him if he hadn't had the slightest clue?

"So, there's nothing wrong with me?" She gnawed her lip until he licked the spot she abused.

"I told you already. You're perfect."

A ghost of a smile tilted her full lips as she rocked her hips, stroking her belly over the bulge of his erection. "It hurts. I want you so bad."

"Believe me, I know the feeling." He leaned in, bumping her shoulders into the wall behind her. He slid his palms along her arms until they reached her wrists. His fingers encircled the dainty bones there before raising them and pinning them to the wall beside her face.

The moan she couldn't repress spurred him on.

Razor crowded her, stealing any iota of personal space she had remaining. They were plastered together from head to toe. She undulated with him, urging him on. As if he needed encouragement. The pebbled tips of her breasts gouged him through the thin cotton of the shirt he'd dressed her in.

Beneath it, she would be bare. He debated his ability to bring her pleasure without seeking his own for less than two seconds before he stole a final taste of her lips, intending to sink to his knees. He would binge on the slick arousal perfuming the air, causing his nostrils to flare in an attempt to catch more of her scent.

As soon as he finished devouring her mouth and her mewling cries for more.

"Razor!" Two fierce knocks accompanied JRad's shout. At the ruckus, they jerked apart like guilty teenagers caught making out. Not that they could put much distance between them in the tiled box of his bathroom.

He had to try twice before he could answer. "Yeah?"

"The network called. You're late."

Damn it! He'd lost track of time. "Give us a minute, okay?"

"No more. We can't afford to tip off anyone watching. Things have to seem normal."

"Understood. JRad, do me a favor? Put out a missing person on Gerard. Something's not right there."

"I'm on it. You two have to move. Now."

After several regulated breaths, Razor turned to the sexy sprite lounging against the wall. Her sparkling eyes and mussed hair complemented the flush of arousal painting her cheeks bright pink.

"Are you sure you're up for this?" Screw the investigation. If Izzy balked over the show, he wouldn't force her do it. "How's your ankle?"

"It's fine." She answered without rotating it or putting all her weight on the injured joint. "I'm ready, James. I wasn't lying during our practice. I need to do well in the competition. I have to prove to myself I can cut it on my own. If I work hard, things will turn out okay, right?"

"Better than, princess." He cupped her cheek in one palm then promised, "I'll do my best for you."

"Thank you." Izzy's lips brushed the center of his hand. "For everything."

She shoved past him, into the other room and began to dress. "Remember your posture. Keep your arms up, shoulders down, chest out..."

Chapter Sixteen

Razor gripped the arm of the makeup chair so tight he expected it to dent. Every minute they kept Izzy out of his sight had him more on edge. The producers had refused to allow him in her dressing room. Too much to do, too little time, until they went on the air in front of hundreds of thousands of viewers kicked back in their ratty PJs while he suffocated in this ridiculous tuxedo.

Why the hell did it take three hours to prepare the dancers for the show? He'd had no idea of the torment actors and actresses suffered before now. No, thank you.

Of course, he'd have endured far worse with a smile if Isabella could have stayed nearby.

"Almost done, sweetie." The perky cosmetics specialist and her shameless flirting would have piqued his interest under normal circumstances. Today, his cock didn't stir. Her ultra-fashionable hair and makeup seemed overdone compared to Izzy's natural beauty.

Neither the flash of her lace-top stockings beneath her short, black skirt nor the not-so-subtle press of her enhanced breasts on his arm could grab his attention.

Not when thoughts of his princess preoccupied his mind. Who watched over her now? Was she nervous? Had they wrapped her ankle well enough?

Lost in his concern for her, he failed to notice his fellow officer slip into the dressing room.

"Who knew you cleaned up so pretty?"

"Screw you, JRad."

"No, thanks. You better behave or I won't tell you the good news."

"What's that?"

Melissa—or was it Clarissa—frowned when he ducked to prevent her from fussing with his over-gelled hair. He'd endured all he could bear of her torture.

"Isabella's ready for a final dress rehearsal whenever you are."

Razor sprang from the chair before his friend had finished his report. The stylist's seat spun in a lazy circle in the aftermath of his lunge. "Take me to her."

JRad consulted his high-tech digital watch as he led them along a bright hallway. The thing had enough gauges it could probably navigate a space shuttle. Razor's dance shoes made rapid-fire taps, which echoed off the white linoleum.

"Nice heels, man."

Razor flipped him the bird, checking the urge to waste time on insulting JRad's mom in retaliation. Besides, Linda was a nice lady. "Any word on the butler?"

"One of the horse trainers we were able to catch off duty reported a scuffle near the barn last Wednesday. He thought it might have been Gerard he heard arguing with a couple of dudes. When he went in for a closer look, whoever caused the disturbance had already climbed into a black SUV. Said they took off quick. Remembers 'cause they spooked some of the horses with the commotion."

"Fuck." Razor rubbed his neck, wincing when he smeared the powdery makeup there. How did women stand this gunk? "No way did he leave willingly. He's what, sixty-five? Izzy said he seemed a lot thinner since last time she saw him too. He wouldn't be able to fight off two bruisers like Buchanan keeps around."

JRad slowed, frowning as he faced Razor. "This is serious shit. I know you care for her, but you have to screw your head on straight. These guys aren't fucking around. This is real cash. They're not going to take kindly to losing out on twelve million, no matter how much they have—"

"Twelve? I thought it was five?"

"Matt nosed around The Black Lily this morning. Stragglers from the private rooms hit the streets after Isabella spilled. With the info she supplied, he was able to dig up more scraps. You know, the usual talk from guys too drunk—or too mellow after a night of fucking or being fucked—to stifle the urge to brag."

Razor cursed. JRad continued explaining.

"They didn't know what the prize was but a couple of Doms overheard talk at the bar about an auction. Five million starting bid had climbed to twelve mil by the time the whales started bitching about how Carrington had screwed someone over."

"Holy shit."

"Yeah." JRad met and held his stare. "She's right. They'll try to take her back."

"They'll have to get through me."

"That's what I'm afraid of." His friend scrubbed his hands over his face. "After the show, I'm going to track the finances. Money will lead us to the big players. Don't give me any shit about it either."

"Not this time." Razor's number one priority had shifted from busting the ring to ensuring Izzy's safety. If JRad could nail the top dogs, maybe they could do both with one cyber sneak and peek.

"I'll make sure not to cross any lines. If I close in, I'll do it official. I won't allow them grounds for a technicality because of me. I swear. After what I saw today, I'd hunt them like rabid dogs if I didn't believe in justice, the law. We have to do this right."

"Thank you, JRad."

They bumped fists before the other man pointed. "Around the corner. She's in the first room on the right. Mason and Tyler are camped outside. I'll be watching the crowd for a while. They're starting to pass people into the studio now."

Razor had forgotten all about the show. The reminder sent a wave of nerves through him. Shaking it off, he turned in the direction JRad had indicated.

From behind him he heard the other man call, "Break a leg, twinkle toes."

He jogged the last thirty feet to the spot JRad had indicated. As he flew around the bend in the hall, he drew up short. His speedy approach had set the men guarding Izzy's door on high alert. They'd adopted a defensive stance, balanced on the balls of their feet, arms loose at their sides, weapons in hand. Shoulder to shoulder, Mason and Tyler blocked the entire hallway.

"It's just me." Palms out, he slowed to a walk. "Man, I'm glad you two are on our side."

"Damn it, rookie." Mason tucked his pistol into the holster concealed by his sport coat. "Give a guy a little warning, would you?"

"Don't mind him, Razor." Tyler patted his hulking partner on the shoulder. "Lacey's inside, chatting with your girl. You know how Mason is when she's around."

"I'm starting to understand a whole lot better."

Mason shot him a sympathetic look. "It's not easy to walk around with your balls in a vise all the time. I'll never forget when trouble dogged Lacey. All you can do is rely on your training. And your instincts. How's that edge coming?"

Razor shrugged. He hadn't believed in himself this morning and the deficit of trust had resulted in unnecessary stress for Izzy. He should've known she would never do those things. Nothing in her nature lent itself to that kind of dominance or the need to humiliate. Not to say she couldn't stand her ground, but she had a submissive streak a mile wide with those she trusted. How else could she have permitted the men in her life to take charge for so long?

"Working on it," he mumbled.

"That's good enough for now." Mason stepped aside, permitting him to enter. "She's sweet, your Izzy. Don't fuck this up."

Isabella laughed as Lacey regaled her with tales of Razor's antics. Odd, he didn't seem like the goofy, rash rookie to her. The recent past had transformed him, and she only now realized how much. Maybe, together, they could learn to have fun again.

God knew hanging out with Lacey came easy. They'd hit it off from the moment Tyler had introduced them. She envied the strong, beautiful woman sharing the sofa with her. Lacey glowed with the love of her two men. Though her desires had been unconventional, she hadn't allowed anyone tell her she couldn't have what she needed. Instead, she'd snagged two hot men in blue with one bold move.

Rainbows winked from the glittering facets of the woman's antique engagement ring. It took a lot to impress Isabella in the jewelry department. She'd seen enormous diamonds before. Heck, she'd worn pieces from her own collection that surpassed the total carat weight of Lacey's ring many times over. Knowing it'd been given with undying love and eternal promises, from two different men nonetheless, made all the difference in the world.

She wondered for the thousandth time what detained Razor. Had he decided not to go through with this after all? He'd remained quiet on the ride to the studio. Thoughtful. He'd taken to her Ferrari like it'd been special ordered for him. The ride had been smooth as glass. His fingers had drummed a mile a minute on the gearshift, though. The idea of exposing himself to another round of vicious gossip might have driven him away.

Dancing together without presenting their attraction for the world to critique would prove impossible. At least for her. She'd understand if he couldn't handle that. To flaunt their connection where Malcolm, her father, or both would surely see… Well, it wasn't smart.

"Earth to Isabella." Lacey waved a hand in front of her face. "Take a deep breath, you're starting to hyperventilate."

The woman tucked Isabella's head between her knees then rubbed her back while murmuring in a soothing croon. "Nothing to worry about. Razor will be here soon. You two will do great. I know it. Don't think about the people at home. Ty says you've practiced a lot. You're ready."

The mantra started to penetrate her anxiety, although her fears lurked so much deeper than the ones Lacey had addressed. She'd started to sit up when Razor called across the room, "What's wrong? Is she okay?"

Relief flooded her. He hadn't abandoned her. How silly to freak over nothing.

Isabella rose, flinging herself into his arms as he reached her side. She didn't care if Lacey saw how badly she'd missed him. Ludicrous! No more than three hours felt more like a decade had lapsed. To her surprise, he hugged her just as tight in return. Her toes left the ground despite her five-inch stilettos.

The loose straps around her bandage allowed one to slip off her foot. James kneeled before her, kissing the injured joint. He slid her shoe in place like Cinderella's Prince Charming then rose, concern etching his brow.

"I'm fine, James. Just worried."

"Why? You're an amazing dancer. Or is your ankle acting up? I can tell the producer you're hurt—"

"No." She took a step back, fixing the wrinkle in his tux

jacket with absent flicks of her manicured nails. "I thought maybe..."

"What?" He trapped her hand against his chest.

"You'd changed your mind. I don't want to embarrass you."

"Where would you get a crazy idea like that?" He glowered at her.

"I'm afraid I'll subject you to gossip again. People will talk."

"There's only one person whose opinion matters to me, princess." He kissed her knuckles. "My instructor's."

The darkened cocoa of his eyes guaranteed she'd become more than a teacher to him. The warmth spreading from her center chased away the dregs of her chill. It would take a while to believe life had turned so sweet. Every time he reassured her, she came closer to having faith. Her luck was changing.

"Your *partner* thinks we're going to kick some ass." She loved his answering grin. "And I also think you look handsome."

Drop dead gorgeous more like it.

"Same here, princess."

Razor's once over turned downright naughty as he scanned the fabulous gown Arthur's shop had crafted. It fit her better than the designer label ensembles Malcolm and her father had insisted she wear. The blue silk complemented her eyes, and the fluffy white edging on the layered skirt made it look like she floated as she moved. The bodice conformed to her breasts like a second skin.

Her cop licked his lips as he evaluated the glittery stockings encasing her legs, hiding the high-tech wrap Lacey had applied to her ankle. When he reached the strappy heels, he groaned.

She had to admit, her legs looked fantastic in them when she spun, flashing the curve of her calves.

"You don't have time to do it right, kid." Mason broke the silence with his teasing. "Besides, I think the team of women who worked their magic would stab you with their makeup brushes if you got her dirty."

Isabella's cheeks heated. She'd forgotten all about their company. She peeked over at Lacey, bundled into Tyler's arms, holding one of Mason's hands.

"Don't mind them." Lacey rolled her eyes. "Sex is all they think about."

"As if you're any better, doll." Mason kissed his woman full on the lips while his partner cradled her. The sight had Isabella's heart kicking in double-time.

Before things could turn any steamier, a woman wearing a wireless headset—carrying a clipboard—rapped on the open door.

"Isabella Buchanan and James Reoser. Time for your practice run. The cameras will use this to block the shots for the live show, so do it like you mean it. Stage Three. Quickly. We're running behind. You're last in the lineup and live TV waits for no one."

"Good luck." Lacey hugged her before heading off, hand in hand, with Tyler. "We'll be cheering for you."

Mason stayed with her and Razor as the stagehand led them to the studio. He took up the rear while Razor peered at each niche they passed. Their subtle vigilance might have escaped her notice if she hadn't understood how much Mason would rather be with his lovers.

Isabella thanked her lucky stars again for teaming her with Razor. How else could she have ended up with a slew of new companions and such qualified protection yet avoided tipping anyone off? If Malcolm—or whichever monster ruled the women she'd seen—suspected her intent to bring him down, he'd do worse than sell her. Of that she had no doubt.

No one would question Razor's buddies attending such a public event, though. Having the other cops nearby put her at ease. They would watch Razor's back, relieving a smidge of her guilt for dragging him into her mess.

Her stress melted thanks to the guys. She concentrated on the dance she'd choreographed. Beside her, Razor mumbled a sequence of steps over and over. She grinned. He'd surpassed all her expectations. Wait until JRad and the gang saw him nail the waltz. They'd have a field day. Underneath the endless ribbing, their support would linger.

What would it be like to have such a strong network of friends? She'd do anything to earn that kind of respect.

When they reached the studio, Mason stayed behind the curtain while Isabella assumed her position on one side of the stage. Razor pressed a quick kiss to her temple before departing for his corner. The flurry of activity from the lighting crews, cameramen, and the crowd gathering made it easy to pretend they were alone. No one focused on the couple as they attended to their own duties.

Only the section of cops and their dates in the front row paid them any mind. Their presence comforted her. She hoped Razor could say the same. Waiting for their cue, she glanced up. Her partner beamed at her from his mark, nodding a moment before the music began.

As if in a dream, she surrendered herself to the song, which had become her instant favorite, and the man waltzing toward her. When James took her in hold, she imagined she really was the princess he called her so often. He certainly placed her on top of the world as he dipped and cradled her.

She spun in his arms, executing difficult turns and leaps with effortless grace. During each combination he supported her—held her, balanced her, lifted her—all the while maintaining his own perfect rhythm. Together they exuded the elegance and nobility inherent in the steps despite their youth and supposed lack of maturity.

Isabella gazed into his eyes, attempting to communicate all she desired and how grateful she was for his strength. He reciprocated, allowing his vulnerability to enhance the gentle sway of their bodies as he whisked her around the floor. More than the accuracy of their steps, their chemistry brought the dance to life.

Her lids grew heavy. She arched her spine. Draped over his arm, she relaxed while he executed the final laid-back arabesque turn. Isabella released her grip on his shoulders without a single moment of hesitation. He'd never drop her. The room continued to spin as the final strains of their song faded.

James had disrupted her equilibrium far more than a million rotations could have. He bundled her close to his pounding heart as cheers and claps erupted from their left. She realized they'd finished in front of Matt and Clint, who had snagged the chairs adjoining the judges' table.

Leaving an impression on the panel had been her intent, but she'd given their cheering section quite a show. The catcalls and whistles of the guys mixed with the clapping of the women until she couldn't deny their approval of both the dance and their friend's rebound. Tonight marked a major victory for James. Satisfaction swelled her heart.

"Razor, Razor." They chanted and hollered for their cohort

in rowdy manner better suited to a football game than the ballroom. Still, he never broke eye contact with her.

He buried his fingers in the glamorous curls the stylists had crafted out of her hair. He dipped his face to whisper against her lips, "Thank you for the dance. Thank you for making me human again."

Isabella tried to respond with a fraction of the list of things she owed him for. Before she could, he merged their mouths in a tender kiss. He didn't hide from his friends, the cameras or anyone else who watched. Unlike the time in Arthur's shop, he no longer cared who witnessed their shared affection.

The men in blue cheered louder.

"Perfect." The woman with the clipboard shouted from the top of the stage. "Save the juicy stuff for the live show. Marissa will touch you up. You've smeared Ms. Buchanan's lipstick."

After a lingering lick, Razor separated them with a smile. Sure enough, red gloss stained his delicious mouth. She swiped the worst of the damage with her thumb, grinning in return at his mischievous smirk.

"I love that you blush at a simple kiss."

"*That* was a simple kiss?" She couldn't catch her breath, breaking the question into segments between pants.

"You're right, Izzy. Nothing about us is simple." He clasped her hand as he guided her toward the station the producer had indicated. "I think we'll surprise a couple people tonight."

One of the judges passed them as he headed to his seat. "If what I saw is any indication, you'll be gliding through to next week. I bet the other judges twenty bucks we'd see you in the finale. Don't disappoint me, huh?"

"Yes, sir." Razor winked at the gentleman.

They rushed up the stairs to the gathering of their competitors. Isabella stumbled. Butterflies fluttered in her stomach when she recognized several of the other participants. A city politician, a local model and a corporate executive had all been guests at balls she'd attended. With her husband.

She tried to shake free of Razor's hand, which gripped tighter to help her stay upright. Oblivious to her discomfort, he high-fived the quarterback of the city's college football team while she waited, dread tainting her happiness.

The censure she braced for never came. Instead, everyone except the politician heaped them with good-natured ribbing along with some moans and groans. It seemed none of the other couples thought they stood a chance. Not after witnessing her and Razor throw down the gauntlet.

As the stagehand ushered them from the crowd toward the waiting attendants, Razor shocked her with his insight. She couldn't hide anything from him.

"Maybe it's time we both stop expecting the worst from people," he whispered.

Razor cringed as the Channel 6 weatherman made an ass of himself in a terrible rendition of a disco. Things went downhill fast when the man, stiff and akward, elbowed his pro in the jaw. Though they smiled for the camera, the woman ripped him a new asshole the instant they went to commercial.

Didn't she realize her outburst would be next week's sound bite? Ah, well, understanding the potential repercussions had never stopped him when annoyed enough. He shook his head.

The order of the couples played in their favor, leaving them last in the show. They'd clean up after this train wreck. He figured the couple who'd face elimination this week had already been locked in. The free pass didn't lessen his anxiety.

A shitload of spectators had jammed into the studio. Stage lighting obscured his vision. Spotlights contrasted with shadow, making it impossible to see the rear of the room. Forget about the balcony. The team in place—not only his friends in the front row, but also other plainclothes officers stationed around the floor—had it covered. That didn't stop the hair on his nape from rising anyway.

Fuck, why couldn't he take his own advice and learn to trust again? Not everyone was out to hurt him. His colleagues were skilled, capable.

Izzy patted his knee from her place beside him. He laid his fingers over hers, stroking her thumb with the pad of his own. The segment of their thighs resting together generated enough heat to distract him for a moment.

"Getting nervous?" She studied him with blue laser vision.

Razor sent her a soft smile. "Not about us."

"Yeah, this is kind of painful to watch." Her face tilted toward the judges, who massacred the current contestants. A wince and her wrinkled nose marred the perfection of her aristocratic features.

"No worries. We'll do better." So why couldn't he shake the panic rising in his throat to strangle him?

As she had done for the nine other not-quite-ready couples, the harried stagehand appeared from behind the curtain to hustle them to their positions. When she shoved Izzy toward the wide-open dance floor, he had an irrational urge to yank his princess into the shelter of his body.

But the opportunity had passed. Izzy stumbled in the dark. She crossed to the opposite side of the polished wood expanse before he could wish her luck or ask her for the dance as he had intended.

Breathe in.

Breathe out.

The announcer read their names and mini-bios in an obnoxious, booming narrative for the sake of the studio audience while God knew what video package played for the viewers at home. He tried to scan the crowd. No luck. In a last ditch effort, he gestured in JRad's direction—a flash of the sign they'd used when attempting to steal home on the department's softball team last summer.

He hoped the man would understand. He wanted Izzy out of here the instant they fulfilled their obligation. The time for strategy ended. The opening notes of their accompaniment settled around him.

He rushed in his haste to touch Isabella, putting him ahead of tempo.

She corrected them by hesitating a moment before stepping into his arms.

Razor's feet operated on autopilot. His brain whirled far out of the game and away from the peace he'd captured during their dress rehearsal. Something tickled his instincts.

Like a kid trapped in a fun house, distorted faces zoomed at him from the darkness, captured in the spotlight when it deflected off him and Izzy. A flash of silver caught his eye from somewhere in the mid-deck.

It didn't sit right.

His bad thigh locked up when he tensed, almost pitching them to the ground. They recovered, Isabella coaching him to stay calm with hushed instructions while maintaining her cover-girl smile. How the hell did she do that?

Afraid of making a fool of her, he suffered through the

debilitating panic, which urged him to shove her to the ground and wait for reinforcements. He concentrated on the intricate sequence coming up, navigating the choreography competently if not with the magic they'd harnessed earlier.

As he berated himself for ruining Izzy's debut over a bad case of the heebie-jeebies, they whizzed past the center stands. His next move would expose her completely.

Fuck! I can't.

At the last possible moment, he retracted his arm. Unwilling and unable to let her go, he switched direction. With the spotlight angled away from him, he couldn't mistake the muzzle of a gun aimed straight at them. He roared in outrage as he continued to spin, attempting to place himself between Isabella and the danger threatening her.

He acted a split second too late.

The flash of a shot being fired seared into his retinas. It was useless. No matter how many times he'd watched *The Matrix*, he couldn't snatch a bullet out of mid-air.

Not even the one headed straight for his princess.

Chapter Seventeen

Isabella jerked in Razor's arms. They crashed to the floor. He rolled toward the shooter until they tucked close enough to the metal chairs to destroy any clear angle the man might have had. Chaos erupted as the crowd caught on. Innocent people scattered, leaving him to pray they didn't end up trampled flatter than a pancake. Screams obliterated any hope of contacting the officers stationed around the room.

"Izzy!" he shouted. No answer, not even a moan, emanated from the limp woman beneath him. Warm, sticky fluid poured over his hand.

Razor couldn't afford to pry his attention from the direction of the threat in case the maniac who'd shot her managed to weave through the confusion. He swore he didn't breathe until JRad landed at his side, gun drawn, to provide cover.

Terrified of what he'd find, he lifted onto locked arms to examine the damage. His shaking fingers flew to the crimson stain ruining the left side of her gown. Please, God, not her heart. If the bullet had struck her there, he'd already lost her.

His hands slipped in the puddle forming beneath her. Christ, he couldn't make it stop, couldn't find the wound.

"Razor! Move!" A woman yelled his name, but abandoning Izzy proved impossible. "Let me help her."

Several burly sets of hands grabbed hold of his jacket and yanked. He fought them until they pinned his elbows behind his back and shook some sense into him.

"Calm down, kid." Tyler finally broke through the sheer panic debilitating him. Razor realized who'd sank to the ground beside Isabella. "Lacey's an ER nurse. She knows her shit. Let her do her job."

His friend bent low over the woman he'd come to care too much for in such a short amount of time. Lacey explained, calm and rational, as she worked through her trauma checklist.

"She's breathing, and she has a pulse." Lacey's touch seemed gentle despite her speed and efficiency as she searched for the source of all that blood. "It looks worse than it is, Razor. You know how much a gunshot wound can bleed."

He roared as visions of *that* night assaulted him. Not now. Not here. Izzy needed him. Bile seared his throat. He swallowed it, leaning into the steady grip of his friends, counting on them to hold him up.

"Her torso is clean." Lacey hummed when she lifted Isabella's arm. "Found it. Upper left arm, three inch gash. In and out. Shallow. More like a burn."

Razor heard someone gag when Mason and Tyler's woman exposed the torn, seeping flesh. Iron tang hit him full force, knocking him into the past.

"She'll be fine, Razor." Lacey never paused. She tore a strip off Izzy's ruined silk dress as she made eye contact with him. Her reassurance had little effect.

Lacey bound the wound, making neat passes with the improvised gauze. When she drew it snug with skilled motions of her adept hands, the direct pressure brought Izzy around.

His princess gasped, her shoulders lurching off the hard ground.

The entire force couldn't have prevented him from comforting her then. He broke loose and collapsed beside her, cradling her head in his lap. Wild blue eyes locked on his.

"What?" She couldn't force out more before a groan interrupted.

"You're all right." Razor hoped he hadn't lied. "Hang in there, Izzy. We'll take you out of here in a minute."

Accustomed to a patient's confusion, Lacey assisted.

"You've been shot. The bullet grazed the underside of your arm. You need a number of stitches, but it's a laceration rather than anything serious. The bleeding has slowed already." She gestured to the mess smeared over Izzy. "I know this looks like a lot. It's not. It's less than what people give when they donate blood. Things could have been much worse."

Isabella calmed as she absorbed Lacey's rational reassurance. Ebbing panic left room for nightmares in Razor's mind. He couldn't stop staring at the blood on his hands. The memory of pain so intense it felt like touching the surface of the sun slammed into his chest. He struggled to breathe. Giant gasps sawed from his lungs.

Izzy started to sit up in his arms.

"I'm fine, James. You're with me." Her teeth chattered as she reached her good hand to touch his jaw. "Stay here with me. Focus. We're both okay."

Christ, had anyone else noticed the dual terrors plaguing him?

"Come here." She winced when she tried to tug him closer. Her fingers buried in his hair as he obliged, descending toward her parted lips to hear her coarse whispers better in the din surrounding them. The squawk of walkie-talkies toted by emergency workers teased the wisps of recollection haunting him. This close, she couldn't help but see the ghosts in his eyes. "Kiss me."

He hesitated, afraid of hurting her further, unsure of his control when demons raged inside him and adrenaline pumped full blast. Izzy protested, straining her neck until their mouths fused. She soothed him with tiny licks over the seam of his lips, which had locked tight to trap the howls threatening to rip free.

The moist heat of her kiss soaked into him, warming the chill around his heart until the solid block of dread, anxiety and regret thawed. He melted in the rays of her affection. Her heartbeat slowed and steadied against his palm, which supported her elegant back. The consistent double thump paired with the glide of their tongues to mesmerize him.

Brilliant colors chased the blackness from his soul.

Isabella came up for air. She nuzzled their noses and whispered, "We're okay."

"This time." He'd ignored his intuition, waltzing her into the line of fire.

Before she could vocalize the indignation in her gaze, Matt and Clint pounded to a stop outside their group, huffing and puffing. "Shit. That motherfucker slipped away. We chased him into the alley, but he had a car waiting. They disappeared before someone could tail them. Sorry."

Mason nodded. "You did your best. At least we know he's gone. Off the premises. I want us all out of the open. Doll, is it okay to transport Isabella?"

"Yeah, she's good to go. I can do the stitches if someone brings me the materials. An IV with antibiotics and something to dull her pain wouldn't hurt either. Once the shock wears off, that will ache like a bitch. Otherwise, we'll need to swing by the hospital."

"No! Your apartment, please?" Izzy's wide eyes begged for her as Razor swung to his feet. "I'm fine. Really."

She swayed as she attempted to stand. He caught her, fussing over her as he cuddled her to his chest.

JRad, Matt, Clint, Mason and Tyler closed rank around him and the two women, protecting them in the center of their circle. They moved in unison, shoving aside the rolling cameras, a producer and even the paramedic who'd finally made it on scene as they escorted their charges to safety.

Though Razor's skin no longer crawled, he didn't plan to stop and chat before ensconcing Isabella somewhere safe. Somewhere private.

"What the *fuck* were you thinking?" The Master's icy hiss terrified Malcolm. "If we lose her, we lose everything. We don't know where she's stashed the best stuff. She's our ticket to the source."

His bladder released. Nothing happened since he'd already pissed his pants at the sight of the fury contorting the idolized face of his ex-lover until it formed an unrecognizable mask. The tyrant before him no longer resembled the man he'd lusted after for years, but instead, someone out of control. Someone who'd abandoned regal dominance in a fit of misguided, egomaniacal, drug-induced insanity.

Buchanan no longer possessed the most successful formula of their salvation. That obviously hadn't stopped him from using whatever close seconds they'd stockpiled.

"I-I instructed him to scare Isabella. To drive her back to us." He shot an incredulous glare at the fuck-up hanging, beaten within an inch of his life, from the iron beam in the dusty warehouse. "I swear. I didn't pay that prick to harm her."

Malcolm screamed when Buchanan grabbed his soggy balls and twisted. He writhed in the bindings, dangling from the rusty chain as his legs curled up, setting his shoulders on fire. His cursed cock pulsed in response.

"Even a moron like you has to know he's an assassin for

hire. How many times do you think people hedge their orders in case someone's listening? Or because they're too much of a pussy to ask for what they really want." A sneer twisted the lips Malcolm had always hoped would kiss him with returned love someday. If only he did as instructed. Too late he'd realized his dreams would never come true. The things he'd done in pursuit of affection turned his stomach. "You should know all about being a coward."

God, please forgive me?

Malcolm shivered when Buchanan turned to a table laid out with instruments of torture. The Master—suited head to toe in black vinyl—selected a long, wicked blade. Malcolm imagined the tempered steel slicing him to pieces and struggled harder to escape. Nothing budged.

When Buchanan turned instead to the hired gun, part of him cheered. Until he comprehended what the older man intended. He couldn't. He wouldn't dirty his own hands.

He never had before.

But this time he did.

"No one destroys what's mine." The Master spit in the nearly unconscious man's face before drawing the gleaming knife across his throat in a single, continuous slash. As the assassin gurgled, blood spurted from his jugular. Buchanan threw his head back, fists clenched at his sides, reveling in the spray of his enemy's life force.

The light faded from the victim's eyes within seconds.

"I'd heard he was the best. That's all." Malcolm sniffled. He hated to disappoint his Master, no matter that the man no longer deserved his devotion. Probably never had. Too bad he'd only accepted the truth when it was too late.

Too late to change.

Too late to atone.

Too late to escape.

"You will pay for your mistakes."

"Please, no." Malcolm sobbed now. "Let me go. I'll bring her home."

"She will never return to you. I see that now." Buchanan flashed a feral grin. "My daughter has bigger balls than you could hope to grow. You are no longer useful."

"Please..." Pointless begging poured from his lips. He

couldn't say what it was he craved—for his Master to release him into the world that had only hurt him or to end it all. Quickly.

He received neither blessing.

Screams echoed off the corrugated tin walls of the warehouse long into the night until, finally, the contrasting silence would have deafened any occupants.

All but one man, who'd found peace at last.

"The IV knocked her out for a little bit. It won't last more than another hour or so, I'd guess. When she wakes, she can take two of these every four hours. Make sure she eats a little or drinks a glass of milk with them even if she complains." Lacey handed Razor written instructions along with the pain pills that had been prescribed for Izzy. "And try to rest with her. I worry about you, James."

He hugged the woman who could have hated him so easily for his past failures.

"Thank you." He raised his gaze to include the two men behind her as well. "For everything."

"Don't mention it, kid." Mason paused before the trio slipped out the door, nodding toward the TV. "I DVR'd the news. You felt it, didn't you? You knew something was off."

"Doesn't matter." Razor shrugged. "I didn't pay attention to the warnings. I trotted her out there like a duck in a shooting gallery."

"Watch it." Tyler clapped a hand onto his upper arm. "You did more than you think. You're honing your edge. This girl is good for you."

Before Razor could argue, they turned and left, shutting the door quietly behind them.

He snagged a few beers from the fridge before flopping onto the couch next to JRad. The other man surfed the limited channels of Razor's basic cable, killing time while his queries ran.

Whatever the fuck that meant.

"You fixed the remote?" He passed one of the bottles to his friend, lifting his own in a silent salute.

"Yeah. What happened to it anyway?"

"Must have dropped it." Admitting his fury over his initial

attraction to Isabella seemed a bit absurd now. A blind man could see the fireworks flaring between them at every touch, every glance. JRad had witnessed far more than sparks this morning.

"Sure." His friend wouldn't believe it for a minute but he knew when not to push. JRad had a knack for worming into people's psyches. "So...you want to see it?"

"Fuck, no." Razor scrubbed his hand through his hair. "And yes. I don't know."

"For the record, I agree with Mason and Ty. Isabella's resurrecting the old you. With several major improvements. You've lost some of the green you had." When Razor opened his mouth to argue, JRad whipped out the stern tone he reserved for special occasions. "I caught your signal. Watch the clip."

Razor blinked. Most times JRad made it easy to forget the geek possessed a core of steel. Solitary, yet an integral part of their pack, he could command a room without trying when he chose. His lazy grace rarely required him to flash the determination beneath. He hid behind a logical, nerdy shell. Almost like a woman who camouflaged a killer body beneath baggy clothes because of some misplaced self-consciousness.

What was up with that?

Sweet visions of their joint examination sped before Razor's eyes. JRad's clear authority had pervaded their interlude, peaking when the man helped feed Razor's cock into Izzy's virgin mouth. His friend knew how to handle a woman yet he'd never had a steady girlfriend in the time Razor had known him.

He contemplated prying.

JRad disarmed him with a shrug and an offhanded, "Whatever."

As though it didn't matter if they chose to hindsight the evening's action or flip on anything from the sports highlights to a porno instead. Either that or his squadmate realized how much he'd revealed.

Razor didn't have the energy to start a tense discussion tonight in any case.

"Fine. Shit. Play the damn thing."

JRad had the segment cued up. Razor grimaced at the introduction. Of course they'd replayed clips from Izzy's interview. Her metamorphosis impressed him. She'd blossomed in the past week alone, transforming from the frightened, battered woman who wept onscreen to the independent beauty who'd emerged.

Isabella amazed him, adaptable and so tough.

Next came the footage of them about to kiss—the very first day in the practice room—along with his fierce, protective reaction to the asshole cameraman. Watching it unfold from this vantage point underscored the futility of struggling to repress attraction so instinctive, immediate and complete. The producers had included a snippet from last night's fire, which revealed the two of them consoling each other while bundled in a blanket on the bumper of the ambulance.

Razor ignored the speculation of the newsroom crew as they aired a portion of his and Izzy's debut dance. He hadn't realized he held his breath until JRad's knee knocked into his.

"She's okay, kid. Relax."

He blew a stream of cold air through numb lips as he watched himself scanning the crowd. The instant of hesitation when he'd almost called her off seemed clear as day. He silently screamed at the video of himself.

Take her and run. Listen to your gut.

He noted the awkward fumbles caused by his stilted gait. Instead of drowning in the approval of Izzy's gaze, he'd had his head up, peering out into the crowd.

His molars ground together as they neared the point of no return. Faster than he could see in the recording, he switched direction an instant before he and Isabella hit the ground. The delayed reaction of the crowd attested to their stunned disbelief. Jesus, it had happened so fast. In his reality it'd seemed like an eternity.

No one else had expected it. No one else had been tipped off.

The network replayed the terrifying moment in super-slow motion, over and over. From every angle. It became clear he'd reacted well before the shot had been fired. The slight turn he'd squeaked had meant the difference between a kill shot to the heart and a graze to the underside of Izzy's arm in their ballroom hold.

While JRad intended to reaffirm Razor's reaction, the near miss left him freezing inside at what had almost occurred. He never could have recovered from losing her. Not like that. Not when he should have prevented it.

"You saved her."

"I let him shoot her."

"You kept her alive. That's all that matters."

Razor didn't agree, but something more bothered him at the moment. "This doesn't make sense. We expected them to try to steal her. Why the hell would they hurt her?"

He couldn't force himself to say *kill.*

"That's what I've been sitting here wondering." JRad scratched his chin. "Doesn't fit. Why risk twelve mil unless it's to protect the rest of the ring. Either they think she knows more than she does, or she knows something she doesn't know she knows. We'll have to question her some more. Dig deeper."

"Not tonight."

"Don't get your panties in a wad. I won't bother your girl now." JRad sighed. "She needs sleep. Tomorrow... We have to uncover some answers so you two can put this behind you and start the rest of your lives together."

"You're making some huge assumptions there." Not that he didn't hunger for the nirvana his friend implied. But how the hell could he convince Izzy to stay with a poor schmuck like him? Once things settled down, she'd realize he had nothing to offer her long-term.

"All I know is you both seem to have found what you need. That makes you pretty damn fortunate in my book." JRad leveled a pointed glare in Razor's direction. "You can't tell me you'd throw that away when hardly anyone discovers what they're looking for."

"What're you looking for, Jeremy?"

"Something I'm not likely to stumble across. Older every day and no luck yet." His friend grimaced as he stood. Razor understood his discomfort had more to do with the subject at hand than the stiffness of his muscles. The guy couldn't be more than thirty-two on the outside. "Well, it's been exciting, but my results await. Matt and Clint are supervising this shift. Mason and Ty will be on after dawn. You're covered."

"Thanks." Razor cleared his throat, debating the prudence of speaking his mind. What the hell? He hadn't lost all traces of his impulsive recklessness yet. He hedged by considered how Tyler would say what he meant. Then he blurted, "You know, friendship is a two way street. I'm here..."

"Yeah. Just not now. Not tonight."

He didn't plan to goad the other man to share before he was ready. Isabella spared them from an awkward parting when she called softly from his bed, "James?"

"Go." JRad nodded. "Take care of your girl. I'll see you tomorrow."

Razor plucked the pills, an unopened bottle of water and a granola bar from the side table then headed into his room. He'd left the bathroom door ajar with the light on so Izzy wouldn't wake up scared, in the dark. A sliver of the yellow glow illuminated the bed. His heart stuttered when his gaze landed on her, tucked under his covers, wearing another one of his shirts.

Waves of platinum hair framed her precious face. Sapphire and diamond earrings dangled beside her cheeks, which had regained some color. Sure, the ice was costume but she probably had a truckload of the real deal in her mansion. A true princess compared to his pauper, she seemed surreal sometimes.

"How are you feeling?"

"Lonely." She winced as though she hadn't meant to admit it aloud. Her arms slid from beneath the comforter, raised and opened, to invite him to join her. He shuffled from bare foot to bare foot instead.

Did she know what she asked for? What he wanted to give?

"I've never been so out of my league before, Izzy."

"What in the world…?"

"When I look at you, I imagine everything you deserve. Everything I could never hope to give you."

"You're all that I'm asking for. A friend." Doubt crept into her eyes, forcing her to shrink into his pillows. "Lie with me? Please?"

Razor couldn't bear to make her think he'd rejected her so he sank to the edge of the mattress. He enveloped her hand in his. "What's between us is more than friendship. I won't pretend it's that basic. But this isn't the time to make important decisions, Izzy. So much has happened. I'm afraid if we rush into a relationship right now, you'll regret it later. Regret hooking up with me when you could have had so much more."

"You really don't understand, do you?" She tugged until his shoulders settled on the headboard then rested her cheek on his abs. "You have purpose. You do something that matters. I'm twenty-two years old, and I have no idea what the rest of my life is for. My existence was isolated and sterile. Years of worthless galas and figure heading stretched before me at home. Raising money for charity events was about the best I could hope to accomplish. You have solid friendships. You know how to share, how to have fun, how to live and how to love. In my book, you're far ahead of me."

She snuggled closer while he weighed her opinion. Her wince reminded him of the medicine he'd brought. He shook out two pills, handing them to her along with the water. As she washed them down, he opened her snack.

"What would you like to do? You know, after all this," he asked as he swapped the empty bottle for the bar. She nibbled the corner then devoured it, considering.

He petted her hair while she chewed, content to sit in silence as she debated. When she angled her face toward him, he traced the elegant arch of her eyebrow with the tip of one finger before sliding her earrings off and setting them on the table along with the crumpled wrapper she handed him.

"I don't have a lot of skills. I enjoy dancing. I'd like to teach. Not people who want to impress their friends or appear more important. I'm talking about people who love the music, love to dance." She yawned around the end of her sentence. Once the medicine kicked in, she'd be out like a light again. "If we win...maybe I'll set up a subsidized studio for special needs children, as physical therapy."

After tonight, were they eligible for the competition? God knew the contest had been the last thing on his mind. He'd call the network as soon as they opened in the morning to check, for Izzy's sake. No sense in upsetting her over nothing.

"Do you think that's a dumb idea?" She worried her lip to fill the gap in their conversation.

"I think it's a lofty goal. You'd do great at it, princess. If you can teach me, you can teach anybody." He imagined her gentle empathy enriching the lives of her students. "You'd be fantastic with kids."

"Do you want a family, James?" She sounded drowsy as she mumbled into his belly. The wash of her breath heated his groin.

"Someday, sure." Why did discussing the prospect with this woman send desire coursing through him? "I told you about my brothers and sisters. I'd love to have my own family."

"Me too." She nuzzled closer. "Someday..."

The quiet pattern of her respiration led him to believe she slept. He lifted her enough to slide out of the too tempting bed.

"Please, don't leave," she protested. "Sleep with me."

He groaned, too weak to resist them both when every cell of his being begged him to burrow as near to her as he could.

"I don't want to be alone anymore," she whispered when he'd snuggled close, careful to avoid bumping her arm.

"Me either, princess." More than ever he acknowledged he wasn't worthy of her.

The praise she'd lauded him with ran through his mind on constant repeat as he held her, listening to her slumber, for hours. Every time he allowed himself to imagine things might work out, he remembered his deception.

How would her opinion change if she knew he'd manufactured their meeting? Their entire relationship rested on a foundation of lies. She'd never believe everything after that had been real.

What if, as he suspected, more than just her husband had betrayed her? If she discovered he'd known yet hadn't mentioned the possibility to preserve the department's investigation? She'd refuse to accept even one word out of his mouth had been sincere.

Razor wouldn't blame her either.

Chapter Eighteen

The jarring ring of the phone finally cut through the drug-induced haze Isabella had rested in. She reached in the direction of the ruckus before she recalled whose bed she occupied. By the time she pieced things together, she'd lifted the receiver off the cradle. She could either drop it, hanging up on whoever called or be rude enough to answer Razor's private line.

What if it was a woman? Maybe a casual girlfriend who'd seen him on TV the night before? *Crap!*

"Hello?" The shrill question cut across the space between her hand and her ear.

She cleared her throat to avoid making a bad impression with her smoky, just-woke-up rasp then answered, "Hello?"

"Oh! Do I have the wrong number?" The voice belonged to a woman, though one too elderly to be any sort of plaything for Razor.

"I'm not sure, ma'am. Who are you looking for?"

"Jimmy."

"James is in the shower at the moment." The splash of water and curls of steam from the partially closed door clued her in once she batted some of the cobwebs lurking in the corners of her lethargic mind. "May I take a message?"

"Who are you?" The woman sounded excited now. "The girl from the paper? Isabella Buchanan, yes?"

Should she deny it?

"How are you, darling? Don't be afraid. I'm Eleanor. Jimmy's grandmother on his father's side." Before Isabella could respond—or offer to put Razor on the line—the woman continued. "I called to give him hell for not informing his family about the incident last night. You made the front page two states over. His mother nearly had a heart attack when we saw the headline. Considering that business with the deranged woman a couple months back, Jimmy's mom is jumpy. But she's too stubborn to ring him up. Doesn't want to intrude, you see? I'm too old to worry about nonsense like that. But maybe I should have waited. Were you sleeping?"

Isabella laughed, loving Eleanor already. "Probably much later than I should have. I'm sorry I didn't think to have him contact you."

Her own father hadn't bothered to find out if she was okay. Not after the incident at her apartment or last night's shooting, and he lived in the same damn city. He didn't intend to forgive her for leaving Malcolm, or for the scene she'd caused in doing so, apparently.

"With such a sweet lady to tend to, I'm not surprised he forgot. One of my granddaughters showed me your dancing on that Internet thingy this morning. My cataracts make it hard to see, but I could tell enough. Perhaps we'll meet you sometime soon?"

"I would love the opportunity to chat with you more, Mrs. Reoser." Isabella dodged the woman's implications. "Though I'm sure James doesn't make a point of bringing his work home with him."

"Who are you talking to, Izzy?"

She choked on her tongue when he stepped from the bathroom, wearing only a low-slung towel around his hips. Water dripped from his dark hair to bead on his slick chest before continuing to roll over the contours of his defined abs.

Isabella croaked, "Here he is now, Mrs. Reoser. So nice to speak with you this morning."

"Same here, darling. It's been a long while since I met a youngster with such impeccable manners. Take care of that arm. And my boy. He could use a good woman to look after him."

"Yes, ma'am."

Chuckles fell from the receiver as she handed it to James. She chewed her nails. Had she given his family the wrong impression?

"Sorry," she whispered.

A huge grin lit up his face when he realized who had called.

"Yes. Yes, she is. Beautiful, generous and sweet, too, Gran E. Don't worry. I'm trying my best to impress her."

Isabella giggled when he waggled his eyebrows at her.

Razor turned serious, apologizing for frightening his family—something she owned at least some of the blame for. She headed to the bathroom to take her shower, granting him privacy to speak freely.

Keeping her arm out of the spray occupied most of her attention while she lathered her body. Pleased by the low-level ache in her biceps, much less painful than she had expected, she relaxed beneath the soothing water until the temperature began to drop. When she finished, she smiled as she drew on the lounge pants, cropped tee and fuzzy hoodie Lacey had hooked her up with.

Though danger and problems galore lurked outside this haven, her newfound friends made the fear less debilitating. She had someone to help. Someone to lean on. With their assistance, the hope she'd lost sight of while secluded reasserted itself in her heart. She wished she'd be able to repay them in kind one day.

Isabella padded into the living room, prepared to brainstorm solutions and facilitate the investigation into her bastard husband's involvement in torturing the women she'd glimpsed. She had to help them, grant them a modicum of the salvation she'd found if she could.

The collection of grim men who turned to face her stopped her in her tracks.

"Izzy…" Razor slammed his eyes closed to avoid her unspoken questions.

"What is it?" She scanned the crowd, her gaze landing on Jeremy. His somber mood screamed something awful. "It's Gerard. Something's happened to him?"

Her knees trembled. She forced them to move, to carry her toward Razor. What retaliation had the butler suffered for her escape?

"No, baby. We haven't found him yet."

"Thank God." She sighed, accepting the hand Razor held out to her. He led her to the couch then sat her between JRad and Clint. He kneeled by her feet.

"It's—" He gulped. "I'm sorry."

Her curious glance flicked to Mason and Tyler. "Somebody

spit it out. You're scaring me."

Tyler nodded then said, "Two bodies were discovered this morning in a warehouse owned by Carrington Industries. One victim is a known assassin who's evaded us for years, likely the man who shot you last night. The crime scene investigators believe the other is your hus—"

He broke off, shaking his head. Surely, he couldn't mean what it had sounded like.

"They believe it's Malcolm Carrington."

"Oh God." One hand covered her open mouth while the other returned Razor's squeeze. "They're not sure? Maybe it's not him? Could there have been some mistake?"

"His identification was found at the scene. But..."

"I can take it. Tell me."

"The body had been mutilated beyond definite recognition. They're conducting lab tests now to confirm. We don't expect a different result. I'm sorry, Isabella."

Shock, horror and regret washed over her in waves. The blinding grief she expected never materialized. Somehow that hurt worse.

"We understand if you need some time to digest this." JRad tucked her hair behind her ear.

"No. No, it's horrible. But I'm o-okay." She sagged against his heat while holding Razor's gaze. "I'm actually..."

Should she admit it?

"What, Izzy? You can tell us," Tyler prompted.

"Relieved." A tear leaked from her eyes at the admission. Did it make her a horrible person?

"That's understandable, sweetheart."

"And those women. Someone can rescue them if we don't have to worry about Malcolm reestablishing his business elsewhere. Lily too. They'll be safe now, right?" She blinked away the moisture blinding her when dead air met her questions. She might have heard the chirp of crickets.

"Ah, shit, Izzy." Razor gathered her to his torso as he crouched between her knees.

She laid her head on his shoulder, inhaling the scent of his soap and skin from the crook of his neck. Her freezing fingers clung to his shoulders.

"The world doesn't work like that."

"Why not?" She hated her sheltered existence, which had left her naïve and ill-equipped to deal with reality.

"There's too much money on the table. This either means someone else has assumed control of the ring or..." His audible sneer made her believe this alternative had actually been his theory all along, "...your piece of shit ex-husband was never the kingpin of this organization."

"I don't understand. Why else would someone k-kill Malcolm?" She stumbled over the question. It seemed impossible. He'd ruled her life for years. How could he be gone? Vanished. Just like that.

"The media is speculating it could have been retaliation."

"For what? They don't know about the women I saw, do they?"

No one answered. Their silence started to tick her off. She looked from one man to the next until the tingling dread in her mind coalesced. "They think *I* did it? Holy crap. Do *you* think I did it?"

Isabella shoved Razor. She popped to her feet, pacing through what little space the men in blue's muscled frames left unoccupied in the living room.

"Honey, none of us believe you were responsible. Even if more than one of us hadn't surrounded you at all times last night, and even if we didn't know about your cash flow issues, we wouldn't consider it of you." Matt spoke for them all. "We need to play this by the book so no one else has reason to doubt either. The public hasn't come to know you as we have."

"We uphold the law. The system." Mason agreed. "You need to head downtown for formal questioning. Let's record everything. Do this right so we can take out whatever scum is behind this once and for all."

"But..." She scrunched her eyes and rubbed her temples. "Can we flash back a second? If I didn't do this. And Malcolm didn't do this. Who did? Who's in charge? Who's responsible?"

This time, no matter how long she waited, none of them responded.

"You don't know? Or you won't say?" Anger rose in her, born of betrayal. Didn't they trust her after all?

"We can't afford to influence your thinking, baby." JRad covered for them all. "Come on. We'll drive you to the station. Let the detectives ask you their questions. Their way. You may know more than you think."

"Promise you won't leave me alone?" She peeked over her shoulder to where Razor sat on the floor. "If someone is out there..."

"I'll stay with you the whole time. I swear." He rose, crossing to her side. "Nothing will happen to you in our house."

She deflated, settling into his open arms, soaking in the strength of his embrace. "Okay. I have faith in you, James. In all of you. I'll do whatever I can to help."

Isabella whimpered as she rubbed her arm. Taking pain pills which would muddle her thinking and dull her senses had seemed like a bad idea when she needed to remain on high alert. Despite the reassurance of the cops she'd come to adore, she couldn't put herself totally at ease around all the strangers who bustled through the station.

So each time Razor had handed her medication from his post in the corner, she'd faked swallowing the capsules then hoarded them in her pocket. More than twelve hours later, her pants bulged like a chipmunk's cheek. When she'd consented to this, she'd had no idea how many different people would pepper her with questions.

For the most part, she hadn't minded. Except after repeating her answers to the basic inquiries time after time, she'd started to burn out. That didn't include the emotional drain of her perpetual embarrassment. She'd suffered when her replies revealed the bareness of her upbringing and the dysfunction of her marriage.

The lowlight of the day had come when they arranged for a doctor to confirm her virginity to support her claims around the horrid images she'd surrendered as evidence. She cringed, remembering her mortification as she'd huddled under the paper gown. Razor had held her hand through the entire ordeal.

"Isabella?" The grey-haired detective working with her tilted his head.

"I'm sorry." She checked the ID at his hip. "Could you repeat the question, Detective Roberts?"

"Joe, I think she's had enough." Razor's palms settled onto her shoulders, his fingers massaging with light pressure. "We're not going to get anything more today."

"I think you're right, rookie." The detective stretched his

hand across the cheap plastic table to shake hers. "Thank you for cooperating, Ms. Buchanan. It's been a pleasure meeting you. If you remember anything else..."

"I'll let you know." She finished for him.

"You really have been here too long." The kind-faced cop shook his head. "Razor and his squad will escort you home. They'll take good care of you."

"I know." Her genuine smile overcame her weariness. "They've done a great job so far, sir."

As if on cue, the door to the interrogation room opened. She flinched into Razor's waiting clutch, relaxing when she recognized Matt and Clint. They must have supervised from behind the one-way glass. Unknown stares had burned into her all day as she revealed some fairly personal business.

Maybe that's what had her so disconcerted.

She accepted Razor's hand as he guided her from the room, through an endless tangle of hallways to the backseat of a patrol car. He settled her in the crook of his arm for the ride to his apartment. The simple space felt more like home after two days than Malcolm's mansion had after two years.

What would she do when this mess had blown over or they were booted from *Dance With Me* and Razor moved on to his next assignment? Would the attraction zinging between them persist or did his endorphins dictate this kind of response on each new case?

She sat up straighter as she wondered.

"What's wrong, Izzy?"

"Did last night disqualify us from the competition?" With everything else that had happened since, she hadn't considered the possibility.

"Nah." Razor stroked her bangs off her forehead. He kissed the bare skin there. "I checked with the network this morning. I guess they played the footage from our dress rehearsal for people to vote on. There's no way we'll be eliminated this week. Besides, an on-air shooting is great for their freaking ratings."

Her eyebrow arched at his caustic tone. She bet someone had received one hell of an earful after making that comment. His concern moved her. She flicked her eyes toward the two men in the front seat. They did a commendable job of feigning disinterest.

If their presence bothered Razor, he didn't show it. He

groaned as he used his knuckles beneath her chin to angle her jaw into position. Then he swooped in, nibbling at her mouth. He tasted like the jelly donut he'd stolen from the desk of one of his friends. Delicious.

His left hand curled around her waist as his arm slid into the gap she'd left between the seat and her back. His palm stroked her thigh, causing her to sigh. She shifted her legs to provide him better access. What would he do with the opportunity?

The heat of his touch brought her alive, forced her to experience more than the exhaustion and pain dissolving her strength.

She loved it. She craved it. She needed more.

Her hips rose, grinding into his roaming hand.

"What the..." He stiffened beside her, yanking his lips and tongue away as though burned.

"Why did you stop?" Had she done something to discourage him? She froze, afraid to make things worse.

"Izzy!" When he threaded his fingers into her pocket, she understood his outrage. "You didn't take any of these? All day? Christ. You sat there and suffered for twelve fucking hours? No wonder you look like shit."

"Gee, thanks." She had an iota of vanity remaining.

"Razor, take it easy." Matt warned from the front seat. "I wouldn't have altered my reasoning capability either. Think about it a minute. She's no dummy."

Harsh breaths reverberated through the car for a solid thirty seconds before James calmed. His forehead touched hers. "I'm so sorry. I should have noticed. I'm angry at myself, not you, princess."

"I did what I had to. That's all." She relished the freedom and easy companionship allowing her to press a gentle kiss to his parted lips. "I'll take them tonight. I promise."

"You amaze me, Izzy."

He returned her affection with interest in a caress of lips that stole her breath. Their exchange escalated until everything outside the two of them ceased to exist. She couldn't say how long they made out, exploring and feeding the magnetism welding them together. Long before she was ready to stop, Clint blasted them with cold air, which gusted through the open door.

Her nipples pebbled against Razor's heaving ribs.

"Get a room, kids. We're here."

James panted in the silence before scooting from the car. It relieved her to see their exchange affected him as much as it did her. Weak-kneed from the arousal coursing through her, she didn't resist when he lifted her into his arms. Instead, she drew a meandering squiggle across the cords of his neck as he carried her up the stairs, which he took two at a time.

JRad opened the door when they approached, ushering them inside. "Things were quiet in here today. The apartment's clean."

"Thanks."

She hardly recognized Razor's growl.

Jeremy grinned, surveying them both, unable to miss the color staining their cheeks or their swollen lips. "Seems like you're in a hurry. I'll hit the road. Have a good night."

He winked then disappeared.

Razor set her on her feet long enough to lock the door behind their friend. When he hesitated with his back to her, she grew nervous. Uncertainty rushed in to occupy the chasm between them. Why had he stopped touching her?

The universe made sense when they met skin on skin.

Isabella drew a fortifying breath. She laid her hand on his shoulder. He twitched beneath the tentative contact, his hands fisting at his sides. Instinct erased her confusion, her pain and the reluctance bred by her inexperience.

"Come to bed with me? Hold me?" She approached him, resting her cheek between his powerful shoulders. Her arms wrapped around his waist. The good one slid higher to allow her to caress his chest. The other lingered above the band of his jeans. Her fingers teased his flexed abdomen, tracing the valleys between his defined muscles. "Touch me?"

"I don't know if I can, Izzy." His honest response broke through gritted teeth. "I want you more than my next breath. You're not ready…"

"Don't you think *I* should decide when I'm ready?" She didn't know where she found the courage for her unskilled seduction, but she rotated her hand until her fingers dipped beneath the denim to cup his erection.

The hard-on encased in cotton she expected turned out to

be hot, velvety bare cock instead. They gasped together.

"You're so thick." She whispered in awe as she recalled how he'd throbbed in her fist the other night and the taste of his come in her mouth yesterday. "Long and salty."

He groaned, but remained frozen like the gorgeous marble statue in the center of her favorite garden fountain while she toyed with his shaft. She daubed the bead of fluid seeping from the tip over the head of his cock with one fingertip.

"I want to know what it's like to make love to a real man. I'd be honored if you'd be my first." When he didn't respond, she blanched. Her hand retracted. "Unless... I mean... That's if you're interested."

"I'm not interested in being your first, Isabella."

Air whooshed from her lungs as she stumbled back a pace. He turned, his arms banding around her, preventing her from tumbling to the carpet.

"I want to be your only."

Chapter Nineteen

Isabella couldn't deny the fire blazing in Razor's eyes as he walked her to his bedroom. He flung open the door, flipping the switch to illuminate the scene he'd set inside with the soft wash from his bedside lamp. His sweet efforts had her turning to him once more, adoration radiating from every pore.

A whimper escaped her chest when he evaded her seeking lips again. Frustration prodded her. "What? What now? I'm not married anymore, James."

"You were *never* married to that piece of shit. He used you. He conned you. Nothing more."

"Then I don't understand." She glanced away from the intensity of his gaze.

"Look, this was a bad idea. When we left this morning... I don't know. As usual, I didn't think things through. I didn't expect to be at the station all day. You're hurting. You just lost one of the only people you cared for in the world, even if he didn't deserve your friendship." Razor knocked his skull on the doorjamb three times in quick succession. "I want you. Desperately. Please don't doubt that, princess. But you should have more than this. You deserve something special. Someone extraordinary."

He gestured to the cheap bottle of wine sans glasses and the flowers, which looked suspiciously like the bushes in his complex's landscaping, overflowing a chipped coffee mug. A handful of petals dotted the neat but mismatched bedding he'd turned down.

"Nothing could mean more to me than your thoughtfulness." She stood on tiptoes, tugging his hair until he met her gaze. "I've had fancy things. They don't matter without emotion. And I can't imagine anything more special than the magic consuming me when I'm with you."

"Izzy—"

She silenced him with a kiss. Talking became unnecessary when they communicated on a primal level more effective than words. Here, they were in tune. When he'd calmed, sipping from her proffered lips, she pled her case.

"Please give me what only you can. I'll try my best to be everything you need."

"You already are, princess."

Her trembling fingers caressed his cheeks as she bracketed his face in her palms, urging him nearer. When his lips hovered a hairsbreadth from connecting with hers, she whispered, "Show me how to love you."

Razor groaned into her mouth. He nudged her hoodie from her shoulders, careful to avoid scraping the area surrounding her bandage. They both paused to wince when he revealed the dark bruises there.

"Are you sure you're up for this?" He deposited a trail of butterfly kisses beside the tender area while his broad hand glided over her ass. "We can wait as long as you need to."

"I've waited my whole life for this moment." She grasped the hem of her tank top, shimmying it up her torso to reveal her belly and her bubblegum pink bra to his appreciative stare.

"God, yes. You're so damn pretty, Izzy." Razor sank to his knees before her. He licked along the protrusion of her hip bone, a fraction of an inch above the top of her pants. His fingers tucked inside the waistband to ease the light fabric lower until it pooled at her feet. "I can't say no when I want you so bad. No matter how much I should."

She blushed when he nuzzled the crotch of her matching panties, drawing the scent of her obvious arousal into the depths of his lungs with a huge inhalation. His hand clenched on her hips, his fingers squeezing her ass as he moaned.

"I swear I'll make this good for you." He ran his hands down her thighs, her knees, her calves until he lifted one foot at a time from the puddle of fabric. The socks were swept from her feet beneath the pressure of his wondrous hands. He stood, taking her fingers in a gentle grasp as he led her to his bed. "Not this time. Not today. Always."

Isabella sighed. She rubbed the aching peaks of her breasts

through the delicate material of her bra while he drew the covers to the foot of the bed. She'd lost the ability to speak beneath the weight of both her emotional and physical desires—needs he promised to fulfill.

Razor had to touch her soon or she'd do it herself.

When he turned, he groaned. "You're sexy. Stunning."

She bit her lip as she considered all the times she'd tried to tempt Malcolm and failed. What if she couldn't satisfy James?

"I'll wipe out all the bad memories lingering in your eyes. Love you until all you remember is the heat, the pleasure...our desire." He placed one hand on her spine, nudging her forward. "Nothing before now matters."

"For either of us." She kissed him as she passed, unable to forsake the opportunity to taste him again before she climbed onto his bed, kneeling with her ass on her heels. "This is *our* first time."

While she watched, he divested himself of his T-shirt, which clung to the bunched muscles of his arms and trim stomach. She preferred the firm leanness of his body to the bulk of some of the other men in blue. All that strength impressed her. Still, she wouldn't feel as comfortable with them, one on one.

Razor's physique didn't appear too skinny or too huge. He was pure perfection. Beneath her searing appraisal, his sleek abdomen flexed in and out in time to his elevated respiration.

Isabella licked her lips.

He hadn't panted that hard after they'd performed their physically challenging waltz. Her gaze wandered up the breathtaking landscape of his chest to the spot where he once again fingered his scar. She didn't care to have anyone else sleeping with them. Not tonight.

"I'll try to forget my mistakes if you will too. I think it's time we both forgave ourselves. At least a little." She reached forward, unbuttoning his jeans while he gaped at her. "Time to build something new. Together."

His cock thrust from the dark nest of hair revealed by the descent of the denim that had so recently encased it. When she started to wrap her fingers around the magnificent length, he dodged her grip and joined her on the sagging mattress.

Razor tucked her close as he pressed them flat on the cool sheets, his larger frame blanketing her. The glide of his skin over hers left her gasping.

"Okay?" He dipped his head to murmer into the curve of her neck. "Does it frighten you to be pinned beneath me?"

He started to rotate. She protested with a whine. The thought of riding his trim hips, using his taut muscles to pleasure herself, sent shivers along her spine. But his strength surrounding her like this intoxicated her. Nothing could compare.

"No, Izzy? You like my weight on you?" He grinned before nipping her lip. "Me too. Good thing I'm no hulk like Mason, or I'd crush you. Christ, you're tiny."

"I was just thinking the same thing," she mumbled into his parted mouth. How synchronized could two people be?

He devoured her smile, lingering before he dragged his lips over her chin. He nibbled a path along her neck to her collarbone. Her eyes fluttered closed when his mouth toyed with the sensitive patch in the hollow there while his fingers slipped under the satin straps of her bra. The privilege of soaking in his attention raced through her veins.

Isabella's hands wandered from his taut shoulders to the curve of his hips. She marveled at the joy it brought her to simply hold him close. The intimacy of their mutual exploration ratcheted her anticipation higher. She squirmed, aligning her pussy with the hard bulge of Razor's cock as he settled fully into the vee of her thighs. The soaked fabric of her thong provided a flimsy barrier between them. Even that was too much.

"Not so fast, princess." His teeth grazed the upper swell of her breast. "I'm going to make you so hot you scream for me to take you, to make you mine. There's a lot more to enjoy along the path."

He growled as he shoved his hands between her shoulders and the mattress. She levered onto the elbow of her uninjured arm to grant him room to maneuver. With a deft flick she couldn't have placed as well, he unhooked her bra.

Razor slid the straps from the main section of the bra with his teeth, eliminating the need to thread her sore arm through the loop. He peeled the fabric from her chest, burrowing his face in the mounds beneath the lace. Her giggles became a gasp when he dragged his open mouth from the ticklish skin over her ribs to the mound of her bared breast.

He feasted on her taut nipples, drawing them into the moist heat of his mouth in turn while he plumped the perfect handfuls she made for him. After more minutes than she could stand of his patient assault, she buried her fingers in his hair, urging him to suckle harder. He obliged with impressive gusto. It spread the current of pleasure from her center outward.

Her pussy clenched in response.

The sight of his large fingers and flushed lips on her lighter skin turned her insides to mush. Not to mention the lash of his tongue over her tingling nipples.

"More!" She cried out when he nipped the ripe tip of her breast, craving intense contact. Empty, aching, she had to have more.

Razor grinned at her. He finally traveled lower, nibbling a path across her abdomen so damn slowly she thought she might scream. He paused to dip his tongue into her belly button, swirling it through the sensitive depression.

Her spine arched, presenting him with the ideal handhold. He wrapped his palms around her hips, positioning her exactly where he liked. The gradual pressure from his shoulders spread her thighs as he nestled further between them.

A shriek rent the air when he lapped at the moisture gathering in the crease of her thigh. Had she made that keening cry?

"Mmm." The vibration caused by his hum of approval zinged straight to her engorged clit, which pulsed in anticipation. "I love your taste, princess."

His rough timbre thrilled her. The approval shining in his eyes emboldened her.

"Then why don't you take your fill?" She lifted her legs perpendicular to her torso, wiggling and tugging so her thong wrapped around her knees. With a twist of her knee and a flick of her ankle, she kicked the scrap into space, toward the living room.

It wasn't until she draped her thighs over his shoulders once more that she realized what an up close and personal show she'd given him. He groaned, tucking his hands behind her knees, propping her soles on either side of his head. When he lapped at the ample arousal coating her labia, she figured he hadn't minded.

Razor's thumb swiped over the apex of her pussy, brushing

the knot of her clit. Electricity shot from the point of contact, driving her closer to the edge.

"Oh, yes." She thrust her pelvis at his talented mouth, begging for his attention.

He didn't disappoint. With teasing flicks of his tongue, gentle pulls of his lips and glancing scrapes of his teeth, he drove her insane. The world spun out of control as Isabella tried to ground herself, to stay there with her lover as a riptide of euphoria threatened to carry her downstream. It would be easy to free fall, easy to drown in the waves battering her senses. But she held on—unwilling to allow the current to take her under before she'd achieved her goal.

For long minutes she endured the sensual torture.

"James. Wait." She had to repeat herself several times before her request sank in.

He lifted his face, his chin glistening with her juices, to gauge her reaction. The billows of his breath puffed over her clit. Even that small tease nearly shoved her into orgasm.

"No." She shuddered, gripping the sheets at her side to keep from flying. "Don't want to come without you."

"I'll take care of you, princess." He stroked her tummy until some of her distress evaporated. "There's plenty more. You can have as much as you need."

"Not this time," she whispered again. "Only with you."

He rose above her, nodding when he realized how much it meant to her.

"Please, no more teasing. I need you." She opened her arms, welcoming him into them. "Now."

She could no longer speak when he captured her mouth with his own. The sweetness of her arousal mixed with his tangy flavor to create a perfect blend, which she greedily ingested. Lost in their kiss, she blinked when he retreated. She shouldn't have worried he'd stray far.

He leaned across her to snag something off the nightstand. A condom. He ripped the foil packet with his teeth then rolled the latex over the proud length of his shaft. She wished she could have tasted him. Wished they didn't need the thin layer between them at all. Not when it seemed like her destiny to be with him.

As though he could read her thoughts, he tipped forward once more.

"I don't know if you believe in fate. Or God. But all my instincts are screaming this is how things were always meant to be." James never stopped gazing into her eyes though he aligned the head of his cock with her dripping folds. He rocked his hips, notching the blunt tip in the opening of her pussy. "I was born to be yours. You were born to be mine. I understand that now. And I'll be grateful for this connection every day for the rest of my life. I swear it, Izzy."

This is really about to happen. Finally. It stole her breath to cradle him at the juncture of their bodies, on the brink of entering. She had to try several times before she could speak over the bliss coursing through her.

"Then take me." Isabella bumped her pelvis into his. The motion drove him the slightest bit into her swollen channel before he stopped. Blocked. She hated the membrane keeping their bodies apart when she'd swear their souls had already merged. "Please."

"Yes." He held her gaze as he pierced her resistance with a sharp jab. Razor continued to penetrate her virgin passage with bold strokes until they united as completely as possible. He filled her beyond bearing.

Flames of passion licked higher until they singed her with their intensity, edging into something unpleasant. She couldn't catch her breath. Her heart pounded. Panic stole a little of her sanity, causing her to squirm in an attempt to evade the pain.

"Shh. I have you, princess." Razor kissed her, soothing her hurt with tender strokes of his tongue on hers. He fed her long, even breaths—his cinnamon gaze locked on her face for any sign of escalating distress—until the discomfort morphed into something brilliant and epic.

She surrendered to his presence inside her, accepting the throbbing flesh that impaled her. Welcoming him into her grasp.

"Better?"

"Much." She sighed though the reprieve didn't last very long.

He frowned, knuckling a tear she hadn't realized she shed. "I'm so sorry. Is it terrible? We can stop."

"Hell, no. It's wonderful." She trembled when his deep exhalation rubbed the head of his cock over ultra-tender nerve endings. Sparkles of color filled her vision at the ecstasy the tiny motion brought her. "I never imagined...and I thought about it a lot."

"It's never been like this for me before." He rubbed their noses together. His cock jerked inside her. "You were right. This is the first time. Of many, I hope."

"If I have anything to say about it." She nipped his lip.

He laughed, kissing her again. Deeper. "Greedy. I like that."

"Do you like pushy too?" She grabbed his ass, coaxing him to move before riding the knife point of pleasure killed her. "I want you to take me hard."

"Not tonight, princess." He withdrew, stroking each untried inch of her pussy with his departure, until just the head of his cock lodged inside her. "But I'd give a lifetime supply of Carnot dinners to make love to you right now. Are you ready for me?"

"Yes." She moaned when he tested her with tiny, light strokes. The sample of him whetted her appetite like the richest appetizer she'd ever been served. Her arousal rebounded, stronger than before.

"You're trembling." He gathered her close as the arc of his hips grew despite his concern.

"Because I need you so much." She whimpered as she recalled the explosion he'd wrung from her the day before. Could she survive something this much more powerful? "Want this to last forever, but I'm close. So close already."

The impact would reach far beyond the temporary reprieve he'd granted her the last time. Where that sensual play had the effect of a gentle spring shower, rinsing away her lust, this encounter whipped ecstasy around her with gale-force, ensnaring her heart and soul in its energy.

"Thank God." Razor groaned as he pumped inside the clinging sheath of her pussy. "I don't know how long I can last. You're so tight. A perfect fit for me."

He twined their fingers together, locking their hands where they rested on the pillow beside her head. When she squeezed, encouraging him, he redoubled his pace then devoured her lips. His tongue thrust into her mouth in time to his cock shuttling in and out of her body. A storm of emotions raged around them. Through it all, he maintained a steady rhythm, flowing rather than slamming into her.

The pressure of his blunt cap parting her flesh and bumping the ring of muscles at her entrance had her welcoming his invading hard-on. Full. He packed her to capacity. When he bottomed out, the base of his shaft dragged along her clit, setting her up to explode. She tensed around his cock, wringing a groan from his chest.

"Shit, yes." He came up for air from their debilitating kiss. "Hug my dick, Izzy. Come around me. Take me with you."

He'd probably laugh again if he knew how much her ability to arouse him mattered. She didn't have the chance to explain. Razor shifted, positioning her hips so he ground against a particularly sensitive patch on the front wall of her swollen interior.

He smiled as he learned the secrets of her body, homing in on the motion guaranteed to induce her moaning until he could replicate the pleasure with each penetration.

Suddenly, she could resist no longer. He knew her better than she knew herself. Her pussy constricted around his erection, rippling along his shaft as she prepared to explode. The last thing she noticed was how he clutched her to his chest, as though afraid she'd disappear while he buried his face in the crook of her neck and shoulder. He roared before his teeth closed gently around the tensed tendon there.

His primitive claim dissolved her inhibitions.

Together, they came. She screamed his name as her body convulsed and he poured his release into the latex reservoir. Unending pulses of pleasure echoed through her system, reverberating with each answering jerk of his hips—proof of their unified desire.

Euphoria surrounded her, buffeting her as she floated, aware only of being held as close as possible to the man she loved.

Sometime later, she opened her eyes. Razor hovered above her, stroking her cheekbones as he alternated sweet kisses with a flex of his hips, which prolonged the aftershocks coursing through them both. They lay together without uttering another syllable until his flaccid penis slipped from her body. She mourned the loss.

The bed dipped as he left to dispose of the condom and retrieve a cloth to wash the speckles of blood from her thighs. While he administered her medicine and checked her bandages, she observed in contented silence. She could hardly believe they'd done it. Finally, she could call herself a woman.

Somehow, though, she acknowledged it had more to do with her connection to James than the tearing of a thin boundary of her innocence.

When he returned to her side, the world seemed perfect. She settled into his open arms, forgetting about all her problems. At least for one night. His unending caresses and romantic whispers lulled her. She pretended nothing could wreck what they'd started to build and that, come morning, everything would be as flawless as it appeared in the silvery moonlight streaming through the window to dance over their joined forms.

Chapter Twenty

Isabella's heavy lids struggled to open. The pinch of discomfort between her legs paired with the throbbing in her arm to inspire a wince. Solid heat generated by the man holding her, protecting her, erased any lingering aches.

"Good morning, Izzy." He brushed a kiss to the corner of her eye from his post behind her.

"Mmm. How long have you been awake?" She angled her face to smile at him without budging from the shelter of his arms. The disarray of his rumpled hair and the slumberous cast to his sexy eyes had her gulping.

"Long enough to figure out your secret." He grinned.

For a moment her mind raced. Her days of deceit were over. She had withheld nothing from this man. "What do you mean?"

"Ms. Isabella Buchanan, I'm sorry to inform you that you snore."

"I do not." She tapped his shoulder with a lighthearted slap.

"Like a chainsaw, princess. How does such a loud sound come out of such a dainty mouth?"

"If it did, it's your fault for knocking me out with the greatest sex of all time."

"I was pretty fucking awesome, wasn't I?" He tickled her while he continued his smug teasing, drawing a shriek from her parted lips. When she squirmed in his hold, she had the last laugh. His half-hard cock awakened where it nestled between the globes of her ass.

She hitched her hips, guiding his erection between her thighs. They rocked together. The arousal he generated with their sensual friction counteracted some of her soreness. His stiffening shaft slipped across her damp tissue, the tip nudging her entrance on each pass.

If she could have purred, she would have. Instead, she dragged his hand to her breast, goading him into smothering her ripe flesh while she rubbed her nipple into the heart of his palm.

Isabella moaned. She tilted her pelvis until her pussy aligned with Razor's prodding hard-on. When he skimmed her opening, she clenched, kissing the head with her lower lips.

The intimate contact had him flexing in reaction, shoving his heated cock the barest bit inside her. She spread her legs, pleased when he shifted to support her knee, holding her open.

Could she be lucky enough to experience the earth-shattering pleasure he'd brought her last night again so soon? She hid her slight wince at the twinges of discomfort prickling her in pursuit of the avalanche of rapture he would trigger.

Hope spread throughout her body when they strained together, burying him another inch into her welcoming sheath. The groan of regret she released when he slid free morphed into a cry of delight as he fucked her slit, rubbing their combined slickness over the tight bud of her clit.

She undulated beneath the delicious pleasure, causing him to tuck inside her pussy once more.

"This is a dangerous game, princess. I'm not wearing a condom." He groaned in her ear. "Even like this, there's risk. But shit, you're like wet satin on my cock. Had my physicals to get reinstated. I'm clean."

"A little more, please."

"It's reckless."

"Don't care." The only important thing in that moment was having him inside her again. Pregnancy didn't frighten her. If it weren't for the timing and how screwed up her life was at the moment, she'd welcome a child. His child. Children. Once she'd digested Malcolm's betrayal on their wedding night, accepting she'd never have a family of her own had delivered the next biggest blow.

Now, things could be different. Her whole life changed by the hour. Improved.

She shuddered, driving James further into her channel. The motion stung a little, reminding her of her inexperience in this world. It didn't stop her from craving more. Curious and eager, she wriggled closer to his heat.

"A few more seconds." His reply pushed through gritted teeth.

He pumped into her from behind, both of them on their sides. She reached down to spread the lips of her pussy, circling the sensitive bundle of nerves hidden there as James had taught her by example.

The angle permitted them both to watch. The sight of his possession set her ablaze.

"That's right, princess. Rub yourself." He panted as he tried to control his own arousal. "You're so hot. So responsive. Can feel you gathering around me."

When he bit her shoulder, she arched. The shift caused his cock to glance off a particularly sensitive place inside her. He maintained his gentle thrusts, accurate and effective. Too soon, her orgasm built in the pit of her stomach.

Isabella focused on the speck of delight until it blazed into a full-on climax.

"That's right, give in." He groaned.

Razor went stock still as she convulsed around him. He allowed her to wring satisfaction from his embedded cock while one hand cupped her neck, ensuring her line of sight. When the contractions quieted, he whipped from her pulsing depths. He flattened her hand, which still petted her pussy with light strokes, over his exposed shaft.

"Feel what you do to me," he growled.

He thrust, wild, between the saturated folds of her pussy and her palm—once, twice, three times—before the purple head flared. The tips of her fingers caressed his balls where they drew tight. His cock twitched in her hand. Jet after jet of hot come spewed from his impressive erection, glazing her hand, coating her belly and decorating the soft blond curls of her pubic hair.

The echoes of her own release had her throbbing in time with the pounding of his heart, which thumped at her back. Before she could recover from the alluring vision, he'd wrapped his arms around her. Razor turned, rolling them from the bed.

He guided her to the bathroom, turning the shower on full-blast with one flick of his wrist.

Isabella smeared the mix of their fluids over her stomach and breast before raising the tip of her finger to her mouth. She licked their unique flavor from the digit while he stared.

"Holy shit, that's hot." He clutched her hips, yanking her close while they waited for the water to warm. "What do we taste like, princess?"

"See for yourself." When he dodged the sample she proffered, she blushed. Had she crossed a line?

"Not like that, Izzy." Razor perched on the low edge of the tub. He tugged her over to straddle his spread thighs. She clutched the towel bar to her left for support. Her right hand dropped to his silky hair when he raised one of her legs, balancing the crook of her knee on his upper arm.

His splayed hand landed on her lower back. The stroking of his fingers tensed and released his biceps, which her thigh rested on. The wanton pose leveled his mouth at optimal height for what she prayed he intended.

Sure enough, he leaned forward, lapping at the evidence of their lust, which glimmered on her flushed skin. He hummed in appreciation. Vibrations shot straight to her core, where the remnants of her orgasm lingered.

Razor amplified the low-level arousal with a series of open-mouthed kisses. When he encountered an errant strand of his come or a trickle of her arousal, he paused to clean her with long swipes of his tongue. By the time he'd meandered to the valley of her pussy, she quaked in his hold.

"I never realized..."

He paused to peer up at her without removing his talented mouth from her soaked flesh, his eyebrow raised.

"How amazing it would feel. Every time."

The end of her statement flew out on a gasp. He redoubled his efforts as though her admission spurred him on. She trembled, her knees wobbling. He held her firm. Steady.

Isabella forced her eyes open so she could witness the care he took in ensuring her satisfaction. When he noticed her watching, he smiled against her pussy before sucking her clit between his tender lips.

Razor slipped the hand not busy supporting her along her thigh, toward her core. She whimpered when he hesitated, a fraction of an inch from infiltrating her.

He lifted his head to ask, "Are you sore, Izzy? I should have thought about it before..."

"It only hurts when you stop." She answered honestly despite how vulnerable the truth made her. If he walked now, she'd shrivel up in a corner somewhere. The need he instilled in her left her completely exposed. And she loved it.

She should have known he'd never abandon her to suffer. The bulk of two fingers parted her moist lips then tucked into her pussy. Before she could beg, he guided them in as deep as he could reach while remaining careful not to overtax her inexperienced flesh. The combination of his fierce possession and the tenderness of his seductive kisses unraveled her resistance.

Isabella felt greedy for taking so much ecstasy and giving none in return. The base nature of the act kept her from insisting they play fair. Not to mention the moans of approval emanating from the man devouring her.

Could her passion be enough to sustain him?

She didn't care, and couldn't spare the brain cells to wonder much longer. He scissored his fingers inside her, stretching the walls of her little-used pussy. Unlike the night before, or the tender loving of this morning, his touch grew insistent as he manipulated her from the inside out.

The intensity of his fingers lunging along the slippery tissue had her squatting to assist, driving him faster, harder. Each stroke added kindling to the bonfire building again in her center. His throaty laugh bounced off the tiled walls. "You like that, huh?"

Against her will, her fingers clamped in his hair. She forced him to return to the amazing job he'd been doing of granting her every wish.

"Harder!" she shouted, not caring about the neighbors or any of the long-forgotten men staking the perimeter of Razor's apartment.

"Like this?" He rumbled into her drenched folds, slamming his fingers to the extremity of her clinging passage. The sudden impact, which obliterated the last of her resistance, teamed up with the scrape of his teeth on her clit, flinging her into a powerful, shuddering climax.

Steam filled her lungs as she drew giant gasps into her chest. While she shattered, the world turned. James cursed as he maneuvered them through the curtain, into the shower. He spun her to face away from him. With one arm wrapped around her waist, he shoved her shoulders until she bent, presenting her ass.

Isabella clung to the knobs for dear life when James seated himself to the hilt in her clenching pussy with one bold shove. The gentle lover who'd initiated her to lovemaking had disappeared, replaced by a man intent on driving her wild as he slaked his lust.

She'd never felt more desirable, or turned on, in all her life.

Razor wrapped the sopping mass of her hair around one wrist. He tugged until her neck arched. She adored the thought of anchoring him as he rode her.

"Yes. Fuck me, James." She screamed his name when the passing of his rock-hard cock triggered several mini-orgasms that pummeled her with the force of a series of waves. "Harder. Don't stop."

"No. Chance. Princess." He adjusted his grip. His free hand left the dip of her waist to smack her ass. The wet slap ricocheted around the shower stall, shocking her. In the wake of the burn it brought, a bone-deep glow suffused her body.

"Again," she begged, loving the bounce of his sac on her clit. When his excitement eclipsed reason, he drove impossibly far inside her. The force of his thrusts jiggled her breasts, teasing her nipples.

He granted her request, lighting them both on fire. He banged into her hard enough her foot slipped on the plastic shower stall. He braced her, steadied her. The knowledge that he'd catch her, even now, suffused her with joy unlike any she'd dreamed possible.

She locked her knees and elbows to meet his powerful lunges, absorbing all he could dole out, surrendering to whatever he chose to do to her. With her.

"Ahh." Intelligent speech escaped him, but she understood his appreciation. Knowing she pleased him set her off. She came around his cock, making him work double to plow through the rings of muscle hugging him.

Though she craved his molten come boiling inside her, overflowing her most private places, he withdrew at the last possible instant. He spilled his seed over her ass and the small of her back, moaning her name with constant repetition until they both capitulated to gravity.

Too weak to stand, they melted into a pile of tangled limbs and soaked skin.

Razor turned to land on the bottom, pillowing her

controlled descent into his arms with his striking muscles. She rode the rapid rise and fall of his chest while warm water streamed around them. She licked beads of spray from his neck.

"God, Izzy." He groaned between wheezes. "You're amazing. I've never been with a woman so wild, so open."

"I have a lot of time to make up for." She nibbled his ear, savoring the salty taste of his skin. "There's so much I want to try."

"Give me a minute." He framed her face as he tilted it so she could see the laughter in his eyes. "I'm young, but I have a feeling you'll wear me out before long."

"I'm going to do my best." She smiled as she kissed him.

"Thank God." He grinned before sipping the droplets from her eyelashes. The throb of his rejuvenating cock grew stronger despite his protests. "'Cause I don't think I'll ever get enough of you."

Razor wore a shit-eating grin as he and Izzy called the guys in to join them for lunch.

"I can't believe we slept so late." She blushed.

Her mind must have run to all the other things they'd done in bed past noon. Damn, now his had too. Just when he thought he'd tamed his everlasting boner. If the guys caught sight of his flagpole, they'd never let him hear the end of it next time they hung out at the station.

"*I* can't believe you've never ordered a pizza before." Razor's stomach growled. He snagged a roll of paper towels from the kitchen as JRad, Mason, Tyler, Clint and Matt piled into the apartment. They toted four grease-stained boxes and a case of soda.

The men in blue shouted hellos, but Izzy kept her gaze glued to the stained carpet. What the hell?

JRad plopped onto the couch beside her and nudged her knee with his. "You all right, Isabella?"

She picked at the hem of her cut-off sweat shorts, nodding.

What the fuck did she have to be ashamed of? It wasn't as if they'd committed a cardinal sin. Did she regret sleeping with him?

Razor stalked to where she sat, cross-legged, about to

question her sudden shyness when Clint hooted from behind them.

"Oh, ho. What do we have here?"

Razor's eyes bulged when the jackass spun Izzy's pretty pink undies over his head on one finger. Not now. Not when she already seemed mortified to have fucked him.

He glanced at Izzy's horrified face. Her jaw hung wide open. A cramp twisted his guts.

Damn it, he'd known she'd regret taking a no-name cop to her bed. Though she sure as shit hadn't been complaining last night. Or this morning. Or even an hour ago. She couldn't intend a lasting relationship if it upset her that the men in blue knew they'd made love.

Shit. Why did he care so much this time when he never had before?

"Give me those, asshole."

Clint flung the thong at him as though it were a slingshot. Razor caught the scrap of lace. He jammed it into the crack between the couch cushions. Beside him, Izzy had frozen. He barely recognized her—so unlike the pliant, sexy woman he'd woken to this morning.

Matt slapped his partner upside his thick skull. "You idiot. Can't you see you're jacking them up?"

Tyler cleared his throat. He laid his fingers on Izzy's hand. Razor resisted the urge to deck the man for daring to touch her. She jumped at the contact, her cheeks flaming red.

"There's nothing to be ashamed of, Isabella." The other man smiled, patient and understanding where Razor probably would have blown a raspberry and spun out of control like the Tasmanian devil. "You're among friends. None of us will judge you."

His princess choked. She rasped, "Judge *me*? I'm worried about James. I'm not capable of hiding how I feel. You all knew immediately. Will I bring him trouble because of...this? After what happened last time, he doesn't need that kind of—"

She didn't have a chance to finish.

Razor cut her off, silencing her with a full-on kiss. She melted before it turned ravenous, unable to resist the pure attraction arcing between them.

Mason cleared his throat.

Razor broke free, surprised to find Izzy had climbed into his lap.

"Listen to me." He grabbed her ass, drawing her lower until she straddled him. She couldn't miss his obvious arousal. Christ, the last time he'd sported wood this often he'd been fifteen and had the mother of all crushes on his teacher, Ms. Dalton, who favored fuzzy, v-neck sweaters. "This isn't a game. I'm not about to screw you one minute then treat you like some dirty little secret the next."

She cringed at his directness, but he couldn't change overnight.

"These guys are my friends. My brothers. They accept you as they accept me. Even if they didn't—if my superiors didn't—I'd never turn my back on you. You're mine, remember? I'm yours. Or didn't last night mean anything special to you?"

"S-sorry." Izzy blinked a several times. She shook her head. "I guess I'm not used to this yet."

"Used to what?" He growled, his rationality impaired by her challenge to his commitment—intentional or not.

"To loving people who stick." The shimmer of tears in her sky blue eyes broke his heart.

"Well, you better adjust quick, honey." Matt dropped his massive hand on her shoulder, breaking the tension.

"Congratulations." Jeremy leaned in to kiss her on the cheek.

"Welcome to the family, squirt." Mason ruffled her hair.

"Damn, enough of this gooey shit. Can we eat?" Clint cracked the lid on one of the boxes, allowing the perfectly blended aromas of cheese and tomato to permeate the apartment. "Listening to a twelve hour sexathon makes a man hungry."

His sweet princess hid her face in the crook of his neck while she giggled.

He nudged her chin up until he could rub their noses together, grinning in return until someone handed over a steaming slice of heaven. "Here you go, Izzy. Dig in."

"You'll never forget your first piece of pizza." JRad winked as they moved on, laughing and sharing stories throughout the meal.

"I had no idea a half-dozen men could eat so much." Isabella refused to listen when they protested her picking up. Not one scrap of mozzarella remained stuck to the corrugated cardboard. They'd blazed through the case of soda and moaned over the beer they couldn't touch while on duty.

"You should have tried it." Matt attempted to stifle a gigantic belch behind his fist, but failed miserably. Izzy only laughed. "It's a match made in heaven."

"I'm good with this, thanks. As it is, I don't think I've ever been so full." Isabella clutched her svelte stomach. "I need some exercise. A jog would be awesome."

The men in blue looked alarmed. She waved them off.

"Don't worry. I figure I'm sentenced to life inside. At least for now."

"Don't pout, princess, or they'll think I can't entertain you."

She shot him a naughty look. He thought he heard Clint curse under his breath. Something along the lines of, "Lucky bastard."

"It's true, we'd like you to stay where we can keep an eye on you for now." Mason turned serious. "We're digging through all the shit around Malcolm's murder. Clint and JRad turned up some more leads on the ring from hanging at Black Lily last night."

Mason flashed Razor an apologetic shrug. The next thing out of the guy's mouth would suck. Big time.

"If you're up for it, we'd like to take you out tonight to have a look around the legitimate side of the club. See if you remember more by being there. Maybe scare some people into panicking. Maybe force them to mess up."

"No fucking way." Razor leapt to his feet.

"It's okay, James." Izzy laid her palm on his forearm.

"No. It's not. It's too dangerous."

"Think this through. We can't hide her forever. Eliminating the threat will ensure her safety." JRad spoke, calm and rational, from behind him.

"This isn't only about me." Isabella persisted with gentle pressure on his biceps until he turned. She wrapped her arms around his waist, tucking her cheek against his chest. "Those other women..."

She shivered in his hold.

"Oh, fuck. I know, Izzy." He savored the silkiness of her platinum hair between his fingers, afraid of doing the right thing for the first time in his life.

"We'll bring Lacey. With all of us on the lookout, it'll be relatively safe." Tyler winced at the death-ray glare Mason issued. "Besides, don't the two of you have to start practicing for next week's show? I heard you drew the samba. This will be perfect. We'll take a look around, have a good time, chase away the cabin fever and be home before you know it."

JRad added, "It's probably not a bad idea. You'll be glad you had the break tomorrow."

"What's tomorrow?" Razor grimaced at the shadows in his friend's eyes. They'd suckered him into the worst of the news.

"Malcolm's funeral."

"Already? I thought—" Izzy tensed as she glanced from man to man, waiting for someone to fill her in.

"Yeah, we didn't expect it so soon either. There are some big guns harassing the administration to be speedy." Mason cleared his throat. "It looks like the commissioner caved."

"Who's taking care of the arrangements? Should I help?" Izzy chewed her lip.

"Everything's covered, honey." Matt dropped the bomb. "Your father's handling it all."

She sank to the couch, her head in her hands. "I guess he always cared more for Malcolm. He hasn't even bothered to find out where I am. *How* I am."

"Actually, Chief Leigh told us he asked for you. More like demanded you be returned to his household. The chief refused to reveal your location. Guaranteed him we have it under control."

"Thank God." She sighed. "I don't want to go back. Malcolm or no Malcolm. Still, it's nice to know he thought about it. Even if it's because he considers me his property."

"Fuck him." Razor squeezed her knee. "You don't need that kind of drama. We're here for you. *I'm* here for you. In fact, I don't think you should attend the services at all."

"What?" She gawked. "I know this whole situation is insane, yet I can't help but pity Malcolm. The more I think about it, the more I'm positive I knew the real man. Sometimes anyway. He was miserable. At least he's not suffering anymore."

“Princess, I’m sorry to say it like this. I’m no good at being subtle. The fact that the funeral is all some giant rush job sets off warning bells in my brain so loud I can’t hear myself think. There’s no reason to do that. It could be a trap. Something to lure you into the open. And that asshole doesn’t deserve jack shit from you anyway.”

“Maybe not. Still, I’d like to say goodbye. *I* need the closure.” She sighed. “Malcolm was the only friend I had. The only person who gave a crap about me after my mom died. Besides Gerard, anyway. And I wasn’t able to see him very often after I moved out. Malcolm kept us apart. I understand that now. Oh God, and Gerard’s probably in trouble because of me. Soon there will be no one left. My entire life is vanishing, changing. I want to go. I have to say goodbye so I can move on. I have to.”

“Okay, okay. It will be okay. We’re searching for Gerard, Izzy. We’re doing our best. And no matter what, you’ll never be alone again.” Razor tried to calm her. His worthless rambling didn’t seem to penetrate. When his reassurance failed to soothe her, he gathered her to his chest and whispered, “I love you, Isabella.”

Chapter Twenty-One

The cops took their cue to slip from the apartment. Razor supposed those dreaded three words scared most of them, though Tyler and Mason nodded their approval as they filed out the door.

Hope replaced the despair creasing Izzy's brow. "You do?"

"Yeah." He rested his forehead on hers. "I definitely do."

"I'm so messed up, James. My life, everyone I've ever known..." She groaned. "I'm not sure I know what love really is. I know I've never felt anything this strong before. I-I think I love you too. And I'm terrified I'm going to ruin what's between us somehow."

"It'd be impossible to destroy this, princess."

He claimed her mouth in a searing kiss, noting the zesty spice of the sauce she'd eaten as well as the sweetness from the soda. So much like her. Life would never be boring with Izzy around.

Razor might have christened the couch with some afternoon nookie if Isabella hadn't winced. "Your arm? Or..."

"Both." She grimaced. "I know we woke up late, but I think I could sleep for a week. There's not much on me that doesn't ache right now."

"I'll grab your medicine and a blanket." He shifted, tipping her onto the wide leather cushions. "Nothing like a day of snuggling, snoozing on the couch, watching cheesy old movies and maybe playing some video games to cure you."

She opened her mouth as her gaze wandered over the bulge in his sweats. He stifled her objection with two fingers over those luscious lips. "There'll be plenty of time later."

Razor reached across Izzy to grab his buzzing Smartphone from the coffee table. She dashed a tear from the corner of her eye. Maybe she figured he wouldn't notice her crying.

So what if she'd enjoyed the romance?

He'd never admit it to the guys, but he had too. Because he'd shared it with her. Her head pillowed on his arm, he'd relished every single minute, spending more time studying her expressions in reaction to the drama onscreen than the films themselves. The sweet smiles, the soft laughter and the sighs of pleasure falling from her lips entranced him.

After three chick flicks in a row he'd started to get a cramp in his neck. His arm had gone numb hours ago. He would have stayed for another triple feature.

Beside him, Izzy stretched her elegant arms above her head.

Razor swallowed hard as his gaze fixated on her narrow midriff. She tugged the hem of her tank down and blushed. He winked.

"Huh? Yeah, I'm here. Sure, send her up." He snorted when JRad made some wild suggestions as to what'd stolen his attention. "Very funny. We're decent."

Before Izzy could ask, a light rap sounded on the front door. She curled into a ball against the sofa's arm, drawing the covers to her chin as if to prevent their guest from seeing her beaded nipples beneath the thin cotton covering them. She hadn't bothered with a bra for their private screening session. Her pert breasts didn't require one anyway.

"It's just Lacey, princess." He pecked her cheek before admitting the other woman.

"Hey, guys." Mason and Tyler's woman tossed them a finger wave as she sashayed across the room. She plopped onto the arm of the sofa beside Izzy. "Ohhh, *Dirty Dancing.* One of the best movies of all time. Damn, too bad I missed it."

Surprised, Razor turned. Credits rolled across the screen. Where had the last hour gone?

"Soooo..." She glanced between him and Izzy. "We still on for tonight? I brought some gear to slut us up good."

"I don't think—" he started at the same time Isabella said, "Yes, if you'll help me with my hair."

She pointed to her injured arm.

"I'll tease that mane so high the girls on *Jersey Shore* will turn green with envy." The pair giggled, frightening him on a level he hadn't experienced in quite a while. What the hell had he stepped into?

Izzy flung the quilt off. She bounced into the other room, elbow locked with Lacey. He might as well have ceased to exist for all the attention they paid him. It made his heart sing to see her so excited. Maybe this wouldn't be such a clusterfuck after all.

"I borrowed a handful of dresses from one of my tiny friends, the bitch, for you to try on. I hope you pick the red halter. It'll look great with your eyes and some fire-engine lipstick. I brought my fuck-me boots too. What size shoe do you wear?"

"Seven."

"Me, too. We're shoe sisters. It's fate." The gleam in Lacey's eye as she glanced over her shoulder proved she'd planned his demise all along. "No peeking. We'll be ready by nine. Not a minute sooner. So tell Mason to chill when he has a bug up his ass to head out."

Two hours later, the squadmates sat around the living room waiting to hit the road. They'd discussed strategy, reviewed safety precautions, handed out assignments, studied diagrams of the club's layout and finger-combed their hair.

In fifteen minutes, they'd prepared for the night with time to spare.

"What the fuck are they doing in there?" Razor shook his head when the lights dimmed for the tenth time. "Building a dirty bomb?"

"Dude, you don't want to know how many goddamn cords there are in my bathroom these days." Mason ticked them off on his fingers. "A blow drier, three different sizes of curling irons and some rectangular tong contraption."

"A flat iron," Tyler supplied with a grimace.

"Whatever." The gruff partner shook his head. He didn't fool anyone. He adored his two companions—beauty products and all.

"Is something on fire?" Razor sniffed the air.

"Nah. That's the smell of hairspray burning off one of those doohickeys."

"That can't be good for you." JRad covered his nose and mouth with the sleeve of his black, button-down shirt.

"I will admit, the end result is usually worth the torture." Tyler squirmed in his seat, adjusting his package with a stealthy shift.

Clint consulted his watch for the fiftieth time in the last ten minutes. The women operated on borrowed time since the clock over the microwave read 9:02.

"Someone has to go in after them." Matt grumbled, "And it ain't gonna be me. That stench won't leave my clothes. How will I find a hottie to take home when I reek of someone else's lady?"

"This is a work outing, remember?" Mason frowned at the junior officer.

"It is until we're finished. The minute you exit the girls from the game, Clint and I are free to do a little clubbing of our own, right? No use in wasting the entrance fees. Have you ever seen the women who hang out there?" He screwed his face into a ridiculous expression. "Like sex on heels."

"Well thank you very much, Matthew." Lacey blew him a kiss as she strutted into the huddle of men. She sported a purple leather mini-skirt so short and tight Razor doubted Mason would let her leave without changing.

The poor guy's eyeballs almost bulged out of their sockets when he followed her seamed stockings to her matching platform pumps with six-inch heels. Mason cursed, his leer turning to the black and purple satin corset shoving her impressive rack up so far Razor feared her girls might tumble free.

"You really want to antagonize him, little one?" Tyler raised an eyebrow. "By the time we make it home he'll be at the end of his rope. You know what'll happen..."

"Yeah, I'll turn her ass red for teasing me before we fuck her senseless."

"Promise?" Lacey licked her glossy lips.

Razor could have sworn he heard JRad heave an envious sigh before the man averted his gaze from the sensual spectacle their friends made. Escape eluded his friend as Isabella emerged from the shadows behind them.

"Christ. How the hell are we supposed to concentrate?" JRad scrubbed his hand over his face, blocking his vision. "These are hazardous work conditions."

Razor traced the other man's line of sight. Then it was his turn to gawk.

Izzy prowled to his side, one hand on her hip. She wore a slinky red dress. The straps twisted around her neck. Tiny strands of ruby beads dangled from the fabric, swaying with each movement she made.

"Give 'em a spin. Show off the back. Well...what there is of it," Lacey chuckled.

Razor swore he'd swallowed his tongue. A band no more than eight inches wide covered the bare essentials. He figured if she got carried away dancing he'd catch a glimpse of her pussy. Was she wearing anything beneath that wicked dress?

Her hair had multiplied to unbelievable proportions, sexy enough his palms itched to touch the voluminous curls and the soft tendrils artfully framing her face. Giant sparkly hoops drooped from her ears. And, holy shit, Lacey hadn't been joking about the lipstick. A flash of imagination depicted those crimson lips wrapped around his cock, obliterating all common sense.

Platinum hair, azure eyes and her matching red nails generated coordinating hues in a vibrant palate. And that was before he noticed the thigh-high, stretch stiletto boots, which showcased her perfect legs. He'd never seen something so sinful, so alluring or so mouth-watering in all his life. "Are you sure you don't want to stay in tonight, Izzy?"

Matt whistled when he recovered.

"As much as I'd like to..." She squirmed, pressing her thighs together. "I have to do this. Please, take me there. Everyone be extra safe. I couldn't bear it if one of you were injured because of me."

"Don't worry, baby." JRad didn't hesitate. "We have it covered."

"Let's go." Razor extended his hand to Izzy. She took it, skimming her thumb over the erratic pulse in his wrist. "The sooner we leave the sooner we come home."

She shivered, but squeezed him harder.

JRad scanned the crowd in a never-ending cycle. The collection of beautiful people gyrating on the dance floor to Ke$ha's "Take It Off" didn't hold much temptation for him. Now the sounds emanating from the hallway to his left... They piqued his interest big time. Whips cracked followed by moans of women—and men—submitting to skilled Doms and loving every minute. His cock strained, harder from the cries than the sight of all the bared flesh presented before him.

He'd tried to avoid opportunities like this. There'd be no reining in the desires dissolving his control after tonight. Could he find someone here to relieve him? Could any of the women handle his true nature? He'd learned long ago that hedging—taking a taste of what he craved—only multiplied his dissatisfaction. Maybe things would turn out different this time.

He scrubbed his hand through his hair, focusing again on the task at hand.

While Razor and Izzy tore up the floor next to Mason, Tyler and Lacey, he'd been placed in charge of locating the establishment's manager. Tracking her whereabouts proved hard enough. Pumping her for information became impossible when he couldn't find the minx in the den of shadowy passages, private rooms and not-so-private play spaces.

Izzy hadn't remembered anything more from visiting the club. He hadn't figured she would. Her captors couldn't have been stupid enough to cart her through such a public place where someone might have recognized her standout beauty. No, they'd smuggled her through the back door, straight into the dungeons he knew existed below.

The spark of desire lighting his primal instinct snuffed out when he considered how many of the women there had been forced against their will. Shit, he was fucked up. This is why he'd avoided the scene for so long. He couldn't be trusted.

Before he could resort to self-flagellation, he spotted his prey. Black Lily. Her raven hair had been woven into a thick braid that reached well past her perfect ass. She strode through the crowd. People jumped to yield to the Mistress. Or begged to be her toy for the night. She ignored all requests, moving unaffected through the sea of willing slaves.

The black latex conforming to every curve seemed like part of her rather than clothing worn on top of her delicate frame. Her attitude and bearing erased some of her diminutive stature, but he saw straight through the persona she embraced like armor. Other than Izzy, she had to be one of the most petite women he'd ever seen.

Hell, she could be Isabella's evil twin.

The thought had his cock throbbing in the black leather pants he'd changed into. He loved how the soft underside conformed to his legs, hips and the bulge at his crotch.

It'd been too long.

He shoved off the wall, ambling after the proprietress with lazy grace designed to mask the urgency of his strides. He'd gotten good at hiding—at playing the harmless geek. So good, he'd almost started to believe the ruse himself. One night here destroyed all that. And this time, he wasn't sure he'd be able to lock his urges away again.

The sultry Domme stalked along the corridor, stopping to check on the observation windows of the private rooms, guaranteeing the safety of her patrons. How could she be so good at her job and, yet, be involved in the horror below?

When she reached a black door, which nearly blended into an alcove at the end of the hallway, he offered a silent cheer. Her office. He'd found it. Matt and Clint's sketched diagrams from their prior recon hadn't shown her hidden headquarters. He'd figured they were buried deep. Now, in the heart of the club, he'd corner her.

He'd secure the information they needed by whatever means necessary.

As the heavy metal panel swung closed, JRad thrust his thick leather boot in the crack. He dropped his shoulder and shoved through the resistance, stepping inside Black Lily's domain in time to catch a flicker of motion in the dim recesses of the office.

His mark snatched something from the wall as she spun. Braided leather snapped in the space a fraction of an inch to the right of his face. The loud slap made him pause. Not for long. When she lashed out a second time, he was ready.

JRad launched his hand to the side, deflecting her strike. He wrapped the end of the lash in his fist then yanked. Hard.

Black Lily teetered off balance in her ridiculous, shiny black boots, which added a deceptive lift to her height with their platform soles. They were sexy as hell, he'd give her that. Practical for evading an assailant—not so much.

Instead of slamming her to the wall, he found himself cradling her close, pinning her with his bulk. His instincts reacted faster than his brain. God knew, something about this woman fired him up, turned him on and had his cock straining to burrow inside her.

"This is dangerous, cop," she whispered, not the least bit frightened.

"You're telling me." JRad groaned when her lips brushed his neck with her speech. Since when did a Domme turn him on? The idea of making her submit flared as bright as the sun in his imagination. She would be glorious in her surrender. If she didn't break. "What the fuck is happening here? You helped—"

He cut off when she bit him hard enough to leave the impression of her sharp little teeth. No one marked him. With a growl, he captured her mouth. They wrestled, tongue versus tongue, lips versus lips and teeth versus teeth until he feared he'd squash her beneath the pressure of his hold.

She blinked up at him in the near blackness, the glitter of her eyes barely visible now that his pupils had dilated. Had she been swept up by the contact the same as he had?

This *was* dangerous.

"Tell me—"

This time she shook her head. A subtle twitch, the gesture spoke volumes. She nibbled a path along his neck, gouging his palms with her nails until he bent closer. She whispered in his ear between sucks on the lobe. "They're watching. Listening. Always. I'm sorry."

Before he could ask what for, she'd wrenched from his hold. Lily drove her knee into his already aching balls. He doubled over, retching from the searing pain, planning decadent retribution. One day she would pay for that.

"Security, I have a pickup in my office."

Before he'd stopped seeing stars, the door flew open behind him and two giant dudes in metal-studded leather harnesses ensnared his arms. He laughed as they dragged him from her stronghold. "Someday..."

"In your dreams, asshole." Her reply held some truth. JRad would dream of her plenty. But he also caught the tremble in her fingers as she brought them to her swollen lips.

Oblivious to everything except having fun, Isabella reveled in the rhythm of the music pulsing through the crowd, moving them all in time to the Latin beat. She rode Razor's thigh as they ground together. Before she could leave a slick spot on the leg of his jeans, he twirled her out and back. She shimmied her shoulders, incorporating some of the samba they needed to prepare for next week.

Beside them, Tyler entertained his partners with a ridiculous dance move that looked suspiciously like starting a chainsaw. She thought she'd imagined it when he started in on rolling the dice, then picking them up. Laughter erupted from her as Mason turned red with embarrassment. Lacey clutched her stomach. The woman tugged Tyler close to do some dirty dancing of her own, sparing them all from his antics.

"What's this song?" Isabella screamed. She might as well have mouthed the question since she couldn't hear herself over the intoxicating music.

Razor guided her into the crook of his arm, bending to shout near her ear. "'Calle Ocho'. Pitbull."

She made a mental note, hoping to convince the producers to use it for their next routine. Though, she almost forgot everything she knew when Razor dragged his palms up her thighs, over her ass. The scrap of material barely covering her allowed his fingertips plenty of access to tease her right there on the dance floor.

A glance to her left and right confirmed many of the couples engaged in their own adventures for all to see. She could hardly breathe at the thought of coming apart in her lover's hands as they danced. Still, having an audience didn't sit right at the moment. Anyone could be watching. Especially here.

When she tensed, James reached out to tap Mason on the shoulder. The big man turned from his lovers, who bumped and grinded before him. Razor gestured toward the sidelines with his chin. Mason nodded.

Razor tucked Izzy's fingers into the waistband of his jeans at the small of his back. He headed for a break in the crowd. She clung for dear life as they wended through the throng. She tried to convince herself the occasional touches on her ass were accidental.

When she could hear herself think again she asked, "Where are we going?"

No answer.

They rounded a divider, coming face to face with a non-descript man perched on a stool behind a black, granite counter.

"A booth."

The man selected a key from the pegboard to his right and tossed it to Razor. "Number seven. Thirty minutes."

"Thanks." Razor dragged her to a more subdued room. A couple dozen tables occupied the center of the dimly lit space. Couples, or more, chatted over glasses of wine and bottles of beer. Japanese style screens formed walls around the perimeter of the room. She gasped when she realized the bright lighting on the other side of them cast naughty shadows.

"There are people inside?" She gasped. "They're..."

"Yeah, just like we will be in a minute." Razor flicked a smile, so diabolical she shivered, over his shoulder.

"Everyone can see..." She moaned when she noticed the silhouette of a woman on all fours. Someone pounded into her from behind while someone else fed her a cock from the front. The throbbing in Isabella's pussy escalated, making her wish she were the lucky bitch.

"Uh huh. Sort of." He grinned. "Where's your sense of adventure now, Izzy?"

Razor might as well have called her chicken. Nothing could be farther from the truth. The steamy show, the admiring gazes of the men and women around the room and the pure effect of spending time in close contact with her lover had her ready to ride him on top of the table if she had the chance.

With the variety of levels to the club, they could certainly have discovered a place where overt fucking would be appropriate and welcomed. She appreciated Razor's gradual initiation to these wicked fantasies. She could go wild and never fear failing.

"Oh, I'll show you that side of me and more." Isabella snatched the key from his hand. She marched to the rice paper and balsa door with the black seven artfully burned into the frame.

When she turned to gauge his reaction to her bold move, she noted Mason, Tyler and Lacey heading for an empty spot less than ten feet away. *Holy shit.*

"How brave are you now, princess?" Razor chuckled against her neck. "Will you show them how hot you really are?"

Chapter Twenty-Two

The crotch of Isabella's thong, already damp, soaked when her pussy generated an instant gush of wetness. This new side of her gentle lover sparked her imagination. What would he do to her? Not one modicum of fear tainted her excitement.

He ushered her inside.

"Is this okay?" Razor whispered in her ear. His arms cradled her from behind. The stiff flesh of his erection ground into the small of her back.

"God, yes." She trembled when his hands slid upward to cup her breasts.

"You're not afraid?"

"Never with you." She spun, showing him the truth. Concern darkened his eyes despite the bright white light in their cubby. She couldn't hide a single thing from him in here.

He nodded with a sexy smile.

"What would you like to try?" He offered her any fantasy she desired with a sweep of his hand in the direction of the naughty vending machine in the corner. "Anything? Nothing?"

Isabella took one step then another away from his fiery hold. She browsed from object to object, dismissing the clamps, inspecting the lubricants and paddles and skimming the row of vibrators before facing Razor.

"You told me you enjoy...bondage." It irked her to stumble over the word. "What about the silk scarf?"

He grinned then rushed to her side, holding out his credit card. He swiped it through the slot on the side and keyed in her selection, adding a package of condoms.

She moaned as their purchases fell into the tray where

Razor collected them.

"This is going to be quick, princess. We don't have much time in here." He murmured against her temple as he wrapped each end of the silk around one of her wrists, punctuating his whisper with a kiss when he tied it off. The ample amount of play left in the middle disappointed her, but she didn't want to ruin his fun. "Later tonight, when we're home, I'll give you a more thorough demonstration."

Isabella nodded, anticipation blossoming once more.

When she stood bound as he wished, he swiveled her to the side. She froze when she saw the elaborate system of hooks on the wall to the right of the spotlight.

"Oh, did you think I was letting you off easy?" His soft laugh did a crappy job of disguising his hunger.

Razor snatched the draped silk, which arced between her wrists. He hung the center over one of the curved brackets above her. Her wrists lifted, though not very far.

"Swear you'll tell me if this hurts your arm."

The command brooked no argument. She nodded.

"Good. Now…" He paced behind her to grip her hips. "Take a couple steps backward, toward me."

Isabella obeyed. She had to tilt forward as her arms extended fully in front and above her. She considered their silhouette. Immediately, she understood what he intended. Isabella bent at the waist, her shoulders straining as she dipped lower and lower.

"Ah, yes. Just like that, Izzy. You're so flexible." Razor stroked her flank, her ass presented for his taking. "Imagine how beautiful you look to the crowd out there. Every man, and some women, will be very jealous of me tonight."

She rocked into his touch as he skimmed along her torso, testing the snugness of her binding and the tension on her arms. He paused near the hook, which held her in place. She angled her face to nuzzle his cock through his jeans.

"Let me taste you. Let me show them how I can please you."

"God, yes." Razor ripped open his fly, his bare cock springing free. He ducked beneath one of her arms to stand directly in front of her. The profile of his cock tunneling into her mouth would remain clear. Unmistakable.

She devoured him as he fucked her mouth slow and deep. The techniques Jeremy had showed her to enhance Razor's experience came in handy. He tasted delicious. The grunts he made spurred her on. After several minutes, her arousal began to trickle along her thigh. She fidgeted in a bid for relief.

"Enough, princess." James tapped her cheek with one finger. She released him despite her desire to taste his hot come on her tongue again. "You need me inside you, don't you?"

"Yes!" She hadn't meant to shriek.

He released a strained laugh. "I need you too."

His shadow blocked the harsh light on the right side of her face for a fraction of a second before he adopted his stance behind her. He used his sneakered foot to kick her boots wider. The crinkle of a foil wrapper drifted to her ears. Spread as far as she could go on the mile-high heels while wearing her miniscule dress, he would have a perfect view of her swollen pussy.

His fingers tested her, dipping inside her saturated folds. They spread her moisture over the hard bump of her clit. She could have come at that touch alone. Instead, she bit her lip, waiting for him to join with her.

"Please, James." She begged without shame. "Take me."

Before she finished asking, he buried his entire length inside her. She felt full to bursting. The pressure of his entry shoved her off balance, but the silk scarf she dangled from kept her upright. His strong hands clamped over her hips, securing them as he rode her hard and fast.

Between the bonds at her wrists and his iron grip, she could only stand there and accept his delicious treatment. The idea had her on the verge of climax after a handful of fierce lunges.

"You're so hot. So tight." Razor groaned as he drilled into her depths. "You're about to come already, aren't you?"

"Yes." She panted, trying to rock on him in return. "Make me."

Razor bent forward, blanketing her spine as he reached one hand beneath her torso. He simultaneously supported her and teased her when his palm massaged her breast, giving her something to lean on. His cock seemed huge inside her, thick and hard, as he continued to shuttle in and out.

Rougher than the other times they'd made love, he didn't temper his lust. His pelvis smacked her ass, driving her forward into his waiting grasp. When he tucked his other hand between her legs, she lost the ability to speak.

Isabella screamed, moaned and shook in his arms. His fingertips danced over her clit. Her orgasm smashed through her, obliterating all sense of space and time. Their audience, forgotten.

All she cared about was the ecstasy assaulting her and sharing it with him. He stiffened behind her, shouting as he filled the condom he wore. Their jagged breaths cut through the air in sync.

"Amazing." He moaned as he withdrew from her quivering sheath.

Both of them jumped when a round of applause and cheers sounded from the other side of the screen while he freed her. The embarrassment she expected at their wanton display showed up in the form of wicked pride instead.

"You're good with that?" Razor tipped his head in the direction of the noise as he massaged the kinks from her shoulders. He kissed the red marks braceleting her wrists.

"I'm only worried about what you think." She strained her neck to kiss him.

After a wild exchange, which drew more whistles, he smiled against her lips. "I think you might've earned an upgrade from princess to queen."

They took a minute or two to straighten their clothes and shake out some of the wobbliness in their bones before emerging from the booth. Isabella didn't bother with false modesty. She stared straight at the place she'd last seen her three friends.

Lacey had vanished.

"Where's—" Razor began. He cut off when the sultry woman appeared from beneath the tablecloth of the trio's table.

"Dropped my purse." She winked as she licked her lips. The satisfied smirk on Tyler's face called her a million kinds of liar.

"Time to go home, kids." Mason's grouchy mandate proclaimed he'd lost the lusty lotto. "Right now."

After a couple additional private lessons in the comfort of his bed, James turned onto his side looking serious.

"What is it?" Isabella traced the slight frown on his

handsome face. She'd never tire of admiring his spectacular body.

"This all happened so fast."

Her heart stuttered when she wondered if he meant their relationship. They bonded together with every passing second, the link between them strengthening until she doubted they could be separated again. At least she hoped... What if he'd changed his mind?

"You and me?"

"Huh?" He tilted his head on the pillow. "Not exactly. I mean, yesterday you were a virgin."

"Technically, that was two days ago." She grimaced, as though one day made any difference.

"You know what I mean, Izzy. You were innocent." He squinted as he considered. "Tonight you're setting my sheets on fire. Am I pushing you too fast?"

"No." When he didn't seem relieved, she shoved his shoulder, rolling him to his back. She climbed on top of him, straddling his hips so she could peer straight into his eyes as she cupped his cheeks in her palms. "Listen, James. I've craved this for so long I gave up hope of securing what I needed. Now I realize it wouldn't have mattered. Unless I'd found you, nothing would have been enough."

"That doesn't mean I need to turn all kinky on you." He scrunched his eyes closed. "Your bastard ex-husband tried to sell you to other men for Christ's sake. What do I do? Flaunt you in front of a roomful of horny dudes and their dates. I'm hardly better than him."

"Don't be ridiculous." She clapped a hand to his chest as she sat upright. "Mason and Tyler share Lacey. Do you think they're in the same league as my ex, who would have shared me?"

"Fuck no." His instant denial had her nodding in return.

"Me either." She winced. "I might have thought so before meeting them. But how can the idea horrify me after I enjoyed you and Jeremy touching me together? Or after I've seen how they look at her? It gives me goose bumps and makes my stomach do flip-flops to stand in the same room as the three of them."

"How do they look at her, princess?" Razor grew quiet as his hands caressed her thighs.

"Kind of like you're looking at me right now," she whispered. "I love you, James."

"I love you too."

"And that makes all the difference."

He guided her hips with unconscious direction from his fingers until she rode the ridge of his awakening hard-on. Still, she could tell his mind lingered on their conversation, which she'd almost forgotten in wake of renewed passion.

"How come you're so smart, Izzy?" He traced the swell of her breast with a worshipping brush of his fingertips.

"Just lucky. So very lucky." She smiled as she leaned forward to kiss him. The slow meshing of their lips and tongues matched the pace of her rocking. With one hand, she searched through the wreckage of the condom box and wrappers, beaming when she secured the last unused packet. "Fate gave me no choice but to figure things out in a hurry when you showed up. I was in the right place at the right time. I thought everything had fallen apart. Until I bumped into you. And I realized this is how things were always meant to be."

The sharp intake of his breath made it seem like he might say something. He closed his mouth, shook his head and scrunched his eyes closed.

She would erase his doubt. Employing one of her newfound skills, she rolled the condom over his erection, eager to cradle him in her body once more. She lifted enough to fit him to her greedy opening then sank onto his shaft, inch by inch.

It wasn't until much later, when she studied his measured breathing as he slept that she wondered what he'd been about to tell her.

"It's a trap." Razor slammed the side of his fist into the refrigerator door. A magnet bounced off, leaving one of his niece's or nephew's artwork to flutter to the floor. "What's the point of having a fucking edge if no one pays attention when it's phoning home loud and clear?"

"We're listening to your gut. Taking extra precautions." Mason attempted to reassure him. Nothing could alleviate the panic rooting in his heart. "We're all attending. JRad will stay right with you, and there will be more undercover cops than actual mourners at this point. It will be all right."

"Son of a bitch, we practically waved the red flag in their

face last night. It'd be impossible to miss the message." He kicked the magnet across the room as he hissed, "Izzy's no longer a twelve-million-dollar virgin. What if they decide she's an inconvenience? A liability?"

"We'll be there to catch them before things spiral out of hand."

"She's been shot once already." He tugged on his hair. "I'd rather not repeat that performance."

"Everyone will wear vests under their coats. We have snipers in the trees onsite. The perimeter is secure. We're prepared." Mason ticked off the points they'd reviewed multiple times.

"Just worry about being there for your girl." Tyler retrieved the drawing. He rested a comforting hand on Razor's shoulder. "She's hurting still over that piece of shit. You have to stay strong for her. We're covering you. Both of you."

Jeremy lingered a respectful pace behind Razor as the young man, decked out in his dress uniform, led Isabella to the gleaming casket to pay her last respects. They'd arranged a private moment so she didn't have to address other guests, especially her father. No one wanted her to deal with that stress on top of her grief.

His gaze flew along the perimeter, checking in with the cops posted at regular intervals. Each flashed a subtle thumbs-up in answer to his silent request. He nodded, satisfied, then positioned himself close enough to protect Isabella's head from any gunmen who might have snuck past their guard. Her tiny stature made it easy to block her from view. At least in one direction. Sandwiched between him and Razor, she had as much coverage as they could afford.

A chill dampness hung in the spring morning air. They tromped across the soggy grass. In places, hints of green shone through the dull grays and browns of winter. The past several months had been long and dark for many of his friends. Hopefully, the change of season would allow sprouts of the new beginnings they'd seeded to bloom into something beautiful.

Yet, the last fingers of winter refused to relinquish their grip. Wisps of fog threaded between the silver trunks of the birch grove surrounding the cemetery. Morose musings fractured his focus as he considered the funerals he'd attended recently—Rob's, Gina's, Jackson's, now Malcolm's. Only one of them a friend. All human. Someday it would be him in the box.

And who would care to weep?

He'd given up hope of discovering the kind of connection Razor and Isabella had made. The soul-deep bond Mason, Tyler and Lacey shared. Because who would accept him when he couldn't accept himself?

Jeremy recommitted himself to his job, to protecting innocent civilians and seeking justice for the victims of crime. That would be enough to matter. His sense of honor affirmed his purpose as the most significant thing in his life. Duty and the unbreakable friendships he had cultivated with the other members of the force and their families.

Crystaline tears dropped from Isabella's glacial eyes. His heart lurched as though her pain were his own, as though she belonged to him because she belonged to his friend and he guarded what was theirs. It was how he worked. He couldn't help it, though he'd learned to veil his possessiveness along with the other facets of his composition modern society deemed improper and overbearing.

Lost in thought, it took him a moment to spot the single anomalous flower among the pile of garish bouquets, sent by people who cared more about the appearance of propriety than the sentiment behind the act.

A black lily.

He spun on his heel, gouging the earth, searching for the one woman he hadn't expected to stumble across at the funeral. The flutter of midnight silk skirts peeked from behind a tree on the fringe of the woods.

Isabella kissed her fingers, touched them to the polished wood and stepped back—her final goodbye said and done. When Razor prepared to lead her to the waiting SUV, driven by a fellow officer, JRad waved them to the side instead. He took point, unwilling to risk dragging them to the departure spot before returning.

What if Lily disappeared in the meantime?

The rookie trained his observant gaze in the direction Jeremy indicated. Once the kid locked onto Jeremy's goal, he followed, tucking Isabella in the crook of his arm. He whispered to her, low enough to avoid exposing their position. She peeked, curious, then kept up with his brisk pace. Smart girl.

Jeremy approached from one side while Razor drew Isabella around the other. They shouldn't have worried about stealth. Lily had collapsed against a moss-covered stump with her shoulders on the bark. Wracked by sob after unrelenting sob, she remained oblivious to their approach.

Isabella glanced between Razor and him for approval. They both nodded their assent. She crouched beside the grieving woman. Lily jumped a solid three inches off the ground when Isabella touched the hand covering her face. Jeremy wished he could have surrounded the broken woman in his arms, soothed her obvious distress.

He'd taken two steps in Lily's direction before he realized it. Something about this woman destroyed his barriers despite the distinct lack of a docile bone in her luscious body.

"Lily?" Isabella crooned in an attempt to break through the shock and pain etched in the other woman's eyes. Black mascara ran in rivulets across the Lily's cheeks, slashing her porcelain skin with onyx strokes. "Are you hurt?"

His stare whipped to Razor. Things could turn ugly if Isabella figured out what they already realized. Lily had cared for the man she'd trained. For Malcolm. The photographs they'd seen guaranteed it. After their brief exchange the night before, he would swear her standing as an amazing Domme meant more than her than her managerial roll at Black Lily.

This woman would never have played so seriously with Malcolm if she hadn't harbored feelings of some caliber or other. The loss of a submissive would stagger her. Had it stopped at valuing his humbling gift or was she in love with the man? It would make all the difference in the world to the situation with Isabella.

Razor tensed when Lily surprised them. She enfolded Isabella in a desperate embrace—which dragged the girl into Lily's lap—holding her tight.

"I'm s-sorry." Lily keened, low and tortured. "So sorry, *sister.*"

"What the—"

Jeremy settled a restraining hand on Razor as they digested the news.

It explained so much.

Sisters.

Of course.

"Sister?" Isabella plopped onto her ass. The women huddled together. Razor's girl studied the features—so similar to hers and yet so different—peering at her, tormented. "What? How is it possible?"

"Half-sister." Lily tried to speak through her tears. "Our father. The same. That m-monster. He did this. I know it. His fault. I should have prevented it. Stopped him."

The choppy confession floored Isabella. Jeremy flinched at the agony twisting her lips into the starring feature in a mask of outrage and disbelief. Razor knelt behind her, his hands cupping her shoulders, which heaved with the effort of staying calm, rational.

"You're saying *my father* is involved in this mess?" Isabella did an admirable job of gathering facts despite the surreal situation. They'd suspected, but they'd had no proof. Nothing she'd told them in her statement had led them closer to their hunches, so they'd refrained from divulging their theories. No reason to upset her further or tip off the man before he made a move they could bust him for. "O-our father. You're...my sister?"

"Yes. So sorry." A fresh batch of tears streamed from Lily's bloodshot eyes when she nodded. She folded her arms around herself, rocking in a futile attempt to ease some of her pain. Her mouth worked. No intelligible sound emerged despite repeated attempts to speak. The breaking of such a strong woman chilled Jeremy.

He couldn't stand to observe a moment longer without going ballistic.

"This isn't the place for this discussion. Let's move somewhere safe. You can tell us the whole story when we're out of the cold. Protected." He swooped in, astonished Lily didn't object when he cradled her in his arms. She settled against his chest, light as a feather—delicate, even bundled in her long black overcoat. How had she seemed larger than life the night before?

"I agree. Let's get the hell out of here." Razor checked over his shoulder. He offered a hand to Isabella. The stunned woman shifted her oversized purse to the opposite shoulder. She enfolded her man's white-gloved fingers in her own, allowing him to tug her upright.

Unwilling to traipse through the media circus at the center

of the clearing with his precious cargo, Jeremy steered the group through the brush to the vehicles waiting on the other side of the hill. While he walked, he whispered to Lily. He couldn't say for sure what nonsense he spouted, but it seemed to work. Her shudders had faded to shivers by the time their car came into sight.

Rodger, the new guy on their team, had been assigned as their driver. He opened the rear door to admit them as they approached. The hair on the nape of Jeremy's neck stood on end, prodding him to secure Lily in the vehicle without hesitation. When he ducked inside the dark interior, he realized his mistake. Someone delivered a sucker punch straight to his jaw. With his hands full, he couldn't block the debilitating blow.

He twisted, sheltering Lily despite the pain obliterating his logic. He tried to call out to Razor. His intended shout sounded more like *oomph* than, "Run!"

The assailant lurking in the shadows kicked him aside. Things happened at lightning speed. Quicker than he could react, the blue spark of a stun gun crackled. Lily deflated beneath him. In the split second since he'd entered the backseat, things had gone straight to hell.

Something pricked his neck. His eyes rolled in their sockets. He struggled to fight unconsciousness, but the jolt to his nape signaled game over. The last thing he thought before darkness enveloped him was that he had to warn Razor before he stepped into the car.

The heavy thud to his right left him no hope. He'd failed Lily, failed Isabella.

Failed them all.

Chapter Twenty-Three

Isabella screamed into the hand muffling her mouth when Razor crashed to the floorboard beside Jeremy's limp, twitching form.

"Get in the car, bitch." The dirty cop slapped her ass as he shoved her. She attempted to bite him, but he avoided her gnashing teeth. Her fists and heels bounced off him as if he were made of steel. "We don't have time for hysterics."

Two other men in uniform stood nearby. She struggled enough to alert them. When they pivoted, she cried. She recognized the goons. How could she forget them drooling over her during her escape from Malcolm? From her father.

Oh God, Lily had told the truth.

Her struggle escalated as she accepted reality. If her father had orchestrated this madness, he had murdered Malcolm—or paid someone else to—as he must have contracted her assassin. Her own father. The moment the hired guns slammed the doors on the SUV, she and her friends would disappear. Like Gerard. Like any competitor who'd ever stood in the path of her father's progress.

Isabella quit fighting. She played possum despite the roaming hands of the dirty cop, who tossed her onto the seat like a sack of potatoes. He chuckled, leering in her direction. "This one's a little delicate. Passed out. Probably too excited over the thought of my giant cock fucking her like her daddy promised I could."

"You wish." The dark-haired muscle sneered. "You ain't packing nothing impressive in those tighty-whities, I bet. Though, after Tiny, your pathetic pecker'd seem gigantic."

The third man snorted at their immature jabs. "The two of

you douchebags can fuck the cops. *I'm* taking first swing at the girl."

As they bickered, Isabella inched her fingers into the open top of her purse. She withdrew the object she sought from the tailored pocket. Her fingertips flew over the bottle until she aligned it as she needed. When the two goons piled in next to her, twisting to fasten their seatbelts, she leapt into action.

Before they knew what hit them, she'd sprayed one then the other in the eyes with her extravagant perfume. The stuff her father had given her. Served him right. The driver turned to investigate their howls, presenting the perfect target to take three squirts to the face.

The men gouged their eyes, writhing in pain. The entire cabin filled with the potent mist, suffocating her. Making it hard to act. She flinched when the side door wrenched open. With a deep breath of the fresh air pouring in, she prepared to spritz as many assholes as it took to break free before losing her lunch or collapsing for real this time.

Damn, this crap is strong.

"Police!" Mason's bark had her sagging to her knees in relief. "Everyone down. Hands where I can see them."

Clint and Matt bounded over her to secure the attackers, dragging the dirtbags from the car. The cops shoved the criminals face down on the ground. Someone grabbed the driver, treating him to a similar introduction to the hard earth.

She couldn't have cared less about what happened to them. James, Jeremy and Lily were all that mattered. Had she gotten them killed?

"Isabella. Stop." Tyler peeled her fingers from the sleeve of Razor's jacket as she attempted to roll him onto his back. "I'll bring him out. Let me through, sweetheart. Let me help."

He wrapped his hands around her waist, prying her from the motionless bodies. The horizon shifted around her as she struggled to find her balance. Mason enfolded her in his arms as he lowered her to the ground outside.

She moaned, horrified, when the motion left her panting. A gush of wetness spread between her thighs. What the hell was wrong with her? This wasn't the time to start lusting after Razor's friends.

"Shh." He tried to soothe her. Gentle passes of his hands made the situation worse, not better. "Are you hurt?"

Isabella bit her lip to keep from whimpering. Heat singed her extremities. Blackness encroached on the fringes of her vision and desire pulsed in her core. Something was wrong. So wrong. "H-help me."

"You're safe, honey." He cocked his head, taking in her elevated respiration even as she attempted to disguise it.

From behind them, one of the other cops gave a shout. "Medical assistance, over here. Something's not right."

She could relate. The universe spun before her.

"Razor!" She tried to check on him. She couldn't find him. Couldn't think past the throbbing in her pussy.

Her frantic gaze whipped from side to side. The three men she'd sprayed grunted and groaned as they undulated on the ground. In her hazy vision, they looked as if they humped the muddy landscape. The idea of their debauchery turned her on instead of disgusting her.

"Whoa!" Mason clamped his arms around her, stilling her unconscious motions as she rubbed herself on his leg for relief. "What the fuck?"

"Help me," she shrieked this time. Unable to stop—unable to find her lover—she panicked, thrashing until Mason lunged for something on the ground. "Razor!"

"I'm sorry, Izzy."

"W-what—" She never finished the sentence.

Mason brushed her hair aside then stunned her into unconsciousness. The blackness delivered relief.

Razor counted several dozen regular beeps of the monitoring equipment before attempting to open his heavy lids. Christ, he'd had some vivid dreams this time. He could have sworn he'd been on the outside. He fantasized about that a lot while in the hospital.

"His hand moved, Jeremy." An angel spoke from beside him. Must be a new nurse. "I felt it."

"I think he's waking up, baby."

"Izzy?" The familiar rasp of his dry, cracked throat ripped through the hushed room.

"I'm right here." Butterfly kisses from her supple lips dusted his forehead, his cheek and his lips.

Holy shit. It had been real. All of it.

He'd found his soulmate then almost lost her. Again.

He blinked sporadically until the blinding glare from the window became bearable. The dark figures between him and the wall came into focus. Mason and Tyler. From the size of the shoulders leaning on the jam, he'd say Matt and Clint had the door covered.

JRad, Izzy and Lily all sported nasty gowns like the one barely covering his ass, but they sat up, alert, while he battled to rejoin the land of the living.

"What the fuck happened?" A hit from a stun gun shouldn't have landed them in this antiseptic hellhole. He started swiping wires from his arm and temple. He'd had enough of that shit to last him a lifetime.

"Damn it, kid." Mason laughed, his relief pervading the room. "You better not let Jambrea or Valerie catch you. They'll tattle to Lacey. Then you'll really be in trouble."

Izzy's soft hand landed over the IV, preventing him from tugging it free. "Leave this. It's almost done. They're counteracting the drug as best they can."

"Drug?"

"Can you run through it one more time, Lily?" JRad brushed a stray lock of raven hair from the woman's forehead. He loomed close to where she rested on the edge of her own bed, not three feet away.

The Domme nodded. Back straight, collected, she briefed him on what she knew.

"I'm not sure how much you remember..."

A gap big enough to drive a semi through ruined his memory. The loss unsettled him.

Isabella must have sensed his unease. She slid beneath his covers and snuggled into the curve of his chest as though made to fit. Because she had been. He squeezed her, grateful.

"Okay." Lily met his curious look dead on. Her confidence impressed him. He noticed JRad's palm lingering on her lower back. She didn't object. "Perry Buchanan, Isabella's father, is my father too."

Somewhere in the recess of his mind the information tingled. He knew that. Hard to believe, but he nodded. Razor curled his arm around Isabella. "Are you okay with all this, princess?"

"I'm working on it." When she glanced up from beneath those sinful lashes, he noted the puffiness around her eyes. Shit, she'd needed him and he'd been lying unconscious, worthless. What the hell had gone down? "I wish I had known. So many years apart."

When Izzy glanced at the other woman, longing seeped from every pore of her being. Despite the past, or because of it, they wouldn't lose each other again. They'd connected. Lily had suffered as much as Isabella.

Maybe more.

"I've always known and wished I didn't." The dark version of his princess locked her hands in her lap as she spoke, almost as though she confessed. Could what she had to say be so bad?

"Buchanan would visit my mother, who might as well have been a whore. She'd spread her legs for that bastard time after time, in the hopes he'd spare his pocket change. She played his kinky games, allowed him to hurt her—anything he liked—while I pretended to be asleep in the corner of our one-room shithole. Sometimes he'd take his fill then leave her with nothing. I swear he enjoyed his ultimate power over her more than the sex. If she'd used the cash to pay the rent, to hold us over and find a real job, I might have understood. But, no... She'd drink it all the first night, leaving us to starve the next day, week or month until he deigned to return.

"Each day she spent dry, her meanness blossomed. My mother tolerated me at the best of times. If I made myself useful. She'd only kept me in the hopes of conning Buchanan for cash. He knew it and used it to keep me in line. I see that now." Lily's fingers balled into a fist. "I grew bitter when I had to choose between stealing or eating out of a dumpster to survive. I have too much pride for either. One of many disgusting traits I inherited from Daddy dearest."

JRad ran his fingers along the weave of her thick onyx braid, which flopped onto the bed after trailing down the center of her back. She shifted several inches out of his reach.

The tight lines at the corner of JRad's grimace and the entranced attention of the audience had Razor wondering if she'd shared the cold hard facts earlier, waiting to divulge the grimy details this once. The telling couldn't be easy.

"Always, always he would remind me of his *real* daughter. Surrounded in a house that looked like a castle. Once, I found a picture of what I imagined on the side of a cereal box in the trash I picked through. I'd focus on the stained cardboard to block out the sounds at night, imagining my sister and how she'd find me and bring me to live with her someday. When he noticed my prize, he cultivated my jealousy. He twisted it into something sick instead of something productive. By the time I turned twelve, I hated Isabella."

Razor tightened his grip on Izzy. Lily's gaze held echoes of the past. The hint of her resentment scared the shit out of him. This woman had allowed a pack of men to abuse his princess. Did she still harbor her malicious intent?

"I tried to find work—tried to look older or dress as a boy." She cursed. "I'm stuck with this worthless body and no one would believe my lies or give me a chance to take on manual labor. They didn't think I could handle it."

A scrawny, younger version of this gorgeous woman wouldn't have inspired his faith either. Plus, who'd be brute enough to pawn something menial off on a child? No man could live with himself after that, even if he hoped to hire some help.

"Not too long after that, maybe two years, my mom disappeared. Went out one night and never came home. I figured she finally chose the wrong John. Pushed her luck too far."

JRad reached for her. She froze him with glare that couldn't have been more alarming if daggers had bristled from her eyes. "Enough. Do not touch me again without permission, cop."

Holy Mistress! His friend nodded and halted his approach. He also refused to increase the space between them. He stayed, a fraction of an inch from contact with her creamy skin. Interesting.

"My father came to the apartment a few days later. He told me he'd give me a job. A position of power. One I could make my own. He said he could see the fire burning my soul. He understood the heat, and he promised to teach me how to tame it."

Tyler spun on his heel, burying his fingers in his hair.

"It wasn't until years later that I learned he'd killed her. And how painful it had been..."

"None of his sins are on you." JRad tried again to soothe her.

"I know. My mother, the fool, had threatened to share information with someone investigating that pig fucker. She was dumb enough to try to play the player himself." She shook her head. "Crazy bitch. No, his black soul will burn in hell for all he's done. But what I did while I was blind is all mine.

"He brought me to his club, thrilled me by lending it my name. I trained with the best Masters in the business, learned to control my rage and honed my desire for success. Sometimes he mandated I observe him with his own pets. Always informative. He has skills. He can worm into people's minds then rot them from the inside out. I'll give the bastard that."

She closed her eyes for a moment.

"I inherited his sadistic talent and his appetite for control. God knows, I never had much of it in my early years. I began to love discovering a man or woman's greatest weakness. I'd use it to bring them to their knees before building them back up. I can harness the power they surrender to grant them everything they want, even if they don't know what that is when we begin."

She sighed, a wistful smile tugging the corner of her mouth. Razor caught JRad rearranging his package.

"One day at work netted me more than a month at any other nine to five I could have scored. Plus, I won't lie. I craved the rush. I'm the best in the scene at what I do."

JRad looked as though he might challenge her declaration until a hand signal from Mason quieted him. They couldn't afford for her to clam up.

"About five years ago, I realized Buchanan had conned me too. I found a camera in one of my playrooms. Not the safety camera. Something completely different." Lily flipped her braid over her shoulder. She slapped the end against her thigh fast enough to produce a sharp sting. Razor winced. "That fucker used me to generate blackmail. God knows how many of my subs he forced to dance to his tune when he had them by the balls."

"I'm not judging, Lily. I swear." Isabella spoke up. "But why did you stay? What made you continue? You're so strong, so free. You're not naïve or a coward, like me. You could have run."

"I don't run from anyone." Lily sneered. "And it wasn't that simple. Around that time, something happened. Something I couldn't walk away from."

Razor squeezed Izzy, bracing for what he knew would

follow. It made perfect sense now.

"Buchanan brought me a new slave. A very willing submissive who begged to serve me. Our father told me the man was my reward. The stuff of dreams for a Domme to train."

She shrugged. "No Hallmark card for this occasion, sister. He gifted Malcolm to me with orders to break the man. Your husband loved our father until nothing else mattered, his devotion pure and unfailing. He'd have done anything I instructed to please Buchanan."

No one could call Isabella stupid. "Daddy ordered Malcolm to marry me, didn't he?"

"I'm sorry. Truly."

Razor couldn't say what he expected. The smile on Izzy's face when she turned to him certainly wasn't it, though. Her grin had him worried she'd lost it. Until she explained.

"You were right, James." A lone tear trickled across her cheek. He didn't detect any sadness in it, only relief. "Our marriage never existed. I'm not crazy. He *was* my friend sometimes. Until Daddy warned him to back off. God, how stupid I was."

"You had no chance at understanding." Lily drew their attention once more. "They're experts at twisting reality. In business they were nearly unstoppable. I didn't see the full extent of their corruption right away, either. Hell, I had more experience by the time I was seven than you did when you were seventeen and even I couldn't fathom it all."

"How old are you now, Lily?"

"The same age as you. Our birthdays are less than a month apart."

"But that means..."

"Yeah, I was barely seventeen. It's just an age." The guys gaped at her, their mouths hanging open. "I was ready for the challenge. You probably don't want to hear this, but Malcolm had a core of goodness. I think, if things had been different, he would have come to love you. Unfortunately, his physical...limitations...combined with his subservient bearing left him susceptible to the evil our father rained on him."

Isabella nodded, her hair brushing the inside of Razor's arm. She lit up each of his nerve endings touching her with her subtle motions. What the hell was wrong with him? He forced himself to focus on Lily's story.

"I came to care for the man. He didn't deserve our father's abuse. I treasured his absolute obedience. I felt an odd connection to him. Fuck knows, I understand what it's like to be manipulated by Buchanan. In the beginning, I stayed because I didn't want anything to happen to my charge. I can't tell you how many times I had to intervene to keep our father from causing permanent damage—especially once he began to have trouble getting it up. He took out his fury over his impotence on Malcolm. The stupid man would have borne it and begged for more. Buchanan destroyed every sacred rule in the D/s lifestyle yet no one else dared to stop him. They're all terrified of the bastard."

Lily gulped.

Razor made eye contact with Mason, Tyler and JRad. They all projected the same determination he felt broiling in his gaze. They made a silent promise to each other. Lily would never discover how much Buchanan had made Malcolm suffer at the end. The crime scene investigators had unanimously declared it the most gruesome case of their careers.

"Then, Buchanan started dumping women in the dungeons. They were fucked up. All of them. I noticed the wildness in the monster's eyes when he would visit. The first few times, I thought I imagined the manic glee. It became apparent after a while. He'd fly into a frenzy and fuck Malcolm until he bled. When that wasn't enough, he'd move on to one of the dozens of other souls who'd fallen under his spell. I couldn't protect them all. Buchanan's control disintegrated. He lost his aptitude for devising twisted power plays in favor of sheer brutality."

"He started using." JRad shook his head.

"Using what?" Razor couldn't contain his curiosity any longer.

"The drug. If it has a name, I don't know it. I think the weak form started out as Harmytal, but who wants to fuck a zombie doped on a date rape drug when you can ramp up the dosage until your victim is so hot for you it hurts?"

Mason and Tyler tensed. They had personal experience with Harmytal. Someone had used it on Lacey last year. The association drove things home. Before they could rage, Lily continued.

"It's so protected, I don't have much info though both

Malcolm and Buchanan take...no, took...it regularly in the last six months." She lifted a sculpted eyebrow in Razor's direction. "You can see why. Even after five hours, the drug's making your impressive cock hard as steel beneath that skimpy sheet and Officer Eveready here has excused himself three times to jack off in the bathroom. Babycakes is doing the best job of hiding her arousal. The fog clouding her eyes reminds me of the vacant stares I've grown used to from women in my dungeon, but she has lots of practice with repression."

"Lily!" JRad snapped. They all turned, shocked, at the iron in his tone.

"Old habits die hard, sweets." The Mistress winked, undeterred, before continuing. "They stashed some of the new formula in Isabella's perfume. I suspect they used a weakened version to coerce her for some time. Hell, you said it was a wedding gift, yes? Probably right from the start. Father's a genius at crafting elaborate schemes. He takes something and twists it until lances of pain jut out in every direction. I can't tell you how much he enjoyed marrying Isabella off to Malcolm when he knew I cared for the man. Or how he delighted in rubbing it in my face at every opportunity—another thing she had that I never would."

"Mother fucker."

"Father fucker in this case." Lily sneered.

Razor could see where she'd excel at intimidation.

"That asshole used the women to experiment on then sold off his damaged guinea pigs as unwilling slaves. How could I stand for that to happen? I've tried, for close to a year now, to unearth more information—to set things right and build a case—before he catches me and shuts me down. He'll take me out. All I want before I die is to see him lose once."

JRad risked his limb, and his manhood, by reaching for her. This time she allowed him to comfort her.

"I smuggled as many of the women out as I could, spent my savings to make it look like they'd been sold. I have no use for his dirty money. I placed a dozen others with men I trust, who are keeping them safe until we can figure this out." Her veneer cracked the slightest bit when her breath hitched. "But I couldn't save Malcolm."

"You tried," JRad murmured.

"Yeah, what, with a bunch of grainy pictures? I gave them

to Isabella, hoping she would leave, save herself as she did." The woman nodded in their direction. "I prayed she'd divorce Malcolm and I'd be there to break him away from Buchanan—to care for him. I should have known diminishing his usefulness to my father would end with him murdered instead."

JRad leaned in slow, as though waiting for her to reject his advance. When she didn't, he whispered in her ear, something meant for her alone. Whatever it was, it worked.

She calmed, sighing as some of the lines of tension faded from her creased brow. "Sometimes fate is a bitch. The manufacturing process for their drug requires precision, which is difficult to maintain when you're hooked on your own junk. God, it must be unbelievably addictive. One of the techs fucked up and started a fire that burned their research station to the ground the day before Isabella escaped Malcolm. That's how I was able to delay the arrival of her buyer."

"So you're saying..."

"Yes. The bottle Isabella has is all that's left." Lily grimaced. "I think they can make more or they'd have hunted her harder. Still, it takes time to rebuild. Now our father knows I've betrayed him. I need your help to destroy them before they can reestablish their operations. They'll be stronger this time."

Razor noted she didn't beg. Not even for something she'd risked her life for many times over.

Chapter Twenty-Four

After the IV of God-knew-what had finished emptying into his system, Razor gathered their clothes then shuffled to the bathroom while Izzy held his gown shut. It'd taken him longer to recover from the stun and the drug because of his recent injuries. Plus, they suspected—since he'd lain closest to Isabella—he'd been exposed to a higher dosage of the drug.

Fuck, Lily had been right. His balls ached like he hadn't had sex in a decade though he and Izzy had gotten it on at every opportunity over the past couple of days.

"James?"

"Yeah?" She snapped him out of his musings. His jeans crumpled in his hands. Their gowns puddled around their bare feet.

"It wasn't me. All that time, it wasn't me. I mean, it was. Just not because there was something wrong with me."

"What the hell are you talking about, princess?" He lifted her until she sat on the wide sink in the stark institutional bathroom so he could look into her captivating eyes.

"Malcolm never wanted me because I'm not...dominant." She blew out a giant sigh. "Our wedding night, it turned him on when I attacked him. He hated when I waited for him to make love to me. He came with me on top of him, when I scratched him. How didn't I notice? Why didn't I guess? He knew it wasn't in my nature. He knew it wouldn't make me happy, so he pushed me away after that. I couldn't be what he needed. That doesn't make me defective."

"Jesus Christ, Izzy!" Razor slammed their mouths together, unable to think beyond his need to prove her desirability. How could she have doubted it?

When she broke for air, she added between licks and nips, “I mean, he needed help. I’ll always wish I could have seen that—could have done more—but it wasn’t my fault. I didn’t make him the way he was. I didn’t drive him to the insane place he ended up. Thank God. Thank God.”

She crushed her lips onto his, sucking his tongue into her mouth as she clawed his shoulders.

He chuckled between searing kisses. “You’re doing a damn fine job of mauling me for someone who claims to be docile.”

Izzy laughed too. “I think it’s the drug, persisting. Can you feel it? My body is humming. Like the day they took me to the dungeon at Black Lily. Do you remember? How I told you about my arousal? How it felt unnatural? Inappropriate. I’m not completely fucked up. It was the drug. Thank God.”

“Oh, shit. I’m so sorry I didn’t understand.” Razor wanted to say so much, to confirm her relief. He hadn’t realized she carried all that doubt and anxiety inside. And, the truth was, he *did* feel the effects. Lust coursed through his veins. His cock jammed, hard as granite, into the edge of the sink where he stood between Izzy’s spread legs. He couldn’t force himself to retreat.

“Not your fault. You couldn’t have known. I didn’t know my own reactions well enough to understand how abnormal this feeling is. It’s like my body’s on fire.” She propped her feet beside her on the porcelain then tipped her shoulders until they rested on the mirror. She ran her hands from her neck over her breasts to her pussy. “James, I’ll die if I can’t have you inside me soon.”

“Fuck, yes. I can smell you.” Her arousal hid the reek of disinfectant he’d learned to despise during his extended stay here. Making one fantastic memory would go a long way toward helping him forget the months of suffering he’d endured between these walls.

Her pink-painted toes curled over the rim of the sink when he bent to lap at the moisture drenching her. She shrieked as she grabbed the edges for support. He feasted on her flesh. He’d barely begun to whet his hunger when she tensed. She shattered, riding his face as she came apart in record time.

Izzy screamed his name

“Everything all right in there?” JRad called from the other side of the door.

"Go away," he and Izzy hollered in unison.

Masculine chuckles drifted into nothing as their friends granted them some privacy.

"Where was I?" He growled into her sodden folds when she began to move. "Stay. I think we need to start over."

"No, fuck me." She tugged on his hair.

"Soon."

"Now."

She changed her tune when his tongue probed around the hard bump of her clit. This time he couldn't deny himself the weight of her perky breasts resting in his palms. He pinched her tight nipples. Izzy came again, flooding his mouth with her juice.

He stood, sharing the flavor with her in a smoldering kiss.

Shuddering with continued pleasure, Isabella wrapped her arms around his neck, her legs around his waist and clung to him. The white-hot heat of her pussy pressed to the stiffest hard-on he'd ever had. It bobbed in time to his pounding heart.

Razor reached below her thigh to grasp the base of his cock. He angled it toward her as she flexed her thighs, rising up to make room. After he fit the leaking head to her opening, he grasped her hips. His hands easily spanned her back, his fingers meshing in the middle, over her spine.

Izzy moaned. She interlocked their bodies with a sinuous gyration of her abdomen. He watched in wonder as she orgasmed the moment her clit stroked his pelvic bone, his cock lodged in the depths of her pussy. Staying stationary proved impossible.

Who wouldn't become addicted to this?

He palmed her ass, spreading the cheeks as he lifted her. Her climax extended, seeming to crest with every full stroke he made into her clenching sheath. She came and came on him, strangling his engorged shaft with impossibly strong spasms.

When gravity ceased to generate enough friction, he spun. They banged into the door. He pinned her chest with his as he pistoned into her, utilizing more force than he thought appropriate. She encouraged him with husky dirty talk, begging for more.

Razor fucked her. Hard, fast and deep until he couldn't possibly resist the animal instincts urging him to release, to fill her greedy pussy with his come. He had to mark her, stake his claim. Because he loved her and no other man would have this with her.

"Do it. James. Make me yours."

He groaned.

In harmony with his every move, her lids fluttered open, sharing the ecstasy he'd given her. Continued to give her inch-by-inch, over and over. The naughty grin spreading across her reddened lips tempted him beyond sanity.

"No one else will ever come inside me. Only you. God, yes." She clenched her pussy around him. The fierce rhythm of his thrusts degenerated into spastic rams. "Do it."

Razor shouted her name. His love. He pumped her so full, his semen overflowed her tiny pussy, dripping onto her ass and his balls. He came as she shuddered, lost in her own euphoric climax. All the while, her gaze stayed fixed on his.

She whispered a thousand times, "I love you."

Nothing had ever sounded so sweet or felt as good as those three words, falling softly from her lips.

Razor grinned at the knowing smile on the face of each woman ringing the nurses' station. During the months he'd spent here, these ladies had become part of his family. He could see them practically chomping at the bit for a peek of his princess.

Izzy's manners always amused him. She knew exactly the right thing to do in any social situation. Even the awkward kind where she emerged, thoroughly fucked, from a public-ish restroom.

"Hello. I'm Isabella. It's my pleasure to meet the women who provided such amazing care of James. Lacey told me a little about you and, I have to say, if you're anything like her...my guy was in good hands." She skipped the handshakes and went straight for full-on squeezy hugs. Another tendency he adored about the sprite. By the time she'd smothered Valerie, giggled with Jambrea and permitted Dr. Joy to envelop her, they'd become fast friends.

God help him.

"That young man is a devil to take care of. You're going to have your hands full," Valerie, sporting some new purple highlights in her silver hair, teased.

"It looks like she knows how to settle him down." Jambrea laughed, winking in his direction. He adored the naughty side he'd found lurking under the shy nurse's exterior.

"Let's hear it, Dr. Joy." He shook his head as he waited. "What do you have to add?"

"I can't express how happy I am you've found someone to bring light back to those sexy eyes of yours." She embraced him with one arm and Izzy with the other. "I hate to see one of my favorite cops off their game. You, my dear, are a miracle worker. And one lucky bitch to score our Razor. There'll be a bunch of broken hearts around the hospital cafeteria today."

Isabella beamed. She rose on her tiptoes to kiss him. "I know."

"Dr. McHottie, is that any way to talk in front of the kids?" Tyler approached from the cheap, plastic bucket chair he'd occupied while guarding their room. "Sorry to break up the reunion. Mason will freak if we're not on the curb in the next two minutes. I told him I'd come in to retrieve our little lovebirds five minutes ago."

"Oh boy." Jambrea winced. "You'd better walk fast."

"Yeah, Captain Hardass puts his crankypants on if I'm a minute behind schedule." Tyler shook his head in mock disgust.

"He worries because he loves you." Valerie waved as they turned to leave. "Stay safe."

Razor tugged his jeans over his hips without bothering to button them. He kissed Isabella's cheek then abandoned the supple warmth of her sleeping form for the cold leather of the couch. Not exactly an upgrade but he had work to do.

He checked the volume on his stereo—nice and low—then flipped through his playlist until a song struck a chord. "Sirens" by Angels and Airwaves flooded the space, which seemed warmer, cozy, when Izzy shared it with him.

A twitch at the corner of his eye forced him to scrub his face with his shaking hands before extracting the interoffice envelope JRad had deposited beneath the sofa cushion. From inside it, he withdrew a manila folder.

Razor opened the file and spread the contents across the surface of the coffee table. A noise from the other room had him tossing a glance over his shoulder. Izzy rolled onto her opposite side before settling into deep sleep once again. His stiff fingers buffed the smile from his face.

Today, hell, the entire week, had been filled with an infinite stream of unpleasant surprises for his princess. She'd taken each lump like a trooper, adapting and making the best of the shitty situations. How long could she keep it up? What would be the last straw? How much more could she take?

If they didn't resolve things soon they'd slip one day and leave her exposed.

Recent developments had convinced a judge to unseal several investigations involving Perry Buchanan. The one Razor selected from the pile had his blood pressure rising until he thought steam might pour from his ears.

Grotesque images of a young, broken woman littered the pages. Isabella's mother. She'd fallen from the balcony of the master suite on the third floor of their mansion. The spikes topping the decorative wrought-iron fence around her flower beds had impaled her, instantly killing both her and the unborn child she'd carried.

Homicide had suspected Buchanan of shoving the woman. As with all the other alleged offenses, they'd never been able to gather enough intel to hold in court and convince a jury. Evidence had gone missing, been tainted and warrants had yielded nothing. With money and power, Buchanan had managed to stay a step ahead of the law for decades.

The pen shook in Razor's fingers as he attempted to add notes to his log. He'd jotted major developments in his reports each night as required for his assignment. Tonight, he couldn't seem to clear his mind and document without emotion. Maybe the drug continued to affect him. He couldn't seem to bury his fury as he had in the past.

When he read the final details of the "accidental death" file, the pen snapped in half.

Below the bullets on time of death, a damning statement followed. "Mole lost. Daughter—Isabella Buchanan—remains on premises per Judge Wineman. Future informant prospects preserved."

Razor could read through the fucking lines. Izzy's mom had helped the authorities. She'd tried to put her husband away, probably to ensure her daughter's future. And how had her sacrifice been rewarded? Not only had Buchanan murdered her, but also, the men who should have saved her daughter had abandoned the girl instead.

In the hopes of a future lead, they'd left an innocent as long-term bait.

Red haze obscured his vision. An organization that would condone an act so heinous wasn't one he was proud to serve. He'd had enough lies, lived enough nights in the shadows.

He stormed to the door and flung it open. "Clint."

Where the fuck had his fellow officer gone? He needed someone to cover the apartment so he could cool down. Take his bike for a quick drive. How the fuck could they have done this to Izzy?

They'd had the power to stop it yet had chosen not to. The knowledge shook his foundational belief in the system.

"Matt."

He glanced down as he fished his phone from his pocket, intending to text the guys on duty. Where the hell had they disappeared to?

Before he wiggled the device free, a whisper of sensation caught his attention. He turned in time to use his forearm to deflect something solid—his Slugger—aimed at the crown of his head. His phone flew out of his grip. It bounced across the landing. His damn pants slid lower as he stepped back, strangling his legs, limiting his movement. The man in the shadows took advantage, shoving him as he teetered off balance.

Razor tumbled ass over teakettle down the stairs, hitting his head on the post at the bottom. For the second time in one day, stars faded to black.

His primary concern was for Izzy but, when he realized he couldn't shout a warning, he hoped he'd at least managed to keep his full moon from hanging out when he died.

He prayed for his princess's safety—prayed for his friends—as the world fell away.

Isabella woke to darkness. She groaned then shifted, trying to stretch the kinks from her shoulders. Her arms yanked to a halt, bound behind her. The abrupt jarring tore her stitches. Blood oozed from her gunshot wound, warming her skin. She blinked several times, waiting for her night vision to clear. It never did. Instead, the pressure of fabric over the bridge of her nose dawned in her mind. Blindfolded.

She whimpered.

"Ah, there you are. Did you miss me, daughter?"

She shivered at the fanatical tinge to her father's greeting.

"Too bad you won't be staying long." He *tsked* then ripped the covering from her face. She squinted, but couldn't make out anything while her vision adjusted. "Couldn't have you peeking if you woke up early from your nap. No more chances for escape. No more mistakes. No more guardian fucking angels. You're as slippery as your old man to catch. Harder still to exterminate."

"Daddy, listen. You need help..." She hated the weak child in her who attempted to reason with him when she had no hope of success.

"Now you sound like your mother." He overturned a metal cart, scattering supplies to the corners of the linoleum floor. The resulting crash hurt her ears. "I don't need your opinion. Don't plan to give up all that I am, all that I have. For what? Some fool's perception of how things should be? Right and wrong are for the masses who can't do shit about where they stand. I make my own rules. My own fate. No one can stop me."

"You can't sustain this." She tried again to reach him, stalling for time. As her sight returned, she scanned her surroundings—white walls, clinical machinery, stainless fixtures. She'd found their new laboratory. If only she could figure out the location and fill in the men in blue, she'd rest easy. Even if they came too late for her. She could help the women he'd victimized and all the rest who would suffer if her father succeeded. Her life could mean something. "They're going to stop you."

"Says who? The puny cop *assigned* to fuck you?"

His taunt imparted a flash of panic. She tried to conceal it. Her father latched on to the flicker of doubt like a pitbull lunging for the jugular.

"You didn't really believe his nonsense did you, Isabella? The same mistake twice? Malcolm first, your cop second? You've always been so fucking gullible it sickens me." Her father zoomed in. She thought he might spit in her face. Instead, he settled for snarling so close she could count his nose hairs. "I fear I encouraged your trust. It made my life easier. I still wish you had some spine of your own."

She had to remain calm and avoid falling into his traps. Why should she believe him over James? Or Lily? What would the strong Mistress do if it had been her chained to the wall instead? "You want me to be more like my sister?"

"Ah, she told you. Nicely played." Sick pride tugged a grin from his maroon face. "Yes, I have to respect her tenacity. Now *there's* a daughter to be proud of. Unlike you. Fuck, the only thing you were good for was trading. The Scientist cut his offer in half. Six milliliters. You're lucky he'll take you at all after that mutt ruined you."

"Milliliters. Not millions." She hadn't meant to murmur aloud. Her fuzzy mind struggled to catch up. Finally, something made sense. "You traded my virginity for drugs?"

"What the fuck do I need more money for?" The hatred churning in her father's gaze soured her stomach. She hadn't really believed the extent of his insanity before now. "The drug is so rare, so strong, no amount of cash could convince the Scientist to part with the supply. Not after the sample he gave us proved its potency. I funded the lion's share of the venture. My sizable investment earned me seven milliliters. One of which we used in your perfume. What a waste. Then again, we didn't want to experiment on ourselves. Besides, for you, the fool would have given me enough to last until full production kicks in. A damn fine bargain. I don't have much left. I have to be careful."

"I thought everything was destroyed?"

"Pay attention." Her father gripped the chains she hung from. He shook them, sending bolts of pain through her arms. "The lies your fake boyfriend told you stretched far and wide I'm sure. You can't believe anything he said."

Lily had told her about the fire, not James.

Isabella should have ignored his delusion, but allowing her father to demean Razor felt like a betrayal. "I love him. And he loves me. Nothing you say will convince me otherwise."

Buchanan—it became harder to think of him as her father by the second—grabbed his middle then doubled over with uncontrolled guffaws.

"Fool." He spun around to rummage through some documents on a desk nearby. When he found the one he sought, he held it aloft in triumph. "Care to read his case notes? His assignment is right here in his own pathetic chicken scratch. I'm shocked he's literate at all. His superiors gave him one last chance to save his career by going undercover on that ridiculous farce of a dance show you signed up for. They ordered him to befriend you. His mission... Dig up information on your darling husband and yours truly. Another pesky mosquito to be splattered. They pop up every so often. I've never met one yet who couldn't be bribed or eliminated without much fuss."

"Razor isn't like that. He won't quit. And he would never take your money. He's honest."

"Really? No trust required here, Isabella. Look for yourself."

The sheaf of papers rustled as he thrust them in front of her face. She recognized the handwriting. Razor had drafted an incident report after the explosion at her apartment. It looked identical. The match screamed his involvement in black and white. Snippets jumped off the lined pages to rip her heart out.

Investigation initiated. Initial contact with suspect successful. Meeting arranged for ten tomorrow.

She pictured Razor's fury the day he'd kept their appointment at the mall. Why else would he have showed?

Suspect avoids discussion of her husband and father. Suspicious behavior following morning break. Message located on cell phone. Confirmed communication intercepted by Officer Radisson.

He'd invaded her privacy. They all had. Stealing her phone to read her messages, misinterpreting the threat she'd received. They'd thought she was involved.

Hell, they'd taken her downtown for questioning.

"No!" She thrashed in her bonds, oblivious to the physical pain assaulting her. Nothing could hurt worse than the knife stabbing through her back, into her heart.

"Wonder if he collected hazard pay for fucking you?" Buchanan shook his head. "It couldn't have been much fun for him. A virgin with no idea how to please a man. He must have been disappointed when you had nothing relevant to share during your pillow talk."

She didn't know she cried until her father ridiculed her tears.

"You'd think marrying Malcolm would have robbed you of your pitiful delusions. Christ, you're a stupid one. As dumb as your mother." He slammed his fist into a lever on the wall. Her bonds cut loose, dropping her to the floor in a pile of chain and wire. "Try not to let the Scientist figure that out until I have my supply. After the fire, we're lucky he had this much remaining in his safe. Otherwise, I'd have shown you what it really means to suffer."

Isabella couldn't find the strength to fight. Nothing mattered. Her entire life had been a lie. Her father was right. She'd been a moron. Again and again.

"I'd love to mark you, but I don't want to give him reason to withhold my due. Guard!" A giant man with a slash across his right eye lumbered into the room. "Take her to the holding area. Keep her there until it's time for transport. If you fuck up, I'll kill you."

"Yes, sir." His grimy hands encircled Isabella's neck as he yanked her from the floor. When she refused to walk, he threw her over his gnarled shoulder.

"Say hello to Gerard." Buchanan's laughter reverberated into the hallway. She bounced with each of the man's stomps. "If he's alive. You might want to hurry."

Chapter Twenty-Five

Isabella clung to the brute lugging her around the corner in the hallway. He picked up his pace, breaking into a trot. Gerard. She had to compartmentalize the portion of her spirit that wailed in agony in order to help her friend. Whether the end came quick for her or took a slower, more painful route, she'd have plenty of time to rehash the damning facts Buchanan had presented. After she'd done what she could for Gerard.

She gasped at the thought of the older man—alone, afraid and broken. What would she find when she reached him?

"Sorry, miss," the mammoth guard whispered. "Have to hurry. Not much time."

His gentle tone surprised her. Relying on instinct, she slapped his back several times in a row to secure his attention. "Put me down. I can run."

"Good. Stay quiet." Ridiculous to trust this oaf. Would she never learn her lesson? Then again, what greater trouble could she find herself in at this point? She no longer believed Razor would rescue her. Would he even attempt it? Probably, because the men in blue had their sights on her father. Clearly, they'd do a hell of a lot for their positions.

If she had any hope of saving Gerard, she'd have to do it herself.

She'd entangled him in this mess, she'd set it to rights. At least she'd try. If nothing else, she'd hold his hand and prevent him from dying alone. It'd always been her biggest fear. One she seemed doomed to live out.

Isabella stumbled when her gargantuan escort took a flight of open, steel stairs three at a time. He checked over his shoulder before unlocking a door on the right side of the landing. She didn't hesitate to ask why he helped her when she spotted the crumpled form cowering in the corner.

"Not again."

The cross between a plea and an oath terrified her.

"Shush, Gerard." She sprinted toward the trembling man. He scurried away in a grotesque imitation of a half-smashed bug.

Isabella dropped to her knees. She crawled the remaining distance between them, hoping her non-threatening posture would penetrate the cocoon of terror engulfing her friend.

"It's me. I would never hurt you." She repeated herself until he stopped retreating.

"Little bell?" His confusion sent a chill down her spine. How out of it was he?

"Yes, Gerard." She subconsciously moved to hug him.

He flinched hard enough he collapsed onto his side and didn't rise again.

"I'm here." She sobbed when she noted the damage to his face, his body. It took her a while to recognize his nudity. Bruises peppered every inch of his skin. Blood oozed from uncounted abrasions. His face had swollen so much she hardly recognized him.

"What have they done to you?" She wept, aching to comfort him. How could she do so when he feared her contact?

"They raped him."

Isabella spun to face the gentle giant who'd delivered her.

"Too many times to count. Mr. Buchanan ordered the lab techs to use tiny droplets of the test formula on the guards until they went berserk. He observed. They documented the frenzy. They didn't intervene. They made us hurt him. Again and again. Couldn't stop. Didn't want to...felt so good..."

His face turned an unhealthy shade of green, matching his dazed eyes.

"When I tried to stop, they turned on me." He gestured to the slice on his face. "I took out three or four before they dosed me again. Said I was too big for one drop. Don't remember much after that."

"They raped you too, forcing you to act when you would have chosen not to." Isabella closed the gap between them, hugging the man before she could think better of it. "I'm sorry."

He patted her shoulder as though terrified to damage her. The vibration humming through him as he trembled didn't escape her notice.

"What's your name?"

"Jonathan."

"It wasn't your fault, Jonathan. Gerard would forgive you."

The giant's stare fixed on his shoes, refusing to meet her gaze.

"B-bella?" Gerard called.

She drifted from the man's side when he nodded, urging her to console her friend. "Yes, it's me."

"No!" He cried with huge heaving sobs. "It's all been for nothing. They found you anyway. They'll hurt you. They'll destroy you. No!"

Nothing she tried could calm the hysterical man then.

"I know a way outside." Jonathan wrung his hands. "But I doubt it will work if I try to take both of you."

"Go, little bell." Gerard shoved her toward the door. "Run! Run from this hell."

"I won't abandon you." She stayed glued to the floor. "Never again. If you can't come with me, I'm not leaving."

"Please, we have to try now, or it'll be too late," Jonathan begged. She could read the futility in his stance. He didn't believe they'd evade the rest of her father's well-trained men.

"I have a better idea." Isabella shot him her best smile from her glamour days. It seemed to dazzle Jonathan as it had most of the people she aimed it at. "You go. Bring help. Contact the p-police."

She stuttered as she considered. Who else could she call? Razor would strive to bust the operation, even if he didn't love her. The importance of his career had never been in question. She should have realized his true motivation. If she made it out of here alive, she'd never allow a man to deceive her again.

For now it was enough that he come. Whatever the reason.

"Ask for Razor."

"You're sure?" Jonathan glanced between her and Gerard.

"He won't make it. This is his only chance."

"No! Take her." Gerard wheezed beside her. "Don't let her stay."

Jonathan shook his head, his hands balling into fists. "I hate it. The little one's right. I have to run on my own. Might actually work."

The former guard drew a gun from the waistband of his pants. He slid it across the floor to them. "It's not much, but it's all I have."

"Thank you." Isabella gulped as their last hope slipped from the room, locking the door behind him. "Be safe."

He passed the key through the barred window. "Maybe this will slow them down."

Before he turned to leave, Gerard whispered, "She *is* right. Not your fault. I forgive you."

Jonathan's face seemed to turn twenty years younger. "I'll fix this. I'll be back. With help. I swear."

"So, if you didn't see the person. And they came from behind you, from inside the apartment, it could have been Isabella who attempted to brain you?"

"No." Razor raged as they wasted time on wild hares. Izzy had been stolen. She was out there. Alone. And she needed him.

"You didn't see..."

"Fuck. Chief, it doesn't matter. I don't care what clues you have or how they implicate Izzy. She did not do this. You're wasting time we need to find her and bring her home..."

He couldn't say alive. The worried looks and grim faces guaranteed the rest of his squad knew what he meant.

"Son, calm down." The chief swiveled in his chair. "You're right. You don't have all the facts. Clint and Matt were away from their posts, investigating a tip. They found documents under the seat of Isabella's car. Records. Payment registers. An empty vial, which looks like it contained more of the drug."

"It's her father's car." Razor refused to lose faith in Izzy. "She has nothing to do with this."

"They also uncovered a flight itinerary. Booked in her name. Scheduled departure an hour after she vanished, headed for the Caribbean. A private island her husband owned. She owns it now. He left her everything."

"You could have found a smoking gun with her fingerprint on it. It doesn't mean shit. I know her. She wouldn't be involved in this. Not to save her life. No one can convince me otherwise. I'm sure of it." He smacked his flexed abs. "Here."

Then he touched his heart, praying he didn't break down and cry in front of them all. "Here."

Silence stretched for eons in the tension of the room.

"I don't believe she's involved any more than you do." The chief stood behind the desk, slapping his palms on the polished surface in a rare display. "The ringer on our team at the funeral proves your girl was right to mistrust us. Her father has men on the inside here. I hate that more than you know. So I'm giving you boys all the lead I can. Run like hell out of here before someone higher up than me reins you in. You're ready. You can handle this."

"Thank you, sir." How could he ask for a better leader? "I won't disappoint you."

"You haven't yet, rookie." The chief cracked a tiny smile. "Now find Isabella. I'll feed you what info I can from this side. I'm afraid it won't be much."

Razor grimaced at the reminder. He struggled to embrace control, taming his impulsive streak. Izzy needed the best of him concentrated on rescuing her. He bolted from the room with the rest of the team in tow.

"I think we should start with properties in Buchanan's name. Having to act fast, he'd fall back on something he already has. Something he can use until the coast is clear."

Before anyone could respond, Payton from dispatch rushed at them, holding out his headset.

"JRad. You know how you told me to keep an ear out..." The heavily tattooed guy thrust the contraption at Jeremy. "I think you're going to want to hear this."

The technophile jammed it over his head in his haste.

"What? Who are you?"

Someone poured out information on the other end of the line.

"Where is she?"

Pause.

"You're sure? When did you last see her? How much time do we have?"

A longer pause followed.

Razor counted to ten, impressed with his restraint.

A long stream of curses flooded the hallways. "They're holding her in a temporary facility on the south side, about twenty miles from the city. It's one of her father's holdings. An unfinished factory."

"Welcome back, kid." Mason nodded as they sprinted for the garage. The other man beamed at the rest of the crew. "Looks like Razor's found his edge."

JRad cut off any possible response as he shouted out the address and general directions while they ran. Their footfalls echoed on the concrete of the parking area. Velcro fasteners on their flak jackets tore and resealed. The men in blue piled into their patrol cars. All except for Razor, who opted to take his motorcycle instead. He could beat them there. Too bad they'd left Izzy's car at his apartment for another team to finish searching.

Hang on, princess. I'm coming.

Isabella sank to the floor beside Gerard, her shoulders braced on the cinderblock wall. She dug in her pocket, thrilled to find the medicine she'd stuffed in her pajamas earlier that evening.

"I'm sorry I don't have any water. You should chew these."

He eyed the pills suspiciously. "What are they?"

"Painkillers."

"Why do you have them?" He scanned her for signs of distress.

"Nothing major." *Just a bullet wound.* She tipped her hand until the capsules rolled into Gerard's palm. No need to worry him further. Besides, her injuries looked like a splinter compared to the trauma he'd sustained.

The magnitude of his agony came clear when he didn't argue. He chomped the bitter medicine to bits and swallowed it dry.

Isabella hooked her pinky with his, one of the few places not swollen, bloody or bruised on his body. She pressed the knuckles of her other hand to her mouth to smother a sob.

"Shh." Gerard soothed her despite his own agony. "Jonathan will bring help. We'll be out of here in no time."

"That's not what upset me." She didn't bother to correct his assumption. If he had to believe the fairytale to keep going, she didn't plan to burst his bubble. She figured the odds to be about a million to one against them, though. Without Razor's love waiting, she found the prospect less devastating.

"What is it?" The man who should have been her father stroked her hair, unconcerned with his own condition—not his injuries, not his nudity and not his imprisonment.

"All this time you've been here. Suffering." She struggled to breathe. "While I was..."

"What, little bell?" He turned to her, serious. "Tell me about something other than this trouble. I want to forget."

"I met someone."

"A man?" Gerard smiled an honest-to-God smile, if a pitiful one since his dry lips cracked. "You work quick, Bella."

She ducked her chin. "Easy when he's assigned to fake a relationship with you."

"What does that mean?" Gerard's hint of happiness disappeared. She hustled to fan it to life.

"Well, he's a cop. It's a long story... I thought I met him by chance, but my father showed me documents—"

"Stop right there." The fragility vanished from Gerard's tone. "Nothing that man says can be trusted. Tell me what you know in your heart. Ignore everything else. What does your soul say about this fellow?"

"Fellow." She giggled. "You make him sound like something out of a black and white movie. He's twenty-four. Handsome. Funny. A great dancer. Noble. Comes from a huge, amazing family. He's sweet..."

Gerard waited for her to finish.

"And I'm completely in love with him."

"Does he know?"

"Wait...you don't think that's crazy? To love someone so soon after meeting them?" She confronted the worst obstacle along her path. Her father had made her doubt it possible.

"I loved Irene from the moment I met her." Gerard sighed. "I bumped into her in the kitchen. She wore a yellow dress with a matching ribbon in her hair. I still have that scrap of satin. She gave it to me after I kissed her in the garden a few hours later. The connection between us existed from that day. The first instant."

"It's exactly like that." Isabella grimaced. "At least for me."

"He'll come around, little bell." Gerard acted like they had a future. "Give him time."

"No, that's not the problem." She sighed. "He told me he loves me. When he..."

She stopped, blushing.

"You slept with him?"

She nodded.

"Because he said he loved you?"

"Even I'm not that naïve." She shook her head. "I wanted to know what it was like. With him. He made it so good for me. I felt like...a princess. He calls me that. It's silly, but he treats me like one. He didn't tell me he loved me until after that."

Would talking about this upset the man after all he'd been through?

"And this cop has been looking out for you?" Gerard narrowed his eyes.

"Yes. He saved my life. A bunch of times, really."

"Maybe you'd better explain, little bell."

She hadn't intended to steer the conversation to serious matters. "Well, my apartment kind of blew up. I got shot at. Umm... Someone tried to kidnap me and Lily at Malcolm's funeral and..."

"You've met your sister?" His finger squeezed hers. "Malcolm's dead?"

Damn, a lot had happened in the past ten days.

She sighed. "Yes and yes."

"Buchanan did it?"

"I think so."

"Dear God." Gerard gripped her pinky harder. "Forget all that, Bella. Believe me, I know it's hard. But all that matters is what is written in your soul. When you meet the one, you know."

"Razor is the man for me. I hope it's truly the same for him. I don't think I'll know unless I can look in his eyes and ask him. Even then..."

"Trust yourself. You'll know." Gerard steered her from the depths of her misery. "They call him Razor? What an odd nickname."

"Ah, yeah. His name is James Reoser. You know, R-E-O-S-E-R so they call him Razor. It's not as bad as his one friend,

Jeremy Radisson. They call him JRad."

Gerard chuckled. "To be young and foolish again..."

She wanted to laugh, but she had one more thing to get off her chest. In case...

"I understand now why you wouldn't leave my father's house. Even though James only approached me because of his job, I can't change how I feel about him." She scrubbed her sweating palm on her pajamas. "His friends, his little apartment, his motorcycle—I love all those things because they're his. I'd never give them up if I didn't have to."

"A motorcycle?" Gerard groaned. "Do you know how dangerous those things are, little bell?"

She didn't see the need to remind Gerard of how much more lethal her father was, content to feign ignorance as he did.

"Yeah, it's bright yellow and super fast. When I ride with him, the wind in my face makes me feel like I'm flying..."

She continued to distract them both with highlights of the prior week. She'd done more living in ten days than in the twenty-two years before. They shared stories until another guard came to retrieve them.

This one wasn't nearly as kind as Jonathan.

Chapter Twenty-Six

Razor ignored years of training in favor of raw reactions. He cut the engine to his bike then ditched the machine in the scrub, approaching the factory on foot under the awning of the woods. Right where their informant had promised to wait, a colossal shadow darkened the ground.

It could be a trap. Or this could be his chance to save his soulmate. He'd take the risk, no matter how foolish.

"Jonathan?" he called softly, not willing to startle the man.

"Are you Razor?"

"Yes." He didn't have time for the pleasantries Izzy adored. "Take me to her."

"I sort of thought you would bring some backup. We have to drag them out of there. The Scientist is coming."

"Help is following." Razor grimaced as he considered how much he'd exceeded the speed limit on his trip here. "Five minutes behind me, maybe. Take me now. They'll catch up."

The pair of them zigzagged across the clearing, ducking behind what cover they could find. Jonathan, light on his feet for someone so large, made little sound as he led James into the cellar entrance. They sped up once inside. Without talking, they wormed deep into the complex.

Up ahead, he spotted a series of gated doors.

"This is where they kept the test subjects." Jonathan broke the hushed atmosphere. "All of them have been moved. Or..."

"Disposed of." Razor supplied to keep the man talking. They didn't have time for pauses.

"Yeah. All except the girl and her friend. I think they kept him to use against her. I've seen them do it before with husbands and wives, family members." He stumbled when he said, "I helped them. I didn't know what they planned."

"You're doing the right thing now." Razor couldn't think about the magnitude of the horrors committed. All he could do was move forward.

They barreled around one final turn. When his guide slammed to a stop, Razor almost plowed into the brickhouse.

"What?" He dodged around the blockade Jonathan created. "What is it?"

"They're gone." The man crumpled to the floor on his knees. "We're too late to save them."

Isabella tried not to finger the cold steel jammed in the small of her back. She'd never used a gun before, never touched one. She had no idea if she could pull the trigger never mind hit a target. She debated the best use of whatever firepower she had, deciding it would be most beneficial to save it for when her captors transported her and Gerard.

If she could disable the driver, as she had at the cemetery, they might have a chance. But every second longer she had the weapon on her, she risked discovery and disarming.

She stood, afraid to breathe, while waiting in the loading area for the man they called the Scientist to arrive. Her father paced. Sweat poured from his brow. He chewed his fingernails, and his pupils dilated until his eyes appeared solid black. He mumbled to himself as he circumnavigated the space, jonesing for another hit of his precious drug.

Isabella had no doubt the chemical destroyed him by the minute. He'd never last after subjecting his system to such duress. Gerard leaned closer when she whimpered. She tightened her arm until her friend stopped wobbling. He couldn't take much more either.

The *whap-whap-whap* she'd assumed stemmed from her pounding heart crescendoed until a sleek black helicopter dropped into view. She averted her face to keep dirt and pine needles from stinging her eyes.

The engine muted from a deafening roar to a mere cacophony when the rails touched down. A man in a trench coat and dark sunglasses alighted, toting a briefcase. He could have been anywhere from thirty to fifty, hard to tell from here.

"Buchanan," he called as he approached. "Finally managed

to secure my winnings, eh?"

The Scientist didn't pause by her father. He tossed over the satchel, blowing past the slobbering man to inspect her face to face.

"You're going to need some serious cleaning up, my dear." He seemed harmless, although she knew the evil he perpetuated had destroyed countless lives. "Don't worry, you'll be back to your old self in no time. You'll learn to behave as I like you. I have plenty of the formula left if you need some motivation to adopt the spirit of things."

"I don't think so, asshole."

Isabella could have cried at Mason's welcome shout. But she stayed calm, waiting for the opportunity to strike—to assist the men who hadn't disappointed her. This fiasco had to end. All of them had to walk away safe. Please, God, protect them.

She grinned at the men in blue surrounding her father and the Scientist. Several she didn't recognize had joined the familiar men who'd protected her, befriended her, made her one of them.

All the guys were there, Mason, Tyler, JRad, Clint, Matt... All but one.

She gulped. Where was Razor?

"Looks like your boyfriend has cold feet." Buchanan turned to her and laughed hysterically. "Or maybe you should fucking learn your lesson once and for all. He never wanted more than to fuck you. Stupid girl!"

"Put your hands up." Tyler trained his weapon on her father.

Buchanan didn't stop opening the case.

"Freeze!"

Her father reached into the foam lining. He withdrew a syringe from inside. They watched—horrified—as he licked the needle, which glinted in the early morning sunlight.

"Yes." He groaned as he depressed the plunger a tiny bit, sipping the dew from the tip. "Fuck, yes."

Their attention diverted for an instant at his lusty gurgle. That was all the opening the Scientist needed. He grabbed Isabella in a headlock, then backed off the dock, toward the chopper.

She smiled at the cops she'd grown to adore, coming last to

JRad. She nodded at him and rolled the dice. Her hand closed around the butt of the gun, her index finger curled on the trigger. She whipped the weapon from behind her back and shot the Scientist point blank in the chest before he could process her intent.

The bang scared the shit out of her even though she expected it. She swore she'd never hear again after the deafening blast. The Scientist gaped at her as he clutched his chest, flying backward in slow motion. The weapon skittered from her limp fingers.

She'd killed someone.

Isabella dropped to her knees, horrified as the world snapped into motion once more.

"You crazy bitch," her father screamed as he charged her. "Without him there can be no more drug. I'll kill you. Should have done it years ago."

He clenched the needle in one hand as he reached for the gun with the other. From this angle, the cops behind her couldn't take a clean shot.

"Noooo." She heard a furious howl before Razor barreled in from the fringe of the clearing. He dove through the air, tackling her father before he could reach the gun. They wrestled on the ground, switching positions as they rolled.

"James!" She shrieked when her father raised the syringe as though to inject Razor with a lethal dose of the compound.

Her cop deflected the enhanced strength of her father's jab, knocking his momentum off course. The needle missed its mark, jabbing into Buchanan's wrist instead of his would-be victim's neck.

Isabella would remember his chilling cackle for the rest of her life. He surveyed the impossible odds and the dead scientist before taking the easy route. Her father jammed the plunger to the hilt, injecting himself with six milliliters of the drug all at once.

"Son of a bitch." Razor ripped the needle from Buchanan's arm. It was too late.

Seconds later, seizures wracked the man's body, bucking Razor from his torso. He convulsed before their horrified gazes, the rapture never leaving his face. Isabella collapsed beside Razor, who engulfed her in his arms, trying to block her line of sight by tucking her head against his chest.

"No." She stared into her father's eyes as he entered the last of his death throes. "I want him to know you love me. That this wasn't some assignment. Tell him, James. Mean it. Please."

"It *was* an operation, Izzy. I'm so sorry I lied to you."

Her heart stopped.

"Dumb bitch." Buchanan spit the curse through the foam gathering on his lips.

"Everything changed the moment I met you. None of that mattered. Of course I love you, Isabella. With all my soul." He ignored the suffering of the man on the ground to face her. "Thank God you're okay. I would be lost without you. I love you, Izzy."

"I love you, James. I'm sorry I doubted you." She turned, horrified by the pitiful husk of her father. She couldn't let him die like this, despite the fact that he deserved it. Isabella couldn't bring herself to touch him, but she gazed into his eyes when she said, "I love you, too, Daddy. I forgive you."

For a second, she swore she saw something other than insanity. Something other than the tyrant he'd become. Then he fell still, his eyes lifeless.

Isabella didn't know what to do. Where to look. She couldn't process all that had happened in the past two minutes. She'd taken a life—an evil one, but a life nonetheless. Her father had committed suicide before her eyes. Her world would never be the same.

The only thing that made sense was the comfort she found in Razor's embrace.

Chaos exploded around them as cops moved in from every side. She blinked, stunned. Her wild gaze flipped between the two bodies, wrecked on the floor.

When one of them moved, she thought she'd gone insane.

She struggled in Razor's grasp. He subdued her, trying to sooth her panic. By the time she realized she wasn't hallucinating, it was too late.

The Scientist rose from the ground—a gaping hole mangling his bulletproof vest—and bolted for the helicopter.

Someone, she thought it might have been Clint, shouted a warning. Everyone stopped what they were doing—securing the thugs who'd helped Buchanan, tending to the injured man behind her or retching into the tall grass at the horror they'd witnessed.

Boots pounded the concrete beside her head as the cops gave chase. Jonathan shouted. He blocked the path only to be mowed down by the Scientist. Razor's solid frame blanketed her while round after round of shots were fired. In shock, all she noticed was the receding din of the motor as the Scientist slipped through their fingers.

Radios squawked. The men spread news of the incident, scrambling for assistance to halt the mastermind behind the drug ring. By the grim looks on each of their faces, she knew they'd failed.

JRad stood in the bowels of Black Lily, one step behind the club's namesake. He'd watched as she freed every last woman, helping them to the waiting ambulances. She'd insisted on doing it herself since she believed she'd contributed to their imprisonment.

He stifled the urge to object, to argue. He saved his breath for later. For a time when she might listen. She wasn't ready yet. So he stood by her side as she did what she could to end the prisoners' misery.

The empty dungeon echoed with the receding rap of Lily's heeled boots on the stone floor. Until she stopped short, her shoulders slumped. She pounded the wall with the heel of her palm.

"Son of a bitch!" Her cry reverberated through the cavernous space. "This is bullshit. Nothing to be proud of."

"The women upstairs may feel differently."

"We've traded a situation where I was able to keep an eye on the place, freeing some of the worst cases, for a complete unknown. The Scientist will set up shop somewhere else. And next time will be worse. The drug is stronger. Their guard is up. Who will help his subjects now?"

"I've been cleared to join the task force working with the DEA." Jeremy shared what he hadn't divulged to his squad yet. The move could mean an indefinite leave of absence. Cases like this often took years to solve. "I signed up."

"You did?"

He turned to face her, taking a step closer so they stood toe to toe.

"Yeah. And I'm not against employing whatever means necessary to find the men responsible for this and make them pay. I'm going to hunt these fuckers. I won't stop until they're out of commission. Do you hear me, Lily?"

The sparkle returning to her amazing blue eyes buoyed his spirit and his cock.

"Yeah." She mimicked him. "I just have one question."

"What's that?"

"How do you plan to use me?"

Oh, Jesus. A million and one possibilities streaked through his mind. In the end, he knew what she needed. "You'll be my mole. Work this from the inside, with my support. We could make one hell of a team."

"Deal." She stuck out her hand to seal the bargain.

JRad grasped the offering, surrounding the delicate bones with his palm and fingers. He tugged her into his arms. "For the record, I kiss my informants. Often. Better resign yourself to it, ma'am."

He covered her sputtering mouth with his. They wrestled for control. She fought long and hard, but he persisted. All objections disappeared without a trace when he explored the glossy surface of her lips. He rewarded her with a nip and a hand on her ass.

Lily moaned. She arched closer before ripping from his hold to glare at him like something smelly she'd stepped in with her favorite fuck-me boots.

This was going to be fun.

And very, very dangerous.

Epilogue

Razor grinned as Isabella bounded past him with a bowl of microwave popcorn and two beers. In the three months since the trauma that had joined them, she'd come to enjoy the finer things in life, as she liked to call them. Personally, he thought anything he shared with her ranked at the top of the world.

He laughed when she hopped onto the couch, cross-legged, then patted the cushion beside her. "Hurry up. It's starting soon."

"Izzy, it's a re-run, and we have DVR." He shook his head as he approached, grinding his teeth to keep from whisking her into the bedroom for another round of mind-blowing love making before the big screening.

"I know, but I want to see it again."

"You know how it ends. You were there." He chuckled when she stuck her tongue out at him.

Damn, the things she could do with that tongue.

"Okay, okay." He pretended to sigh in resignation. "We'll watch it as many times as your heart desires. But, uh, I have something for you first."

Isabella paused, the seriousness of the moment penetrating at last. She read his emotions like no one else. A finely tuned instrument couldn't pick up on his moods quicker.

"Is everything okay?"

Razor hated that even now, she panicked sometimes. He understood—every person in her life other than Gerard had betrayed her. Still, he hungered for the day she didn't doubt he intended to stick around for the long haul. He'd debated the best next step for weeks until the perfect solution came to mind.

"Everything's great, Izzy." He smiled despite the nerves plaguing him all of a sudden.

She held out her hand and he took it, kneeling in front of her by the couch so they were at eye level.

"I have to talk to you about something. Now that things are starting to settle down, you've made plans for the future. I'm proud of how you handled Malcolm's estate. The money you donated to charity will do so much good."

"I kept enough for my studio. For Gerard. Moderate savings, enough for a house..."

"I know. That's what I have tell you." He couldn't help himself. He kissed her knuckles. Every moment he spent not touching some part of her was torture. "We're young. A lot of things have happened. I swear to you if it's up to me, we'll spend the rest of our lives together."

"Why do I sense a *but* in there?"

"I think you need time to enjoy a normal life before deciding if this is what you really want. Don't rush into something permanent. I couldn't stand it if you came to regret the decision." Weight lifted off his shoulders as he confessed his fears.

"James, are you dumping me?" She chewed her lip.

"Hell, no." He scrubbed his hand through his hair. "I'm screwing this up. I just thought you should know why I bought you...what I did. It's not a ring, Izzy. I need time to save up for something nice anyway."

"What?" She shook her head, confused. "I don't need a rock to tell me you love me. And I don't need time to know I love you too. Forever."

He leaned forward to kiss her with soft, lingering strokes of his lips on hers.

"Then our timeline won't matter. Someday, in a year or maybe two, we'll get engaged. Married. Have a family. But, for now..."

He got to his feet, crossing to the door. When he opened it, Leo waved from the landing. Izzy had tracked the homeless man down and helped him find a job, an apartment, a new start. He'd always enjoyed animals and had hoped to train as a vet before life had screwed him over. With two hometown heroes vouching for him, it hadn't taken long for the local animal shelter to snap him up.

"What's going on?" Isabella asked from behind Razor.

Before he could explain, the puppy he'd picked out from the pound rushed between his legs in a beeline for his new owner. Izzy dropped to her knees with a squeal of delight as the silly thing's ears flopped, its tail wagged and its tongue lolled. Razor silently apologized to the little guy for the ridiculous red bow tied to its collar.

The puppy didn't seem to mind as it launched itself at Izzy, knocking them both into a heap of excited joy. Their friend laughed before he winked and turned to go. In the time it took Razor to promise Leo they'd come by to visit later and lock the door behind him, Isabella and the puppy had become inseparable.

She hugged the bundle of energy to her. It licked her face.

"You gave me a puppy." The adoration in her eyes bowled him over as he sat beside her.

"A starter family, I guess." He grinned when she flung herself into his arms, the puppy squirming between them.

"Look at the size of his paws." Her eyes grew wide. "He'll need a yard. A big one."

"Yeah." Razor nodded. "If you're up for the house stage, I thought we might all move in together. Until we're ready for whatever comes next."

Isabella didn't say anything. Tears pooled in her eyes.

"Oh shit, are you disappointed?" Maybe he should have proposed after all. God knew, he'd never change his mind about her.

"No." She set the dog on the ground. He immediately ran off to find trouble. Neither of them minded. "He's perfect. You're perfect. I love you."

"I love you, too, Izzy."

"You know, James. You were right..." She wrapped her legs around his waist and licked the column of his neck. Her breath washed over his ear. "We should watch this later."

"Hmm, I don't know. I'd like to see us kick ass in the finale of *Dance With Me* for the twentieth time." He gritted his teeth as he tried to ignore the undulation of her steaming core on his abdomen. His cock begged him to quit teasing them both. "You were smoking hot when we danced to 'Calle Ocho'. Almost too sexy for network TV. I swear that dress earned them a big, fat fine."

"Blame Arthur, not me."

"Oh, I think I owe that man a hefty Christmas present this year."

"If you want, I'll wear it for you while you..." she whispered the rest in his ear.

His resolve cracked, his hands flexing on her ass.

"Razor." She growled before nipping his ear. "Bedroom, now."

"At your service, princess."

About the Author

Jayne Rylon's stories usually begin as a daydream in an endless business meeting. Her writing acts as a creative counterpoint to her straight-laced corporate existence. She lives in Ohio with two cats and her husband who both inspires her fantasies and supports her careers. When she can escape her office, she loves to travel the world, avoid speeding tickets in her beloved Sky and, of course, read.

Jayne is a member of the Romance Writers of America (RWA), the Central Ohio Fiction Writers (COFW), International Heat and Passionate Ink. To learn more about her, please visit www.jaynerylon.com, send an email to contact@jaynerylon.com or join in the fun at International Heat, internationalheat.wordpress.com.

Nothing's sexier than a man, or five, with power tools.

Kate's Crew

© 2010 Jayne Rylon

Sultry summer heat has nothing on the five-man crew renovating the house next door. No one could blame Kate for leaning out the window for a better view of the manscape. The nasty fall that follows isn't part of her fantasy—but the man who saves her from splattering the sidewalk is definitely the star.

When Mike personally attends to her injuries, she realizes her white knight in a hard hat has a tender side, giving her no choice but to surrender to the lust that's been arcing between them since day one. In the aftermath of the best sex of her life, she whispers her most secret desire: to be ravaged by his crew.

She never expected Mike would dare her to take what she wants—or that the freedom to make her most decadent desires come true could be the foundation for something lasting...

This book may cause you to spontaneously combust as five hot guys bring a woman's wildest fantasies to life during one blazing summer affair.

CPSIA information can be obtained at www.ICGtesting.com
Printed in the USA
LVOW060252240911

247672LV00001B/28/P